Children of the Enaisi

L.S. King

Cover Design: Miblart Copyright © 2020
miblart.com

Loriendil Publishing
loriendil.com

DEDICATION

Shannon McNear, my Good and Dear Friend: thank you for everything!

CONTENTS

Acknowledgements

Thanks to:

Dr. Jonathan Crofts - My Very Own Physicist™ who has patiently waded through my questions and tried valiantly to keep me from breaking the laws of physics. Without him, the technology of this world would be much diminished, although to be honest, his brain would probably be in a much better state if he didn't have my stories twisting his mind into knots.

To Jane Lebak: you know why!

Sarah Hulett, Rick Copple, Moira Hartwell, and Cameron and Corrie McNear for your feedback and support.

And as always:

Johnston McCulley and Guy Williams—for my love of capes, swords, and brave deeds.

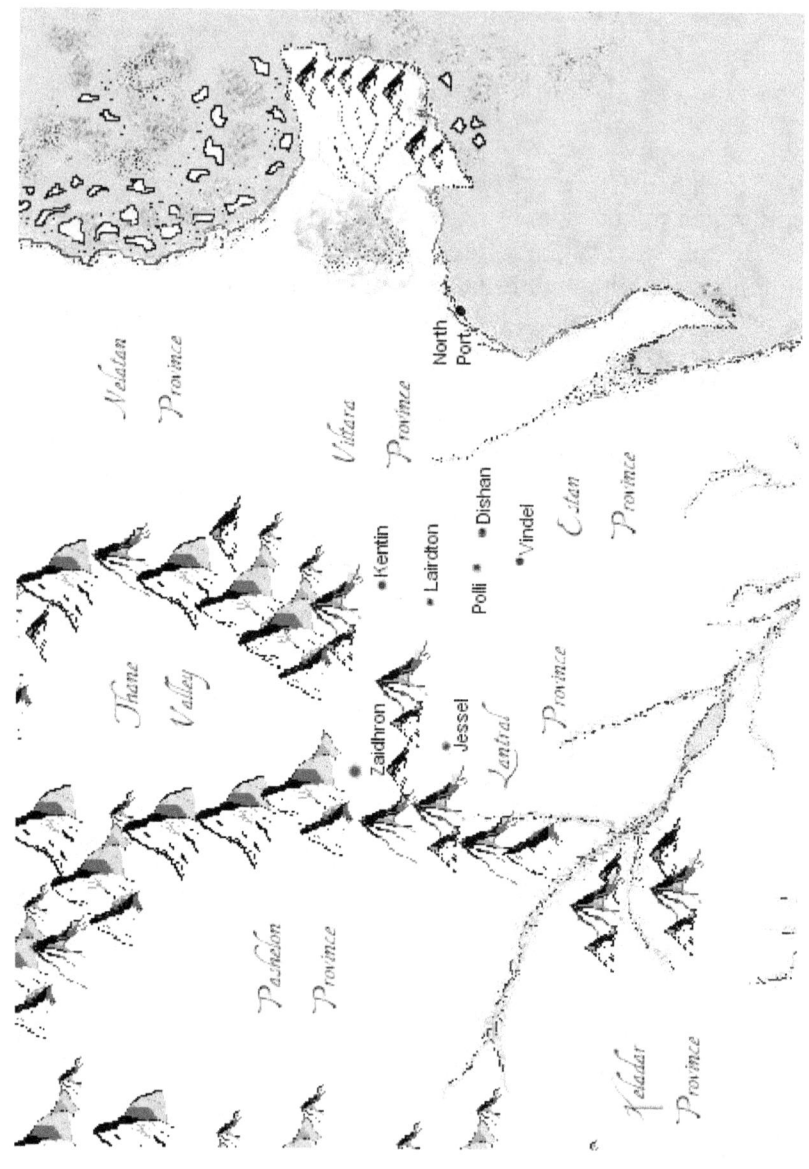

North Port

Nedalan Province

Vittara Province

Thane Valley

Kertin
Lairdton
Polli
Dishan
Vindel

Estan Province

Zaidhron
Jessel

Lanthal Province

Pashelon Province

Veldar Province

PRONUNCIATION OF NAMES

Teldheri:
- ' indicates a glottal stop except when used after ch, in which case it indicates the ch is a hard sound (as in Scottish lo**ch**)
- dh indicates a fricative **d** (as in mo**th**er or **th**en)
- a is **ä** (as in f**a**ther), except in an accented syllable, in which case it is short
- e is short as in **e**gg
- i is short as in p**i**t, except as final vowel, then it is long **e**, as in Teldheri (or when followed by double consonants, such as is common in female names)
- ai is a diphthong, with the separate vowels pronounced as given above: **ä** and long **e**
- ei is a diphthong, with the separate vowels pronounced as given above: short **e** and long **e**
- o is long **o**
- u is long as in r**u**le
- gh indicates a soft g (as in **g**eneral)
- jh indicates a sibilant s (as in mea**s**ure)

Male names:
- accent is on the first syllable except when it is a three syllable name beginning with a vowel with a closed second syllable, in which case the accent is on the second syllable, therefore *El'adhrel* but *Alcan'dhor*

Female names:
- in names such as *Sarinna*, or *Colinn*, the i is pronounced as a long **e** and carries the accent, as indicated by the double consonant after the vowel
- in names such as Amara or Aleta, the accent is on the second syllable
- in names such as Sherel, accent is on the first syllable

"enh?" used at the end of a sentence to indicate a question does not carry a long **a** sound, but rather the nasal enh sound similar to "hein" used by the French.

CHILDREN OF THE ENAISI

Discovery - Chapter One

year - 1038 (five years before current events)

Delgan stopped to puff steamy breath onto his hands and rest a moment from the climb up the steep mountain, high above the pastured slopes. The snow had mostly melted, creating a treacherous ascent. More than once, he and his companions had to grab one another to steady themselves, not always successfully. The mountainside mud was as much on them as on the mountain now.

"There, history-keeper." The herder pointed at the flat, greyish-white slab. "This is what my father and I found. There are several above too. They aren't natural, are they?"

Delgan knelt in the mire and ran his hands over the smooth surface. He yanked out tufts of soggy grass and brushed away snow and mud to reveal more of the substance. Oldstone. This substance dated to a time before his people came to this planet.

His stomach shuddered slightly, and he looked up at his two comrades. Their wide eyes met his with expectation. Even the wind seemed to still. Delgan swallowed to clear his throat. "This is of the Enaisi."

Bivnat's face, flushed from both the exertion of ascending the slope and the cold, showed open awe, and he fell to his knees to touch the stone.

Delgan pressed his lips together to keep from saying anything to the Worshipper. He had read too much about the aliens called the Enaisi, and things written by them, to believe they were gods.

"But what is it?" asked young Vadmar, whipping his dark hair out of his eyes with a snap of his head. "I mean, not the oldstone, I know what oldstone is."

Delgan peered up the incline. Good question. The rock-like substance, half-buried aslant in the ground, was once probably perfectly horizontal. "It might be part of a path." He stood, wiped his hands on his trous, and pulled his cloak tighter. "Let's find out."

~*~

Vadmar wiped his arm over his face, smearing mud across his forehead. His black hair hung in damp strands. He shook his head at Delgan. "We aren't going to find anything. We've been digging and searching around here forever."

Forever. It had only been five days. *Time goes so slowly for the young.* Delgan leaned on his shovel, breathing heavily, wishing his wife were there to rub his sore back. "That's the way of things." The clouds hung heavy and low. A rumble echoed in the distance. "Let's go farther uphill and have luncheon. The outcropping above has some sheltered spots. We're likely to get a downpour before long."

Splatters of icy rain pelted them before they got to the tor, and they rushed upslope amid missteps, slips, and spills. Delgan heaved for air as they reached cover. Grey-blue tanglevines hung down thickly, obscuring most of the rock face even though bare of their summer foliage. He'd wager those were the reason why herders didn't use this land more so than that the heights and rocks and almost vertical angle. And also why they had plains herdbeasts rather than any of the variety of hillbeasts, which could certainly climb and graze here. Tanglevines, besides being a bane for their sharp spines, were poisonous to ingest. And hillbeasts were stupid enough to eat anything. Especially kinchou.

Delgan crowded in the small space with the other two history-keepers. Lightning flashed nearby and a heart-stopping *boom* made him jump. Bivnat gave a shout and closed his eyes, his lips moving in silent prayer. Delgan turned away from the Worshipper with a curled lip and scuffled his feet. His eyes widened. Under the thick layer of dirt lay flat, smooth stone. He wheeled about and stared at the thick fall of spiky vines covering the rock. "Men, when the rain stops, we're starting a bonfire nearby. Then we're pulling down these vines."

Bivnat snorted. "You're mad! Those things will rip us to shreds."

"We have axes. We'll cut them down." Delgan pointed at his feet. "Look what we're standing on!"

~*~

Delgan smeared crown plant salve on the scrapes covering his arms. At least the tanglevines were gone, burning in the fire down slope. His companions ran their hands over the flat, grayish-white wall recessed in the rock face.

"All this," Bivnat said, dropping his arms with a sigh, "for a blank bit of stone? The seams near the edge are regular and even, but other than that, there are no scores, no marks of any kind."

"Except this." Vadmar tapped the surface.

Squinting, Delgan stepped closer to spy a slight, perfectly round indentation about the size of his thumb tip. He inhaled sharply, exultation like lightning shooting through him. "I know what that is." He straightened. "I need to send a message to Zaidhron."

Vadmar's mouth dropped open at the mention of the Ranger city. "Zaidhron? What for?"

Delgan eyed his fellow history-keepers. "Only the Thane can open this."

"The Thane?" Vadmar blinked. "How? Why?"

Bivnat crossed his arms. "Alcandhor would never help us. He despises history-keepers—and Worshippers."

"With reason." Delgan's lip curled. "Some of you treat him as though he is a god for having Enaisi blood. But why do you say he hates history-keepers? He's one himself."

Bivnat's eyes glittered. "I've heard he hinders the efforts of any history-keeper who wishes to directly study the Enaisi writings at Zaidhron."

"Not true. I've studied there. And spoken with the Thane many times. Of course at the time, he wasn't Thane, just Second at Table under his father. But Alcandhor himself took me on a tour of the Portal Complex. I know he'll be interested in this discovery."

Both men gaped at him.

"You're serious!" Bivnat exclaimed. "You truly think he'll come here?"

Delgan gazed again at the small concave spot marking the key port on the smooth door—for that was certainly what it was, and grinned. "Ha, I think I can guarantee that. Come, let's go down to the village, and find a messenger-runner. We must send for the Thane."

~*~

Alcandhor stood atop the tor at the west side of the Pashelon Pass, surveying the lush, spring-green land below him, pasturelands and farms disappearing into the distant haze. A beautiful province, deserving better than the greedy Lord Lorwith. The noble kept his hand tight on his people but always within a sword's edge of the law to prevent the Laird and Alcandhor from being able to bringing charges.

What would the legendary Avadhron, first of the Rangers to claim bounds and roam this beautiful land, have thought of the current lord? By reputation, he was stern, stolid, and unafraid to face down anyone, including the other chiefs, lords of the provinces, or their alien mentors themselves. A Ranger's Ranger, the most respected in all their history. Their move to this planet—their very salvation as a race—was owed directly to him.

Lorwith might quake in front of such a man; he certainly did not fear the current Thane.

As Alcandhor descended the mountainside, he pondered what he might learn about Lorwith from journeying through his province. Those of Pashelon had a quiet disposition, not easily provoked. Yet they had a fierce independent spirit, partially due to three sides of their land being walled in by mountains. Only the pass which Alcandhor came through from Lantral province and the south border into Keladar offered any interaction with the other provinces.

Once near the bottom of the switchback, he surveyed the land. Keddek, the tiny herder village where Delgan waited, lay almost due north, at the edge of the mountain range, two days' journey.

He stopped at a rill, swollen from the spring thaw and foaming over the rocks, and splashed icy water on his face. Dark clouds roiled on the western horizon. He would likely trudge through rain all the way to his destination. Adjusting his pack, he sighed and headed north.

~*~

Alcandhor had hoped to find the village and Delgan before this second day ended. But the western sun's slanted, orange rays winked occasionally through trees, and still he found nothing but the wild. At least the rain had stopped, although every gust of wind brought down an unwelcome splatter of water drops from the budding leaves, and the muddy ground slowed his journey.

A path lined with flat stones lifted his spirits, and he eagerly followed its course northward.

He soon came across a cottage. Two children playing in the yard saw him and darted inside. A man rushed out, wielding a staff.

"I don't take to no one crossing my land, Ranger or no."

Alcandhor halted, his fist lifting and then opening palm forward, indicating friendship. "I merely pass through."

The man waved his hand. "Pass some through somewhere else."

Alcandhor fought the urge to sigh and ran his thumbs under the straps of his pack to ease the weight, glancing at the draggled children peeking around the doorway. As Thane, he could vaunt his authority, but that would lead to resentment. He could defeat the man easily, probably without serious injury—except to the man's pride, leading to even more ill will toward Rangers. "I will pay to cross. I am journeying to Keddek, going around would slow my journey."

"I want no money. I want you off my land. There's a good road to the west, use it."

"But—"

The man hefted the staff. "Be off!"

With a deep inhale, Alcandhor inclined his head and turned west, hoping the road he sought would not be too far away.

Dusk deepened before he found a well-used, deep-rutted cart track and followed it north, staying in the grass to avoid the sucking mud. "Good road, indeed," he muttered.

~*~

After stumbling in the dark for the third time with his mud-weighted boots, Alcandhor wondered whether to stop and make camp for the night. Just a little farther; he would fain sleep indoors than in the damp cold. Did he see a light? He blinked and rubbed his eyes. Aye—there, uphill, beyond those trees and shrubs.

He drew closer to find a small cluster of buildings. A flickering torch illuminated the sign over one door—a drawing of the backside of a hillbeast with the name "The Buck's End" underneath. Alcandhor's short laugh puffed warm mist into the night air. *Someone has a wry sense of humor.* His rascally cousin Haladhon would likely find great amusement in the name.

He pushed open the door to find a large chamber with tables scattered throughout. The warmth was as inviting as the delectable odors, and his stomach growled as he wiped his boots at the threshold. Mats piled in one corner told him this place had no sleeping chambers; 'twas a pub more than an inn.

Two herders at a table near the fire, tankards in their fists, shot him sidelong, curious looks. No history-keepers about. Or innkeepers, it seemed.

Alcandhor sat at a side table, stowing his pack underneath. A woman, sturdy but not fat, came from a side door wiping her hands on an apron as she approached the table. "A Ranger! And where are you from?"

"Zaidhron, mistress."

"We rarely have Rangers up here, much less one from the Rangers' own city." She brushed straggles of brown hair out of her face with a frown. "Not trouble brewing, is there?"

Alcandhor smiled. "Perhaps just the opposite. Do you have history-keepers staying here?"

The lines in her face eased. "Yes. Up on that mountain, likely. They'll be in soon. You'll be wanting a full stoup?" She rubbed her palms against the sides of her skirt.

Alcandhor barely hesitated before replying, "Aye, please." *Full stoup.* Stars above. Did that term for a tankard throw back to something in her clan's dialect, or did Pashelon use such archaic expressions?

"There's bashi at the hearth. Mind you don't spill it. Bread on the sideboard."

"Aye, mistress," Alcandhor said, rising. *Archaic indeed—to have guests serve themselves.*

A large kettle hung on a crane swung away from the fire. Alcandhor smiled as he saw the poached eggs floating on top of the soup. Aye, he had stepped into Pashelon truly. Bashi was rarely served anywhere but this province. A hearty dish of vegetables and spiced sausage in a redfruit sauce, eggs were dropped onto the top, thickening it and giving it a unique flavor.

Sensing with amusement the woman's hard gaze on his back, he ladled soup carefully into one of the large earthen bowls and snagged one of the small, round loaves.

A boy perhaps having ten years filled a tankard and set it on the sideboard. Alcandhor took his food to the table and returned for his tankard. The boy stared at him with open curiosity before going back to the fireplace.

He ate the soup slowly to savor it. And by the Bells, the ale had a strong bite! He might find out if this was their own brew and have it shipped to Zaidhron. Lorwith had high border taxes, but Alcandhor would pay these people's portion to get such good ale.

The door opened, and three men entered, talking quietly among themselves. Except for a few wrinkles and being a bit on the portly side now, Delgan had not changed. And aye, his curly hair had more silver now, granted, but his eyes were as keen as ever.

Alcandhor grinned and stood. A rumbled "Ha!" escaped the history-keeper and he hurried over to Alcandhor. The two men grabbed each other's shoulders in greeting.

"How are you, my friend?" Alcandhor asked, grinning up at the older man.

"I'm fine! And how are you, Thane?" Delgan hesitated, his smile fading a little. "My condolences to you."

Alcandhor inclined his head in acknowledgement. The fresh pain of losing his father still ached raw inside every time he heard himself called by that title. Discerning of Delgan. "Thank you." He glanced past his friend to the other men. One, with light hair and a broad, ruddy face, watched with a wary gaze. The other, young and thin, with mop of unruly black hair, goggled open-mouthed. Alcandhor smiled at them. "Get you some food and join me. I wish to hear what you and your colleagues have found."

Soon they all gathered around the table, introductions made. Bivnet's stony face and crossed arms indicated his disapproval. Of Alcandhor? Of Ranger clan? Alcandhor was certain the man would let him know.

Delgan, between spoons of soup, told how a herder had contacted their guild upon finding strange-looking rocks in a high field his family had been trying to clear for grazing, and their subsequent findings. Vadmar, the young, dark-haired goggler, occasionally interjected a comment or clarification. Bivnat said nothing.

"This stone is not white—not shimmerstone?" Excitement coursed through Alcandhor, but he suppressed it for propriety's sake. The Thane should not caper in hysterics or run off trying to find a key port in the night. He settled for twisting his clasped hands on the table. Could this possibly be the lost western entrance to the Portal Complex? Best not to say rather than get these men's hopes up.

Vadmar shook his head. Face flushed and eyes alight, he looked ready to rush out into the dark. "Not shimmerstone, Thane. Oldstone." He edged forward, his elbows on the table. "Delgan says you can get us inside. Sir."

"Indeed." Alcandhor returned the youth's smile. "Tomorrow we shall see what is inside this place. 'Tis not on any map. My curiosity has crested."

Discovery - Chapter Two

"Oldstone, indeed," Alcandhor murmured as his hand brushed over it. Dawn barely gave light under this rocky overhang, but the smooth surface could be nothing else.

Delgan felt along the stone and pointed to the indentation. "There, Thane."

"Aye." He pulled the chain from under his shirt and jerkin and took the bio-crystal key in his hand. It glowed faintly, and Bivnat gasped, closing his eyes in muttered prayer. *Oh, by both moons, not a Worshipper.* Teeth gritted, Alcandhor ignored Bivnat, and set the key to the spot.

Silence fell.

Nothing happened.

Delgan's eyes met his in disbelief. "Could...could there be more than one key, one type of key?"

Alcandhor lifted his shoulders slightly. "Nay, but then, our knowledge of the Enaisi is limited." He squinted at the edges of the door, his fingers probing the fine, straight cracks.

"Should have known this would be useless," Bivnat grumbled. "Did you even bring the real key?"

Vadmar exclaimed, "You fool! You saw it glow."

Alcandhor ignored the outburst and squatted to examine the base. This door might not swing open, but slide sideways as did some in the Portal Complex, but he could see no tracks, only years of dirt encrustation. "Get you shovels, picks, whatever equipment you have. The threshold needs some cleaning, I think."

Before long, they gathered back at the door, and Alcandhor and Vadmar used the edge of shovels to scrape along the bottom. Buckets of water, hefted up the slope, helped wash away some of the loosened buildup.

The sun shone high by the time they cleared the tracks. Alcandhor wiped his face on his sleeve and pulled out the key again. This time the door moved, a stuttering slide against how many centuries of dirt? He placed his shoulder against the edge of the door and lent his weight to the unseen aged machinery straining to do its work.

The door stopped with a handspan still projecting from the rock face. Good enough.

Alcandhor straightened and peered into the darkness of the interior, taking a deep breath. The air smelled musty but not foul. He took a step inside, and the other three crowded behind him. A slight glow emanated from tracks of lights embedded in the beveled corners between wall and ceiling, stretching down the long corridor of grey-white oldstone. Doors lined the hallway to the left and right.

The two young history-keepers gasped.

Alcandhor had seen interiors similar to this in two places: some areas of the Portal Complex and in the structure on the Forbidden Peninsula. He dared not openly mention he had visited the latter place years ago with his father; too many considered it blasphemy to even set foot on the edges of the peninsula, while others feared it contained evils too vile to be imagined.

The history-keepers surged forward, exclaiming over smooth walls. The two younger ones entered the chamber to the right.

"This place is unknown, what was it?" asked Vadmar's muffled voice from inside the chamber.

"Who can say?" Bivnat replied.

Alcandhor followed Delgan into the left-side chamber to find a laboratory. Work consoles lined the walls and tables bore various scientific equipment, all under a thin layer of dust. Interesting, that. The Enaisi had a method of automated care which eliminated most dust and kept the air pure. How long had this place been deserted if dust could actually accumulate to any noticeable extent? He touched a microscope reverently. Slides scattered over the table; this place had been abandoned in haste. Another point of curiosity.

So many questions... Alcandhor turned about, wondering where to start.

His friend gazed in open awe about as he whispered, "What is your theory, Thane?"

"I have a few thoughts..." Alcandhor's voice trailed off as he peered into the microscope, adjusting the sight mechanism. Whatever had been on the slide those many ages ago was gone—naturally. Disappointment tingled in him anyway.

Delgan's hand ran across the top of a console and then ran a start sequence. Alcandhor came closer, and when nothing happened, exchanged a wry grin with his friend.

"These chambers and equipment remind me of the Portal Complex, Thane."

"Aye. I cannot say for certainty, but..." he hesitated, and Delgan lifted his brows in query. Alcandhor cleared his throat. "'Tis not well-known, but there was, at one time, an entrance to the Portal Complex on this side of the mountains. Where one accesses it from the complex itself, we know not."

Delgan leaned against the console. "By the Bells! An entrance lost—

on both ends? That...that sounds deliberate."

"Aye. Could be. But we know not for what reason. One thought is that it was to limit access to the complex. The Enaisi were known to be mysterious about their own past on this planet. It could be there were secrets here they wished kept from us."

"Like the Forbidden Peninsula."

That had not been a question. Alcandhor shot Delgan a measured look. *How much does he know?* "Aye. We know not what they feared we should find there, but respect of their wishes was why we initially avoided that land."

"And rumor and superstition did the rest."

The two men shared a smile.

"But this place, Thane. Shall it be a secret?"

Alcandhor shrugged, his mind torn. Safety for the Portal Complex warred with his yearning for knowledge, and for sharing that knowledge. "We shall see."

Delgan squinted upwards at the lights. "The power is still on after all this time," he murmured with a sigh. "Would that we had that technology."

"We did have."

Delgan glared, but Alcandhor only grinned.

"*Still* had," Delgan amended.

They shared a chuckle, then Alcandhor asked, "Shall we explore the rest of this place together, my friend?"

"Yes, let's do."

~*~

Delgan eyed the Thane. Alcandhor was more closed than he used to be. *Still feeling his fa's death, yes, but is that all it is?* He certainly seemed genuinely happy to see Delgan again, and although more restrained than when younger, his eyes gave away his excitement at this find.

This place definitely did give one pause. The long corridor opened into various work chambers and sleeping quarters, but just as with the Portal Complex itself, only the lights functioned, and those only dimly.

At the back of the corridor they discovered a lift—nonworking, of course; they took the circular stairs that wound down into the mountain. Delgan gasped for air by the time they reached the next level. *I'm getting old.* Taking slow deep breaths, he peered down a corridor dimly lit with beveled lights that looked much like the one above. Here, they found corridor directions on the wall: north, west, south, and section numbers, all written in Enaisi. Again, they wordlessly split into two teams, the younger two together, and he with the Thane.

They wandered into one chamber then another with no more findings than the level above them. Alcandhor stood by a console, his lips pursed.

"Disappointed, Thane?"

Alcandhor huffed a laugh. "Aye. And nay. I know I should expect to find nothing, yet finding nothing is...discouraging."

Delgan chuckled, understanding. Despite being forced into what was largely a political position, Alcandhor was, at heart, a scholar. Sciences, languages, history—those were his passion. An expedition such as this was his heart's delight, perhaps just the thing to help take his mind off his father's recent death and his ascension to Thane.

If only they could find something worthwhile here—and not just for Alcandhor. Delgan wouldn't mind either.

~*~

Delgan squinted up the steep slope, hoping this day's endeavors would bring some results. A way to the Portal Complex on the other side of the mountain, insights about the Enaisi. Something. Anything.

However, as the day wore on, his hope flagged. He sighed at yet another chamber bereft of evidence, of reason for the abandonment. No findings at all. Nothing. He swept a hand across yet another console. *Unless one includes dust as something.*

A shout came from across the hall, and he and Alcandhor rushed toward the sound. The two younger men almost collided in the doorway, chattering wildly like curvins flocking to overripe keeberries, interrupting each other.

"A light! A light blinking—"

"On a console!"

"We tried to activate it, but—"

"Do we need a special code?"

"Will the key work?"

All four men raced to the inside chamber. Delgan skidded to a halt in front of a console with a blinking light, set against a near wall, and then gazed about the huge, almost bare chamber.

"Still active after all this time?" murmured Alcandhor.

"How long, Thane?" Vadmar asked.

"Thousands of years, if this truly is an undiscovered Enaisi structure from before the time we settled this planet," Delgan replied.

"Aye." Alcandhor pored over the readings on the console. "*If.* Delgan, does this say what I think it does?"

Delgan's brows drew down. "Your knowledge of the Enai language is the most perfect of history-keeper I've ever known, Thane. Why do you

11

ask me?"

Alcandhor grinned. "I am not infallible."

Delgan chuckled and peered closer. "This console appears to be for a holographic imager."

"Aye, and I believe this light indicates a message or record, which is ready to be viewed."

"After all this time?" Vadmar asked.

"The Celestials could certainly—" Bivnat began.

"Keep your inane Worshipping to yourself," Delgan spat, "especially in front of the Thane."

"Just because he's—"

"Enough!" Alcandhor's voice echoed in the large chamber. "Let us see if the holographic imaging is still intact."

Delgan gazed at Alcandhor in anticipation. The Thane had longed for a moment like this his whole life. But he smiled at Delgan. "See if you can access it, my friend."

He cannot mean it! "Thane, you wish me—? You should be the one!"

"You are one of the few who have studied their technology including their computers. Go to, man!"

Delgan glanced at the other two, wide-eyed but silent, and ran his tongue over his dry lips. His hands hovered a moment over the board. Did he remember the coding to "wake up" a "sleeping" computer? And would his theoretical training mesh with the reality before him? And further, would bringing this computer online wake up other systems too? Was it too much to hope?

With slow exhale, he touched the screen in what he hoped was the right sequence. It seemed to work; the console activated, and a key port pulsed.

"It doesn't require a password, Thane, but it does a key. Will yours work for this, do you think? Or...?"

"This is supposed to be the master key. But let us find out." Alcandhor whipped the chain from around his neck and set the key to the port. A flash erupted behind them, and they whirled.

A table appeared in the center of the chamber, with men sitting around it, in styles of clothes so foreign, odd. They seemed solid, real. Vadmar gasped and stepped forward, swiping one arm toward the nearest man. His hand passed through the image, and he jumped back.

Alcandhor gestured for them all to be still. Delgan needed no urging; even breathing seemed difficult at the moment.

At the end of the table, stood a man with long, dark hair and a firm jaw. His black jerkin hung down to the thighs of his dark brown trous. From portraits and sketches, Delgan recognized the man. *Avadhron!*

"I will be heard."

The accent made Delgan frown, but with effort he could understand what Avadhron said. The official phrase *I will be heard* was used even in those times, it seemed, indicating someone was registering their objection, usually to some law or proposed law. *What did Avadhron object to?*

The older man with silvering blond hair sitting at the opposite end of the table lifted an arm. "You may speak, Commander Avadhron."

Next to him, Alcandhor inhaled sharply. Delgan realized why. The legendary Zaidhron! Their only king on this planet and first Thane of the Rangers. Stars! His heart thudded, and he took a measured breath.

"As I have stated in previous sessions, I do not agree with the new system of government you are attempting to implement since the war. It fractures authority, allowing the provincial lords too much control with too little oversight. Ch'shalna has no direct means of stopping abuses. Not only that, this shift of authority has blunted the teeth of our constabulary role."

"Our laws haven't changed. This merely shifts the burden—"

Avadhron spun to his right and addressed the man who spoke. "This is my Airing, Viltara! I am not here to argue." He squared his shoulders and again faced the table. "And of course I expect you lords to promote this new system as it increases your own status and power." Avadhron pointed with a sneer to the dark-skinned man with long, straight black hair seated at the far end. "You know this is true, but will not say because you 'do not wish to interfere.' At least Ismari is more honest about it than you!"

Delgan's whole body froze: an Enaisi! *The* Enaisi: Mattan! He could not have one of his breathing attacks now! *Inhale slowly...exhale slowly...*

Mattan lifted a hand. "Now wait—"

"I will not!" He gazed about the chamber. "The time will come when your government shall fall from corruption. I have seen it. I now record it for future generations to be aware. A Ch'shalna thane will have to take the throne back to save all our people from destruction."

The men at the table all exchanged glances, fear and doubt on their faces. Avadhron inhaled and continued, "And as I cannot back your new government, I officially resign as head of our security forces."

Most of the men jumped to their feet, exclaiming their dismay and protests. Mattan remained seated, rubbing a finger across his lips.

Avadhron raised a hand and glared at the men until, one by one, they fell silent.

"There is no room for discussion. I have decided. I am moving to Pashelon province. I will be a patroller and judge for the area in which I live." He reached forward and touched the center of the console. "I have chronicled my objection for future posterity."

The imaging faded.

No one spoke right away. Delgan certainly could not find his voice.

Alcandhor fell back against the console, his face pale.

Could it be true that Avadhron had opposed their new government? That he foresaw a Ranger thane making Claim? Wait—how could a Teldheri have foresight? Was this a true history? And was this something he should ask openly, or wait to speak privately to Alcandhor?

"Did you see them? That was them!" Vadmar exclaimed, bouncing on the balls of his feet. "Wait until we show the world! Living images of—"

"We cannot." Alcandhor said.

Delgan held his breath, trying to sort through this revelation and Alcandhor's proclamation.

The Thane met the others' gazes of disbelief. "We dare not. Not now."

"But this is history!" Bivnat sneered, his face dark. "You would deny our world their history? That was an Enaisi, a *Celestial* sitting with them! Mattan, wasn't it?"

Alcandhor chopped a hand through the air. "People are denied nothing. They know our history. How we came to be here, who we owe for it. This...this would cause contention. Too many fear the Rangers already— fear I might make Claim and try to restore the original rights of my clan."

Delgan sighed, trying to absorb that implication.

"But what difference does that make?" Vadmar clenched his fists. "That's history, not now. What does one opinion from a thousand years ago make on today? We have the chance to show everyone not just paintings or statues but the actual *people* who kept us alive through all the catastrophes and brought us to this planet!"

"Besides the fear of making Claim, we show that those venerated leaders did not all agree." Alcandhor crossed his arms. "One of the most respected pillars of our past objected to the change in rule proposed by our leaders, and gave up his position because of it."

Delgan raised a hand as Vadmar opened his mouth to speak again. "I have to agree. We have been taught all our leaders agreed unanimously to the new government. I never knew Avadhron was against it. I find that very unsettling."

Bivnat snorted. "It also gives new insight as to why the Rangers of this province are..." He peered at Alcandhor, eyes narrowed, and continued, "are a bit...independent."

With a chortle, Alcandhor replied, "That is an understatement. The Sons of Avadhron follow the law and answer to their Thane but keep to themselves, and within their sept have their own prescripts."

"But we can't *hide* this!" Vadmar waved his arms.

"Not forever, nay." Alcandhor said. "But...to just expose this, openly, would cause the current unrest to escalate. My clan is entrusted with keeping peace. I am concerned this revelation could hinder that."

Bivnat eyed Alcandhor. "You've surprised me, Thane."

Alcandhor lifted his eyebrows. Delgan was surprised, too, at hearing the Worshipper use his friend's title for the first time.

"How?"

"You truly do not want the advantage this could bring, do you? You could press for it—state your precious ancestor Avadhron wanted a king, that he foresaw the need for a king, and make Claim."

"Claim is only for exigencies, a temporary stratocracy. My ancestors gave up their right to be sovereign rulers. Why is this so impossible for people to comprehend?"

"It's your clan who wield the swords. It's feared they could wield more." Bivnat shrugged. "So I've heard it said."

"Let's return to our dilemma." Delgan said. "What is your suggestion, Thane? What do we do with this discovery?"

"I can't believe you would even consider siding with him," Vadmar said. "This is history! It's the truth of our past. The truth can't hurt us."

Delgan exchanged a wry smile with Alcandhor.

"You think it can't?" Bivnat sneered. "Foolish boy. You know history, how men behave."

"But it's the past! It's been one thousand years. Avadhron was wrong—our government works."

Alcandhor chuckled, scrubbing his face with his hand. "Does it now?" he murmured.

Delgan pursed his lips in thought. Some of the provincial lords, including Lord Paltor of his home province of Keladar, made life difficult for those under their dominion. Families struggled to survive while Paltor, well-warmed and well-clothed, dined sumptuously in his hall—as evidenced by his growing waistline.

If a king ruled with a firm hand instead of the Thane and Laird attempting to keep the rebellious lords in check, how would their lives be different? And if the lords thought the Thane might consider Claim, what might they do? Subvert what little oversight kept them in check and openly declare themselves independent? Delgan had no doubt of their despotic ambitions. "Give those who seek to undermine the Rangers a tool, a fear to use as a lever, and they will. Most assuredly."

Bivnat chewed his lip with a frown. "I...think you might be right. Yet I cannot help but want this find made open."

Alcandhor cleared his throat. "I think we should forestall any more investigating today. 'Tis already late. Let us return to the inn and ponder this revelation."

"We should call a meeting of the chiefs of the history guild. They

15

should know about this. And maybe they'll talk sense into you three," Vadmar spat. "Once they see that holographic file themselves."

"They shall not see it," Alcandhor said. "Not right away. That is my duty and my burden."

"Yours?" Vadmar clenched his fists. "Who are you to make that decision? Granted, you are Thane, but that doesn't give you full sway over all the history-keepers!"

"This complex and the imager itself were only unlocked by using the bio-crystal, which meant the original chiefs, perhaps even Avadhron himself, or Zaidhron or Mattan"—Alcandhor nodded at Bivnat—"sealed it. They wanted not the information within known generally. Thus, as with all things pertaining to the Enaisi, the keeper of the bio-crystal key is considered steward. It is at my discretion should anything be revealed."

"But—"

"I—have—spoken." The thunderous authority in Alcandhor's voice brought compliance from young Vadmar, who visibly wilted. He paused for moment, glaring at the young man, nostrils still flared, then ordered, "Let us return to the inn."

Delgan followed the other two history-keepers out with a smile. The soft-spoken Alcandhor could indeed be Thane when needed. His heart lightened. He had never harbored doubts that his friend had the wisdom, strength of will, and forbearance needed for the task, now Delgan knew he also could wield authority. Their world certainly needed that now!

His mind returned to what they had seen today. Was Avadhron right? Was the "fractured authority" to blame for the troubles their world had now? Each province left largely to its own rule, the people left to the whims of their lords? The lords were meant to be answerable to each other, but with so many corrupted, their self-governance was a sham. Not even the Thane and Laird together could stop the abuses and excesses.

Yet the abuses and excesses of their last king on the old world of Teledhar, and fears of it reoccurring, eventually led to this change in governmental structure. Perhaps all governments were merely as good or bad as those in authority. Was there even a proper answer then?

No one said a word as they climbed the stairs—still in the near dark, with only minimal light—and exited the place. They must all be as introspective as Delgan. *What turns are their thoughts taking from this discovery?*

Another thought plashed depressingly in his mind: nothing else had been activated when the holographic computer came online. He supposed it was the lot of history-keepers to be continually disappointed.

The sun barely peeked over the mountains, making their descent even more hazardous than usual. Halfway down, full gloaming forced Delgan to give all heed to where he placed his feet by feel more than by sight. He jumped at a call from down slope. Two men climbed toward them, their outlines barely seen in the growing dark.

"What brings history-keepers to our province with no word to its Rangers?" called one.

"History-keepers do not answer to Rangers," Bivnat said.

The two Rangers set hands on their swords as the first said, "This is our province."

"You do not belong here," snarled the second.

Alcandhor held out his arm. "Hold, cousins. You need not draw weapons."

"Do we not?" the first Ranger retorted. "That is to be seen."

Delgan frowned. The Pashelon Rangers held themselves apart from their kin in the other provinces, but this—this was disrespectful.

The second Ranger unsheathed his sword. "Ranger or not, you are not welcome. This place is ours, to guard. Even from other Rangers, even from history-keepers."

"Who gave you orders to guard this place?" Alcandhor asked.

"Rangers cannot command history-keepers!" Bivnat sneered.

"Shu!" hissed Delgan, digging an elbow into Bivnat's side.

"A place such as this is our right!" Vadmar cried.

The second Ranger marched uphill and shoved his face close to Vadmar's. "You have no rights here. Leave now."

"Just when we've discovered a whole vast complex in the mountain?" Vadmar shouted, waving his arms. "Laboratories and an—"

"Enough!" ordered Alcandhor.

"'Tis not possible," the first Ranger said. "Only the *key* can open—" He plodded up the short distance to Alcandhor and peered at him in the near-darkness. Delgan smiled in anticipation.

The Ranger fell to one knee. "Thane."

"Ordhral, is it not? And this other Ranger's name?" Alcandhor asked.

"This is Hosdhron, sir." He slapped his fellow Ranger's leg. Hosdhron also belatedly knelt.

"Well met."

"My Thane, we need to discuss your discovery. It has been the task of our sept to guard its secrets for almost one thousand years."

The two younger history-keepers both spoke at once.

Again, Alcandhor raised an arm, and they fell silent. His tone dry, he replied, "By all means, let us discuss this."

Alcandhor set his bowl and mug on the table, glancing about at the patrons. As usual, only a few herders. He frowned at the two Rangers gathered with them in the corner, then set his gaze on the older blond. He knew the man. As principal chief of his sept, he had attended Thane Saldhor's funeral. Like Alcandhor, he was one of the few who was a Child of the Enaisi and could make a key glow. The few lines around Ordhral's eyes belied his age. Alcandhor knew him to have over seventy years.

"So...you knew of that hidden complex?" he whispered, not wishing any to overhear.

"Aye, Thane. It was delegated to the chiefs of our sept to guard it," Ordhral replied in a low tone, his deep-set blue eyes fixed on Alcandhor.

"Even from your Thane?"

The two Rangers shifted in their seats and exchanged glances but did not answer. Alcandhor leaned forward, hands clasped on the table before him. "Who delegated this task to you?"

Ordhral hesitated, then said, "Ismari."

Alcandhor sat back. "Ismari?" *Mattan's sister—an Enaisi...*

Bivnat inhaled with a choking sound but said nothing.

"Aye." Hosdhron gulped from his mug. "Avadhron had made her promise to preserve his objection in her people's system, so it could not be lost or destroyed."

"However," Ordhral continued, "Ismari had foresight that a revelation of Avadhron's objection would cause grievous harm. So she kept her word to him but in the western portion of the Portal site which had been sealed and hidden from our people when we settled here."

"So this *is* the lost western entrance to the Portal Complex!" Alcandhor whispered with a grin at Delgan.

"Aye. And she then shared her sight and instructions with her sons, the original chiefs of our sept."

"I don't understand why you would worry anyway, it's not as if just anyone could open the place," Vadmar said. "The door won't open except for that bio-crystal."

"They could try—using force if necessary," Hosdhron said. "As a precaution, tanglevines were seeded around the area centuries ago to discourage anyone from getting too near."

The three history-keepers rolled their eyes, groaning.

"Was that truly necessary?" Delgan grumbled, scratching his forearm.

"Probably not. But our ancestors were zealous to obey Ismari, perhaps overzealous."

"And 'tis how I realized you must be the Thane, if you had been inside," Ordhral stated. "Only your key would open that door."

"So you know of the objection then?" Delgan asked.

"Not the details, but that he objected to the new rule. And only we"— Ordhral twirled a finger to indicate himself and his companion—"chiefs know. It has been handed down as law from our first mother."

"And when laws conflict..." Alcandhor murmured. "What then?"

"What conflict?" Hosdhron asked. "Keeping our charge from you?"

"Ha. Nay." Alcandhor relaxed against the back of his chair with smile. "You are caught at odds between the wishes of a husband and wife."

Ordhral snorted softly. "Aye. The command of our first father, and that of our mother, who was an Enaisi. How would you choose, Thane?"

Alcandhor fingered his mug, shaking his head. "'Twas not my choice, happily. But foresight of an Enaisi has always been given the weight of law. I do not disagree with your ancestors' obedience to her."

"But what happens now?" Vadmar asked. "How can you keep such a place hidden—"

Bivnat slammed his hand on the table, making Vadmar jump. "Do you not understand yet? Ismari, a *Celestial*, had *sight* and ordered this kept secret!"

"Quiet," Alcandhor ordered, glancing at the locals, who now all watched them with open curiosity. Wonderful.

The two Pashelon Rangers exchanged disgusted looks at Bivnat's outburst, then gazed expectantly at Alcandhor. He shook his head.

Vadmar sagged back in his chair. "I understand all that. What I mean is, the locals all know about it now. Do you really think we can conceal it?" He nodded toward the people sitting nearby. "Especially since you just shouted we are keeping a secret loud enough for the whole inn to hear."

Alcandhor ran his hands through his hair, breathing out long and low. "Let us rest for now. Tomorrow we shall trek back up to the complex and investigate more thoroughly."

"But Thane, what of the decree from Ismari?" Bivnat asked.

Alcandhor eyed the two Pashelon Rangers. "Know you why the western entrance was sealed?"

"Nay, Thane," Ordhral said, as Hosdhron shook his head.

"Then we return tomorrow. We few know and respect her wishes. But I wish to know *why* this entrance to the complex was closed off ages ago, *if* it is possible to discover thus."

~*~

"You are not worried about the locals knowing of this place?" Ordhral asked.

Alcandhor shook his head, paused, then shrugged as he set the bio-crystal to the key port. "A little, perhaps. But think you anyone will truly find a way to enter without the key? Especially with your sept aware and keeping eye here?"

"Aye, there is that." Ordhral's eyes widened as the door bumped and ground its way back into the rock wall.

Besides..." Alcandhor grinned, gazing about at his companions. "How can we leave with a mystery still to solve? *Why* was this side of the complex sealed?"

The two Rangers gazed in open awe as they passed through the corridors.

"To actually see what we have guarded," whispered Hosdhron.

"You have not yet truly seen it," Alcandhor said.

Bivnat blinked, his mouth dropping open. "You...you aren't going to show them the Airing, are you?"

"Aye. They have a right to see what they have guarded all these years." With a chuckle, Alcandhor added, "Besides, I want to see it again myself."

~*~

The imaging faded, and in the dim light, the men all stood silent.

"By the Bells and both moons," murmured Hosdhron.

"Aye, 'tis awe-inspiring," Alcandhor said.

Ordhral nodded. "In so many ways. We are seeing our ancestors, direct and collateral."

Whispering drew his attention to the corner. Was Bivnat praying? Alcandhor stifled a groan.

The Pashelon Rangers noticed, and Ordhral stepped forward, teeth gritted. "Stop that blasphemous muttering now, Worshipper!"

"This place is holy. Mattan is seen here. You can't stop me from—"

"You think I cannot? Ismari is my foremother, Mattan her brother." Ordhral's fists clenched. "They were no more gods than I am. If Ismari were with us, she would surely box your ears."

"How can a history-keeper, one who has studied our past, and our mentors, believe they were gods?" asked Hosdhron. "Worshippers are deluded. I would think you would know better."

"Simply because some of the divine dwells in you, lives in a diluted form in your blood, you think they are mortal as you are. Look at the powers the Children of the Enaisi have." Bivnat pointed at Alcandhor. "You are one, Thane. Don't you have powers that are unnatural?"

Alcandhor barked a laugh. "Unnatural? Nay. You know I am a Child of the Enaisi—you have seen the key glow. But simply because their race had abilities ours does not—"

"How long will you live, Thane, if you die of old age? How many hundreds of years?"

Stars, this would get them nowhere. Bivnat obviously chose to ignore the science, the genetics involved. "I will not engage in a discussion on this. Let us—"

"Do mortals live forever?" Bivnat crossed his arms, and Alcandhor lifted his eyes to the ceiling, sighing. *Bells above!*

"Their blood in you gives you unnaturally long life. Just because you deny—"

"The Enaisi do not live forever," Ordhral said, waving a hand, his voiced choked.

"They were here for hundreds of years, unchanging. They didn't die. They all went back through the portal and shut it down. Mattan, Ismari, Treyor, Dassel, Ashani—all of them, they're still alive."

Fists clenched, Ordhral stepped forward. Alcandhor lifted his arm to forestall the sept chief, pursing his lips and shaking his head. "Ashani is not. She died and is buried in my family's crypt. I would think you would know that, *history-keeper.*"

Bivnat lifted his chin. "Your clan claims that, but you have no proof. She went through the Portal—"

"The Portal closed before her son Zadhras was born," Alcandhor said, "years before she even married Tirdhal. Tell me how she used it then?"

"She's a Celestial. She would have known how to activate it."

"And how would she deactivate *our* side once she passed through? Tell me that," Ordhral said.

"They have ways—"

"Great Bells, what nonsense!" Hosdhron exclaimed as Alcandhor groaned.

As Ordhral opened his mouth in reply, the Thane held out a hand. "'Tis useless. You should realize that. Let us press on and explore."

After a scathing glare at Bivnat, the two Rangers strode forward with Alcandhor, out of the chamber and toward the interior of the structure. The rest followed.

Two more levels of laboratories, work and storage chambers, sleeping quarters, all with equipment and personal effects left behind. As they descended yet another flight of circular stairs, Alcandhor could hear Delgan gasp for air. As they reached the bottom, he turned and put a hand on Delgan's shoulder. "Do you need a rest, my friend?"

"No, thank you, Thane. It's only too much studying and not enough exercise." He patted his stomach with a grin. Alcandhor returned the smile, then glanced around. This new level seemed to be the final one—no stairs descended lower. It branched off not only to the west, north, and south, but east—toward the Portal Complex.

The six explorers simultaneously gave various shouts and exclamations and hurried down the east corridor. They gave the chambers on each side cursory examinations but their attention unanimously focused on heading east. Soon the walls showed signs of stress—slight bulges, cracks, streaks from moisture. Some of the panels of track-lights were dark. The damage grew worse and before long, in the glow of the few working track-lights, they could see the corridor ended abruptly in a cave-in.

"Think you this is natural, Thane? A quake, perhaps? Or was this caused to block access?" Ordhral asked.

"'Tis hard to say." Alcandhor set a hand against a large chunk of fallen oldstone, a strange feeling overcoming him. "I would guess a natural disaster. That would explain why everything was abandoned in haste." He froze as an image wavered and grew before him of the portal, shimmering black in the center, the ring framing it bright blue, the silhouette of a person walking toward him. He rarely had such an obvious vision. But did he see the future or the past? He took a deep breath, closing his eyes, struggling to hide the emotional impact of the sight. Dare he hope he saw an event to come?

"But why not return later?" Vadmar asked. "Why not clean up the laboratories, reclaim personal items?"

"Perhaps they thought it unsafe," Hosdhron said.

Vadmar scratched his head. "Wouldn't they have ways to determine that?"

"If anyone would, it would be the Celestials," Bivnat said.

Alcandhor shot a disgusted glare at the Worshipper.

"What caused the damage?" Delgan asked, his voice a murmur. "Why the immediate abandonment? Why did they not return? Why hide this place from us? Without bringing in engineers to assess this"—he waved a hand at the cracks and crumbled walls—"we cannot know if this was natural or planned. Even then we may not know. And I don't think the Thane will allow anyone but us in here."

They all looked at Alcandhor, who raised his eyebrows with a slight smile. Delgan had the right of it. He would not, could not allow more people in here. Ismari had given orders, he would not abrogate that.

"So that's it? We stop?" Vadmar threw out his arms.

"We have not explored the rest of this level." Alcandhor gestured back toward the stairs.

After a long, futile investigation, the group gathered once again, staring at the blocked corridor.

"What now, Thane? Do we give up?" Delgan's gaze swept over the rubble before them, his face a mask of frustration.

"'Twould be sweet to find answers as to why the Enaisi sealed this place." Alcandhor stared at the rubble, frowning. "Did Ismari truly think no one would ever open this place, see her husband's Airing? What were her thoughts? Her motives?" He took a deep breath and let it out slowly, defeated. "Let us return to that chamber and view the Airing once more. I would delay leaving here."

Alcandhor need not reach out to sense his companions to know what they felt, their silent trudge up the circular staircases bespoke their despondency. They all gathered in the imaging chamber again, and Alcandhor set the key to the port.

The image that came up, however, was not Avadhron's Airing. Instead, Mattan stood before them, smiling. His long, straight, black hair, tied with a leather thong, hung down his back. His leather jerkin bore the embroidery indicating his status as a chief of Ranger clan, but he wore trous and shirt of a black material, not the traditional colors worn by Rangers.

"Greetings, my curious children." Mattan's warm, dark eyes seemed to bore into Alcandhor's. How could an image *see*? "I assume the Thane of Ch'shalna clan himself is here since the bio-crystal key is necessary to enter this place and activate this console." The smile spread into a grin, white teeth against such dark skin. "To answer your question, Thane, this device can sense the key, therefore my statements will be directed at you."

Stars, could this Enaisi read minds across time and through a machine? Alcandhor felt faint. He inhaled deeply and let his breath out softly, his heart drumming against his chest. He could not help but devour every detail of Mattan's face. This was his forefather!

Mattan continued: "My sister told me of her duplicity concerning Avadhron's Airing. I agreed with her reasons, but foresaw something more—the insatiable curiosity of your people. I knew somehow, someday, this place would be found, and if it occurred after my death, I wanted to safeguard not only her secret, but my people's." His grin widened. "As a matter of fact, if you are viewing this, it is most likely I *am* dead."

The Enaisi paused, his animated face sobering. "Your people know of the area you call the Forbidden Peninsula. That place is a shameful part of our past, and I will say no more about it." Pain flitted across his face, and he swallowed before continuing. "This place also carries shame. And I will say no more of that either."

His smile returned but with effort, it seemed. "I can understand your elation at a historic find such as this, but I must ask that you honor the wishes of my people and not reveal what you have found." He lifted his chin, his head tilting slightly. "My respects to you, Thane, and to any colleagues accompanying you. I wish you a felicitous future on this world. It was, and is, my gift to you." He brought his fist to his heart in salute, then bowed.

The image faded.

No one made a sound in the subsequent emptiness of the chamber. Alcandhor felt it would take a long time to absorb everything he had encountered here. He wished this chamber had seats; he needed to sit down right now. Fortunately, the others must all feel as overwhelmed; the silence continued for some time. He stepped back and rested against the wall, his mind awhirl.

After awhile, a boot scuffed.

Ordhral murmured, "Thane?"

Alcandhor cleared his throat. "I think we should leave, as Mattan requested." His voice came out a harsh whisper.

"So we will never know what this shame is?" Vadmar asked.

"Nay. As the Pashelon Rangers respect and obey their mother in the task of guarding this place, so I will respect and obey my father in guarding their shame. It is my duty as a son. And as Thane."

With reluctance, Alcandhor pushed himself up from the wall. He noticed then that Bivnat had been kneeling with his eyes shut—at least his "prayers" had been silent. He pushed down his irritation, ignored the Worshipper, and left the chamber. The others followed.

The silence in the trek up the stairs and out of the edifice was broken only by the sounds of footfalls and breathing.

Once outside, Alcandhor touched the key to the port, and the door shuddered shut. He set his hand upon the old-stone. *Good-bye, my forefather. Would that we could have met.*

Dare he share this with the chiefs of his clan? He had a long journey home to ponder that question. He turned away from the mountain and began the careful descent down the treacherous slope. A thought made him halt mid-stride—if only his father could have lived to see this event. Another tragedy in his father's early death. To keep his mind off his morbid thoughts, he concentrated on the muddy ground.

As they all trudged downslope, Ordhral touched Alcandhor's sleeve and jerked his head. Alcandhor slowed and bent his head to Ordhral's.

"My Thane. . .what that Worshipper said about the Enaisi living forever. What do you know of the truth of this matter?"

Alcandhor frowned. "Why ask you me this?"

"They *do* have extraordinarily long lives."

"Aye. You should know thus being a descendent of them."

"I do. I just...have you had reason to believe any of them are still alive, here? Now?"

Alcandhor chewed the inside of his cheek before finally asking, "Do you?"

Ordhral stared at the ground as they walked, and finally shook his head. "Nay. The last we knew of was your ancestress Ashani, the second to marry into your line years after the portal closed."

"Aye, and was killed by Isandhral during the Uprising. So much for immortality."

Ordhral blew out a quick breath and nodded. "Aye."

Ahead of him, Delgan's footing slipped, and Alcandhor hurried forward, chancing falling himself to steady his friend. The history-keeper nodded thanks then whispered, "Thane, I would talk to you about something. And perhaps the sept chief as well."

"Oh?"

Delgan's sharp blue eyes in his craggy face bespoke something important, and Alcandhor called for Ordhral.

The Ranger trudged over to Delgan's other side, grasping his arm with concern. "Do you need help, history-keeper?"

"Not of that sort, but a pretense might keep our conversation more private."

"Now my curiosity is crested," Ordhral said with a crooked smile. "What would you discuss that must be private?"

The grey-haired man squinted ahead, then at the men next to him. Now Alcandhor's curiosity crested as well.

"I don't know that it must be private, but I'd rather exercise caution than have regret."

"Admirable. Say on, sir."

Delgan licked his lips. "Avadhron said he had foresight. But he was Teldheri. How could he possibly have an ability that is exclusive to the Enaisi or their offspring?"

Alcandhor's mouth fell open. Bells, he had been so excited by their extraordinary find that he had not thought of that! He stared at Ordhral, but the man grinned. "I take it, Sept Chief Ordhral that you know the answer?"

"I know many answers. I am not certain which ones I am allowed to share, given the instructions left by my first parents."

How much information did this man have that he would not, could not, share? Alcandhor ground his teeth. "Bells, you gall me!"

"I apologize. It is not my desire to do thus. But, let me share this. I have sight, too. And I know you have. I share your vision that our world will see change. It is close. We shall see it, and then the question Delgan posed will be answered."

"Shall we, Ordhral? Sometimes I falter in believing."

"Do not, Thane. Hold fast. And know that the Sons of Avadhron back you, and will be wherever you need us to be." The sept chief nodded to them both, and turned to join his cousin waiting downslope.

Hold fast. Most days, Alcandhor felt his hold was slipping.

"Well, Thane," Delgan muttered, "this has been an interesting bit of exploring, with many eye-openers. But at least, we have seen a great thing."

"Aye. Keeping it secret is the bitter medicine."

"But that medicine is for our health."

Despite his melancholy, Alcandhor chuckled. "Aye. True." He clapped a hand on Delgan's shoulder. "My thanks."

They shared a smile.

A laugh brought their attention to Vadmar, downhill. The lad grinned. "Mattan said he must be dead. The Enaisi *do* die!"

"No," Bivnat shot back, glowering. "He was jesting. Couldn't you tell?"

Alcandhor closed his eyes and shook his head as the rest all groaned.

~*~*~

CHILDREN OF THE ENAISI

Chapter One

current year - 1043

Nandhal rose before daylight and broke camp. He must keep ahead of the Rangers trying to find his trail, if indeed they had not already found it. His lip curled. Cursed clan-lovers. He would show them one day.

As black gave way to grey, the breeze picked up, showering the forest floor with autumn foliage. He hurried on, pleased that the heavily falling leaves might help hide his tracks—anything to slow the Rangers even a little.

Mists rose, shredding into vaporous rags that vanished as pale dawn presaged another day. The dim boom of drums rolled through the forest, and he grimaced at its message that he, the Ranger Nandhal, had gone Rogue. They had given him twenty-six hours, a full day, before drumming out the first message. *Rangers always play by the rules.* He tossed his long, blond hair over his shoulders with an arrogant snatch of his head. *I will not stop long enough for them to find me.*

He needed to find Monadhal's Rogue band. But how could he find the Rogues when Monadhal was so adept at eluding Rangers?

If only the plan of his confederates had been successful, the Thane would be dead along with all the Ranger chiefs. But he would get revenge on them. All of them. Especially Thane Alcandhor and his little favorite, Tam.

~*~

Tam adjusted her pack and her quiver, slung her bow over her shoulder, and hefted her staff. She pulled her cloak close around her in the chill pre-dawn air, and gazed around the torch-lit bailey at the large company she would be journeying with. She knew few of them, save the chiefs and Marcalan.

Being a Child of the Enaisi, she had the ability to sense other people's emotions, and all these strangers' feelings and moods assailed her, making it hard to breathe. She put up a block and sighed at the respite from the onslaught, then stood on tiptoe, seeking her uncle, Thane Alcandhor. Where was he in this throng? She could not see her great-uncle Lamadhel either. His red-haired older son stood near.

"Andhrel, where is your father?"

The lean, blue-eyed Ranger smiled at her. "Talking to the Thane. Father is staying here, you know. Alcandhor has asked him to stay on to give guidance to our new, young Laird."

"Could that not cause trouble? Laird Hall and Zaidhron are autonomous of each other."

"You have a law-keeper's mind. 'Tis true, but with few ministers left to give counsel to the Laird, it is probably a wise decision. Lamadhel's guidance is not official, just the wisdom of a friend." Andhrel grimaced. "Which detractors will not distinguish in any case. They already accuse Laird Hall of being our puppet."

"Aye, Lord Paltor said as much at his trial," Tam said, speaking of one of the nobles who had been found guilty of being a traitor after the siege. But what was a puppet? Her father had taught her Ranger ways well, but had left her untutored in so many others. Would Andhrel mock her if she asked what a puppet was? She forbore asking and instead said, "I am glad the trials, and hangings, are over."

"Almost over. Do not forget Tanadhon."

Tam shuddered. "Stars, aye. Where is he?"

"That traitor will be accompanying us back home. He is bound and under heavy guard. Once back at Zaidhron, he will be hanged for his crimes."

Tam could not even nod. She had liked the former Ranger, and was sorry he had to die. She would probably have to endure the sight. With a deep inhale, she pushed such a dark thought from her mind.

A call sounded, and the Rangers all moved out. They passed Lamadhel standing at the gate, and Andhrel stopped to clasp his father's shoulder. Tam waited a turn, then hugged her great-uncle. He returned the embrace with a smile and kissed her cheek. "Be well, niece," he murmured.

She nodded and gave him a second hug, then hurried with Andhrel through the Rangers to find the Thane. There—he walked in front with Haladhon and Eladhrel, two close cousins and Ranger chiefs. Andhrel smiled over at his brother, Eladhrel. Haladhon grinned down at her as she walked next to him. The tallest Ranger she had ever seen, he towered over Tam. He also had the most beautiful, thick, black hair. As many Rangers did, he held it back in a thong at the nape of his neck, and the wavy mass covered most of the pack he wore, save one short lock that curled down on his forehead.

Alcandhor gestured to his niece. She moved over to walk next to him. She let her block down so she could feel the affection from her uncle, even as she pondered the dissimilarity between him and her father, in looks and in personality. Her father's hair had been such a dark brown that it appeared black, his eyes narrow and grey. He had been broad-shouldered and heavily muscled. Her uncle's hair was a lighter brown and his eyes more blue than grey. He had a more lithe build than his older brother, and unlike her father, was openly emotional. When angry though, her uncle's eyes darkened and jaw set just as her father's had, and she could more easily see the similarity in their features. At times the resemblance was comforting, and at times, melancholy.

"Sleep well?" he asked.

"Aye."

"No dreams?"

Nightmares had plagued Tam for several years. She would fight against a blackness pulling at her and awake sweating and gasping for air as if in a dire sparring match. But her uncle said these were not true dreams, and that she should not struggle against them. "Nay, Uncle. But I have remembered what you said. When I have a dream, I will try not to be frightened."

"Good girl."

"I am glad you are feeling well. Your pain is almost gone except in your shoulder. Can you move it much?"

Alcandhor groaned. "Girl, you will be the end of me. I can keep no secrets from you, even about my health."

"'Tis possible for you to block your emotions from me, but not your pain. Your arm and shoulder are much better, but movement is still limited, is it not?"

"Aye. The healer has exercises I am to do to help gain movement and strength back. That arrow was very damaging."

"I am so glad you are all right," she whispered, trying not to think about the fact she had lost her father to an arrow only moments after her uncle was hit. He gave her a quick hug around the shoulders and kissed her forehead, sorrow emanating from him. He must be remembering, too, that his brother died that day.

She looked up into his kindly, sad eyes. "Does it ever stop hurting, Uncle?"

"Nay. After awhile it dulls and you can live with it easier, but it never goes away. It took a long time for me to think of my father without the grief overwhelming me. He was a great man. I wish you could have known him."

"Have you ever wished you were not Ranger clan? That you did not have to worry about kin dying all the time?" Would he think it offensive for her to ask such a thing?

"A few times. Especially when grief was fresh."

Tam felt better then. Guilt plagued her for having such thoughts right after her father died.

"Feelings are neither right nor wrong, Tam," her uncle said, reminding Tam he also could sense emotions, if not as strongly as she could. "It is what we do about them that can turn us wrong. Never apologize for what you feel."

Tam pondered that as they continued walking, but her uncle's physical pain bothered her. She sent him feelings of comfort and love. He glanced down at her with a smile. "Thank you. But what was that for?"

"Your pain." She hesitated then asked, "Do you take any tincture to help you heal, Uncle? Like withan, perhaps?"

His eyebrows lifted. "How know you this?"

"'Tis in my book."

"The one you spoke of before? I would like to see this book. Where is it now?"

"I gave it to Sarinna to keep for me," Tam said, speaking of Alcandhor's sister, her aunt.

"We will retrieve it when we get home. I would fain read that book."

"I think you would fain read any book. How many did you stow in your pack?"

He laughed and it lightened Tam's heart; she wished he were not so sad all the time.

"Too many. And other Rangers carry more, plus copies of the charts from that hidden chamber you just discovered in Ranger Hold. We will have much to study, my dear niece."

Haladhon, walking on the other side of Alcandhor, gazed askance at Tam. "The chiefs will all have to study these new books, Tam. See what trouble you caused, finding that chamber of the Enaisi?"

"Typical woman," her prankster cousin Marcalan interjected. "Turns everything topside down. It must be the reason they were never allowed to be Rangers, Thane. A nuisance, that is what they are."

Haladhon tossed the hood of Marcalan's cloak over his head with a suggestive wink as he commented, "Pleasurable nuisances, cousin."

Marcalan flipped the hood back as he snorted, shooting Tam an indignant look. She suppressed the urge to giggle and sent happy feelings to her cousin. He returned them, and the sending of their emotions to each other continued without either trying. Neither Tam nor Marcalan had heard of such happening, of not just sensing another's emotions but of a sustained connection without conscious effort.

'Twas strange, but Tam could not ask her uncle about it right now without giving away Marcalan's secret. Neither of Marcalan's parents were Children of the Enaisi, therefore Marcalan should not be. But he was. He had hidden the knowledge for years, until Tam inadvertently gave it away.

Until Uncle could talk with Marcalan's parents, and unravel the mystery of his abilities, they were to remain known only to Alcandhor, Haladhon, and herself.

~*~

Keeping his emotions light and happy had never been difficult for Marcalan, but now, knowing he must, it seemed a chore. How he and his beautiful—oh, so beautiful!—and delightful, young cousin had developed this ability to keep their emotions connected without any conscious effort confounded him, but he dared not let his feelings for her be known, not even to her. Especially not to her. She was too ingenuous and might mention something to her uncle. And Alcandhor had made it plain he would brook no romantic involvement for his young niece for the foreseeable future, due to the extensive training she must undergo to become the next Thane.

Marcalan stared at the grass as he hiked next to his kin, his thoughts turbulent. He had never been in love, but that changed before he even met Tam, when he heard stories of her from his kin. He'd long had a prescience of whom he would fall in love and his heart pierced with the knowledge it was his newly discovered cousin. But he dared not admit he had the gift of foresight—indeed, he dared not admit he had any abilities passed down from his Enaisi ancestors, as neither of his parents had inherited those gifts. The only possibility, that Marcalan's mother had broken her marriage vows, was not something Marcalan could believe nor would wish to bring to light.

How he had known at an early age that he must keep his Enaisi heritage a secret, he knew not. It seemed an instinct, although how likely was that? Had his parents discussed something that he overheard as a child and understood not? He had never dared ask.

He felt a touch on his arm and looked up to see Tam walking next to him, her oval, golden eyes filled with concern. He had let his feelings become perturbed while connected to Tam. At least his melancholy mood could be laid at the feet of his secret burden about his heritage, not his secret burden of being in love with her.

She whispered, "Worried about—"

Marcalan snatched her staff and ran off with a mocking laugh, her shock at the abrupt act jolting him. Hoots of Rangers filled the air and shouts for her to chase him down and thrash him. He pivoted quickly as he sensed her near and spun her staff above his head with a taunting grin. Her surprise and confusion settled into understanding and humor and she crouched into a fighting stance, her eyes alight.

"Marcalan, you truly are the rascal Uncle says you are!"

"Why thank you, cousin." He bowed, but with one arm raised, keeping the staff above his head.

With a swift leap, Tam grabbed her staff before Marcalan could straighten or jump back, pulling him off balance. They fell to the ground, still struggling for possession. Tam had both hands on the piece of lorzwood and grinned through gritted teeth. Her closeness had an unintended effect on Marcalan, and he let go of the staff and rolled away, blocking, hoping she sensed nothing untoward. He slowly rose, as if out of breath, and kept up the teasing. "Not fair being so young and picking on an old man!"

The Rangers' laughs renewed amid jeers at his easy defeat. Tam's confused and hurt expression gave way to a smile as Marcalan gave her a fleeting wink and headshake. How much had she felt—and understood? By the Elders, he must keep more in control!

Chapter Two

Why did Marcalan pull away and block? Had Tam done something wrong? Surely not her attempt to ask him if worry over his Enaisi gifts caused his anxiety or else why did he playfully take her staff? Or perhaps that was just a way to stop her from asking, then he blocked to chastise her? Nay, 'twas not until that strong burst of passion from him hit her that he blocked. He had not allowed their connection to continue since, and she felt bereft and lonely without his cheerfulness bubbling in her.

She reviewed the feelings expressed in that moment of arousal. 'Twas not the first time she had felt thus from him, but truly never had it been so forceful. The effects still tingled in Tam's stomach and spread downward. Uncle had explained growing up to Tam, and warned her that she should avoid any man with such desires. But this was Marcalan. Oh, if only she could talk to him!

She tried twice, but he skillfully managed to evade her by jesting or taunting Rangers and creating a scene. Finally, she sighed in resignation. She would have to wait until they had the chance to be truly alone. He would talk to her, she was certain, once no one could overhear. She resisted the impulse to sulk as it might draw her uncle or Haladhon's attention, and she dared not explain.

They came out of a stand of trees, and her concerns over Marcalan were displaced by the sight of smoke curling out of several chimneys in the long, wooden building sitting atop the hill before them, a tower standing tall behind it. Tam stared at the strange structure which resembled not at all a house, well, not any house she had ever seen.

"Roads heavily traveled all have stations along them where there are no towns, about a day's journey apart. A day's journey for most people anyway. Rangers generally travel much faster." Haladhon nodded toward the structure rising high behind the station. "Many of them also have drum towers."

So this was indeed a journey station. She peered at the building as they ascended the path. "Will there be room inside for all these Rangers?"

"Nay. And you are about to see a debate concerning that, too." Haladhon pointed to Alcandhor.

Tam's uncle already stood atop the rise, arguing with two Rangers, one fair and one dark. Never had Tam seen Rangers openly argue with their Thane before, and she climbed up quickly to listen. She knew them both.

33

The black-haired one, Cordhan, had been one of her father's old match partners, and was now one of hers. The second, Zandhral, sporting a full beard—rare for a Ranger—was also a Child of the Enaisi.

"We will not have you sleep outdoors, Thane, when there are cots or mats inside," Cordhan said, his arms crossed and his stance denoting his determination.

"I will sleep with my Rangers. Since there is not enough room for all of you—"

Zandhral interrupted. "You slept in Ranger Hold, Thane, and many slept outside—"

"If you remember, I was injured and had no choice."

"You are still injured." Cordhan pointed at the Thane's shoulder and sling. "Tell me you could match with that arm now, Thane."

"It affects not my ability to sleep on the ground."

Haladhon shot a grin at Tam, then gestured to Cordhan and Zandhral that he needed to speak to the Thane in private. The two inclined their heads to the Ranger chief, and Alcandhor and Haladhon walked off to the side, their heads close as they talked. Tam frowned curiously at Cordhan, who shrugged. Her uncle's gaze shot over to her, then he almost stormed toward the journey station, muttering to himself.

Haladhon chuckled as he strode back to where they stood.

Cordhan's green eyes sparkled. "What said you to convince him, Haladhon?"

The tall Ranger smirked, winking at Tam. "I used a very old trick—fatherhood."

Cordhan crossed his arms. "Explain that, please."

"If he sleeps out here with his Rangers, does that mean he wishes Tam to sleep outside, too?"

"What difference does that make?" asked Cordhan.

"Think you, man. He is suffering from a bad case of fatherhood right now and despite the fact that our Second at Table has lived much of her life in the wild with Valdhor, he would wish her inside the building to sleep, not out here."

"Well...granted." Zandhral shrugged. "She is a lass, after all."

Tam stepped forward at that insult, but Haladhon raised his hand to silence her. "I would be careful making statements like that, Zandhral, or she may show you she is truly Valdhor's Trained heir. But back to what I was saying, the Thane is taking his duty as her foster-father very seriously and aye, he does wish her to sleep inside—"

"I would fain sleep outdoors, Haladhon," Tam interrupted.

"Peace, girl, and listen. My point to him was, if he is sleeping outdoors, who is indoors with Tam, chaperoning her in a room of men?"

Zandhral and Cordhan both laughed as Haladhon proudly chortled.

"Haladhon!" Tam's face warmed as she glanced at the other Rangers.

"I am sorry, Tam, but it is the truth. It is not a matter of not trusting Rangers. I know that not one of these men would dare think of attempting anything inappropriate. It is a matter of propriety."

Tam planted her fists on her hips. "But need you talk of it so openly?"

Cordhan winced, ducking his head toward Tam. "She is young to hear such talk, Haladhon."

"It is nothing she does not understand. And in my opinion, it is something she needs to take into consideration, being the only female Ranger in our entire world. Not to mention, if she is a Ranger, she needs to inure herself to such discussions as might take place among Rangers."

With a playful punch to Haladhon's arm, Cordhan asked, "With or without you present, you rake?"

Haladhon grinned, a mischievous twinkle in his eyes. "With, of course."

Zandhral rolled his eyes. "There are grown men who have never inured themselves to some of the conversations that you have had, Haladhon. And would you truly talk of such things around Tam?"

Haladhon shrugged, grinning, and Cordhan gave a soulful sigh. "'Twill be a sad sight to see what the Thane does to you if you do, Haladhon."

Tam did not quite understand all the subtleties of their jesting, but the subject matter alone made her blush.

~*~

Never before had Alcandhor been bothered by the fact that journey stations did not have separate chambers for sleeping. But as mats were set out in the one long room after the trestle tables had been taken down following the meal, he wished it had sleeping chambers as an inn would. He put Tam in the corner, then took the next mat. Only a few days earlier, his niece would not have understood why; at least now she knew it was a necessity and did not make a fuss.

Her father had never taught her anything about growing up or becoming a woman. He had raised her high in the mountains and she had rarely met anyone. She grew up knowing nothing about mores or propriety, and less about relationships between men and women. Alcandhor had wanted to wait until he could take her back to Zaidhron and let his sister, Sarinna, be foster-mother to her, teaching her what she should have already been taught.

The situation at Lairdton's Ranger Hold had been problematic, though. The only young lass among hundreds of Rangers, and empathic as well as beautiful, Alcandhor dared not wait to explain the feelings she had to have sensed from some of the men. It had been a difficult and long discussion, as he did not easily talk about such personal matters.

He watched with affection as she took off her boots and settled onto her mat. In some ways, he felt she was truly his daughter instead of his niece. That made no difference now; as an orphan, he—by law, as nearest kin—became foster-father to her. He wondered, as he had before, who her mother had been. The light gold of her large, oval eyes contrasted against her brown skin. And although dark, almost black, like Valdhor's, her shoulder-length hair did not wave, but hung straight.

She smiled over at him, all dimples, then rolled herself into the blanket, curled up on her side, her eyes closed. His heart ached that Valdhor had not shown that precious child any love. He sighed as he stretched out on his mat. At least she was loved now.

~*~

Tam watched her uncle sleep and thought of the night less than two lunations ago when she first met him. She had watched him as he slept on the floor of the cottage then, too. So many changes had occurred in her life in that time. The sorrow of her father dying twisted her insides into knots. She would not cry, not here, not with all these Rangers. She tried to sense Marcalan but he still blocked; she would not give in to loneliness and sadness. She closed her eyes and breathed deeply, forcing her mind to happier thoughts: Uncle, Haladhon, Marcalan, all her new kin and friends...

The blackness of her old dream came. Her uncle said she need not fear it, but terror gripped her anyway. She tried not to fight this time, but instead she allowed herself to be carried toward it. As she approached the blackness, she could discern a glow from its edges—as she had seen in the chart in the secret chamber she had discovered. The blackness seemed to slowly rotate and as it did, the glow increased. She felt snatched into, then through, the blackness and on into a bright light as if she stared at the sun. The light faded, and a face appeared with high cheekbones, dark eyes, and warm, brown skin. He smiled at her, and although he did not speak, she could sense his elation.

My child! she heard him say in her mind.

Fear gripped Tam, and she pulled back despite her resolve, waking so suddenly she sat up with a gasp as if hit in the chest.

Alcandhor stirred, then shot upright. "Tam! Did you dream?"

She gulped then managed to say, "Aye, Uncle. I passed through the blackness, and I–I saw someone. He called me his child. I...grew afraid and then...then I woke up."

Alcandhor stared at her, mouth open, then closed his eyes, bowing his head. Relief, elation, anticipation, excitement, joy—so many emotions roiled in him. She knew his ambition was to somehow contact the aliens called the Enaisi that had been their people's mentors, ages ago.

Other Rangers sat up now, a few murmuring quietly.

"Thane?" asked one Ranger, after a silence.

"I think, men, we are heading out of darkness after all these years. As my father saw, and as I have seen," the Thane replied, not looking up, his voice thick with emotion. He paused then cleared his throat before continuing. "Our world is balanced on the edge of a sword, and there is going to be trouble in the days coming. People fear change." He hesitated, gazing around the chamber at them, then added, "Even some Rangers."

"Not us, Thane," answered one Ranger. A murmur of assent came from the others.

The Thane peered over at Tam. "Think you that you can conquer your fear and talk to him, the next time? Or can you only hear him talk?"

"It was not talking. I could hear him in my mind. I will try to talk to him. What would you like me to say?"

Her uncle chuckled. "I have a million questions, Tam. I will see if I can make a list of a few that I feel are the most important. I need to think about it."

"Aye, Uncle."

"Tam?" Alcandhor's eyes glittered in the dim light of the hearth. "What did he look like?"

"He was beautiful." She paused, tipping her head in thought. "Um, I guess handsome. I do not think men like to be called beautiful."

Some of the Rangers chuckled.

"He had very dark skin, much darker than mine." She paused again, not knowing what else to say. She gazed down. "I am not good at describing, Uncle. I am sorry."

"'Tis all right, Tam. If he can tell us what to do to get that portal to work, perhaps we can all see what he looks like one day. For now, I suppose we should try to get some sleep, though I doubt it will come easily for me tonight."

Tam curled up again in her blanket, and shared a smile with her uncle as he stretched out on his mat, too. She closed her eyes, fearing sleep and that strange man who had called her his child.

Chapter Three

"So, cousin Tam..." Tam turned to see Maradhor, a Ranger-scribe and sword-master, walking toward her with Jonadhan, another scribe, tagging after. All around the hillside, hundreds of Rangers—looking like herdbeasts milling in the grey morning mist—readied to continue their journey toward their home city of Zaidhron. She could not see Marcalan, and he still blocked; was he avoiding her? She brought her attention back to her scribe cousins with a smile.

Maradhor ran his thumbs under the shoulder straps of his pack. "Tell us again about the man you saw. Was he truly an Enaisi?" Intense curiosity filled his wide-set brown eyes.

"Uncle believes so."

"Does he look like us?"

Tam adjusted her own pack and nodded, noticing many Rangers had gathered to listen. Word traveled swiftly to those in the camps from those few who stayed at the inn.

"Aye. But he has a much darker complexion."

"Like you?" Maradhor asked.

Tam shook her head. Her skin was brown, unlike anyone else she had ever met. Until she saw the Enaisi. "Oh, much, much darker than me."

"When do you think you will dream again?" asked Jonadhan.

"I know not. It just happens at times."

Cordhan grinned at her. "You are an amazing lass."

Tam shrugged, blushing, not knowing what to say.

"You had best expect attention." Cordhan's green eyes crinkled in a kind smile. "You will receive it for being a Ranger lass, and also for being a Child of the Enaisi."

"I do not like it," she shot back, then bit her lip in self-chastisement; Rangers controlled their tempers. "But I know I must get used to it."

"Many of those journeying home with us do not know you and would fain talk with you." Cordhan glanced at the men around them with a nod. "The more you tell us about yourself, the easier it will be to accept you. We have not been raised with you, and are curious about the lass who will be Thane."

Tam frowned. "Who *might* be Thane."

Cordhan laughed. "Is it doubts about yourself that make you wish to dispute the conclave?"

"Nay." She hesitated. "I know not." She paused again and shook her head. "I think not about it. I just know my uncle is Thane, and I want him to remain Thane."

"Understandable. But the law is the law."

"Conclave decisions are not law."

Cordhan raised his eyebrows in surprise. "You understand that distinction?"

"Nay, not really. I need to study. And I need to find a way to keep Uncle as Thane."

"Why are you so adamant about it?"

Tam stared at Cordhan—was he a simpleton? "Because he is Thane."

"Argue not with her, Cordhan." Haladhon stepped behind the Ranger, clasping a hand on his shoulder. "She is a typical female and her favorite argument is 'just because.'" His eyes twinkled at her.

"Careful, cousin," Cordhan replied over his shoulder, chuckling. "She may make you pay for that."

Tam arched an eyebrow. "Aye, Haladhon, we have not matched yet."

Her tall cousin walked closer and bent over her with a smile, his green-grey eyes snapping with a good-natured threat. "Any time, my dear cousin."

"Now?"

Haladhon grinned and started to remove his pack, but just then, the cry to move out sounded. The Rangers standing near groaned with disappointment.

Haladhon chuckled as they began to walk. "You win a reprieve, cousin."

"It is you who won the reprieve."

His grin broadened. "We shall soon see."

Cordhan shook his head. "Do not be too cocky, Haladhon. I have matched her. She is a wicked fighter."

"Aye, Haladhon. I agree."

Tam spun to the older Ranger striding toward her. Edhron had been her father's match instructor. How could a lean man, not much taller than Tam, have taught and bested Valdhor?

She shyly returned his smile. "I am honored you say so, Edhron, but you best me in every match."

"You fight well. And learn quickly." His gaze pierced her. "You do know that I will be your instructor upon our return."

Tam's eyes widened. "I–I thought you only trained striplings."

Cordhan slapped a hand on Edhron's shoulder. "Our combat master also trains with a select group of more seasoned Rangers. To keep himself and us at our best. I think you would be a happy addition to our circle."

They would wish her as a match partner? "Truly?" she whispered, glancing at both Edhron and Cordhan.

The lines around Edhron's eyes deepened as he grinned. "Perhaps tonight we can match again."

"I would like that."

"Oh, stars," came a new voice from behind her. "March all day, then match in the evening? You both must love pain."

Tam turned to see the Ranger that had spoken. She found him not overly tall, with curly, dark hair, his frame lean save for his arms. Despite the loose sleeves, the bulk of his arms could be observed, especially his right arm. Even without the exquisitely carved longbow at his back, Tam would have marked him a master bowman. His grey eyes sparkled as he inclined his head. "You know me not, cousin Tam. I am Bardhal."

Tam nodded in recognition. "One of the four bowmen besieged inside the drum tower within Laird Hall. I saw you the night the siege ended, and I had to read the reports."

He raised his eyebrows, surprise on his face. But why? Did he not expect she would read the reports and know of him? She was Second at Table, after all.

Edhron moved over and let him walk next to Tam.

"It was a great shock to us to see a lass dressed in Ranger garb that night," Bardhal said.

"Aye, I imagine it was. It always is." Tam tried to keep an irritated edge out of her voice. "I would fain practice my bowman skills with you."

He bowed his head. "I am honored. And I also eagerly wait seeing you match Edhron tonight."

"He is a great fighter."

Bardhal chuckled. "Aye, he is. Many are the thrashings I have received from him."

Cordhan grinned over at Edhron. "Are you speaking of Ranger Training or the thrashings you received at home?"

Edhron and Bardhal laughed.

"Both," they replied together.

Tam glanced from one to the other. "Is Edhron your father then?"

Bardhal nodded, exchanging smiles with his father. Tam sighed. She needed to learn her clan tree. To know their kin was as breathing to her clan; they understood not how lost she felt.

"Glad to be returning home, Bardhal?" asked Haladhon.

"Aye. That siege was horrible." He shook his head. "I hope we never have to do such a thing again."

Haladhon nodded. "To see it all happen and be able to do nothing must have been a nightmare."

"Aye, cousin. Never was I so relieved as when we were able to drum to you that it was over."

The talk turned to what they saw in the siege and from there to other events concerning the traitors, now all dead or exiled. Tam was glad it was over too. She remained quiet, listening to them talk in grave tones, then felt a wave of mirth wash over her almost making her giggle. Marcalan! He had stopped blocking. He walked ahead with her uncle, and by his animated expression and gestures he must be telling some outrageous story. He looked not at her, but he need not. Their connection let her know he thought of her, even as he acted out some tale. Oh, how she had missed this!

"So, Tam." Haladhon nudged her arm. "Are you going to match me before or after Edhron tonight?"

Tam blinked, forcing her mind to Haladhon's question, not Marcalan. "After I think. Edhron is a very tough fighter. Matching you will be easy after fighting him."

She heard several Rangers hoot at that, and one shoved Haladhon in the back, laughing. Haladhon grinned down at her. "We will see, my young cousin."

~*~

Tam felt Alcandhor's pride in her as he watched her spar. Here and there Rangers matched in the large field near the inn, but most crowded to see her fight. Edhron pushed her more than the last time. She was beginning to get a feeling for his style though and managed to get a few good moves in on him. Surprise and pride surged with each one, but he would just smile and come in with a new technique. He bested her during the whole match, as she expected. But she did learn—and enjoyed it.

Tam and Haladhon grinned as they faced each other and put their fists over their hearts before starting. Tam knew hard fighting but that would not be an advantage against her ever-so-tall, broad-shouldered cousin. She had to use Haladhon's height against him and use what she had learned from Edhron to score against him. Haladhon had years of experience and his opponents were all smaller than he was. And he had another advantage, he had seen her match and she had never seen him. She did not know his weaknesses but he had had the chance to assess hers. Why was she so determined to do well against her cousin?

His mischievous eyes twinkled at her, daring her, as they circled. She wanted to laugh, then realized he was trying to distract her. It nearly worked, but now she concentrated on the match not the taunting gaze of her cousin.

41

He fought hard. She deflected blows or circled under them and came in with quick, sharp strikes, trying to dance out of his way before he could counter.

Finally, he caught her with a blow to the chest that knocked the wind out of her, and she fell hard onto her back, redoubling the effect. She gulped, trying to get her lungs to draw in air as she kept a wary eye on him. A jolt of worry shot through him, and he dropped his guard, his brow furrowed. How she could continue without breathing she did not know, but she must. She tried once more to get her lungs to work as he reached down to offer her a hand up.

Her father taught her that during a match you never approach your opponent with defenses down. Never assume they are hurt or are giving up the match unless they actually call it. She sensed his concern as she took his hand, then used his arm to brace herself as she leaped up to kick his face. He blocked but never loosened her hand and smirked as she tried unsuccessfully to break free of the vise-like grip.

Insolent, mocking grin! Ignore the wrist and just attack. She moved close, punching to his chin and mid-section, to keep inside his defenses and avoid his feet. He grabbed her tightly around the torso, trapping her free arm between them. Her fist could easily snap down between his legs, but during a match that was not a sanctioned maneuver. She smashed his instep as she slid her arm down and out. She twisted quickly under his left arm, forcing him to let go of her wrist. As she danced away, he grinned with a taunting expression. "You could have used a better move and won the match."

"My father taught me that move was never done in a match, although he said it was an easy method to bring an opponent down in a real fight." Tam hesitated. Had her father been mistaken in his Training of her? "Shall I target your groin the next time?"

Haladhon stared, his mouth open, while the Rangers hooted or burst into laughter. Tam stayed in position, although her face grew hot. She obviously erred again, but knew not how. Haladhon joined the men in their laughter and threw up his hands, calling the match. "I do not think that is considered a proper match technique, cousin." He wiped his eyes.

Tam slowly straightened. "What?"

"Making me laugh so hard that I cannot continue."

Tam blinked hard as frustration and irritation grew in her. Need they laugh at her for not knowing all the match rules? She felt like stalking off, but dared not walk away from those taunting her. She set her chin. "I know not what I said that was so humorous. I thought my father had taught me proper match rules, and you tell me he did not."

Haladhon's smile faded. "Nay, he did teach you how to match

correctly. I was merely teasing you."

"But you turned his jest around and caught him with it, cousin," Marcalan called out. "'Twas sweet."

"Aye." Loch'alan, Marcalan's brother, sauntered over. "I think 'tis the first time that rake would not fain have a woman interested in his—"

"Enough." Her uncle's voice fairly rang with dark authority. "Regard what you say around a lady, Ranger."

Loch'alan flushed and his eyes darted to Tam then away. "I apologize, Thane. Cousin Tam."

Tam felt her face warm as she finally realized the implication.

Edhron crossed his arms. "I wish to know what you thought you were doing by grabbing Tam that way."

"Self preservation, cousin," Haladhon said, chortling. "I thought she was after my—" He stopped and his eyes met Tam's, widening as he finished the sentence: "anatomy."

The nearby Rangers all laughed.

Ire rose in Tam, replacing her abashment, and she strode over, fists clenched. "I hope the next time we match, cousin, you do not forget I am a Ranger and start thinking of me as a lass."

"Why say you that?"

"I felt your worry when I had the wind knocked out of me. I am not the cousin you love when we are matching, Haladhon. I am your opponent. You fought me as if I were a lass the whole rest of the match. If I were like my father, I would have thrashed you to dust."

"Next time anyone forgets you are a fully trained Ranger, Tam, you do just that," Alcandhor said. "It will teach them."

"Aye, sir."

Haladhon threw up his hands again. "You are right. When you fell, I saw my cousin instead of my opponent. It is difficult, though. Your appearance creates an illusion of vulnerability."

Edhron pointed at Haladhon. "You are guilty of what you have lectured us about. You saw her as a lass, not a Ranger."

Haladhon chuckled. "I do not think I will make that mistake again." He leaned over Tam with a challenging smile. "Next time I will see only an opponent."

"Good." Tam crossed her arms. "If you wish me to learn, and be a solid fighter at your back, you had best not think of me as a lass." She turned and stomped toward the inn. He, of all the Rangers, was the one she thought would match her well, without regard of her being female. If even he could not see past that, how could she expect the rest of the Rangers to do so? Did her uncle not see how impossible it was to think a lass could be Thane?

Alcandhor came up next to Tam. "Why are you so angry, child?"

Tam clenched her jaw and hissed, "Even Haladhon thinks of me as a lass, after all. I cannot be Thane if they think thus. What you wish is impossible." She swallowed, her throat tight as she fought tears. She certainly did not sound like a calm, reasonable Ranger with emotions controlling her.

"It is not what I wish, it is conclave decision. And five years will make a difference in how they see you."

She shook her head. "It will not work."

His knowing smile maddened her. "We will see." He put an arm around her shoulders. "Now, I have been thinking about what you should ask if you dream."

Tam closed her eyes in a silent groan as fear overcame her anger.

"There is one question I wish you to ask. How do we get that portal to work? What can we do to open it? That is the one thing I need to know. Can you remember that? To ask about the portal?"

Tam swallowed. "Aye. I will ask." But could she? Could she bring herself to even talk to an Enaisi, an alien?

Chapter Four

Nandhal awoke as he was rolled over, a sword at his throat.

"What say you, Ranger Nandhal?" a mocking voice asked.

He blinked into the dark, his stomach churning with fear. The gravelly voice seemed familiar, but he could not place it. Had Rangers caught him? "Who are you?"

"Why do the drums call you Rogue?"

"I ran."

"Why?"

Who found him? The moons had set, and only the nebula high above gave any light. But although the Bells' glow did silhouette the men standing over him, 'twas not enough light to make out any features. He reached out with his ability to sense emotions and found mostly gloating, scorn, and suspicion, as well as some curiosity.

"I will not say more."

The quiet laughter that followed sparked Nandhal's memory. He tried to sit up but a foot on his chest stopped him.

"Monadhal! Curse you, let me up. I have been looking for you."

"Have you indeed?"

Fear clutched at Nandhal's insides. What if they did not believe the drums that he had gone Rogue? In that case, he was dead.

"Why did you go Rogue, *cousin*?" Monadhal spat the familial name with derision. "Why would you turn outlaw?"

"I could feel their suspicion and distrust of me. I dared not wait and take the chance of a trial."

"Why would they be suspicious of *you*?"

"I was the one who set the ambush that was supposed to kill the Thane and the chiefs. But it failed. The only chief who died was Valdhor. The Thane was wounded but survived."

"Why would you set an ambush on your own kin?"

"I was working with a circle of conspirators. We were going to kill the Thane, the chiefs and any others of the first table we could, as well as the Laird, and the Laird's son all the same day. The upheaval would allow us to take over. I was to be Thane after all the chiefs were dead."

"You, as Thane?"

"I sit at first table."

"You mean you did. Your plan cannot work now, can it, since you are

Rogue?" Monadhal's voice still mocked.

Nandhal scowled. "Nay. But I will still find a way to get revenge against them all."

"For what?"

"For keeping me tied to menial tasks as if I were a stripling and dismissing me as inconsequential even though I have Enaisi blood." Nandhal lifted his chin. "Mostly, for not Confirming me."

"You sought to become Thane when you are not even Confirmed?" Monadhal laughed and the Rogues joined in.

"As highest rank and aye, because I am a Child of the Enaisi, they would have had no choice!"

"You either know not the law or are deluded."

"It would have worked!"

Monadhal snorted, then asked, "So, you have Enaisi blood and can sense emotions, do you? I might find a use for you."

The foot came off Nandhal's chest, and he sat up.

"And it might come in handy having one not branded to go easily into hamlets or among people for news."

Nandhal breathed easier.

"Come with us. We know a sheltered place not far from here with fire and food. There we can talk."

Nandhal scrambled to his feet and joined the Rogues walking through the woods, his steps careful in the near-darkness. He sensed the emotions of the men around him to gauge hostility in case any of them might wish to attack but felt mostly mistrust and curiosity, nothing to warrant immediate danger.

They soon came to a cave, the entrance behind scurry bushes, whose hard, shiny leaves gave some small reflection of the Bells. He blinked once inside, straining to see in the blackness, while Rogues pushed and guided him forward. After a few turnings, a dim light shone ahead, and he could see he was in a passage. One more turn and it widened into a rather large cave with torches on the walls, bedrolls, sacks of what was probably foodstuffs, and a fire in the center.

Nandhal could now see Monadhal clearly. Living wild had changed him much from what he remembered of his uncle's son. 'Twas not just the several days growth of beard and unkempt gold-blond hair, but the lined and hard face that gave him a look much older than his thirty years. And of course, the broken sword branded on his forehead drew the eye. Monadhal's blue eyes glinted with cold ice, and Nandhal lowered his gaze; it seemed wrong to stare at that sign of a Ranger's permanent exile and mark of being an outlaw. And truth be told, he feared the day when he might be caught, tried, and branded. Although his own fate would likely include hanging afterwards, if his part in the ambush on the Thane were known.

Monadhal gestured for Nandhal to sit on the ground near the fire.

"I have heard the drum messages about the siege, and about it ending. What know you of these things?" Monadhal asked, sitting on a bulky sack nearby.

The Rogues gathered close. Whether standing, sitting, or squatting, their eyes all fixed on Nandhal. Ten of them, altogether. Eleven now, if they accepted him. A Rogue dipped cups in a pot over the fire and handed them out.

Nandhal accepted one with a nod. "I told you our plan. It went wrong somehow. The Rangers put Laird Hall under siege with almost all of my fellow conspirators inside. From the news drummed since I left, they are all now either dead or exiled. We killed the Laird, but his son lives and, despite his youth, is our new Laird. It was all in vain, curse it." He paused, and took a sip of the hot liquid. Tea, he guessed it was supposed to be, but it tasted like wet grass to him. "And although Valdhor is dead, we have a new chief to take his place."

Monadhal leaned forward. "A new chief? How? No others have children of Age yet."

Nandhal stared into Monadhal's face, his gazing flicking to the broken sword again. He suppressed a shudder and brought his mind back to the subject at hand. "This you will not believe. Valdhor came down out of his hole in the mountains with a Ranger-Trained daughter. A young lass who looks barely old enough to be a stripling."

The Rogues laughed at that, and Nandhal bristled. "It is on you if you believe me not. She is Second at Table and the Thane dotes on her as one would a favored child. She is the one who somehow found and rescued the young Laird from where he was imprisoned."

"A lass who is a Ranger?" Contempt filled Monadhal's blue eyes. "I knew not you enjoyed jests, Nandhal."

Nandhal sneered at his cousin; he despised jests, and being laughed at. "I do not. It is true. Her name is Tamissa. I jest not."

Monadhal sat back, regarding Nandhal. "If what you say is true, it seems madness has taken Ch'shalna clan." He stared at the fire for a few moments, then murmured, "I wonder if we can turn this to our advantage."

"Have you any plans, then?"

"I always have plans, my dear cousin. Right now we are gathering supplies for the winter. After that, we will get as close as we dare to Zaidhron."

"Zaidhron? A city filled with our kin and the chiefs of our clan? For the Bells' sake, why?"

"Not all of your news was news."

Nandhal bristled. "Why did you—"

"Fool. How easily should we trust you? We had heard of the ambush and are hoping to get a chance to pull one of our own, while they are still a-tilt and grieving from the last one."

"An ambush on Rangers? Near Zaidhron? You are mad."

"The chiefs at times go roaming. What think you the chances are of ambushing one—or more than one if we are lucky?"

Nandhal stared at Monadhal. Was he truly mad or a genius? "And why would you wish to ambush chiefs?"

"To hurt Ch'shalna clan, why else? We got one chief last year and the two Rangers who were with him."

"Bardhor?" Nandhal sat back, his mouth open. He remembered his cousin Haladhon weeping at his father's crypt. How pleasurable it had been to see that arrogant by-blow knocked down. "If Haladhon knew you were the one who killed his father, he would hate you doubly."

Monadhal laughed. "Perhaps we can let him know before I kill him. And this time I would make certain he was dead."

"Aye. I remember—years ago, you left him for dead, but somehow he survived."

"Haladhon will not live the next time we meet." Monadhal's eyes glittered like shards of ice.

"But how think you that you can possibly do this and not have every Ranger tracking you to the ends of our world?"

"If we execute our plan well, we will be gone for days before any bodies are found, and our tracks will be gone—covered by snows or washed away by the rains. It is what we did last time. I have plans, as I said, Nandhal. They go slowly, so as not to make mistakes." The Rogue smiled. "But I am taking my vengeance on the Rangers."

Chapter Five

"I cannot wait to get home," Marcalan moaned as they walked up the sloping road. The Rangers all hurried; their longing to return to their city drove them now on this last day.

Tam tried to get Marcalan away from the others to talk, but although he had not blocked, he also had not fallen for her attempts. After the last one, he frowned and shook his head. She sent him her exasperation, and he had mouthed, "Wait." So she would. But not happily. And not for long. But at least most of the time, neither had reason to block and so had their secret connection. It was becoming almost normal and, most of the time, subtle. Not the overwhelming feeling of another person in oneself, aware of their emotions and physical sensations, but just the touch of knowing the other was *there*.

With a smile at Marcalan for his overt impatience at getting home, Tam asked, "How long until we arrive?" She gazed over at her uncle. He walked in the lead with the other chiefs and seemed well, despite the accelerated pace. The only distress came from the constant, deep ache in his shoulder and arm.

"Two or three hours," Marcalan said.

"Closer to three, I would say," Haladhon said. "'Tis about an hour to the sentry tower and entrance to the plain, and another hour to the gate of the out-wall and then not only to the city itself but crossing the sward. We might arrive in time for afternooning."

"Where will Tam stay?" asked Marcalan. "In one of the family ranges with the single females?"

Alcandhor shook his head. "She will use a servant's chamber behind the Great Hall. It will put her between the Training range, giving her easy access to the Training halls, and Thane Hall in the chiefs' range, where she will spend much of her time."

Marcalan chuckled. "Oh, stars, to have such fortune."

Tam frowned at her cousin in curiosity.

He grinned. "You will be close to hand to sneak and filch food from the main kitchens very easily."

Several nearby Rangers hooted and jeered. Haladhon rolled his eyes. "And incur the wrath of Ganill? Stars, do not lead our young cousin astray where it concerns our head cook. No one dares brave her."

"Not even Uncle?" asked Tam, wide-eyed.

Alcandhor snorted. "Not even Uncle."

Everyone burst out laughing.

What would life be like living in such a place? Her brief visit to the white-walled city had allowed her to see little and understand less. As the laughter quieted, Tam asked, "Can you tell me more of the ranges, Uncle?"

"Your father did not explain the layout of Zaidhron?" Alcandhor asked, browed raised.

"Aye, but only in generalities. He told me of its hexagon shape and the size of it, and he explained its defenses. I think I know the purposes of the six ranges, but I have not many details."

"You are familiar with the west range, of course, where the Great Hall is?"

Tam nodded. "The main kitchens and guest chambers are there, also."

"The southwest range called the Training range, and also sometimes the barracks range, since—of course—that is where the barracks are for single Rangers, and also the Training halls."

"'Twould be difficult to grasp that without explanation, aye, cousin?" Marcalan grinned. "However,"—his voice raised so all the nearby Rangers could hear—"we can pass on telling Tam about the barracks. She need not know of the overpowering odor of boots and sweaty men, and what it is like listening to a cacophony of snoring."

"Marcalan." Alcandhor's tone held a warning.

Tam rolled her eyes. "Stars, I endured that these past nights in the journey stations. I will fain have my own chamber."

Haladhon chuckled, leaning close. "Good one, cousin."

Tam smiled up at Haladhon. "The northwest range is the chief's range, is it not?"

"Aye. It is often just called Thane Hall although that is but a part of that section of the city. The law library, and meeting and study chambers are there," Haladhon said. "It is also where arbitration takes place."

"It is the administrative range for not only all clan affairs, but city business as well," Andhrel said.

"You will be there much of the time, studying." Alcandhor clapped a hand on her shoulder.

With another nod, Tam said, "And I know the northeast and east ranges are called the Family ranges—Family North and Family East, and house not only all the families of Zaidhron but single females as well, yes?"

"Aye. And the last is the craftsmen range," Andhrel said, "and naturally, that is where most of our craftsmen ply their trades. Most of the markets are in that range as well."

Tam nodded, remembering the little she had seen on her visit—

blacksmiths and women with baskets and children playing and vendors calling out.

"Aye, although a fair amount set up at the Valley Gate between Family East and North as well," Haladhon added.

Andhrel lifted his shoulders. "True, although those are mostly for trade coming and going from the valley."

"I will have to give you a grand tour of the city," Marcalan said. "With special consideration given to places that have warm memories for me, such as the hallway between the second level barracks and the privs, eh, Haladhon?"

Haladhon laughed. "Stars, I had forgotten about that, Mar."

Tam glanced between her two cousins. "What did he do?"

"He poured honey on the floor, and as the Rangers got up that morning to use the priv, they walked in the honey either in bare feet or their stockings. Stars, you should have heard the yelling and cursing."

Cordhan grinned. "Even better was seeing Marcalan roasted by Ganill for stealing honey to use for a prank."

"And I did not use her honey, either." Marcalan gave an indignant sniff, winking at Tam. "I found some wild. That is what gave me the idea. But no one believed me."

Cordhan snorted. "I wonder why."

Maradhor cut his eyes to Marcalan. "We got even with him."

"Aye, a good one it was, too," Marcalan said. Before Tam could ask, he continued, "They poured honey over me while I slept, then sewed me into my blankets."

"And did you get angry?"

Maradhor rolled his eyes. "Great Bells, he was jealous he had not thought of it himself."

Tam shook her head as Marcalan laughed. Oh, how she wished she could throw her arms around the rascal. Her cousin ducked his head, frowning, but did not block. What bothered him thus? He must have sensed her worry and confusion because he glanced at her, shaking his head.

Tam offered a small smile, and tried to keep her emotions mellow. She did not want Marcalan to block. She hoped they could find a way to talk alone soon. Very soon.

~*~

"'Twill be bittersweet," Cordhan said as they heard the sentry tower drum their approach.

Several Rangers muttered agreement. It brought back to Tam's mind her father's death. Six Rangers, including Tam's father, had died during the ambush that preceded the siege of Laird Hall. Five had been from Nelatan province, and their bodies were carried thence. Her father's body had been sent ahead to Zaidhron and interred already in the Thane's family crypt.

Tam had avoided being near Tanadhon. Indeed, her preoccupation with Marcalan crowded out thoughts of the traitor. She glanced back to where he plodded, white-faced, guards well around him. With a deep inhale, she turned away and focused on her surroundings.

Tall grasses, faded to yellow in the cool of autumn, swayed against the white stone out-wall that bisected the flatland known as the Settlers' Plain. Passing through the gate of the out-wall, amazement of the city struck Tam all over again as she took in the commanding structure rising before her. Beautifully set against the high mountains and waterfalls behind it, the white stone of Zaidhron acted as almost a beacon in the sunlight. The towers rose high above the imposing height of the curtain walls.

As they passed through the gatehouse of Zaidhron about a half-hour later, cheering erupted, family rushing forward to meet their returning Rangers. Sarinna found her brother, Alcandhor, and clung to him. They cried, and Tam knew it was for her father, their brother.

Tears smarted in Tam's eyes. An arm closed around her shoulders, and she looked up at Haladhon's wet face. He pulled her close, and tears slipped down her face despite all her efforts.

Tam remembered what she had told the young Laird: that the hardness of the lives of the Rangers was not so much the rigorous Training or journeying or the hard duties, but the grief they had to endure so often. Ranger blood spilled too often. She buried her face in Haladhon's chest and cried. She could feel the grief of those near her as well as her own and it overwhelmed her. Haladhon did not move. He just held her.

Arms wrapped around her—a woman, grief-stricken, her body wracked with sobs. Tam turned to her. Slender with a proud bearing, dark hair with only a strand of grey here and there, and deep-set blue eyes. Haladhon embraced this woman with one arm and Tam with the other.

The woman touched Tam's face, a tentative smile on her lips, love flowing from her, even as tears streamed down her cheeks. "Tam, I was not here when you came home the first time. Let me hold you, girl."

Tam shot a quizzical glance up at Haladhon.

"This is Valdhor's mother. Your grandmother."

This was Taniss? Thane Saldhor's widow? She had not considered that her grandmother might still be alive. She must be very old.

The woman gently took her in her arms. Taniss' deep grief caused Tam to cry afresh. The woman held her and stroked her hair, and a measure of peace fell over Tam. Finally, she was able to control herself and straighten. Taniss caressed her face, smiling. "Hungry, child? The Rangers are going to bathe then will gather in the Great Hall for a feast. Come."

She kept her arm around Tam as they walked toward the west range. Tam found herself timidly putting her arm around the woman's waist as well. Taniss gave her a quick squeeze, and Tam felt again her love although they just met.

Her grandmother did not try to talk, which was a relief because Tam still fought tears. The lengthy walk helped. Tam gazed with longing at the gardens as they passed them.

Many enormous tents had been erected near the grounds to the Great Hall, with trestle tables crowded underneath. Bright banners lent cheerfulness to the scene as servants scurried here and there, laughing as they worked. Under one brightly colored tent, musicians played lively tunes. Torches and braziers set here and there would provide not only additional light but heat against the cool tangy air as evening fell.

"With the entire city celebrating, we have not the room inside the Great Hall," Taniss said. "Many more will be outside, and within some of the ranges, folks have their own festivities as well."

As they entered the Great Hall, Taniss murmured, "I will show you to the chamber prepared for you upstairs. You can leave your belongings there, then bathe and change before the feast starts."

With the huge fireplaces on each end of the hall and the central hearths ablaze, and all the candelabras lit, the Great Hall offered warmth and comfort after the autumn chill. Aromas of foods whetted Tam's appetite, as it had her first visit here. As she walked through the hall, some of the Rangers backed away with respectful bows to make room for them to pass. Taniss must command a great amount of esteem.

Ascending the stairs behind her grandmother, Tam gazed down at the Great Hall. Servants bustled about, setting gleaming dishes on tables covered with white linen, amid Rangers milling with their families. Musicians tuned their instruments in the southwest corner, their discordant noise mingling with the chatter and laughter, somehow a proper part of the organized chaos of the Great Hall being prepared for the welcoming banquet.

Two flights of stairs left the Great Hall behind, then they walked along a corridor. Taniss opened a door. "I believe this is the same chamber you had before, Zaidhron's Chamber."

"But Uncle said I was to have a servants' chamber."

"Rangers may be honored to serve, but they are not paid servants in their own homes. Sarinna ordered this chamber readied for you. 'Tis not elaborate, but comfortable. It will be yours permanently since we have no barracking for female Rangers. It is not appropriate for you to have a chamber with the single females above the family quarters. You know where the bathing rooms are?"

"Aye." Tam leaned her staff in the corner then dropped her pack to the floor. She took off all her weapons save her knives, and hung them up, then removed her cloak.

"There are spare clothes in your wardrobe so you can change into something clean. I must say, it does take getting used to, seeing a lass dressed as a Ranger. I hear my son Trained you well. It is what I would expect from him."

Tam did not know what to say. She retrieved the clean clothes, and as they left the chamber, Taniss smiled. "I will see you at table, child. Take your time and enjoy the bath."

Tam smiled back, still uncertain what to say to her grandmother. The woman left, and Tam descended the back staircase to the bathing rooms.

~*~

Her damp hair freshly combed and wearing clean Ranger garb, Tam slowly walked down the staircase, surveying the crowd below. Despite her connection to Marcalan, she could not find him in the throng of people, so she concentrated on him: he was not here yet, but close by, filled with excitement, mirth, and a sense of haste. She focused even more and almost stumbled on the steps—only her hold on the railing saved her from a fall. She could actually sense his own damp hair, the swing of his arms as he strode along, and underlying it all a banked-down passion. For her? Oh, she hoped so!

Tam gripped the rail. Why did she hope so? Was it possible she had what Uncle called *in love* for Marcalan? Tam knew her cousin loved her. Did he have *in love* for her as well? That would explain the desires she sensed.

She bit her lip as a new thought came to fore: if she could tell thus about him, could sense him so deeply, could he sense *her*? When she was bathing or using the priv? Her face grew warm. She would say not, as her abilities were so much stronger than anyone of the other Children of the Enaisi, even her Uncle and Zandhral. They could not even tell Marcalan was a Child until she told them. But how could she sense him so strongly? Was it their connection? If so, did it allow him to sense her more deeply than he otherwise could? Tam felt almost dizzy trying to sort out her own questions and guesses. And frustrated. Stars, she needed to talk to him! But, dared she ask him about this physical sensing? Or having *in love*?

Chapter Six

With a deep breath, Tam lessened her focus until all that remained was their thread of a connection.

Worry washed over her, and Tam smiled despite herself. Marcalan. He crossed the Great Hall, pushing past people, gazing up at her, concern on his face.

He took the stairs three at a time until he was standing just below her, his face anxious. "What is it?"

"What did you feel?" she asked, not certain if she wished him to say nothing or everything.

"Surprise, worry, embarrassment, confusion—I cannot name all I felt."

With a slow exhale, Tam managed a smile. "I cannot tell you here. But we need to talk."

"So I have concluded from your efforts as we journeyed. But not now."

"Later?"

Marcalan hesitated then slowly shook his head. "I doubt we would find a time and place to talk in true privacy tonight. But aye, we need to have a serious discussion very soon."

"Tomorrow?"

Marcalan laughed. "Stars, you are persistent!"

"When, Marcalan?" she asked, grabbing his sleeve.

"Tomorrow. *If* an opportunity presents itself." His eyes had no humor in them as he gazed into hers. "Leave off the idea of a talk tonight. You know not how impossible it would be. Let us just be friends and cousins enjoying the feast."

"So...we are more than that?" Tam's heart leaped that perhaps she was right.

"Not tonight." He turned and hopped on the stairway rail, and as Tam watched with mouth agape, he slid all the way to the bottom. He whirled and grinned up at her with a sweeping bow then sauntered to the table.

Merely friends and cousins. All right. For tonight she would give no thought to their *in love*. If indeed they had *in love*.

She walked to the head table where the Thane stood, holding his little girl in his arms, his two boys on each side of his chair. Trestles had been added, adding length to the tables—to accommodate the families of the

Rangers, she assumed.

Tam sat in her place, save that she was moved down to allow for Taniss, Sarinna, and Alcandhor's wife Aleta since it was a family meal.

People milled around the hall, laughing and talking. Except Aleta. She stood quietly by her place, with a sour expression. Taniss and Sarinna came over and hugged Tam again. The Thane stood at attention by his chair. The hall quieted and everyone hurried to their seats. He sat down and the gong sounded.

The two boys sat down on the left side of the table. A young woman took the little girl by the hand and sat with her on the end.

As everyone settled onto the benches, Tam could sort out a few of the emotions she had been sensing. Aleta was furious, and had a coldness that Tam could not fathom. Curiosity filled her two young Ranger cousins, and they stared at her when they thought she was not looking. The little girl was just happy. She kept wiggling and smiling at her father.

The young woman helped to serve the little girl as food was passed and several times kept her small cup from tipping over. Why was Aleta not doing this for her own daughter? Tam knew little of mothers, so perhaps she was not correct in her assumptions of what mothers did for their children. Or perhaps things were not done that way in Zaidhron.

The coldness and hostility from Aleta kept Tam from speaking to her. Haladhon talked with the older woman on his other side. Tam felt a bit alone. A spurt of cheerfulness and merriment bubbled through her— Marcalan, of course! He had probably sensed she was lonely. Her friend and cousin.

She glanced down the table to see him grinning at her. If only she could thank him, not just by sending but in some tangible way.

An inspiration hit her. Small flagons of vinegar sat on the table for those who liked it over their greens. She picked up the nearest one and, glancing at Haladhon to make sure he was still engaged in the conversation with the woman on his other side, poured some into his tankard of ale. Marcalan nearly slid under the table cackling. Loch'alan looked at his brother as if he had gone mad and pulled on him to get him back up on the bench.

Tam returned her attention to her meal. Before long Haladhon picked up his tankard and halfway through a large gulp he stopped, his face contorting. He glanced about, as if trying to find a way to rid himself of the sour mouthful, then with what appeared almost a painful effort, he managed to choke it down. Marcalan almost convulsed with laughter, and Tam saw her uncle bent over his plate trying to hide his mirth as well. His sons and the others across from her giggled. Sarinna and Taniss asked Alcandhor what had happened. He explained once he got his breath.

Haladhon chuckled, his gaze on Marcalan. "How did you get me from down there, you rascal?"

Marcalan laughed so hard he could not answer, tears rolling down his face. He shook his head and spread his hands.

"But then, who?" muttered Haladhon, glancing around, then his eyes lit on Tam. She hoped the expression she gave was as innocent as the ones Marcalan used. He stared amazed for a moment then threw back his head, roaring with laughter. When he got control of himself, he gave her an embrace that almost lifted her off the bench, then kissed her on the forehead.

"My dear, dear cousin! Congratulations. Has Marcalan been teaching you?"

"He has had no need. I have been around you enough to learn a few things."

"She got you, Haladhon!" Alcandhor pointed his eating blade at his cousin. "The look on your face was worthy, and yours as well, Mar!"

"I could not believe it, Thane!" Marcalan wiped his eyes. "She was so matter-of-fact, as if she were pouring him a cup of tea." He boldly stood, stepped over the bench then walked around the table to Tam. Stars, what Marcalan could get away with! One did not get up from the Thane's table during a meal without permission. He bowed low before her. "My Lady, you got the Master. You have my undying devotion."

"Go sit down, you vagabond," Alcandhor ordered, chuckling.

Tam heard Aleta click her tongue in disapproval but forced herself not to feel anything from the woman. Instead she concentrated on the merriment from Marcalan as he walked back around to his place. Such a scamp!

Marcalan's joyous mood, enhanced by his hereditary ability, easily overrode Aleta's negative feelings, even though she sat next to Tam. And it was better than blocking. She did not like the loneliness of blocking. It did make Tam more mischievous though, being attuned to Marcalan. Such a happy feeling.

Haladhon nudged her arm. "Want to get Marcalan?"

"How?"

"We will just sit here and talk, and you keep glancing down at him. When he looks at you, smile innocently then pretend you are saying something back to me."

She leaned forward to see Marcalan. He grinned at her, and she beamed back. "But what will that do?"

"He will begin to believe we are scheming, and it will drive him mad waiting for something to happen."

Tam smiled up at her cousin, then over at Marcalan.

"Will that truly work?"

"Aye, my dear Tam. Aye."

The roguish twinkle in Haladhon's eyes made her giggle. "You are horrible, and I love you."

A spike of mingled guilt and sorrow jolted Haladhon for a brief moment, but he blinked and grinned broadly with a forced lightheartedness. He bent close and whispered back, "I love you, too. But be careful what you say, and how, and in front of whom, as it could be misinterpreted."

"This I understand, but Uncle knows there is nothing to worry about between us." *Only about Marcalan and me, but not tonight. Friend and cousin... Friend and cousin...*

"He knows nothing of the sort. I have a reputation, Tam. I would not fain have Alcandhor angry with me, nor fear losing his trust. You must not give any opportunity for idle talk."

"If you say so."

"Trust me."

She arched an eyebrow. "With my life but not with my mug."

He chuckled. "You are wise for your years."

"Experience is a hard teacher."

He laughed again, a joyful, musical sound.

As the meal ended, servants carried out pastries and other sweets, but set them on trestle tables to one side. Tam rose as did everyone else so the main tables could be cleared and moved out of the way. The quiet music played during the meal was replaced now with livelier tunes.

Marcalan scurried around the table to her. "We can sit over here." He pointed to a table at the north end near the sweets. They walked over and sat. "By the way, what were you and Haladhon talking about a little while ago?"

Tam frowned at Marcalan, confused, then realized what he meant. "Nothing really. Just talking."

The uneasiness in him made her realize Haladhon truly had been correct. She wanted to laugh, but kept her face and emotions light and innocent.

"Just talking?"

"Aye. I cannot even remember about what."

"Just...making conversation?"

"Aye." She swallowed hard to keep herself from smiling. She gestured toward the table. "When may we have sweets?"

"Any time, but let us have some ale with it. Or do you prefer wine?"

"I have not had ale, but it does not smell good. I do not care for wine."

"But there are different wines and you might like one kind and detest another. Why do we not see if we can find a wine you like?"

Feeling his insistence and not wishing to disappoint him, Tam smiled. "All right."

~*~

Alcandhor threaded through the tables, smiling inanely at various people, feeling eyes on him. Would anyone approach, ask about Tam— about her birth not being properly recorded? Would they call Question on it?

His little girl skipped up, asking for a sweeting, and he forced the dread away, lifting Amara into his arms.

Quest of the Sweeting achieved, Alcandhor sat, his little girl on his lap enjoying her treat. He gave her a squeeze and held in the anger that her own mother had no time for her and that Amara spent her days mostly with the young widow Jholinn.

He turned his mind to happier thoughts, such as his mother's joy at seeing Tam. All through the meal she asked questions about her granddaughter. He discussed his niece with Taniss and Sarinna, who both agreed that Tam needed a foster-mother. Perhaps now, with Tam here, his mother would stay in the city instead of living quietly on her own in the valley.

"...and we had to wash the mud off my feet, but Jholinn did not scold me."

Alcandhor smiled at Amara, guilty that his mind had wandered instead of paying attention to her. "Jholinn is a good friend to you, is she not?"

"I love her, Papa."

His smile deepened, but he did not answer. Jholinn had proven her love and loyalty to Amara, but pointedly did not like Alcandhor. Her emotions turned into a cold, tight knot when he drew near.

Before he could think of a way to turn the conversation to another topic, Amara wiggled. "May I go play with Natinna? She leaves for Ranger Hold tomorrow to be with her papa again."

Natinna was the second of Capalan's children. His family had been brought to Zaidlhron for safe keeping about a lunation before the siege. Now they, and the families of other Rangers stationed at Lairdton's Ranger Hold, would be returning home.

"Go ahead, child." He kissed the top of her head, stroking her curly hair before she slid off his lap. He smiled after her. Such a beautiful little girl. Now that he must spend time here instructing Tam, so he would be able to see his children every day.

He sat alone, watching his people. Haladhon had already found companionship. What was her name? He did not remember. His cousin became involved in a passionate kiss with the woman, and Alcandhor looked away. Haladhon enjoyed more of the prerogatives of marriage, although he had never worn a necklet, than Alcandhor had in all his years of marriage.

He sighed, glancing around the hall again. Where was Tam? Ah, talking with Marcalan. Those two seemed to spend quite a bit of time together, but he had neither seen nor sensed anything inappropriate from Marcalan. Quite amazing considering his reputation, but at least the man had the good sense to not try anything with her. Had his earlier talk with Tam opened her eyes to the fact she was growing up and had to be on guard around men, especially Marcalan and Haladhon's type? He could only hope, but he would also keep watch.

And now both Sarinna and his mother could offer her help and advice, if needed. Taniss adored the idea of mothering Tam. But would Tam mind the attention too much, not being used to having any mother at all?

Aleta walked over to stand in front of him, arms crossed, interrupting his thoughts. "What's this about Tam being her father's heir to Thane?"

Aye, my wife. So these are the first words you speak to me upon my return? She had been absent at the gate, as usual, and had given him no greeting upon seeing him at table.

What happened to the exquisite girl he had met in Estan Province so long ago, alive and flirtatious and so taken with the young Ranger who had eyes only for her?

After their marriage, she found out he was one of only few Rangers with Enaisi blood, able to sense her feelings and send his to her. She forbade him to do so, claiming it made her uncomfortable and that it invaded her privacy. He had pleaded with her, explaining how it could bring them greater joy and intimacy, but she remained adamant. Being too honorable to break his vow, Alcandhor blocked when around her.

Over time, he withdrew, and his love for her withered. Had the death knell come to their marriage when he discovered she had been unfaithful to him or when she rejected Amara, wanting nothing to do with a mere girl-child? She did not even wish to nurse the baby and passed that duty to Jholinn, recently widowed and grieving her own stillborn child. Alcandhor could find no affection for his wife, no feeling of any kind. He ignored her, and she, him. He allowed her concessions for the sake of peace and they lived their own lives. His heart had dulled over time; he lived within himself, blocking most of the time, especially at Zaidhron.

But Tam changed that, somehow. Was it because he enjoyed feeling her love for him, and her adoration? He could not deny that was part of it. But her ability to sense his sadness and doubt had forced him to take a look at himself and at what he had allowed. In his desire for peace, he had been too tolerant of Aleta. That would now change.

He need not permit her sullen attitude that bordered on disrespect, especially in public. After all, was he not Thane? And she would begin to take on the traditional duties of the Thane's wife, which she had shunned all these years, saying they taxed her, and that she could not learn to cope with such matters, not having been brought up in such grand surroundings.

Such grand surroundings. Aye, she had thought it grand when he first brought her home. She had been in awe. Until she found life at Zaidhron was not one of luxury as at the other nobles' halls.

Her mercurial moods, biting tongue, and childish attitudes had been difficult to live with, but he had endured, knowing he had no one to blame but himself that he lived with such a selfish woman. In his youthful naïveté, he had mistaken desire for love, rushing into marriage after mere days of acquaintance.

Aleta had doted on their first born, Teldhor, bragging that she was now mother of the next Thane. Eladhor she was not so fond of, although at times she would fawn on him as well, boasting that he would be a fine Ranger chief one day.

She showed more interest in gaining finery for herself, and speaking with eagerness of the day when Alcandhor would be Thane. When his father died unexpectedly and he did become Thane, she crowed how he had become the most powerful man in their world.

"You have control now," she had said, her eyes bright. "You can do as you please. If you do not like what is happening in Keladar Province, you can send your Rangers to stop Paltor, and set your own people in power. If the old fool of a Laird will not listen, you can—"

"I can—I will do nothing, Aleta! Understand you not our laws? My power is not given me to conquer, or subvert, or dominate, but to keep order and—"

"That is the talk of a weak man! One who is afraid!" Her shrill voice had made him wince. She stopped and drew herself up, a seductive smile curving her lips as she put a hand on his arm. "Take control and show you are powerful. Show that you are a man to be feared!"

Alcandhor had snatched his arm away, disgust rising like bile in his throat. "You do not even know me if you think I would ever misuse my rank and position in such a way."

Her eyes had narrowed as she stepped back, her face contorted into a repulsive mask. "Oh, I know you. Yes. A weakling. A coward. A man who is too afraid to take what lies before him. Too weak to grasp opportunity. I thought perhaps once your father was dead, you would come from under his shadow and the loyalty you felt for him, but I should have known you were as insipid as he was. What a fool I was for marrying you!"

61

Alcandhor pulled his mind back to the present, to the woman who awaited his answer. Her face no longer appeared beautiful to him, even if exquisite in loveliness. In moments it would be twisted into rage.

With strange irony, he realized he longed to bait her, but that would not do. He struggled to keep the smile from his face and remain composed. "It is true. It was decided in conclave."

Disbelief rose in her, with worry and irritation.

"You cannot mean it."

"I do. My duty is to Train her so she can assume her rightful role as Thane."

"You are mad!"

"Why say you that?"

"You cannot give up being Thane!"

Hysteria joined the swirl of worry, anger, and confusion in her. Her breathing grew to short gasps, her fists clenched.

Alcandhor turned up the palm of his right hand in his lap, lifting his good shoulder slightly. "I have no choice in the matter. The conclave vowed that if Valdhor presented an heir, Ranger-Trained, then that child would be Thane."

"No!" Aleta's body shook. Hot surges of rage and bitterness emanated from her. "You are a fool!" She stalked off.

He stared after her retreating figure, letting his breath out in a slow exhale before muttering, "Aye. I am."

Chapter Seven

Tam sighed as yet one more Ranger poured wine for her. One after another of her kin had refilled her pretty, stemmed glass. Although she and Marcalan did spend much time together, they were never alone enough to talk. He had been right. Over and over she reminded herself that tonight they were only friends and cousins.

She smiled at the nameless cousin who had refilled her glass. He bowed and backed away. Tam looked around the Great Hall and murmured to Marcalan, "This is all so strange to me."

"What is?"

She gazed up at her friend-and-cousin's curious blue eyes. "All this. The music and dancing, and so many people. I–I had never been around people at all until Uncle brought me here."

"I know you lived alone with your father, but surely you met people."

She shook her head. "I saw Rangers from time to time. I cannot say I really met them, for my father never introduced me. Other than accepting a mug of tea from me over a campfire, I cannot say I ever talked to a Ranger other than my father until I met Uncle."

Marcalan's brows drew down. "Surely you went with him when he checked his bounds? Were there not towns you visited?"

"When I was very small and could not be left alone I would go with him and had to stand quietly during any arbitration. He allowed no one to talk with me. I was punished once because a woman gave me something to eat. I had not asked for it—she was just being kind, I think. But I did not go with him into the villages once I was old enough to stay alone. He said I did not need to learn about arbitration, since I would never actually be a Ranger."

"Then why did he Train you at all?"

Tam shrugged and shared her own guess at her father's reason. "What does a Ranger do with a small child? He had to keep me with him—I could not be left alone then. He taught me the only thing he knew, being a Ranger."

"He could have brought you here. There is no shame in a widower leaving his child with his clan when he is in a difficult strait as it must have been for your father."

"But that would mean admitting he could not take care of me, and I think my father's pride would not have borne that."

"Why not? He was not too proud to admit he felt he would not make a good Thane."

Tam sat up straight, staring at Marcalan in astonishment. "That is what Uncle meant!"

"What? What did he mean?"

"When they had the fight. Where is Uncle?" She searched the hall until she saw him sitting by himself, watching the dancing couples. He looked lost and alone. "I must talk to him. Excuse me, Marcalan."

A smile brightened her uncle's face as she approached. She sat, and their hands clasped. "Uncle, I just realized something. I was talking to Marcalan, and he said something, and I remembered the fight you had with my father, and I wanted—"

"Wait, girl, slow down!" He laughed. "Start again."

Tam took a deep breath. "I heard the fight you had with my father the night before we arrived here, and I did not understand it. But I was just talking with Marcalan, and he said something that made me understand it, or I think I understand part of it, but I wanted to talk to you about it."

"All right, I think I can make enough sense of what you said that time. What is it you wish to talk about?"

"You told my father..." She paused and closed her eyes to remember. "You said, 'You refused your traditional responsibility to our clan and the Rangers, but in your pride you kept the girl.'"

Alcandhor's eyebrows raised in surprise. "You remember what I said so exactly?"

Tam nodded. "Father taught me to do that. He had no books and would recite the laws, then I would have to repeat them. He did not like it if I remembered incorrectly."

"I can imagine," Uncle replied in a flat tone.

"I did not understand any of the argument at the time, but after I found out that my father had renounced Thaneship, I at least understood what you meant that he refused his traditional responsibility to the clan. But you talked about pride. I could not understand the connection until Marcalan asked why my father had kept me instead of giving me to the clan to raise. I said I thought his pride would not let him, and that is when he said it—"

"Wait. He said what?"

"Marcalan said pride did not stop my father from admitting he felt he would not make a good Thane."

Alcandhor huffed a short laugh, shaking his head.

"But, why would he give up something as venerated as being Thane yet not give me up when he—" She stopped, dropping her gaze to her lap, then she swallowed and made herself meet her uncle's eyes. "When he did not want me?"

He put his arm around her and pulled her close. She relaxed and nestled into his embrace.

"Tam, I cannot answer your question. Your father would not. I know not that you will ever find an answer. I am sorry."

~*~

Alcandhor continued to hold Tam, wondering at the small enigma at his side. She seemed so small and young just now, so hurt by her father's harsh method of raising her, and so starved for love. He smiled at the deception her appearance created. Her father had indeed Trained her well. She was tough and capable, able to fight and kill if necessary, and able to easily survive in the wild. Yet, still a child.

Her emotions bubbled right on the surface, which was not usual for her, not in a chamber full of people anyway. Aleta approached, her face set and hard, interrupting his thoughts about Tam. From her glazed look, his wife had been too much at the wine.

Tam stiffened and started to rise, but Alcandhor held her.

"So here the two of you sit. All cozy, are you?" Her accent had lapsed to her native Estan, another sign she had been drinking or was spitting angry. Or both.

Tam did not answer. Alcandhor spoke softly. "You have had enough wine, Aleta."

"Going to tell me what to do, Alcandhor? You haven't the backbone. You're the weakest excuse for a Thane your clan has had, and when you give it over to this girl"—she waved her hand wildly toward Tam—"it will be the end of the Rangers."

As if Aleta cared about Ranger clan. That line of thought would only cause more fighting, and Alcandhor would not sanction a disruption of these festivities. Certainly not for the mere satisfaction of baiting the woman. "You are talking too loudly."

"Not loud enough, you mean!"

Tam pulled free of her uncle. Her indignation rose as she did. Alcandhor stood, whispering, "It is nothing, Tam. She is drunk. You cannot reason with her."

"She should not talk about the Thane that way, Uncle. It is disrespectful."

"She has had too much wine—"

"I have not, and don't speak about me as if I were not here!" Rangers turned toward them at her shrill exclamation.

"Aleta, do not make a scene."

"Why? You do not wish your Rangers to hear what you really are?"

Tam's anger threatened to boil over. He put his hand on his niece's shoulder and sent feelings of peace to Aleta. His wife's face softened slightly. Now if he could gracefully get Tam away from her.

"Have you had any of the sweets yet, Tam?"

"Only one."

He bowed slightly to his wife. "Excuse us, Aleta." He turned, a hand on Tam's elbow. With a shriek, Aleta grabbed his left arm, sling and all, and pulled hard, trying to turn him around. Hot fire shot through his shoulder. Aleta let go, gasping, and backed up, holding her stomach and moaning. Alcandhor need not be told what happened. His niece had felt his pain and reacted to protect him, sending some strong emotion to debilitate Aleta.

"Stop, Tam," he ordered gently. Tam regarded him with a hurt expression, as if rebuked.

Aleta slowly regained her composure, regarding Tam with a mixture of fear and loathing. Before Alcandhor could tell her to leave, she lifted her skirts and stalked away.

Alcandhor smiled at Tam, sending her peace as reassurance. "Get you something sweet from the tables, Tam, before they are all gone, and go have fun with some of the younger Rangers."

"But I would fain stay with you, Uncle."

Alcandhor pressed his lips to her forehead. "Thank you, child, but I am going to spend a little time with my children before they all are sent to bed."

She dimpled. "Then I will find Haladhon and Marcalan and try to keep them out of trouble."

"Haladhon has probably already disappeared with whoever his current distraction is, as I have not seen him in awhile. However, Marcalan is over there, tormenting those Rangers. You might rescue them."

She kissed his cheek and ran off. She circled the hall and approached Marcalan from behind. One of the Rangers saw her, his expression giving her away, but as Marcalan turned, she ducked under a table.

Alcandhor watched in amazement as she stalked her cousin. She stayed behind the table, hidden by the long cloth, for quite a while. She finally peeked around. Marcalan gestured as was his wont while recounting some tall tale or when bragging on a prank and seemed completely immersed in the telling. She crept until she squatted right behind him. A Ranger's glance clued him and he turned, but she ducked down and to the side. He turned the other way to try to see who was there, but by that time she dropped to her back and cross-swept his legs. He let out a yell as he hit the floor. She rolled up, giggling, and the Rangers howled with laughter. Marcalan lay stretched out on the floor, laughing helplessly.

Alcandhor walked away, shaking his head and chuckling. She was definitely a different person than the suppressed child he had met in that small cottage not so long ago.

~*~

Tam laughed, waiting for Marcalan to rise.

"You scamp!" Marcalan gasped between laughs. He jumped up with a mock menacing expression. Her first instinct was to match him then and there, but Loch'alan yelled, "Run, Tam!"

Tam hesitated, then darted for the door, Marcalan not far behind. Once outside, she avoided the crowds in and around the tents, veering to the right and toward the gardens. Torches lit the paths well, or she would have been lost in the darkness. Rangers gathered outside to watch the race, laughing and cheering for one or the other.

Tam pelted through the garden walkways. She was a fast runner, but felt him slowly gaining. She grabbed a metal torch pole and used it to change her direction by spinning around it and took off on a different path back toward the Great Hall. He gained again! A Ranger cried out to warn her, but too late—she felt hands grab her waist. She tried to spin around, but her momentum still carried her forward, and they both tumbled to the ground. She landed almost on a Ranger's feet before she could stop. He backed away, and she scrambled up, panting from the race. Marcalan lay still on the ground, face down. She could sense nothing from him. She stopped smiling and glanced at the Ranger, who shrugged, shaking his head.

Chapter Eight

Breathing heavily, Tam called, "Marcalan?"

No answer. She sensed him, but felt nothing although he was not blocking. A chill passed through her. She walked close and bent over him. Without warning, he twisted, grabbing her by the arms, and threw her over to the ground. She rolled up with a grin, waiting for him. He got up, laughing, and faced her.

"You have wanted to match me, you prankster," she challenged, feeling strangely grand.

"Oh, Tam, you really do not wish to match me, do you?"

"Do I not?"

"Nay."

"And why not?"

"Because I am half topside down from drink."

Tam was not going to ask what he meant. She only knew she wanted to have fun. "I care not."

Rangers called into the Great Hall as the two put their fists over their hearts. People flocked outside to watch them match, calling out suggestions, cheering, and yelling encouragement.

"Come, Marcalan, you can do better than that," called one Ranger.

"What? Being more than half tipped back, I am fortunate to be on my feet." He grunted at the word *feet* as he blocked a kick from Tam and countered. She blocked and wheeled about, intending to hit him in the face with the back of her fist, the thought flashing through her mind too late that he would expect that, since she had used it on Loch'alan. As she feared, he ducked and tripped her as she spun. She fell hard and stayed still.

The Rangers quieted as she did not move. She felt Marcalan's trepidation grow and wondered if he could be fooled. She kept her mind as still as she could, as if she were unconscious. Not blocking because he would sense that. He had just tried this ruse with her. Could she do it? Calm. Still. Quiet. He took a step nearer and gave her a gentle nudge with his foot.

"Tam?"

"She looks like a young child sleeping," murmured a Ranger.

"Is she truly hurt, Marcalan?" asked another.

"She...she is not moving," he replied, his voice shaky. He took another step closer.

Now! She kicked at the back of his knee, and he hit the ground with a loud *whuff.* Laughing, she sat up and pointed at him. "Got you!"

The Rangers whooped and cheered as Marcalan slowly pushed up, trying to catch his breath. He grinned at her and pointed back in warning. This was war now; when she least expected it, he would get her back.

They all headed back into the Great Hall, Rangers clouting both Tam and Marcalan on their backs.

Marcalan got Tam another glass of wine, and she stood near him, sipping it as he told how he had returned to Ranger Hold from journeying to Estan right after the siege started. He had found Haladhon going without food and sleep in his misery of having to be 'acting Thane' since Alcandhor was still recovering from the injuries of the ambush.

"I made sure he thought I had put something in his cup, by paying close attention to it, and he never realized I had drugged his stew until after he woke up."

The Rangers laughed while one said, "I am surprised you pulled one over on him, Marcalan."

"It shows how he had overreached himself. He was so sleep deprived he could not think."

"What did he do to you when he woke, Marcalan?" Tam asked, then blushed that she had spoken amidst the crowd of Rangers.

"Well, he raged about, trying to find me for awhile, from what I heard—like a rabid ballan, teeth showing, snarling, you know." He acted it out melodramatically, winking at her. "When I came into the meeting chamber, he just picked me up and threw me against a door." Marcalan shrugged. "One of the easiest punishments I was ever meted out."

Gardhal, a Ranger who had been with them in Lairdton, rolled his eyes. "You never get what you deserve, Marcalan."

"And that is my fault?"

"I know not how you do it. You even got up from the Thane's table during the meal tonight, and he said nothing."

Marcalan chuckled. "He was too busy laughing at what cousin Tam did."

"What did she do?" Gardhal's curious gaze rested on Tam. "We poor kin at the other tables missed that one."

Marcalan bowed and gestured for Tam to explain. She shrugged, sipping her wine. "I just poured vinegar into Haladhon's ale."

"And you should have seen his face!" Marcalan acted as if he struggled trying not to spit out something foul then having to swallow it. The Rangers howled at his dramatic efforts. Tam laughed with them, almost feeling a sense of belonging with all these strangers who were her kin.

"So what other trouble did you get into at Ranger Hold, Marcalan?" asked a young Ranger. His jerkin collar did not have a cluster of leaves embroidered on it denoting being Confirmed as Trained as Ranger, so he was still a stripling.

"I had little time to get into any trouble. I was too busy trying to keep up with Tam."

Warmth rose into Tam's face.

"Why? What trouble was she getting into?" the stripling asked.

"Trouble? She just turned the whole hall topside down."

"But how?"

Marcalan rolled his eyes and glanced about. He gestured toward Gardhal and several others. "Help me out, cousins. Can we make a list?"

"She is a Child of the Enaisi." Gardhal smiled at Tam, which surprised her, as he seemed of a sour disposition.

"Like the Thane?" asked one of the Rangers, awe in his voice.

"Nay," came another voice. She turned to see Maradhor approaching, along with Zandhral. Maradhor's deep brown eyes sparkled with gentle humor as he gazed down at her. "Not like the Thane."

"Nor me," Zandhral added, a smile splitting his soft, blond beard.

"She is like the ones we have read about in the times of the Enaisi themselves." Maradhor said. "She saved the Thane from an ambush by Uardhel's Rogues by seeing it before it happened and stopping it without even being there. She dreams and actually has seen an Elder. She discovered a secret chamber of the Enaisi under Ranger Hold filled with books and charts, which the Thane says he hopes will allow us to get the portal working so we can all meet the Enaisi."

Many of the Rangers murmured at that and stared at Tam. She sipped her wine, keeping her head down. How did Marcalan not mind being the center of attention? She liked it not one bit.

"What else can you do, cousin Tam?" She did not see which Ranger asked. Her face grew even warmer with all of them looking at her. Nay, 'twas the hall that was warm. It made her light-headed.

"I know not," she replied to her drink. "Uncle has to teach me."

"I wish I could see her make a key glow," a Ranger said. "How many of us have ever seen that?"

"Few, cousin," another Ranger answered.

Tam braved a timid glance about her. "Think you Uncle would mind, Marcalan?"

He laughed in surprise. "You are Second at Table. You need not ask permission. And why should the Thane mind? It is one more proof of your rightful place in our clan."

Several Rangers asked questions at the same time. Marcalan simply pushed past them with a proud grin, gesturing for Tam to walk outside. She led the way and searched for a spot not too near a torch. Rangers crowded around her. The cooler air outdoors eased her giddiness.

She pulled on the chain, bringing the bio-crystal key out from under her shirt and jerkin. Gasps and sounds of astonishment filled the night air at its brilliant glow.

Tam looked over at Marcalan, smirking with his arms crossed, then she dropped the key back inside her shirt.

Loch'alan shouldered his brother away. "Tell us about the attack on the Thane by the Rogues, Tam. How did you do it?"

"This is a mistake, Loch'y, for two reasons," Marcalan interposed before Tam could open her mouth. "First, Tam is not good at story-telling. It comes from being too shy and not liking to talk about herself, I think." She glared at him, but he just grinned wider. "This means I will have to retell the story afterwards, since I was there and saw it all. And storytelling is thirsty work, so why do we not go inside, commandeer a table and some ale, and I will tell the story properly."

Loch'alan crossed his arms. "You just want to be the center of attention, Mar."

Tam shook her head. "Marcalan is right. I do not tell stories well. Uncle chides me for not reporting properly. He says I leave things out. Marcalan was there. He could tell it better."

Marcalan struck a superior pose. "See?"

Loch'alan's lips twisted in a wry grimace. "Then let us return to the Hall so we can hear the telling."

Marcalan made Tam finish her wine so he could get her another before he started relating the story. Tam stood at the end of the table and tried to pay no attention as he told the story, but his dramatic presentation was too compelling to ignore. He did not just talk; he acted it out. She found the memory disturbing. She remembered too clearly seeing her uncle crumpled on the floor of the crypt and her fear for him. Tam wished she could forget the whole incident.

She was startled out of her reverie by laughter and realized Marcalan had gone on to tell about Tam accidentally spraying the Laird's white surcoat with grub guts while in the garden. He caught her eye and winked, and she knew he had done that on purpose. He could sense the remembrance bothered her and diverted the conversation. That made her want to hug him. *Friends and cousins!*

Surprise swept over her, and she looked up at Zandhral standing next to her. Stars, he could sense. Did he feel something more than friends and cousins?

Chapter Nine

Tam smiled at Zandhral, and he returned it, but said nothing. She gulped and, hoping to keep the conversation away from dangerous topics like *in love*, offered, "Zandhral, how many more of us are there?"

His smile widened in a maddening way that made her afraid he might have felt, or at least guessed, that there might be more than just "friends and cousins" between her and Marcalan. But his reply was unrevealing.

"I am not certain. There some in the Sons of Avadhron, but I know not how many."

Tam nodded. The Sons of Avadhron were the sept of their clan that claimed the famous Avadhron as ancestor, and his wife Ismari. They ranged the bounds of Pashelon Province, where Tam grew up.

Zandhral shrugged, continuing, "The Thane would know. In direct line of Zaidhron, from which you and I are descended, there are...twenty-three. That actually live in this city, we are ten, but only six of us are here at the moment, the other four including my father and grandfather are in search of the Rogues."

"Does that count include Nandhal?"

"Aye."

They neither said a word, but Tam felt Zandhral's pain over their cousin Nandhal. She searched his face earnestly. "How can someone feel others' emotions yet be hardened to them?"

"I know not. But it happens."

Tam remembered the way Nandhal had looked at her, and how he had talked to her—so cold, arrogant, and hateful. She shivered.

"Think not about him, Tam. He is not our concern any longer."

Tam tipped her head, pursing her lips. Zandhral grieved over Nandhal; did he think he could hide that from her? "Forget you that I also feel? Tell me something you believe yourself."

Zandhral laughed, gentle and quiet. It fit him.

"I will have to get used to you, cousin."

Tam sighed. "Uncle says the same thing. But I am as well. My father did not like me to sense his feelings, and I had to block all the time."

"I am sorry. That must have been difficult."

Tam sipped her wine. Ah, this glassful did not taste as sour as the last stuff a Ranger had pressed into her hand.

Aleta stormed across the Great Hall in their direction.

"Ah, nay!" Zandhral murmured. "I wonder who stuck her with a star-flower thorn."

Tam bit back a snicker, never having heard that saying before. Star-flower thorns would burn and sting miserably for days even after being removed if you did not know the right herb to apply to ease the poison. It fit Aleta's mood—lurid as if one had left its poison in her and driven her mad.

The group of Rangers sitting at the table all turned. A knowing expression grew on Marcalan's face as she raised her fists above her head, screaming obscenities. He grabbed her wrists, then quickly stood and stepped over the bench.

She writhed furiously in his grip, trying to break free. He sidestepped as she tried to kick at his legs and groin, then twisted her arms above her head and down around her, forcing her to spin and face out. Her own arms entrapped her against his body.

"Let go of me! You think you can get away with so much, being Thane's pet! I hate you, you incestuous clan-lover! You never quit your stupid pranks! I will kill you one day, you by-blow! Let go of me so I can kill you!"

Eladhrel and Andhrel ran to where Marcalan restrained the screaming, writhing woman.

"This is doing you no good, Aleta," Andhrel stated, while Eladhrel pleaded, "Aleta, please calm down."

She screamed and kicked at them, paying no attention to their entreaties, as Marcalan continued to hold her tightly, his concentration not totally chasing an amused expression off his face.

Tam stared aghast at the scene. "Stars, Zandhral, she is going to hurt Marcalan or herself. What can be done?"

Zandhral shook his head. "There are few who can handle her. Neither Alcandhor nor Haladhon are in the Great Hall, and I do not see Sarinna or Taniss. It is not done to grab or manhandle the wife of the Thane, and you can see that both Andhrel and Eladhrel are having no success talking to her."

Tam thought back to earlier that evening. "I can stop her."

Zandhral gave her a quizzical frown, and Tam smiled. How could she be so calm? As a matter of fact, she felt wonderfully at ease. Aleta was no problem. The hall being a-tilt was. She turned her attention and emotions to her uncle's wife.

Aleta gasped. Marcalan let go of her as she bent double, moaning.

"That is not proper behavior for the Great Hall, Aleta." Tam walked with slow, careful steps to keep from falling over. She had no idea what she should do, but knew from her father's instruction that a Ranger chief had the right to keep order, and as highest rank present it fell as her duty to do thus. A cool head would be her best ally. She fought down the strange, giddy feelings assailing her and concentrated on being in control. She thought of what her uncle would say and do in such situations. She eased the intensity to see how the woman would react.

With malice replacing the pain in her eyes, Aleta slowly straightened. "What would you know about it, being raised in the wild like an untamed animal?"

Tam considered asking who was behaving like an untamed animal, but remembered her father saying that insults only increased tempers. She certainly had no desire to do that, so she had best ignore it if she wanted that odious woman out of here. "What did Marcalan do?"

"The door to my suite fell off! It scared half the life out of me. That insane whoreson—"

"I simply asked what he did. Thank you, Aleta." She looked over at her friend-and-cousin, hoping she looked as sure of herself as her uncle always did, and also hoping she did not break into giggles. "Marcalan, would you be so kind as to fix the door?"

"My pleasure, Second at Table." He bowed, his eyes twinkling. He slapped Loch'alan on the chest and the two of them left.

"It was a simple prank and no harm done, Aleta. It is being fixed. You may go."

Aleta opened her mouth to argue, but Tam heightened the intensity again. "I said, you may go." After a few moments she decreased the emotions to allow Aleta the chance, again, to leave.

The woman shot her a hateful glare before making a hasty retreat. Tam turned to Zandhral. "Marcalan will not get in trouble for having grabbed her, will he?"

Zandhral shook his head. "He was merely protecting himself." He chuckled. "'Thane's pet.' That is one I have not heard before. I wonder what Marcalan thinks of being called the Thane's pet?"

Tam knew not what to say. As they watched Aleta cross the hall, Andhrel and Eladhrel walked over. Tam hoped she had done the correct thing; she had already discovered that often law in fact was not law in practice.

Before either chief could say anything, Tam asked, "It was my place as Second at Table and highest rank in the hall to keep order, was it not?"

Andhrel smiled. "It certainly was, and greatly welcomed."

Eladhrel nodded, wide-eyed. "I have not seen her so angry in a very long time. Many thanks, Tam."

They left to go back to their families, and the young Rangers gathered closely around Tam again, watching the retreating figure of the Thane's wife in silence. After Aleta flounced out the hall, the nearby Rangers burst into quiet laughter.

"Well done, cousin," several Rangers commented almost at the same time.

"Remind me never to cross you!" one Ranger exclaimed.

"What did you do to her?" another asked.

"I sent her a strong emotion to stop her." Tam flushed. She supposed it was from all the attention, but stars, would not the hall hold still?

Confusion and puzzlement crossed the faces of the Rangers about her. She turned to Zandhral. "You know what I mean, do you not, cousin?"

"I can send my emotions, but I cannot do whatever it was that you did."

"I know not how else to explain it. I just picked an emotion and sent to her as strongly as I could."

"You 'picked' an emotion?"

She nodded at Zandhral, and at the others who gathered around, listening. "I had not the time to choose carefully so I chose the first one I could think of, and make myself feel, and send."

"And that was?"

"The best way I can describe it is the broken heart one feels with compassion."

"That is what you did to Ch'oralan when he contested you, is it not, cousin Tam?" asked Maradhor.

That turned the conversation in another direction. Tam inwardly groaned. More stories about something she did. She let Maradhor tell how Ch'oralan contested her abilities as a Ranger because she was female and how they fought for such a long time yet he would not concede she could hold her own in a fight. Her uncle arrived and took all rules of contest off then, and Tam stopped Ch'oralan with sent emotions until he yielded.

It was not what she had wanted, but it had ended the contest, and Ch'oralan's mouth, although she was certain it did not make him more friendly toward her. She wondered what would happen if ever they had an assignment together. She was glad Ch'oralan had gone home to whatever province was his bounds.

After Maradhor told the story, the other Rangers asked questions about Tam and what else she had done, so Maradhor recounted how she had gone to spy in Laird Hall and escaped by fighting several men—sword fighting one while armed with only a hearth poker. From there, he told about her finding the secret chamber under Lairdton's Ranger Hold. Embarrassed by the attention, she stepped back, away the Rangers, sipping her wine. She backed into Zandhral who chuckled at her.

"They are very curious about you, cousin, and you had best become inured to it, and the attention you will draw."

"I cannot bear it."

"So I can sense. Did your father not teach you to face your fears?"

She lifted an eyebrow at him in irritation. "Do you always speak so impertinently to those you just meet?"

With a grin, he replied. "Only to those who have Enaisi blood. We are all a special kin, you know."

Tam smiled and sat down at the nearest table, afraid she would tip over if she stayed on her feet. Zandhral joined her. Her smile faded. "It is not easy being special."

"For you, being raised alone, it must be difficult, and doubly since you are so much stronger. Our abilities are very weak. It is rare that one of us becomes aware of what we can do without guidance. And sensing another person with Enaisi blood—as you did with me—is indistinguishable for us unless an emotion is sent to us."

Tam sighed. "It is hard to understand. No wonder Uncle was so overjoyed when he found out about me."

"Indeed. He must have been ecstatic."

"He and Haladhon both. And the Laird. They all said it gave them hope, although I am still not certain why or how. For my uncle, it has a special meaning as he hopes to meet the Enaisi."

Zandhral smiled gently at her. "Aye. His private ambition."

"Rangers are not supposed to have ambitions."

Zandhral chuckled. "We make an allowance for our Thane. He deserves it."

Tam finished the wine and put the glass down on the table. No more. She did not like the taste. Cordhan came over and sat down, grinning. "That was a worthy sight, Tam. What think you, Zandhral? Will she not make a good Thane?"

Tam glared at Cordhan. "Leave off. You know I do not fain talk about it."

Cordhan chortled and clouted her arm. "Rangers are making wagers on who wins that battle." Tam groaned in dismay but Cordhan laughed.

Zandhral frowned. "What battle? What wager?"

"Tam does not wish to be her father's heir and become Thane when she comes of Age. She has stated she is going to study the laws and see if she can challenge the conclave decision."

"I will not tell you which side of the battle I have wagered on, either," Marcalan quipped from behind Tam.

"I take it you got the door fixed?" Tam asked, twisting and looking up. He was breathing heavily; he must have run all the way back across the city.

"I did indeed, Second at Table," he replied with a formal bow. "I would have laughed in her face, but that would have made her more angry, if that was possible."

The Rangers again assembled around Marcalan. Loch'alan said his brother wanted to be the center of attention, but it seemed he had no choice; wherever Marcalan was, a crowd gathered.

"What did you do to the door?" asked Cordhan.

"I took the pins out of the hinges. I wish I could have been there to see her lift the latch and the whole door just fall down. *Whoom!*" Marcalan slapped one hand into the other, laughing. The Rangers joined him. "I meant it for Alcandhor. She usually stays at banquets and he goes to bed early." He shrugged. "But it went wonderfully in any case."

"Stars, man, you are ever up to something," a Ranger said.

"And you would have me no other way!" Marcalan bowed.

"Wait, Marcalan!" another Ranger said. "The hinges are on the inside of the door—in the chamber. How did you get the pins out, keep the door on the hinges and close it?"

Marcalan smirked. "A secret shared is power lost."

The Rangers groaned, and one exclaimed, "By the Bells, Marcalan, you make new meaning out of that old adage!"

Amid the renewed laughter about her, Tam lifted a foot over the bench to straddle it and peered up at Marcalan. "When did you have time to do it?"

His eyes twinkled as he held up his hands. "I said I am not giving away my secrets." He pointed at Tam. "By the way, have you had any sweets yet?"

"Just the one."

He held out his hand to her. As she took it, he said, "Excuse me, men, I am going to steal away our Second at Table."

She stood and the hall moved. He steadied her.

"I think you have had too much wine."

"Is that why I feel so funny?"

"Ah nay, I have been a fool." He stopped, staring at her, his brow furrowed. "Perhaps food in your stomach will help. Put your hand on my shoulder as we walk across the floor."

They approached the tables, and Marcalan again explained to Tam what some of the sweets were. Tam had never heard of most of them. She decided on pie this time; it had fruit in it, and she liked fruit. He steadied her with one hand on her elbow, holding two plates in one hand, as they walked to a table.

The pie delighted Tam. She thought her own cooking good but limited. Mostly meals that did not take much time, as her father had wanted her time put into Training.

She pushed the plate away, pie only half eaten. "I wish the chamber would stop spinning, it is making my stomach queasy."

"Stars, Tam, indeed you have had too much wine."

Tam tried to stand up, but he had to help her; her foot caught on the bench.

"Tam, I am so sorry. I did not think that you are not used to wine. You are going to thrash me tomorrow."

Tam did not think so. She tried to tell him thus as he took her hand in his and walked her across the hall.

"Sarinna," Marcalan called, steering Tam toward her aunt.

Sarinna strode in their direction. "I was told Aleta came in raging and Tam—Marcalan what have you done?"

"She has had too much wine. I am sorry, Sarinna. I truly am."

"Help me get her up the stairs."

Tam let them put their arms around her and walk her up the stairs. Her feet had trouble finding the steps and she ground her teeth. Control, she told herself, and she concentrated on the steps. Then they were gone and there was a floor again.

"You wait here," she heard Sarinna say. She sounded angry. "I want to have a talk with you."

Sarinna helped her into the bedchamber and onto the bed then lit candles. A fire had been lit in the fireplace but had burned low. As Sarinna added some wood and poked at it, Tam watched the chamber slowly spin.

Her aunt straightened from the hearth and turned to Tam. "Let us get your clothes off."

"I am a Ranger, Sarinna. I can take off my own clothes."

"If you can manage those laces, you have my admiration, my sotted niece."

"I know not what sotted is but I can do my own laces." Tam looked down at her boots, and blinked, trying to get the whirling feeling to stop.

Sarinna smiled. "Sotted means drunk. As in too much wine, dearest Tam."

Tam leaned over to undo the laces on her boots but sat upright as her stomach knotted. "Ooh, that makes my stomach feel funny." She put her feet on the bed instead to work on the laces.

"Not good," she heard Sarinna mutter, then she heard the door open. "Get a small basin, just in case. And if she has to use it, I will thrash you myself."

"Who were you talking to, Sarinna? Marcalan?" Tam asked, still giving diligent effort to the laces of her boots. They were being stubborn. Had Marcalan knotted them without her noticing? It was the sort of thing he would do.

"Aye, Tam. Do you need help?"

Tam shook her head. She got the knot and loosened the laces then pulled the boot off. She chucked it somewhere and started on the other boot.

"Be nice to him, Sarinna." She smiled up at her aunt for a moment. "He has a very tender heart."

Sarinna folded her arms. "Has he? He told you this?"

"Nay, I feel it in him." Tam stopped talking. Drat the boot! She bit her lip in concentration. "Got it!" She kicked the boot off the bed. Stockings were easy and they flew into the air. Tam got her jerkin off and gave it a happy toss toward the chair. It missed which seemed funny. She giggled.

"Great Bells, Tam! When did you get that key?"

"Uncle gave it to me. Oh, stars, I have to use the priv."

Tam rose, wobbling, and Sarinna put a hand under her elbow to steady her and with her other hand opened the door. Tam smiled as she saw Marcalan walking toward them carrying a basin. He did not seem happy. Sarinna took her by the shoulders and guided her toward the back stairs, saying over her shoulder, "Put it in her chamber."

Tam did not mind Sarinna helping her find the priv. She had only been here the one other time and the back hallways still seemed like mazes to her.

On the way back, Sarinna asked her how she was feeling.

"I am fine, Sarinna. But the floor keeps moving."

"Oh, stars," was all Sarinna said.

Looking forlorn and worried, Marcalan paced in the hallway outside Tam's door. Tam tried to walk over to him but Sarinna guided her into her bedchamber. Tam had trouble with her balance and could not resist.

Sarinna shut the door. "I cannot believe Marcalan would try to get you drunk."

"Why are you angry with Marcalan, Sarinna?" Tam pulled off her shirt. "He has not done anything wrong."

"He got you drunk. He should know better and I am going to roast him."

Tam loosened the laces on her trous. "Please do not, Sarinna."

"Are you such good friends that you would let him get away with doing this to you? My dear girl, you are quite beyond tipped back."

"He meant no harm. I do not wish him to get in trouble because of me."

"You seem to like Marcalan quite a bit."

"I do. He is funny and makes me laugh..." she trailed off as she fell back on the bed to pull off her trous. She pitched them across the chamber, too. The giddy sensations assaulting her gave her an impulse to say more, but Marcalan's serious appeal earlier that night somehow stayed with her. "He is my friend and cousin!"

"Hmm, well, you may not find him so humorous in the morning. You will likely have a tremendous headache, and no one will blame you if you thrash Marcalan thoroughly."

Tam giggled as she lay down. "I thrashed him tonight. We matched outside the Great Hall."

"And with both of you tipped back, I imagine it was a sight to see." Sarinna smiled as she covered Tam up. "Night's rest, Tam. There is a basin next to your bed in case you need it."

She kissed Tam's forehead and quietly walked to the door.

~*~

Sarinna gave Marcalan a withering look as the latch clicked shut. "I cannot believe you got her drunk."

Marcalan spread his arms. "Sarinna, I did not try to get her drunk. I used poor judgment, I admit. But it was not a prank, I assure you."

"I do not want to hear it, Marcalan. You are a grown man having what, twenty-three years? Twenty-four? And if you have no better sense than to offer wine to a lass with but fifteen years and think she can handle it as you do, then you have no sense at all. Give me one reason why I should not tell the Thane what you have done."

"Sarinna, sense me. I did not intend to get her drunk. I was so happy to be home and wanted to show her what fun a banquet could be. I would never do anything to hurt her."

Sarinna did as he requested and sensed him. He seemed to be earnest, but this was Marcalan, after all. He could appear so sincere.

"And what about the Thane?"

Marcalan shoulders hunched. "He will find out she was drunk one way or the other. He will roast me, I am sure. But it all means not as much to me as knowing she will likely want to thrash me in the morning. I was a fool. I deserve whatever I get."

Sarinna did not know what to make of that speech. He seemed truly repentant.

"Aye, you do, Marcalan. I will not tell the Thane. But there had better never be a 'next time.'"

Chapter Ten

In his family suite, Alcandhor lay in bed, staring at the ceiling. Aleta's words—and feelings—that evening had opened his eyes. How he could have let himself stay so blind for so long? He cared not that she did not love him, but she did not recognize his authority. She had manipulated and used him, never accepting her role or responsibilities. She never would. Time to end this farce.

His mind whirled too much to let him sleep. He rose, dressed as silently as possible, leaving that dratted sling off—who would see or report him for not wearing it right now?—and slipped out; the last thing he wanted to do was wake her. Where could he go at this time of night? He decided to go down to their hall's main kitchen and cadge something to eat.

A pot of stew hung over the embers of the hearth fire, for those who had night duties. He ate a bowl slowly, trying not to think. While washing the bowl afterwards in the back kitchen, he heard Aleta's chiding voice. "What do you think you are doing?"

He turned to see her standing in the doorway, clutching a long, heavy robe around her.

"What care you about my comings and goings?" He rubbed his hands on a drying cloth.

Her contemptuous laugh made him bristle. "I thought perhaps you were going to a tryst." She walked forward a step, her mocking eyes raking over him. "But I shouldn't have been so foolish, should I? You are too 'good' to actually think of taking a woman, aren't you?"

Alcandhor's face grew warm, and Aleta laughed at him again. In a taunting voice she asked, "So then, what are you doing, 'Thane' Alcandhor?"

"You cannot tell?" He gestured around him in irritation.

Her lip curled indignantly as she drew herself up. "If you wished something to eat, you should have had a servant bring you something. It is beneath you to be in the kitchen yourself, much less cleaning."

He threw the cloth in the basin. "It is not the duty of servants to wait on me. And it is *beneath* me to be waited on as I am a fully capable man."

She laughed, her eyes filled with scorn. "Are you truly?"

"You would not know, would you?"

"What do you mean by that?"

"You know exactly what I mean."

"If you weren't such a weak, pitiful excuse for a man—" she stopped, her eyes raking over him once more. "Thane." She spat the name. "The Thane is supposed to be strong but you are the weakest man I've ever met."

She strode over and snatched locks of his long hair, twisting them in her fingers, her robe falling open to reveal nothing underneath. She pressed her body against his, her mouth open, inviting, so near his.

"If you were strong, you would—" She gasped as he grabbed her wrists, his fingers pushing on pressure points until she let go of his hair. He shoved her back, ignoring the piercing fire in his left shoulder and arm.

He clenched his jaw against the pain. "You are right, Aleta, I am weak. If I were strong, I would not have put up with your games all these years."

Roiling hateful emotions flowed over him. Why had he never been honest before? Why had he blocked her? Why had he not allowed himself to open to her and feel her before? He truly was weak. He had let her do as she pleased and turned a blind eye, all in the name of keeping peace.

Her face twisted with her hatred. "Games? What do you call what you do? Prancing around as Thane with no idea of the power you have. You could easily rule this world. Be king! Ranger clan is the richest of all yet you all live as paupers. This place is a jest. It is more plain than any noble's hall I have ever seen. You Rangers are so proud of a stinking, silly piece of leather vest when it is the ugliest, meanest piece of clothing imaginable. You will not even allow your servants to wait on you."

"Servants are here to keep this city running smoothly, Aleta. They are not here for us to pamper ourselves."

Aleta waved her arms over her head. "There is no clan in power who has that notion but Ranger clan. It is absurd! You have the most warped ideas and I have never been able to fathom them."

"You have never tried. Not to adapt to life in this clan, not at anything, Aleta. Not because it was your duty, not because you cared about other people, or what people would think of you, and certainly not to please me."

Aleta snorted. "Oh, haven't I? What about you? When have you ever tried to please me?"

Alcandhor threw his good arm out in exasperation. "How can you say that? I have never demanded you take on your traditional tasks as wife of the Thane. Taniss or Sarinna have carried those extra responsibilities all these years. I have allowed you a personal maid, despite my clan's custom against such. I have increased your allotment so you could buy more clothes and jewelry, and allowed you leniency in every way imaginable to try to please you, even allowing another woman to raise our daughter since you tired of the role. So tell me, Aleta, how have I not pleased you?"

She rolled her eyes in derision. "You really don't understand, do you?

You aren't even half a man. You don't have any desire to try to please me as I would like. You refused to try. You have no idea how to give pleasure or how to—"

"By your notions of pleasure I am sure I do not." His face again grew warm. "I have never understood those things that cause you pleasure and have no desire to understand them."

"Too bad." A suggestive smirk crossed her face. "You don't know what you have missed."

"I know what I have missed, Aleta. All too well." He sighed, regret and sorrow filling him. "A wife who loves me. One who would support me when I feel overburdened. And come into my arms and share her heart when distressed, letting me comfort her. Who would allow me to feel her softness, and who would let me love her."

Aleta gave a scornful laugh. "'Love.' You think it should be some romantic dream. You live in fantasy. Love is hot and wild and exciting. You have no concept of how to love."

Alcandhor shook his head at such a futile conversation. He walked past her toward the door.

"Where are you going?" Aleta screeched. "Don't you walk away from me when I'm talking." She grabbed at his left arm but he jerked away from her, gritting his teeth.

"What is there to talk about?"

"About you. About how you refuse to take what should be yours." Her voice rose and she waved her arms. "I am sick of it! I thought I was marrying a man who would have power and prestige some day. A strong man who would take what he wanted." Her eyes raked over him again. "But you can't even take a woman. And now you intend on giving up being Thane to some upstart girl, you worthless by-blow!"

"That will be enough."

She sneered. "Or you will what?"

"I have tried to never lose my patience with you, but you have reached your limit. Do not push me."

She opened her mouth, but he sent her his anger as he met her eyes in challenge. She backed up several steps in fear, swallowing, then ran out.

He leaned on a table, anguish and failure washing over him. He left the kitchen, and without thought, his steps took him to the gardens in the center of the city. He wandered aimlessly through Avadhron's Sward. Finally he stopped, breathing heavily at the weight of this decision, each exhale forming a slight mist. Clenching his teeth in resolve, he hooked his fingers around his marriage necklet and with a sharp snatch, the fine, woven cord broke and beads clattered onto the stone path.

There. It was done.

He strode to the Thane's Solar in the chiefs' range, a suite unused these days save for family times with his children. It had a luxurious, comfortable bedchamber attached, but Alcandhor was unable to find sleep.

~*~

Alcandhor rose early and went in search of his sister. He found her in the back hall near the steward's chamber, talking to the grey-haired Ianalan, master of the western range. He hung back while they discussed a problem concerning a servant.

"Where is she?" Sarinna crossed her arms.

"I know not. We cannot find her. She has complained she was ill for quite a few days, but her only symptom seemed to be fits of tears. And this morning, she has not been seen, and we need the extra help in the Great Hall."

Brushing a strand of hair off her face, Sarinna sighed. "If Casinn will not perform the duties for which she was hired, she may return to her family's home in Jessel. Her impertinence has been trying, but this is too much. Find her, and give her the choice."

"Aye, Sarinna." Ianalan bowed to Sarinna, then to the Thane before leaving.

Sarinna turned with a smile. "What brings you to me this early, my dear brother?" She frowned. "And where is your sling?"

"I will retrieve it in a little while. But right now, I need you to supervise a task."

"As if I do not have enough duties as city steward?"

Alcandhor shrugged. "This task I fear you will enjoy."

"Oh? And what is that?"

"I would like all of Aleta's things removed from my bedchamber and taken to a single females' dorm in Family East, wherever there is a chamber available. Also, she is no longer allowed any prerogatives but is to be treated as a single female in every respect."

"In *every* respect?" His sister's gaze strayed to his neck, and her eyes glinted.

"In every respect. No private maid. She is to take part in tasks, as are all other members of our clan, to earn a basic allotment. She has no more allowance for clothing or other ornamental trappings. She has no authority whatsoever."

Sarinna did not try to hide her pleasure, which was just as well, for Alcandhor could sense it anyway.

"And if she is not pleased with her new status?"

"She is free to leave. The boys would stay in any case as they are in

84

Training, but if she leaves, Amara stays here, with her clan."

"And who will tell her of this change?"

"I will. And as soon as I have, you may have the servants begin moving her things."

"I would fain tell her myself." Sarinna's smile had a predatory edge. "Please, allow me."

"I will do it."

"When?"

"I doubt she will bother to bestir herself before this morning's meal. We can go over afterwards. I would rather eat first, or it might spoil my appetite."

Joy and relief radiated from Sarinna. Alcandhor wished he felt relief; all he felt was misery.

Chapter Eleven

Tam jumped awake, vaguely aware that some loud noise had roused her. She could not believe the headache she had. The evening before seemed a blur. Her clothes were strewn all over her chamber, instead of neatly folded next to the bed or on the chair. What in the names of both moons had she been thinking last night? She did not remember. She gritted her teeth, her head throbbing, as she bent to pick up her clothes and get dressed.

Getting to the priv was a chore; she had to move slowly. She never had a headache like this. Or felt so incapacitated—except the time she broke her leg; that, of course, had been worse. She left the priv and searched for the Great Hall. She knew she was close when she smelled food. She came up the hallway next to the kitchen and into the Great Hall. It was empty. Had she missed morning meal? Oh, stars!

Sarinna swept over, concern on her face. "How are you feeling?"

"I am fine, Sarinna." Tam glanced around. "Did I miss breakfast?"

"Nay, my dear. It is not for a little while yet. The horns only sounded a little bit ago announcing it is near mealtime. Are you sure you are all right? You seem pale. No headache, or stomach ache?"

"A...a little. Why?"

"Do you not remember? You had too much wine last night."

"Did I? Nay, I am sorry, I remember it not."

"Do you remember me helping you to your chamber?"

"Nay."

"Never mind. Say nothing of this to Alcandhor. We will talk later."

"Aye, Sarinna. But what do I do until mealtime?"

"A walk in the fresh air might make you feel better."

"Aye." Tam brightened. "Thank you, Sarinna."

"Stray not far, as mealtime will be soon."

Tam nodded with a wince, then hurried as fast as her headache would allow through the Great Hall and outside. The sun had not risen high enough yet to shine into the city, but lit the cliffs above Zaidhron, sparkling in the cascading waterfalls high above. She stood, watching it, enchanted, then wandered through the gardens, thinking of the banquet and the fun she had, and all the Rangers that she met. Why did she not remember going to bed? What was the last thing she did remember? She thought hard. She talked to Zandhral—about Nandhal...and also about their abilities... Oh, she remembered Aleta ranting about the prank Marcalan pulled. What else? She could not remember. How frustrating.

Ah well, she enjoyed the gardens. Not much remained this time of year, but still, it was familiar and comforting. A few Rangers and some families passed her, heading for the Great Hall, and Tam turned back, following their lead.

The hall seemed rather empty, or at least compared to the two other times she had eaten here. But then, this was breakfast not evening meal—and not a banquet.

The Thane awaited at his chair, staring at the table. He sat, and the gong sounded. Tam winced at the noise as she slid into her place on the bench. Her uncle looked haggard as if he had not slept all night. Tam eyed him with concern as she ate, or rather did not eat. Her stomach did not accept food well. The tea was much more soothing. Sarinna patted her hand once or twice. Where was Aleta? Tam did not ask the question aloud but was pleased she was not there. How did her uncle live with such a person?

The same young woman from the night before again sat with Amara, helping her with her food, but Amara was more interested in looking around and asking questions than in eating. She was also difficult to keep still. At one point, she gave Tam an unflinching stare, which disconcerted Tam, although she knew not why. Her brother distracted her by telling her to eat, and she turned her attention to him, making a wry face. "You do not tell me what to do, Eladhor!"

"Hush, Amara," the woman whispered. "He is right. You need to eat. Come, another bite for me."

Despite her resistance, between Alcandhor and the woman urging her, she finally ate a little more.

Tam felt left out. She did not know most of her near kin, and they did not know her. Marcalan was too far away to talk to. Haladhon smiled, his face pale, but said nothing. Most everyone was quiet. Tam sipped her tea, wishing the throbbing in her head would cease.

Finally her uncle stood, ending the meal, and walked off. Sarinna held Tam's hand a moment. "Are you feeling better?"

"A little, thank you."

Her aunt smiled. "The headache will ease. I wish we had time for a talk now, but a task has arisen that I must attend immediately. But, perhaps later in the day?"

Tam nodded. Sarinna smiled again and hurried away.

"I apologize for last night, cousin."

Tam turned to see Marcalan with an unusually serious expression.

"What should you apologize for?"

"For giving you too much wine. I imagine you have a rather vicious headache this morning."

"Aye, but it is slowly passing off."

"Good." A smile slowly spread, but his blue eyes examined her face with intent curiosity and not amusement. What did he seek? Before she could ask, his expression changed, his eyes now twinkling. "So, what are your duties this morning?" His lilting voice banished all seriousness.

"I know not. Uncle left without giving me instruction. He did not look well."

"Aye, he has an overbusy morning, I warrant." Before Tam could ask what he meant, he continued, "You might get a few matches in if your headache allows. I can imagine the sparring this morning will be quite tempered by the overindulgences of last night."

"Do you not have a headache? You were drinking wine with me all evening."

"I never suffer the-morning-after-a-night-before. Some small gift, I dare say." His eyebrows lifted as his eyes searched her face again, and she sensed a gentle urging. "You need a tour of the city. I know you like gardens and such. Shall I give you a tour of Avadhron's Sward?"

"What is that?"

"The whole center of the city. Although only bits of it are actually a sward, being filled with gardens and fountains, and the family crypts and small woods. You know who Avadhron was, of course?"

Tam nodded. "One of the original chiefs who worked with the Enaisi to move us here from Teledhar."

"Aye. He wanted the city to have as much nature in it as possible, and thus the buildings were set in sections along the walls. In his day it was mostly grass, with only some saplings and small gardens planted. It was named for him, thus Avadhron's Sward."

"I think I would have liked Avadhron very much then." Tam's brain slowly caught up with his suggestion—and meaning. He was trying to find a way for them to be alone to talk! She smiled. "Aye, please, show me his sward."

They walked along the paths in silence, people passing too often to try to say much. An herb garden drew Tam's attention, and she asked, "Are we allowed to enter?"

"I am certain the Second at Table may do as she pleases," Marcalan said with a smile.

Passing through the various herbs, Tam felt more at home. She bent close to a tai'ala plant and breathed deeply of the strong, aromatic scent. Was it her imagination that her headache eased a little? Their connection, which had seemed dulled, revived a bit.

Marcalan squatted next to her. "So tell me about these herbs, cousin," he said, then softly added, "We can speak here, but not for too long. Say on, quickly."

Tam took a deep breath and blurted out, "Do we have *in love*?"

Marcalan's easy grin spread. "Do we have what?"

"*In love*. Uncle told me about it. I know he does not have it with Aleta. Do we have it?"

If Marcalan's expression were any indication, he was about to laugh. Tam could not bear the thought he was about to mock her. Tears smarted her eyes. She tried to rise, but he grabbed her wrist.

"Tam. Look at me."

Reluctantly, she did. His sober face, his blue eyes—oh, she could see the love! She felt it from him! He licked his lips and leaned close, then whispered, "I am in love with you."

Joy surged through Tam, and she started forward to throw her arms around him, but he rose too quickly, still holding her wrist.

"Nay," he hissed, then let go and stepped back.

Unable to move, Tam gulped back her hurt, blinking.

Marcalan made a show of pointing to a nearby bush. "What is that big, shaggy-looking thing?"

Oh. He was just being careful. Tam relaxed and tried to smile. "That is sheena." She sensed around them. "'Tis tasty with poultry or in a dish of vegetables." She felt no one near. "We are alone."

"A sharp-eyed person may see quite a long distance, my cousin. And your uncle would act quickly if any flapping tongues took a tale to him."

Tam had to admit that was true. "But we do have *in love*?"

"Aye," he said with a grin. "We *are* in love."

Tam wrinkled her nose. "That does not sound right."

Marcalan laughed. "Sound right or not, we must behave as if it were not true for now."

Oh, Tam wished to dance and shout, and hug Marcalan, and laugh. They had *in love*! They did have *in love*! She sent her feelings to Marcalan, but instead of being happy with her, he blocked, his face showing disapproval. Tam felt as if her insides wilted. What had she done wrong now?

"You cannot, Tam. Do not send to me thus. 'Tis difficult enough hiding how much I love you, how I wish to hold you, to...kiss you. Such sendings make it almost impossible."

Tam did not understand, but she did not wish him unhappy or angry with her.

Marcalan shook his head. "You cannot know how this rends me. To love you. To know I must deceive my Thane. We must not admit to our love. Please, Tam, please understand."

With effort, Tam tamped all her emotions, both her jubilance at having *in love* and her confusion at Marcalan's reaction. She wanted Marcalan to be happy so she nodded. "I understand. We are friends and cousins."

Marcalan straightened, and the twinkle slowly returned to his eyes. "Good! Then, *cousin*, let me show you more of Avadhron's Sward."

Chapter Twelve

Aleta did not wake in time for breakfast. She rarely did. She would rise when she pleased and expect the kitchen to prepare a special meal for her.

With Sarinna and servants waiting in the corridor outside his family suite, Alcandhor entered, strode through the archway to the bedchamber, and threw the covers off the bed. The sight of her lying there nude stirred him not at all, except maybe to nausea. "Get up. You are being moved out of here."

Aleta rolled over and sat up, irritation and scorn on her face. "What in bloody Bells are you talking about?"

"Moving you out of this chamber and out of my life. Now clothe yourself so the servants can pack your things."

"But I am your wife!"

"Not for years. I am tired of living this lie. You can accept your new chambers and status or you may leave."

Her eyes narrowed. "What new status?"

"You have the status of a single female. You will be assigned duties as all others are, and receive the corresponding single female's allotment. You have no authority. And if you cannot abide by the rules of the city and our clan, you will be asked to leave."

"You wouldn't dare," she hissed. Her lapse into use of contractions and her natural accent was a sign he had, that easily, gotten her full attention.

"It has already been done. Notice has been given. The servants no longer obey you. You have missed the morning meal so you will get no food until luncheon is served. The privileges I have allowed you in a failed effort to make you happy have been revoked. No more special rules for you."

Aleta stared at him, mouth open. He walked over to the door, having said all that needed to be said, but she suddenly lunged at him, screaming in rage. He grabbed both her wrists as she tried to claw at him, his head swimming from the agony spearing through his shoulder, and threw her onto the floor.

He clenched his teeth, forcing his mind to the task, not the pain. "This will gain you nothing, woman. Dress yourself. The servants will be in to pack your things." He smiled in contempt. "Unless you would prefer to do the work yourself."

She picked herself up off the floor, hair wild, her face contorted with hatred. He needed not use his abilities to know she was going to launch herself at him again. Another jolt to his shoulder would be too much. He waited for the attack, and backhanded her with his right hand—not hard, but enough to deflect her assault. The shock on her face matched that in his soul that he had struck a woman, but he kept his face hard. "Presume to attack the Thane again, and I will have you in stocks."

"You wouldn't dare!" Her challenge was repeated with apprehension this time instead of derision.

"I care not if you wish to brave the stocks, Aleta. Try me, if you think I am bluffing."

Her eyes widened. "You wouldn't. You know how it would hurt the children."

Disgust rose in Alcandhor. "Aye, it would," he replied in an implacable tone. "Care you enough about them to spare them seeing their mother in stocks?"

She gaped at him, turning pale. Did she finally realize she was not going to manipulate him anymore?

"I tell you, Aleta, your games are over. You no longer control me. I offered you everything I had. I loved you, adored you. Why was it not enough? You have lost it all." He stopped, shaking his head, then said softly, "I pity you."

She slowly got to her feet, her breasts heaving. From fear, Alcandhor sensed. Fear of losing her status? Of her allotment? Fear of what? He cared not. He just wanted her out.

"Clothe yourself! I want you out of my bedchamber."

"Do you think I'll just meekly obey you? Why should I get dressed? I won't help you move me out. And what right do you have anyway to put me out? Give me a reason, as it states in the law."

Alcandhor wanted to laugh at her attempt to use the law to her advantage, since she flouted it and tried repeatedly to coerce him to do thus as well. "You have never fulfilled one obligation required by a wife of the Thane in the five years or so you have held that title. You never ordered the west range as is your duty or undertaken the least of the—"

"I have been hostess to visiting nobles the few times any would bother to come to this stark, inhospitable place!"

"You mean you displayed yourself and fawned over them. You were not the one to see that their chambers were prepared, or that proper—"

"Sarinna is steward of the city, she takes care of all such matters. Why should I bother?" Aleta waved a hand in flippant dismissal.

"Ianalan takes care of such matters with Sarinna's assistance because the wife of the Thane has been too proud and vain to bother with her duties. And if our clan hall is inhospitable, you have yourself to blame, as that is the duty of the Thane's wife. You have no desire to be cordial or gracious to anyone, save when it serves your purposes. So tell me, what duties of Thane's wife have you fulfilled that I should not put you out?" The acrimony in his own voice surprised Alcandhor. Aleta was too, by the startled look she gave him.

She lifted her chin with martyred affectation. "I have borne you three children."

Alcandhor snorted. "A mistress could have done me that favor, and not had the benefits of rank that you have enjoyed."

"Not that you would ever take a mistress," she sneered. "You are too moral for such a thing, aren't you, most noble Thane? No matter how badly you might wish to bed a woman. Why not ask Jholinn? I am certain that slope-shouldered, soft-bellied commoner wouldn't refuse you."

Alcandhor rankled at Aleta's description and opinion of Jholinn. Did she despise the woman who had taken on care of Amara? She should be grateful. But nay, Aleta would not see it that way. Her thinking was such that she would consider that Jholinn was trying to insinuate herself into a better position. Stars, the Ranger widow avoided Alcandhor. But he refused to let the argument take that direction. Accusations would fly, and nothing would be accomplished except giving servants more meaty tidbits to chew on. For the same reason, he did not mention her numerous affairs. Let that remain buried as well, for his children's sake.

"Since you can name no duty that you have performed as Thane's wife, I tell you again, to put clothes on."

"I will not!"

"So be it."

He walked to the door and opened it. Several servant girls entered with Sarinna to supervise them.

"Get them out of here! I am not dressed!" Aleta screeched, pulling the coverlet off the bed to wrap around herself. "Especially her!" She pointed to Sarinna.

How had he ever thought her attractive? Her beauty was like shining ice on a walkway, treacherous and best avoided. "If you are not dressed by the time they have packed your things, you will be forcibly removed from this suite, clothed or not."

Aleta stormed over to her wardrobe, snatched items from the servants' hands, and pulled on garments.

"Do you have it in hand?" Alcandhor asked his sister in an undertone.

Sarinna picked up the sling from the chair by the bed and handed it to her brother with an arched eyebrow. Her smile grew pernicious. "Go on

about your duties, brother. I will take care of everything."
     "Of that I have no doubt," he murmured.

Chapter Thirteen

Alcandhor pondered all the duties crowded into this morning as he crossed Avadhron's Sward to Thane Hall. Before all else, he had best tell his children about putting out Aleta before they found out through city gossip.

His steps slowed. Rondhrel walked along the paved path with a set jaw and pain etched between his eyebrows. The Ranger bowed low. "Thane."

"I cannot imagine your grief, cousin."

"I did not believe Tanadhon had truly conspired with traitors. I visited him last night, and again this morning, trying to talk to him, get him to say it was a mistake. He wavered between rage at our laws and fear. He begged me to talk to you about sparing his life."

Alcandhor shook his head. "Your nephew plotted twice against his own clan. The first was the ambush which killed five Rangers and Chief Valdhor and wounded me, and the second was with the Rogues led by Uardhel, who attempted to kill me. I cannot abrogate the law with such serious charges. Murder and attempted murder have but one sentence."

"I...know," Rondhrel whispered. "I do not ask it. I could not. As a Ranger my fealty must rest at your feet, regardless of blood."

Alcandhor rested a hand on Rondhrel's shoulder. "We of Ch'shalna must rarely choose between our loyalty to our clan or of that to our family. When we do, the struggle is difficult. And Tanadhon was not just a cousin, but a close friend—or so I thought. I know not how such anger festered so secretly, nor how it turned to such betrayal."

"I am as bewildered as you, Thane. And shocked." Rondhrel hunched, and he dropped his gaze. "When...when must it happen?"

A gut-punched ache radiated from the Ranger, and Alcandhor tightened his grip on the man's shoulder. "Soon," he said softly. "I will visit him myself first, and likely Haladhon will too. We were all close since children. When I have done that, I will set the day of execution. I will have you and your family at my shoulder so as to let no one say you are to blame. Also as a statement that you are not to be shunned."

Rondhrel inclined his head, his throat working and lips pressed together. "I thank you, Thane," he managed hoarsely, then strode off, shoulders bowed.

Alcandhor inhaled deeply. Yet another duty of the Thane that he despised. But now, he had a different duty to perform, this one as a father. He did not look forward to it, but delay would not be his friend. Setting his jaw, he quickened his stride.

He tossed his cloak on a peg upon entering the Thane's chamber, then pulled the cord to summon a servant.

A stripling appeared in the door and bowed. Alcandhor's brows raised. "You are my attendant?"

"Aye, Thane."

"And how long do you pull this duty?"

"One lunation, sir."

"'Tis not much of a punishment, serving in Thane Hall."

"'Twas not punishment but my request, sir. I am to serve as attendant to you and to Chief Andhrel."

"Considering law-keeper then? Your name?"

"Feladhrel."

Alcandhor nodded. "I wish my children brought to me at once. And I need to see Tam, Haladhon, and Marcalan as well." Alcandhor hesitated; this would be personal, but since it involved the Children of the Enaisi... "And also Zandhral. They may wait in the forechamber."

The stripling bowed and ran out.

Alcandhor pulled a pile of reports across the table to read while waiting for his children to arrive. 'Twas difficult to remain focused with the fiery pain in his shoulder, but he persevered, especially on the reports about Monadhal's Rogues. No sightings had been confirmed, but a farm in the hills of Lantral Province had been raided of most of its harvest. No one had been awakened nor injured. Bandits did not normally take supplies needed for the winter, but items they could sell. The local Rangers had attempted to track the thieves, but lost them—a rare thing, which added to their suspicions that Rogues were the culprits.

Jholinn brought Amara to the door. Alcandhor pushed all the papers back and beckoned her in. Amara ran to her father and climbed into his lap. The woman stood just inside the doorway, clutching her skirts in her fists. He wished he knew how to make her less ill at ease around him. But at least she did not hold whatever negative feelings she had for him against his daughter.

"Jholinn...you have been a steady presence for Amara since she was a baby. I...I do not know what I could do to thank you."

"You need not, Thane," Jholinn whispered. "I love her."

"It makes my thanks no less, though. And..." he stopped, not wanting to say it, but knowing he had to. "I need to ask more of you. But I need to talk to the children first. Would you stay until afterwards?"

"Certainly, Thane. I will wait in the forechamber."

The boys entered the chamber just then. She curtsied and slipped away.

Alcandhor's heart ached at what he had to tell his children. Amara was content, cuddled in his lap, but both boys had a foreboding expression. Could they know?

He gestured for them to come close, Eladhor edged in by his right knee, leaning against him, and Teldhor stood to his left, lips pressed together. He looked too wise for his almost-twelve years.

Alcandhor cleared his throat. "I have something to tell you that is going to be difficult to understand." He licked his lips, but they were still dry. Meeting his children's gazes was difficult. "I, uh, I have put out your mother. She is no longer considered my wife."

Eladhor blinked, anguish on his face. "But why, Papa?"

"There are many reasons, and they are quite personal, and private, between her and me."

"But where will she live?" Eladhor asked.

"She will have a chamber in the dorms of Family East, with the single women. I would not send her out homeless, son."

Alcandhor glanced down at Amara. She was untying the laces on his jerkin with a single-minded studiousness. Did she understand at all?

"I wanted to tell you three before you heard it through city gossip. And to let you know that if anyone approaches you about this, it is acceptable for you to say this is a family matter and you will not discuss it. Rumor and gossip may fly faster and farther than birds in this place, but we need not give wind to their wings." He peered at each one in turn. "I know this is difficult for you, and I would that it did not have to be thus. I am sorry for the grief this brings you."

The children did not speak, and Alcandhor fought the urge to fidget. He nodded at Teldhor. "What say you, son?"

Teldhor swallowed. "I know not what to say."

Tears welled in Eladhor's eyes. "I do not understand, Father. Not at all."

"I do not either." What else could he say? The boys were too young to understand, and the shame of his failure sat like a stone in his stomach. "I am sorry."

Eladhor sniffed, rubbing his sleeve across his eyes, Alcandhor pulled him into an embrace. Amara pushed at her brother, whining. She did not seem bothered by any of the conversation, only with being crowded.

Alcandhor shushed her. "You are not my only child, Sweetling. You need to share."

She slapped at Eladhor with a sulky pout. "I do not want to!"

Alcandhor tapped her hand with his finger in warning.

"You let her sass too much, Father." Teldhor tousled Amara's hair, pulling his hand back before she could swat at him.

"Aye, I do." He hesitated. "So, have you boys anything to say?"

Eladhor shook his head.

Teldhor pursed his lips. "I–I can sense, and I know you and Mother have not...do not...care for each other. But I did not think something like this would happen."

"'Twas a difficult decision, son."

The children remained silent. The boys avoided his gaze, and Amara pulled again at the lacings of his jerkin. Stars, but they all were growing up so fast. Teldhor would soon be a stripling! Hoping to change their mood, he said, "I will be staying at Zaidhron more now. What say you to that?"

Eladhor brightened. "Will you really, Father?"

Pride exuded from Teldhor. "Why? Because you were able to take care of the traitors?"

Alcandhor smiled. "Aye, partially because of that. And because of your cousin Tam. She is heir to Thane and I must Train her." He peered at his older son, who was being displaced as next Thane. "What say you to that? How feel you about your cousin being Thane in five years?"

"But why?"

"She is my elder brother's heir. What does Clan Law, and Ranger Law, say about that?" Alcandhor asked, smiling down at Amara as she tickled the whiskers on his chin.

Eladhor stared, mouth agape. "Even though she is a lass?"

"Andhrel and I searched and there is no law against a female Ranger or against one being Thane. Our only restriction is that Thane of our clan must be a Ranger."

Teldhor averted his eyes, a resentment simmering, and whispered, "Then she will be Thane."

"And how feel you about that?" Alcandhor asked again, despite sensing his son's feelings. Amara pulled on his chin beard, and he clasped her hand. She wiggled and he hugged her tightly, murmuring for her to be still.

Teldhor shrugged. His emotions became unreadable; he had blocked his father from sensing him. "I know not. Sometimes I would think it would be grand someday when I would be Thane, but then I would think about all the worries you have, and how every decision must be so wise, and I am afraid I would not be a good Thane. But now I need not worry about it."

Alcandhor peered into his son's face. "If Tam and I both were to die, you would be Thane one day, so say that not." He hesitated then added, "It will take time to adjust to this change, but remember you will always be a

Ranger chief with many heavy responsibilities. You are not long away from being a stripling Ranger. How goes your studies?"

"Well, I think. But the last lunation had so much upheaval. Most of the Rangers were gone, and our studies were left to us without the sort of supervision we are used to. Some of the Trainees did not study as hard they should have, but I tried to keep up."

"I know you did, Teldhor. But now I am here and can undertake your studies as I should. Unless I need to be out of the city, I will be able to instruct you both regularly, as is my duty. And begin Amara's studies as well."

"I think Jholinn has been teaching her. She knows her letters and can read a little." Teldhor smiled at his sister. "Can you not, Amara?"

"I can read, Papa," Amara said proudly.

"That makes my duty a little easier, I had worried about that since I knew—" he stopped and Teldhor finished the sentence for him.

"Since you knew Mother was not teaching her."

"Teldhor." Alcandhor's voice held more warning this time.

"I did not say so disrespectfully, but it is true."

Alcandhor sighed. Teldhor was too perceptive. And also withdrawn. Not as Valdhor had been, but still Alcandhor worried. How much of his reserve was Teldhor's way of keeping himself from hurt at his mother's neglect and his father's long absences? Things would be different now.

"So from now on, unless I am out of the city, you three will come to me after luncheon. Is that satisfactory?"

"Will you also be matching us then, Father?" Eladhor's expression was hopeful.

"When I am healed, aye."

Both boys stared at the sling.

"What happened, Father?" Teldhor whispered.

"We did not drum it out as it would have alerted the traitors that they had struck a more serious blow than they thought, but the day the siege began, we were ambushed. Tam's father died, and I would have too, if it were not for both Valdhor and Tam."

"But what was the injury?" Teldhor asked.

"I had many injuries, but at the time I was aware of an arrow in my shoulder. My left shoulder. That arm is still weak as you can see."

"How did Valdhor and Tam save you?"

"Valdhor fought alongside me the whole time, trying to protect me— as Thane I was their main target. And after they felled him, and had shot me, I wielded my sword with but one hand, trying to fend them all off. Tam killed several including the traitor who was besting me at the last. If she had not come..." He shook his head.

Both boys grew pale. Amara wrapped her small arms around Alcandhor and squeezed. She looked up at him, tears in her eyes. So she did pay attention, despite her playing.

"Then...I am glad you brought Tam back, Father," Teldhor said in a quiet voice.

"I am, too," Eladhor said.

"When will you be healed enough to match, Father?" Teldhor asked.

"As soon as the healer lets me remove this sling, I will start matching lightly with a few Rangers, Cordhan and Edhron perhaps. They are older and vastly experienced. They can keep me fit and help me to slowly regain use and strength of the arm without risking further injury. But occasionally I will be watching you Train in the morning. I will probably bring Tam with me, as she will become one of your instructors. Now, here is a question for you both. Do you feel you can go back to your studies this morning, after the news I have told you?"

Teldhor nodded. "Rangers do their duty, Father, no matter what."

"Eladhor?"

"I will be fine, Father," his younger son murmured, his head down.

"Eladhor, you are still young, much younger than your brother. It is not wrong to share your feelings. Think you I slept last night knowing the decision I was making?"

His son's head snapped up, eyes wide.

"Sometimes we face difficult things in life, son. And it is not always easy to roll with those things that hit us hard. And it is not wrong to admit it if you are overwhelmed. What think you I would do sometimes without Haladhon and my other close kin? The Thane needs his chiefs to help bear burdens as well as offer advice." He gazed at Eladhor closely. "Would you rather not go back to your Training this morning?"

"Nay, Father. I will go."

"Are you certain?"

"Aye, Father."

He nodded at both boys. "All right. Go, then."

Amara sat up, grinning, as the boys left. "Now I do not have to share."

Alcandhor laughed. "You are an imp, you know that?"

"What is an imp?" Amara asked, giggling.

Alcandhor touched her nose with his finger. "You, Little One!"

Amara grinned, and knelt on her father's lap and gave playful tugs to his long hair. He caressed her curls.

"You are not going away for a long time?"

"I hope not. I have no plans to go away for now. Sometimes I will have to, but hopefully not for the long times I have had to in the past. Does that make you happy?"

She nodded and threw her arms around his neck.

"Do you understand about your mother, Sweetling?"

"She is in a different chamber now. And in Family East. That is many paces across the sward."

"It is, indeed."

"Jholinn and I like to count together. Perhaps we can count all the paces from here to Family East one day. Shall I count for you Papa?"

"What shall you count, Little One?"

"I can count anything! I am very smart. Jholinn says so."

Alcandhor chuckled. "I wish to speak to Jholinn for a few moments. Would you play in the forechamber by yourself for a little while?"

"Why can I not stay?"

"Because we need to discuss adult things, and you are not yet an adult, Littlest."

Amara scowled a little, and Alcandhor feared she would start one of her infamous temper tantrums so he sent her calm, peaceful feelings. It seemed to work for she merely wrinkled her nose. "I want to grow up now!"

He chuckled, hugging her, then stood. "Let us go find Jholinn, and you can wait in the forechamber for her while we talk."

He held her hand as they walked out. "Stay here and play, Amara. Jholinn will be back very shortly."

Amara climbed into a chair under one of the windows. "May I watch the striplings matching?"

Alcandhor peered out. Why were striplings matching on this side of the city? Edhron was the most likely reason. He was notorious for sending striplings on a run around the circumference of the city, stopping them at intervals to match as a rest period.

"Aye, you may," Alcandhor replied, then gestured for Jholinn to enter the chamber.

The young widow stood by the door, her hands clasped tightly, her gaze averted. He sat on the edge of his table. "Jholinn, I need to ask a tremendous favor of you. Amara is going to need you as never before. I..." he hesitated, still finding it hard to talk about, and in front of a stranger, it was worse. He made himself plunge ahead. "I have put out Aleta. I think Amara does not yet completely comprehend what has happened."

"I understand, sir."

"And I truly appreciate that you sit with us to care for her during family meals, although I suppose I should be the one to do that."

"I am honored you allow it, sir. And you are away so much that it just became routine."

"I know. That is changing also. You will have more time for yourself.

101

Now that I will be here more often than not, I will have my children with me after luncheon, as is customary. Amara enjoys you near her though, so I want you to feel free to join any family activity if she desires it. I want this time to have minimal stress on her."

"You are very thoughtful of Amara. She is fortunate to have you for a father."

"I have not been much of a father, having to be away so much." He grimaced, then shrugged off the ache and guilt. "But things will be different now. And I do thank you, Jholinn, for caring for Amara. I...I wish I knew a way to let you know what it means to me to know she is cared for and loved."

"It is a pleasure and honor to care for the daughter of our Thane. And as I have said, sir, it was good for me too, when Landhral died."

"I am glad you found a positive way to work through his death. It was hard on you, being a new wife."

And a grieving mother. But Alcandhor did not wish to bring up such a sorrow. Before the silence became too uneasy, he stood with a quick smile. "But I should not keep you and Amara inside while I talk endlessly. Go, Jholinn. Take her for a walk, or whatever you two do together. I will see you both at luncheon."

Chapter Fourteen

Alcandhor sat and let his breath out slowly, then pulled a report off the stack. Might as well do his duty while waiting. He stared blankly at the page in front of him and finally rubbed his eyes. Too many things rushed through his mind to concentrate.

"I hear you have finally come to your senses."

Alcandhor looked up to see Haladhon in the doorway, no attempt to hide his grin. Alcandhor cupped his chin in his hand with a wry grimace, eyeing his cousin, who sauntered in and perched on the edge of the table.

"Considering how much prurient speculation there has ever been about my marriage, I do not wish to know any details of the current gossip. But I will say that if the speed at which knowledge is communicated around this city could be done throughout our world, we would have no reason for drum towers and message runners."

Haladhon chuckled. "In this case, she was ranting so loudly, no one could miss it. Taniss and Sarinna both finally had it out with her, and now she is shut up in her new chamber and refuses to come out."

Alcandhor shrugged. "If she causes contention or trouble, she leaves. She has been told this."

Haladhon crossed his arms. "I hope she causes trouble, then."

"You never liked her, did you?"

"I have always been honest about my feelings."

"Aye. Which is more than I can say. How can a man be so foolish, cousin?"

Haladhon chuckled again. "As long as there are women, men will be fools."

Alcandhor sighed.

Haladhon cleared his throat, then said, "But I have other business, Thane, although it has to do with her."

"And what is that?"

"Are you aware she stormed into the Great Hall last night with the intent of thrashing Marcalan because he pulled a prank? He claimed it was meant for you since you usually retire early while she stays up late."

"Aye, I was up later than usual. The boys and I played backhand and tile games in the Thane's Solar until late. What did he do?"

"Took the pins out of the hinges on your family suite door. It crashed down when she tried to open it."

Alcandhor put his hand over his mouth to muffle his laugh. When he caught his breath, he said, "That scoundrel! Does he spend his nights thinking of pranks instead of sleeping?"

"Who knows, cousin." Haladhon shrugged, his eyes twinkling. "But he never runs out of ideas, it seems. Anyway, what I wanted to report was this. She was ranting and cursing at Marcalan, and he grabbed her to keep her from trying to scratch, hit, and kick him, and neither you nor I were there to stop her."

Alcandhor groaned. "Stars! What did she end up doing?"

"Nothing. Tam stopped her."

Alcandhor stared at Haladhon. "What?"

"You heard me. Tam sent an emotion to disable her then told her to leave. Aleta left."

"I am certain there was a little more to it than that."

"A few words were spoken between them, but Tam was very calm, according to my sources, and took care of the situation very quietly and effectively."

Alcandhor shook his head. "That child is amazing."

"You had best not think of her as a child, cousin. She is not. She may only have fifteen years, but she is a woman. What will you do when some Ranger catches her eye?"

Alcandhor glared at his cousin as he snorted. "I will worry about that when it happens."

"If you do, you will not be prepared. You are very farsighted. You foresaw the traitors' schemes, the siege on Laird Hall—so many things. But when it comes to such things as a young lass growing up, you could not see it if hit you in the face and made your nose bleed."

"And you do notice such things, enh?"

"Think of it as my specialty." Haladhon grinned, then he grew serious again. "And I know it is a raw spot right now, but admit it, you have never had any sense when it came to women, cousin. You cannot see clearly concerning them."

Alcandhor stared at the table. Aye, 'twas the miserable truth.

"I am not jesting, Alcandhor," Haladhon said. "I know you have plans for her, but to expect that woman to wait five years if she finds a man—you are inviting trouble."

"She has obligations to the clan."

"Aye, and among them to marry and have children, as any other Ranger. Clan first, cousin."

"This is immaterial. Let her tell me she has an interest in a young man, then I will deal with it."

"How? Will you accept her choice? Tell her she cannot marry? What will you do?"

"I know not!" Surprised at his own raised voice, Alcandhor inhaled, then cleared his throat.

"Think on it, cousin. I have not your sight, but I can see other things. It will not be long before she will be thinking of making a necklet for some Ranger."

Alcandhor gave Haladhon a sharp glance. "Did something happen last night?"

"Not to my knowledge." Haladhon crossed his arms, his tone implying if he did not know about it, then it did not happen. And Alcandhor knew that with Haladhon's nest of information gatherers, that was likely. "But Rangers buzz around her like honey-collectors or nectar-birds, certainly you have noticed that."

Alcandhor groaned, dropping his head into his right hand. "It is too much! I have dealt with numerous troubles as Thane and always thought I was able to meet any problem head on. I admit, perhaps not with the wisest or best solution, but at least something workable or that usually turned out well. But between my own troubles and worrying about Tam, I feel buried."

"It is as I said. Where it concerns women, you are in Hillsdown, cousin."

"Thank you for such helpful advice, cousin," Alcandhor retorted. "But you need not tell me repeatedly I am lost about women. I am aware of it."

Haladhon laughed, but his smile faded. "Think about it, Alcandhor, and about your response, before you are blindsided."

"Speaking of blindsided, there have been no reports on Nandhal?" Alcandhor hoped the quick turn of conversation would end Haladhon's nagging.

"Nay."

Alcandhor sighed. "I saw this morning's reports. Monadhal's Rogue band is suspected to be moving through central Lantral Province. I think there is a good chance Nandhal will try to join them."

"Stars, if he does, they will be that much more of a threat. He is not branded and can sense. Imagine if he—"

"Nay, thank you, I wish not to imagine." Alcandhor rose and, rubbing his aching shoulder, turned to view the map on the wall behind his table. Haladhon followed. "So far, we know not where Nandhal is. Monadhal's band were mere brigands until last year—"

"When they killed my father!"

Alcandhor darted a look at his best friend. "We know that not for a fact, but aye"—he raised his voice over Haladhon's sputtered contradiction—"aye, 'tis very likely." He met his cousin's gaze steadily until Haladhon took a breath and nodded. "Now that the threat to Laird Hall is gone and the traitors found, we can put our undivided attention into searching them out."

"Good to know I am not always the highest priority," quipped Marcalan from the door.

"Only if you are clogging the privs with sansil again," Alcandhor shot back, with a glance over his shoulder. Tam was with the prankster. Good.

"Come, Tam. You need to know this." Alcandhor pointed to the map, his finger circling the province of Lantral located directly south of Zaidhron. "This has always been Monadhal's domain, but with Uardhel's band gone, Monadhal may decide to go west to Keladar or northwest to Pashelon."

"But why with Uardhel gone?" Tam asked.

"Uardhel and Monadhal developed a rivalry." Haladhon crossed his arms. "Which may have been a good thing. Imagine if they combined Uardhel's abilities as a Child of the Enaisi with Monadhal's cleverness. They could have—" Haladhon stopped with a sharp inhale and grimaced.

Tam put a hand on Haladhon's arm, her large eyes gazing sadly up at her cousin. "We will capture Monadhal."

Haladhon lifted his hand with a slight shake of his head, then nodded at the map. "The cave systems on both sides of that mountain range offer far too many places to hide. We have never been able to track him yet, and now the area in which he can roam is much enlarged."

"Aye," Marcalan added. "I see not how we can succeed now where we have failed in the past."

"After the siege, I sent most of the Rangers to those provinces with the task of joining the search, so I think we have increased our chances significantly."

Marcalan mouthed a silent *ah*.

"And the bulk of the Rangers that came back with us from Lairdton will be leaving to join the rest already sent to holds in all three provinces. Rangers are to journey in larger groups for safety, and to seek them diligently as highest priority. I set several cipher experts to create a new code for both drum and carried messages, and the Rangers leaving here will take those new codes with them. I will take no chance that the Rogues or Nandhal might intercept or understand our communication. When their thereabouts are discovered, the chiefs currently in the city shall all go."

"Is that wise?" Marcalan inclined his head. "Your pardon, Thane. I know I am not a chief to question your decisions."

"We shall go with a large contingency for safety's sake. And I expect our men will apprehend them before we arrive, but I mean to be there to at least bring them back here for trial."

"And if they are killed while being captured?" Haladhon asked.

Alcandhor shot Haladhon a cold glare. "No Ranger is to put himself in danger for capture, as you well know, but I had best find no Ranger has killed any Rogue without cause. Vengeance is not our province, but justice."

Haladhon's jaw clenched. He hesitated before bowing his head.

Alcandhor adjusted the sling, walking to the front of his table. He tapped the papers to change the subject. "And although you are no longer Second at Table, when you are in the city, I do want you here for the morning reports until Tam is more at ease with her duties. It will be your part to tutor her."

"Aye, Thane."

Alcandhor sat back against the front of his table and gestured for Tam and Marcalan to be seated in the chairs across from him. "Now, then we only need wait for Zandhral."

"For what purpose, Thane?" Haladhon asked.

"I wish to discuss you"—Alcandhor inclined his head at Marcalan— "with all the Children of the Enaisi who are currently in the city present."

"What of Sarinna?" Haladhon asked.

Alcandhor closed his eyes with a groan. "Great Bells! Send for her, please, Haladhon. And let her not know I forgot my own sister!"

With a chuckle, his Third at Table pulled the cord.

"'Tis quite an opportunity you just handed us, my Thane." Marcalan leaned back in the chair, stretching his feet out with a devious expression.

Feladhrel entered and Haladhon sent the stripling on his errand.

"Thankfully, she is usually attending her duties in this range at this time," Alcandhor muttered. "If Feladhrel finds her quickly, I may win a reprieve." He shot a glare at Marcalan. "Allowing that mouths stay shut."

Marcalan raised his eyebrows with an infuriatingly innocent gaze.

"I was summoned, Thane?" Zandhral bowed in the doorway. His beard had been trimmed back to the traditional moustache and chin beard, probably at the request of his wife.

"Aye. We await only Sarinna, then we will start."

Without a word, Zandhral pulled a chair away from the wall and sat facing Alcandhor, next to Tam. His eyes flicked to Marcalan then he smiled at Tam. "How did you enjoy your first feast?"

Tam dimpled. "'Twas fun." She frowned. "Although I found I should not let so many Rangers pour me wine. My headache is almost gone now though."

Headache? How much wine did his Rangers give his niece? Tamping down his anger, for it was not directed at Tam, Alcandhor asked through gritted teeth, "You were drunk?"

"'Twas not her fault, Thane," Marcalan said hurriedly. "I should not have given her wine."

"From what I have heard," Haladhon put in, "many Rangers toasted her and offered her drinks. I am not certain why you would wish to claim this as an accomplishment, Mar, but I think you cannot."

"An accomplishment? I claim being a fool! She obviously did not know the effects of too much wine, and I was thoughtless enough to not realize. Think you I would wish to—"

"Enough!" They all fell silent and Alcandhor added, "We shall call this closed. Tam, in the future, be judicious in what you drink. You are over young to have more than a glass or two at most."

"Aye, sir." She tipped her head. "I do prefer water, actually, or tea. But I did not wish to appear rude."

Haladhon burst into laughter, and Zandhral chuckled. Marcalan's subdued attitude vanished as he doubled over cackling. Alcandhor rubbed a hand across his mouth in an attempt to hide his smile.

"Stars, Tam." Marcalan wiped his eyes. "Merely say you care not for wine."

"But then I am offered ale."

"You can say you prefer water or tea, without insult," Alcandhor said.

"Aye, Uncle. Thank you."

Alcandhor stared at his niece. Great Bells, she needed to learn so much! At least now Sarinna and Taniss could take over, at least for those things a girl should learn from a mother. But today's task was to learn more of Marcalan and Tam's abilities both.

Tam fidgeted. "Uncle?"

"Aye, Tam?"

"I...your–your necklet is missing."

Alcandhor huffed a humorless laugh. "You must be the last in the city to know: I have put out Aleta. She is no longer my wife."

Tam's large, golden eyes grew larger. Her hands twisted in her lap, but before she could say anything, Sarinna's voice cut in, "And past time, too!"

She came in, smiling, head high, and held out her hand. "Here is the new key to your chamber, Thane. She cannot enter and take anything not rightfully hers."

Alcandhor took the key and set it on his table. "You think of everything."

Her smile grew smug. "Aye, I usually do. And although you probably know, Nadinn is preparing to leave for Laird Hall tomorrow to join Lamadhel."

"Ah, I had not known. I can understand wishing to join her husband since they have been parted overlong as is, but she is older, and the weather is turning cold."

"Aye. Andhrel and Eladhrel both had words with their mother, and Eladhrel wished to accompany her, but she slapped them both down. You know her. Two Rangers will journey with her, along with a travel-man hired to carry her things. She says that is sufficient." Sarinna lifted her chin. "Now, what business does the Thane of the Rangers have that would concern me?"

"This concerns the Children of the Enaisi. Haladhon, close the door, please."

His Third at Table did, then brought another chair forward for Sarinna, after which he stepped back to stand by the wall.

Sarinna sat and smoothed the skirt of her bodice-gown, then folded her hands. "If this regards the Children of the Enaisi, why are both Haladhon and Marcalan here?"

"Haladhon, because he is—was—my Second at Table, and my closest counselor. Besides he is already aware of the circumstances we will discuss. I would fain have his opinions and advice." Alcandhor glanced around the chamber. "Unless anyone has objections?"

Tam and Zandhral both shook their heads. His sister shrugged with a tight smile at Haladhon.

"And Marcalan?"

"Aye, in a moment. Sarinna, I have told you that Tam is a Child of the Enaisi, but we need to ascertain the strength of what she can do. I am not certain this is possible in one meeting, but I wanted to apprise you of what we know. Also..." Alcandhor paused and met Marcalan's eyes; his mischief-making cousin faced everything in his life full-forward, whether it be a brigand or the victim of a prank wanting revenge. But now uncertainly, even fear, filled his gaze.

"And this is to be strictly between those of us in this chamber unless I say otherwise..." He stopped and stared hard at Zandhral and then at his sister, who merely raised an eyebrow. He glared at her, then finished, "We have discovered that Marcalan is also a Child of the Enaisi."

Chapter Fifteen

Alcandhor bit back a smile at his sister, who, for once, stayed silent. Zandhral frowned, but said nothing.

Fingertips over her mouth, Sarinna stared at Marcalan as if he were a puzzle to solve. "Do your parents know?"

"I do not think so," Marcalan replied with a shrug, "but I cannot know for certain. How would I ask them?" Fists on his thighs, he stared at Sarinna. "Please, tell me. How should I have asked my mother why I am a Child of the Enaisi when she and my father are not?" He swallowed, grimacing. "I tried to think of a way. From the time I was a child, I tried. How does one pose such a question when the answer can only be one thing?"

To a person, everyone in the chamber dropped their gaze.

Sarinna cleared her throat, and her eyes met Alcandhor's. "How did we never tell Marcalan was one of us for the whole of his life?"

"Neither of his parents could make a key glow," he said, shrugging, "and since the Enaisi always asserted that such abilities could only be directly inherited, he was not tested."

"But, for none of us to have even sensed anything unusual—"

"How easily do any of us sense another with Enaisi gifts? Unless one of us send directly, how do we know another has those traits? Stars, look at Nandhal. We knew he was one of us because he could make a key glow but did he ever appear to have or use any inherited traits?"

"I used to wonder if he had no emotions at all or merely blocked to keep them private," Zandhral said.

"He blocked almost all the time," Tam said. "One time he did not, and it was...troubling."

Alcandhor snorted; the others all made similar sounds of agreement.

"So then, what about Marcalan's eyes?" Sarinna asked. "You have what, twenty-four years, and no one has ever seen your eyes darken with anger?"

"Have you ever seen this rascal angry?" Haladhon quipped.

"I am being serious, Haladhon! Marcalan, for all his pranks and jesting, has a fine sense of injustice." She turned in her chair to look full on at her cousin. "You have said you did know you were a Child of the Enaisi."

"Aye, I did," Marcalan murmured. "And tried to hide it."

Sarinna's mouth opened, then closed. No one said anything for a long moment, and finally Sarinna softly asked, "So how did you not show your eyes darkening in anger?"

"By trying to not become angry. I suppose having a personality naturally inclined to find humor in life, I have not had as much trouble as some might."

"But still, I know you. Injustice scours you raw. How has no one seen your eyes turn black?"

Marcalan dropped his head into one hand, rubbing his eyes.

"Marcalan, please answer me!"

"I am," he muttered.

"By the Bells!" Haladhon burst into laughter. "Aye, I have seen Mar do that, and thinking back, 'twould be in cases where he was furious!"

Marcalan lifted his head and winked at Haladhon. Alcandhor stifled a groan, Sarinna rolled her eyes, and Tam and Zandhral both smiled.

"Have you talked to Lantalan and Kalinna?" Sarinna asked.

"Not yet. This is delicate, concerning them, aye, but this is important for us also. We are as a family in a unique way, and I would have us reserve nothing that concerns our gifts."

"Would you say that if Nandhal were here, or would you exclude him?" Sarinna asked, pointedly.

"I...would have reservations, and since he has gone Rogue, I will claim they are well-founded. That question, however, is moot. He is not here."

Tam stirred in her chair. "Uncle? Back at Lairdton, you mentioned a prophecy. A Teldheri child born with Enaisi abilities. Could not Marcalan...could it be he?"

Marcalan slid down in his chair, crossing his arms. "Ah, nay. That prophecy speaks of a child born to two Teldheri who has full Enaisi abilities, even able to read minds. And the Thane himself said he believes not the prophecy was real."

Tam's shoulders slumped.

Alcandhor cleared his throat. "We need to concentrate on our two new additions. Now, Marcalan seems to have abilities similar to ours: he makes a key glow dimly as we do, and can sense and send in a limited way, and can block. We know not whether he has foresight, but that is the one gift which seems to be arbitrary. However, Tam's abilities are much stronger."

Sarinna tilted forward around Marcalan to see Tam. "How so, niece?"

"I can send emotions," Tam replied.

"We can do that."

"Not as she can," Marcalan said. "She can send emotions so strong they debilitate or inflict pain. 'Tis how she stopped the Rogues that had ambushed and tried to kill the Thane. She sent to them all to stop them."

Sarinna sat back, mouth open. "She can send to more than one person? And that strongly?"

"Aye, and she can also sense emotions from everyone without trying."

"All the time?" Sarinna's eyes riveted to Tam now.

"Aye, when I am not blocking. Father wished me to block all the time, and it became a habit. But Uncle said I need not block unless I feel the need, so 'tis not so..." Tam stopped, tipping her head with a frown. "It used to make me feel like I could not breathe. So many emotions all at once. But you know how in a place like the Great Hall there are so many voices and they all just melt into noise and you can ignore them unless they become too loud? 'Tis like that now. I only notice if they are strong."

"Stars," Sarinna said. "We can generally only sense emotions if we try."

"Unless they are unusually intense," Zandhral added.

"And the person—or persons—must be near us as well," Alcandhor said. "Tam's ability spans more distance, for both sensing and sending."

Tam bit her lip. "Uncle...that day in Ranger Hold, you did not sense the emotion you had me send to Haladhon when you were trying to discover what abilities I had, is that right?"

"Aye, I felt nothing unless directed at me."

"But could you if you tried?"

"I would imagine so."

"Perhaps we should experiment." Alcandhor thought a moment. "Let us all relax and not try to sense. Tam pick one of us and send an emotion."

"Do you know how difficult it is to relax when it is an order?" Sarinna asked dryly.

Alcandhor shrugged, recalling a jest from years ago. "Feign it."

Sarinna's lips twitched as she hid a smile, but her eyes sparkled.

"Did anyone sense anything?" Tam asked.

With a start, Alcandhor stared at his niece. "Nay, I did not. To whom did you send."

"Me." Haladhon's voice cracked. "I am ever the experimental subject."

Alcandhor grinned, but Sarinna lifted a hand. "I know what you wish to do next. So I have a question. Do we concentrate on Tam or on Haladhon to see if we can sense anything?"

"Why not one of each?" Zandhral suggested. "The Thane concentrates on Haladhon to see if he can sense something has been sent, you, Sarinna, on Tam to see if you can sense what she sends, and Marcalan and I can both just try to be aware of any sent emotions."

"Stars, I feel as if I were back in science-law classes," Marcalan said, "and need I remind you that I did not fare well in them."

"Hush, and concentrate," Alcandhor ordered. "Tam, send again—and let us know when you do so we can be ready."

"Aye, Uncle. I am sending now."

A slight waft of affection floated about Haladhon. Nay, 'twas not an accurate description, but he did feel an emotion not from Haladhon that was—stars, how did one convey feelings in words? "I did feel something around Haladhon. Affection. I could not tell from whence it originated."

"I felt the sending from Tam," Sarinna offered. "But not to whom it was sent."

"Affection, aye, but as if..." Zandhral brushed a hand over his chin beard. "I will use Tam's analogy. As if one has heard the faintest whisper, but is not sure exactly where it came from, or what was said." He peered over at Sarinna, who nodded.

"How long did you send, Tam?"

"Only a moment."

"Send again, for a longer time."

Again, Alcandhor could feel the affection. He concentrated and sensed the direction. He could not discern it was specifically Tam, but came from where she and the three others sat.

Haladhon took a ragged breath and wiped a hand across his face. "'Tis not fair, Alcandhor."

"I am sorry, cousin," Tam said. "I just sent you love."

"Nay, Tam. Not just love. Love from a lass who adores me. I know not whether to rail against such unmerited affection or give in to tears."

"I apologize, Haladhon." Alcandhor ran his hands through his hair. "Indeed 'tis not fair. But how do we continue to discover what she can do without a test subject?"

"We can take turns. Only do not send me pain, cousin Tam, as I am deathly allergic," Marcalan said.

Alcandhor sighed.

"Send pain?" Sarinna asked. "You mean you can send physical pain to someone?"

"Aye, Sarinna. Well, emotion so strong it is painful."

Her aunt stared at Tam. "I missed much being here, I see. So 'tis not actual pain you send?"

Tam tilted her head, frowning. "I have never tried to send pain, nay."

Alcandhor leaned forward. "Do you think you could?"

"And to whom would you have her send pain?" Haladhon crossed his arms.

"I volunteer," Zandhral said. "But I hope it would be not be acute, nor of long duration."

"I could try to send the pain I feel in Uncle's shoulder and arm," Tam offered.

"You are in pain, Thane?" Zandhral frowned at Alcandhor.

"Can you not all feel it?" Tam asked.

"Ah, aye," Zandhral murmured.

The others nodded. Alcandhor shifted uncomfortably at the scrutiny he knew he was now undergoing empathically, his face growing warm.

Marcalan chortled, and the others smiled.

"I can see that my brother does not appreciate attention," Sarinna said.

"Can we return to the question of whether Tam can send physical pain?" Alcandhor asked.

"Try, Tam. I am prepared. I hope," Zandhral said.

Tam bit her lip and nodded with an apologetic look.

Zandhral winced. "Stars. She can indeed send pain. Thane, you are having the healer see to your injuries, are you not?"

Alcandhor waved a hand. "I will attend to that."

"I will see to it you do." Sarinna's fierce expression dictated that she would indeed.

"'Tis not that—"

The mealtime horns blew, interrupting Alcandhor's protest. He straightened from leaning against his table. "Since this was private and we had no scribe, each of you will write your own notes on what happened here, add any thoughts you have, and questions as well." He nodded in dismissal. "We will be having further discussions."

They all stood, and although his sister gave him a withering look, she departed with the rest of them. Haladhon stood next to the door, looking expectant. "I have a request."

"And what is that?"

"I would like to go to Thane Valley for a few days."

Alcandhor sighed. "You may leave in the morning, after we go over the reports."

"You seem not pleased."

"I would be if I thought you truly went to see your daughters."

A dour expression flitted across Haladhon's face then disappeared. "I do go to see my daughters. Not just her."

"Well, go see them, then," Alcandhor ordered, then added, "At least I will only have Marcalan here to deal with. And his delicate problem."

"And other things as well."

Alcandhor scowled. "Leave, you. I need a few moments alone."

With raised eyebrows and a smirk, Haladhon bowed deeply, arms wide—an old sign between them that his cousin was chastising his closest friend—and backed out the door.

Exhaling slowly, Alcandhor adjusted that dratted sling yet again. Marcalan's delicate problem. If only he had access to the fabled store of scientific knowledge in the Portal Complex—he stopped mid-thought, mouth open. He fell back into the chair and stared at the shimmerstone ceiling, laughing.

~*~

"Thane!"

Alcandhor stopped just outside the main doors of the Great Hall. Edhron strode up, face dark. "If you wish that lass to become Thane, she needs a serious schedule of Training. I waited in vain for her to arrive."

"That is my fault, Edhron. I apologize. There was a private meeting, and with all the distractions this morning, I did not think to apprise you."

Edhron's stance relaxed slightly. "I can understand the...*distractions*, but regardless, she needs to Train."

"Aye. Draw up a schedule for her. We will review it after luncheon."

~*~

Marcalan sat at a table in the library across from Tam, chin in his hand, reading. Early afternoons had not been reserved for study since he was a stripling. Since Alcandhor could now personally tutor his children daily, the Thane had given the two of them a list of books to read with the injunction to report to him what they learned.

Suppressing a sigh, he glanced at Tam. Even without sensing the beautiful girl, her furrowed brow as she read indicated she was truly engrossed in her book. Stars. He could understand reading about the Elders' abilities but why the history of their moving to this planet and the Enaisi marrying into their clan? Tam he could perhaps understand; Alcandhor would want to ensure she did not have gaps in her learning. But Marcalan—ah, he had to admit to himself he had not savored studying.

Still, to have twenty-four years and sit as if he were a student? He gazed around the immense chamber, tables strewn throughout, the walls filled with books on two levels. Stairs at various intervals led to the gallery and the more advanced tomes as well as the tables used by scribes in recopying old texts and scrolls before they were lost to age. At least a few adults—law-keepers most likely—sat on this lower level as well, not merely students and striplings.

Having others present while they studied did pose an advantage: it kept Tam on a picket. Marcalan could not say which worried him more, Tam inadvertently exposing her feelings for him or the idea of approaching his parents about his abilities. Both definitely were detrimental to his health and well-being.

The fact they had this strange connection except when consciously blocking was his only consolation throughout all this, although at times it brought him to the edge of madness in longing for her. He must keep control though. And continue to lie to his Thane. How he would manage either one he did not know. But he must. He must!

Taking a deep breath, he forced his attention back to his ancestress Tarnill and her husband, the Enaisi, Mattan.

Chapter Sixteen

Alcandhor finished tutoring his children early. He entered the library and spied Tam and Marcalan at a table near the windows. His niece rested her elbows on the table, hands clasping the book, intent. Marcalan fidgeted, glancing up at Tam from time to time, then hunched over his volume with an obviously resigned air. A smile tugged at Alcandhor's lips; he felt no pity for Marcalan's predicament. At least, not this one.

He wove between tables to where his niece and cousin sat. Nodding to Marcalan, he pulled out a chair and sat down next to Tam. She looked up with a smile. Hoping he kept his excitement contained, he said softly, "I think I might find answers about Marcalan in the Portal Complex itself."

"Then let us go there now, Uncle. I do want to help Marcalan with this mystery."

"'Tis a half-day journey, Tam," Marcalan said. "We would arrive after nightfall."

"Aye, 'tis true, but..." Alcandhor ran his tongue over his dry lips, trying to suppress a smile. "Perhaps 'tis not true any longer." He stood, trying to keep his voice steady. "Come."

The pair followed as he strode through hallways and across courtyards. Other than random greetings or hails to passersby, neither of them spoke, but he could feel their curiosity. Finally, in the back corridor of the Great Hall, Alcandhor stopped before an embrasure in the glittering, shimmerstone wall.

Marcalan gaped a moment, then blurted, "Stars, Thane, are you in earnest?" Then immediately answered his own rhetorical question: "Aye, of course you are." He grinned at Tam. "This is the girl who, after all, found the Enaisi's secret chamber in Lairdton's Ranger Hold."

Alcandhor smiled as his cousin's gaze met his, and Marcalan continued, his voice lilting, "But can she activate this not-secret yet not-usable door, which has slept for centuries, mocking every attempt to awaken it?"

"Shall we find out?" Alcandhor nodded at a small, square panel at the side of the embrasure. "Tam touch this."

She did, and a low rumble grew. Something in the walls seemed to almost groan then the door shook and slowly moved.

"By the Bells and all the stars in heaven," Marcalan muttered.

This bane of his childhood, the first barrier to the secrets of the Portal

Complex, opened by a mere touch of his niece. He blinked the tears from his eyes, and lifted an arm to gesture them forward into a small antechamber. Another door stood before them, this one metal, the surface as smooth and finely polished as a blade but with little reflection. And to the side, another small, square panel. "Tam—" His voice caught and he straightened, clearing his throat. "Please, try again on this one."

She placed her hand on the spot and the metal door slid aside, disappearing into the wall. Alcandhor almost choked, caught between a sob and laughter. *Second barrier, swept away as easily as the door.* He gestured for them to enter the circular chamber. Inside, next to the door was yet another panel, much larger. A touch screen with many rows of little squares, all marked with combinations of letters in En'ai, the common tongue of the Enaisi. Alcandhor chewed the inside of his cheek as he pondered this riddle. He could read and write—and speak—Enaisi fluently, but he had no thoughts as to what reference these letters might have.

After a silence, Tam offered, "Do you need me to touch something again, Uncle?"

"Ha, nay," Alcandhor murmured. "I believe not. I am merely trying to decode the meaning of the letters."

"So we stand in this tiny chamber while you contemplate those squiggles and lines?" Marcalan asked, sounding vastly amused. "What is this place? Other than the entertainment of those letters, it seems to serve no purpose. It has no other exit, it leads nowhere."

Galled by Marcalan's flippant words, Alcandhor punched one of the little square buttons. The interface cleared then a new set of buttons appeared with different combinations of letters. These made no more sense to him than the others. He touched one at random.

The door slid shut, and the chamber vibrated ever so slightly. Alcandhor felt as if his stomach had risen to his throat. Tam clutched Marcalan's arm, eyes wide, as their cousin exclaimed, "Bells!" The vibration lessened for a moment, then the chamber seemed to shift, making them all take a step sideways to maintain their balance. Again, the vibration changed, and a sense of his stomach moving, lurching down to his feet, made Alcandhor swallow. Then, all motion stopped. The door slid open.

A hallway of grey-white oldstone stretched before them, dimly lit by glowing lights running the length of the corridor in bevels between the walls and ceiling. Doors dotted the walls at intervals.

Alcandhor stepped out, the other two on his heels. The door slid shut behind them.

Tam jumped and gasped, but Alcandhor put a hand on his niece's shoulder with a smile.

"Uncle, this looks much like that place you sent me to on the

Forbidden Peninsula!"

"Aye, Tam. 'Twas the same builders, after all."

"Stars, Thane, we are truly in the Portal Complex?" Marcalan whispered. "That small chamber moves from place to place?"

"Aye. 'Tis called a lift. Now hush. I must try to orient myself. I know the basic layout, but not where we are. This complex not only occupies a vast area inside the mountain behind Zaidhron, but also stretches underground. And I have only explored those areas readily accessible from the stairs which wind down from the entrance at the top of the mountain. We could easily become lost." He paused, chewing the inside of his cheek, then said, "I think we should try to find the mountaintop entrance. From there I am on familiar footing."

He turned to the lift door and nodded at the small plate next to it. "Tam, if you please."

"Stars, she is our door warden here as she was at the Ranger Hold," Marcalan quipped as they entered the small chamber again. Truly. She had accidentally discovered the Enaisi chamber by touching a panel which only one with certain of the Enaisi genes could activate.

Alcandhor stared again at the large panel. This was Enaisi technology, and he had studied that as passionately as possible without sacrificing his duties as Thane. With one glorious exception, he had only theoretical knowledge of the working of the Enaisi's computers. Through Tam, he hoped to change that.

He wished he knew the significance of the letters. There must be a way to decode the meaning. At the top of the panel, a familiar symbol caught his eye. He pressed it, and the panel returned to original display. The letters—were they acronyms, some kind of shorthand, or have some meaning beyond his ken? He reached a finger toward the panel, not quite touching it, and the display changed again and dimmed while the button closest to his finger now lit up brightly. A hologram—the second one he had ever seen—now overlaid the rest of display and read *Medical*.

"Bells!" Marcalan exclaimed. "'Tis magic!"

"Not magic. Technology of the Enaisi." Alcandhor snatched his hand away. The display returned to normal. He puffed a laugh and put his finger by another button. *Staff quarters*.

"What does it say, Uncle?" Tam whispered. "Can you read it?"

His finger slowly drifted over the buttons. "Aye. I believe I can find what I—" *Portal*. He could not withstand the temptation—he stabbed the button. The lift shifted sideways then upwards. The door opened and true enough, Alcandhor had indeed been here before. A half day's climb up the mountain, then trekking down the stairs, level after level, and now he arrived in mere moments.

The two followed him down the corridor and through an antechamber, and into a huge, domed chamber. A massive circular frame reached from floor to ceiling several times the height of a grown man. The center was empty as usual, but the frame—the last time he had seen it, years ago, it had barely glowed a dull orange, almost impossible to see. Minimal power, just like the dimly glowing lights in the halls and chambers.

Now the frame pulsed with blue light. Because the Enaisi who had spoken to Tam had activated it from the other side? Stars, would the portal soon allow someone to pass through?

"Stars, Thane, is that what I think it is?" Marcalan walked close, craning his neck. Tam stayed in the doorway, eyes wide, saying nothing.

"Aye. That is the portal."

"Can...can Tam—make it work?"

"Nay. 'Tis missing the index key. Even if activated, it could do nothing without that key."

"'Tis not the one she wears?"

"Nay. The index key is a compilation of all the various coordinates needed to connect this portal to one on another planet. But if we had specific coordinates, we could manually program the portal. Remember that one chart from the chamber under Ranger Hold, which I had the scribes copy? It said 'portal configuration.' I hope that, with study, I may be able to understand it. And if Tam can talk to this Enaisi, he may be able to help us." Alcandhor smiled at his niece, who stood frozen, as if a statue, by the door.

"This is what your studying all these years was for?" Marcalan's eyes twinkled. "No ordinary dreams for our Thane, nay!" He laughed, but not in mockery. He seemed in awe.

"Uncle," Tam said in a small voice, her wide eyes locked on the portal frame, "I thought you wished to find something, some books or something, to explain Marcalan."

The rascal's eyes twinkled, and Alcandhor could not resist remarking, "I doubt if anything can explain Marcalan."

Tam glared, and Alcandhor swore she barely stopped herself from stomping a foot. With a chuckle, he turned back to the antechamber. "I have not been here in years, but I believe this floor may have computers we can access, with Tam's help."

"What are computers?" she asked.

How to explain? "A machine with a remarkable way of storing and retrieving information. Come."

Not waiting for them to follow, he continued through the antechamber and back down the corridor. He approached door after door, waiting for each to slide open then peering inside until he found one with work consoles. "Here."

The two younger Rangers crowded in beside him.

"'Tis not lit to see well," Marcalan murmured.

"Tam, can you find a panel to switch on the lights, as you did in that secret chamber under Ranger Hold?"

"The panel there was inside the doorframe on the right side, perhaps there will be here as well," she said, running her hand along the wall next to the door. The lights abruptly came on.

Alcandhor blinked for a moment to adjust his eyes then strode to a console. "I know not if all the work stations are connected to a central database, or if they are compartmentalized," he muttered. "Assuming I can activate a computer. None of these has ever responded to any command or coding sequence. But they may require a bio-touch, as the panels did to open the doors for the lift and to light this chamber. Tam, see if you can find anything that will bring this thing to life. A panel, a button, anything."

"Aye, Uncle." Tam's hands flitted over the surfaces of the console. Marcalan watched without comment. Had something finally awed him into silence?

The work station chirped and lights came on. Tam jumped back, and Marcalan muttered, "Stars!"

Only once before had Alcandhor actually seen the Enaisi's computer technology active, and he had passed on gaining access to an old, dear friend—stars, he needed to send for Delgan to share in this! He had sent word to the history-keeper about the find under Lairdton's Ranger Hold, and that he had brought many of the books and charts back to Zaidhron. No reply had arrived and neither had his friend. He hoped Delgan was merely busy and not ill. Alcandhor would have to write to him this afternoon about this new access and hope he heard back soon.

But for now, it seemed, Alcandhor had a second chance to use a computer. He sat, staring at the console, his heart thudding. He knew the words of the sequence by rote. As a child, he would pretend he sat at a computer, just like this one, and not only would he get it running, but use it to learn all the secrets of the Enaisi.

"Why are you waiting, Thane?" Marcalan asked.

"Hush," he whispered. He lifted one hand and passed it over the base. A hologram flickered and solidified to display the phrase *password required*.

Mouth gaping, Alcandhor stared at the words, then rubbed his hands over his face. He wavered between laughter and tears. So close. So bloody close!

"What does it mean, Uncle?"

Alcandhor fought for composure. After all, the Thane of the Rangers should not wail and weep. He slowly leaned back in the chair. "It means I shall have to try to find the information I need from the tomes stored in our library. That will be a long, tedious process."

"You were hoping for a quick answer, Thane?" Marcalan asked.

"Aye."

Marcalan chuckled, pointing at Alcandhor. "You hoped to have a solution ready before facing my mother!"

Alcandhor lifted his hand conceding the point. He rose, weary with disappointment. By now, he should be used to it, but again, he let himself dream to no avail. "There may yet be treasures I can uncover here with Tam's help, but I fear any further excursions into this place must wait for another day. Let us return to Zaidhron."

Chapter Seventeen

Marcalan's stomach settled into place as the lift doors opened. A bevy of astonished faces met them. He could not help but laugh aloud.

Sarinna, of course, stood in the front, arms crossed. "Stars, brother, what have you done?"

"I? Nothing. 'Twas Tam."

"You understand me."

"Great Bells, Sarinna, he has ever wanted to get these doors open. Can you blame him when he has a ready key?" Marcalan lifted an arm and pointed down toward Tam's head.

Tam twisted and looked up, then swatted at Marcalan's hand. Her pretend irritation was endearing, and Marcalan could not help but smile. Nay, he must control his feelings and focus on the humor of the situation around them, not the adorable lass at his side.

Sarinna still glowered. "You should have told someone where you were going. No one could find you. Then we discovered the Enaisi's door was open—we have been in uproar. And the afternooning has been totally disrupted. Ganill is quite put out."

Marcalan tamped down his smile and tried to look meek, even though 'twas the Thane being roasted by Sarinna, and likely due for one from their head cook as well.

A barrage of questions pelted at them, and Alcandhor held up a hand. "Aye, through Tam we were able to access the lift and have gained a new, shorter way to access the Portal Complex. Any secrets in that vast place are still a mystery. As my duties permit, and with the help of select history-keepers, we shall delve farther. That is all."

Amidst the resultant chatter, the three trooped through the corridor toward the Great Hall. True enough, the old cook stood at the door to the main kitchens, hands on her spare hips, glaring up at the Thane with steel-grey eyes.

"I should have known. You and Marcalan together. I am only surprised Haladhon was not a member of your party. Are you through throwing my cooking schedule to the wind?"

"Aye, Ganill. My apologies."

The woman sniffed and turned back to the kitchens. Marcalan stifled a chortle, but Ganill spun back around, pointing at him. "And you!"

Marcalan blinked. "Aye, Ganill?"

She took a deep breath, lips pressed tightly. Finally she just shook her head and retreated into the kitchen, muttering to herself.

"Got out of that without harm, Thane," Marcalan murmured as they continued on to the Great Hall.

"Shu, in case she hears you."

"But why did Tam receive no censure? 'Twas her fault."

"Careful, cousin," Alcandhor smiled at Marcalan then down at the object of their discussion. "Tam might censure you for such a comment."

"Thrash is more likely." Tam raised to her tiptoes, frowning about the vast chamber. "And where is Haladhon anyway?"

"Here." Haladhon descended the stairs to their right with a smile. "I understand I missed an adventure."

"Aye," Tam said. "Uncle—"

Their cousin lifted a hand. "I know." He pointed at Alcandhor. "Next time, invite me."

"Next time, be available."

Haladhon spread his arms. "Someone has to attend to duties while our Thane goes wandering off."

"You? Attend to duties?" Marcalan quipped. "Keep eye, cousins. That vagabond must be scheming something. I would check my chamber, Tam—he was coming downstairs."

"Leave off." Alcandhor pulled out his chair and let it drop with an exaggerated *thump*. "I would like to eat in peace."

Marcalan exchanged grins with Haladhon, but wordlessly walked around to his seat.

~*~

Tam rose with everyone else as Uncle did, indicating afternooning was over. Edhron gave her a schedule of Training with strict admonition to be punctual: archery before breakfast, and after morning reports she would report to Edhron himself, until luncheon. Then studying until afternooning. The first hour after that repast she would train weapons, mostly with sword-master Maradhor. Then another fighting session two hours after the evening meal. Tam had much free time compared with her father's Training.

She looked around for Maradhor. He stood at a side table, arms crossed, talking earnestly with two men. Both had stained fingers. Scribes. Should she go over to him or wait for him to come to her or go to the Training halls ahead of him? Nay, for she did not know where within all the various chambers Maradhor taught. He met her gaze and held up a finger, then turned his attention back to the two men. So Tam was to wait.

With one eye on her new instructor, she gazed up at Haladhon. "What do you usually do now?"

"The schedule 'tis the same as at Lairdton Hold. This is a free time for most of us. Some use it for sparring, some"—he nodded at the Thane—"for studying, others for a personal interest."

"Personal interest? Like what?"

Haladhon grinned. "I do some smithing work at least every two or three days, if duties permit. Being Chief of the Elites, my free time is more rare."

Tam blinked. Did she wish to ask about smithing first or his being Chief of the Elites? The latter won out. "What are the Elites?"

With a mischievous grin, Marcalan joined them, leaning against the table and crossing his arms. Tam returned the smile, basking in the warmth of their connection. As long as she did not purposefully send, he did not block. She must learn to be content with that, and resist the strange yearning growing inside her.

"Stars, cousin, you do not know about the Elites?"

"If I did, why would I ask?"

Marcalan snickered. "A point."

"Andhrel is correct," Haladhon remarked, "she would make a good law-keeper."

"So tell me about these Elites."

"Specially Trained Rangers," Marcalan replied.

"What sort of special training?"

"They are given extra diligence in fighting of all kinds, training in ciphers, languages, tracking—the list is long."

"But why? What do they do?"

"I think a brief history lesson is in order," Haladhon said.

"Stars, not more history," Marcalan moaned softly, but Tam felt more a sense of amusement than actual annoyance. Rascal!

Tam glared at her cousin, belying her own humor toward him, and lifted her chin. "Then tell."

"Back on Teledhar, the Elites were a highly Trained group of Rangers whose duties included high-risk tasks such as protection details, as well as threat assessment, gathering intelligence on groups that jeopardized security, hostage rescues, and so on. The Elites were not disbanded when we came to this planet. The last Chief of the Elites on Teledhar and the first here on Elyria was Avadhron—"

"Pardon," a voice interrupted in an irreverent tone.

Behind Marcalan, a girl, the one who had shown Tam to her chamber when she first arrived—what was her name? Casinn?—pulled on the tablecloth. Marcalan stood to allow her to remove it. The girl's red, swollen eyes indicated she had been crying. Tam wanted to feel sorry for whatever was wrong, but the girl met her eyes for a moment with a hateful glare. Tam remembered the girl's condescending, arrogant attitude from when they first met. Why should that have grown into enmity? Casinn's open hostility stopped Tam from any attempt to comfort her.

Tam pointedly turned away from Casinn. "Say on about Avadhron."

Both cousins smiled at Tam with understanding. Haladhon's eyes twinkled. "Avadhron knew that although their duties did not change, how they accomplished them would, as they had not the means to carry them out the same way here."

Tam nodded. Having seen some of the marvels of the Enaisi in the Portal Complex, she could only wonder what those 'means' were on their old world.

"One of the most important tasks Elites do on our world is gather information. They send or bring it to me, and I order it and make it available to the Thane and the rest of the Chiefs."

"Who are the Elites? Can any Ranger Train for this?"

"Some apply, some are noticed for special abilities and given the opportunity to join."

These men must be very special Rangers indeed! "Stars, have I met any Elites?"

With a chuckle, Marcalan turned to face her full and bowed deeply.

Tam's eyes widened. "You, Marcalan? You are an Elite?"

"'Twas inevitable. With his abilities to be stealthy—"

"Much needed in order to be successful at pranks," Marcalan put in.

"—and his quick mind, he has been a great resource for information gathering. He not only learned languages quickly but can mimic accents so well that he can dress as a local in any province and be taken for one of their own."

Marcalan's smug amusement made Tam want to give him playful slap, but she dared not. She sniffed and turned back to her tall cousin, remembering her other point of curiosity. "And smithing?"

Haladhon's infuriating smile tempted Tam to give *him* a slap.

"What about it?"

Or stomp a foot. "You are a smith?"

"Not as good a one as I could be, no, but I do enjoy smithing. Both my knife and sword are of my own making." Haladhon, as most Rangers, did not carry his sword with him in the city, but did have his dagger. Rangers never were without a knife. He drew it and offered it to Tam, handle first.

The haft and blade were straight, and the dagger felt good in her hand. Tam supposed it bespoke Haladhon's penchant for showing off that the symmetrical blade had some pretty tracery etched in it. This was not only functional, but beautiful. Haladhon had a knack for not only excellent smithing, but creating art.

"You do splendid work." Tam gave the dagger back to her cousin.

"My thanks."

Tam glared at him. "Stars, you are ever pleased with yourself."

Haladhon shrugged. "Why pretend humility?"

Marcalan laughed, and Tam rolled her eyes.

"So," Tam asked, "what will you do today then, in your free time?"

"For now, I spend much of my 'free time' waiting for reports from my Elites, from drum messages, and from any other messengers who arrive with news about the Rogues. While waiting, I work with my men to try to ascertain where they might be. I have a map in the Elites' chamber in Thane Hall that is overrun with markers, flagging sightings, or rumors of sightings, and our best guesses as to where they might be headed." Haladhon smiled, but it seemed tinged with sorrow. He did take his responsibilities seriously despite his dissembling, but did his father's death at the hands of these Rogues drive him even harder? "And 'tis where I am going now." He bowed and strode away.

"And you?" Tam asked Marcalan. Over his shoulder, she saw Maradhor approach.

"I am tagged for chores in the Ranger barracks. We all take turns scrubbing and cleaning. You"—he touched her nose with the tip of his finger—"miss out on that one, Lady Ranger."

"But am I not required to clean my chamber as any Ranger would?"

"True, that. But 'tis much less work than an entire barracks."

"Yet I will be require to do thus daily, not as part of a rotation schedule."

With a disgusted expression, Marcalan said, "Andhrel was right. You would make a good law-keeper."

"That may be," Maradhor said, "but for now, let us see if you will make a good swordsman."

"Swordsman?" Marcalan grimaced. "Swordswoman? Swordslass? Bells, Tam, you are going to wreak chaos on our language!"

"Uncle said the masculine is used for collective pronouns. Would it not be the same for this?"

"Perhaps," Maradhor said. "Although perhaps not. We do not use 'lords' to also include ladies."

"So if we say 'lords and ladies' would we also say 'swordsmen and swordswoman'?" The twinkle in Marcalan's eyes belied the seriousness of his question.

Maradhor glared at him. "I will let our language experts battle with that one."

"But you are a scribe. You have in-depth knowledge of words."

"I merely record them. Neatly. Which is more than I can say for you."

"Oh, you wound me, cousin!"

"Come to sword practice and I will truly wound you." Maradhor inclined his head, asking Tam to follow him.

From behind them, Marcalan laughed.

~*~

With great dread, Alcandhor wended his way through the paths of Avadhron's Sward to the western tower for the inner gate. The young Ranger Baidhrol stood guard. He nodded in passing and entered the tower which held the detention cells. The white stone steps glittered in the dim light from the torches.

The guard at the entrance to the cells raised his fist to a salute over his heart. "You wish to see him, Thane?"

"Aye."

With a jangle of keys, the guard unlocked the metal door, then stood back, hand on his sword, and his head inclined.

Tanadhon seated on the stone shelf that doubled as a bed, lifted his head from his hands, blinking. Even in the dim light provided by the open door, Alcandhor could see his wet face and red eyes. His former friend curled his lip.

"Making your obligatory visit to the condemned, enh?"

"Visiting with a man whom I considered a close friend."

"You want to know how I could betray my kin, do you? I said it all before. Our laws are unjust! What was done to Monadhal—"

"Monadhal had many chances to turn aside, to give up being a Ranger, if that was not his desire. He chose to continue in his Training, then to accept bribes to thwart justice, and extort, threaten, and rob those he was to protect—"

"He still did not deserve the punishment he received!"

"He refused to decry his actions for lesser punishment, even with Haladhon willing to stand for him. You know this. Just as you know after his trial he tried to kill Haladhon, leaving him for dead."

Alcandhor stopped and took a breath. He did not disagree that some of their laws extracted a too severe penalty. His private nightmare of Question being called over Tam's birth record loomed as a familiar shadow. He inhaled a second time. "You are not the only one who feels our laws are, at times, too harsh. But—"

"Then change them! You chiefs could call conclave and make a ruling—"

"It has been tried! Know you not our history? Not only many in our clan, but the provincial lords rose up in protest when it was proposed. Would you wish the chance of another such as Isandhral the Cruel and the Uprising?"

"I would! Much better than what was done to Monadhal, and what will happen to me!"

Alcandhor's back stiffened. "Your fate became your choice when you conspired to kill the chiefs and your Thane. That is a law that never will change."

Tanadhon spat on the floor at Alcandhor's feet, then fell back against the stone wall, arms crossed, glaring. Memories of camaraderie flooded over Alcandhor. But this man—this was not his childhood friend. Somehow, somewhere over the years, that man died, leaving a bitter shell which had worn a convincing façade, even to those with Enaisi blood. Alcandhor backed out, jaw clenched, and nodded for the guard to lock the door.

He ascended the steps from the cells, then continued to climb to the allure atop the wall. He surveyed the Settlers' Plain: the yellow grasses rolled as waves of the sea in the breeze, glinting gold in the sunlight, the out-wall stretching from tor to tor, shining like a white ribbon. He leaned out between the crenellations, his fingers gripping the shimmerstone, finding no solace in the sight nor in warmth of the sun.

"Thane?" a guard called, his voice quavering slightly. "'Tis not recommended to...be so close to the edge."

Alcandhor drew back with a swift inhale. "All is well, Ranger." He cast a hard smile and nod to the guard and strode back toward the tower. All was not well.

Chapter Eighteen

As an instructor, Maradhor was intense. Of course, he seemed intense about everything. Perhaps that was how he had become both master scribe and master swordsman. He watched her match several other Rangers and corrected technique again and again. Elbow higher, more wrist—watch your stance, move faster! Her father's Training had been physically harsh, but Maradhor taught a lighter approach, almost a dance. Again she felt her father's methods were being judged as too rigid. Perhaps they were. Maradhor's teaching seemed to match Tam's strengths—her size, quick reflexes, and agility, instead of compelling Tam to master brute force.

Tam left the Training halls, pondering these thoughts as she wandered through the gardens, then toward the markets near the entrance to the city. What was she to do now, with this free time before evening meal?

Various vendors called to her, but Tam shook her head. She had no interest in their wares and besides, had no money.

"Pretty beads, Ranger girl," called a grey-haired woman with a slight accent, lifting several necklaces and turning them so they shone in the slanting sunlight. They were indeed very pretty.

Tam walked closer. "I cannot pay. And Rangers do not wear necklaces."

"Ah, but the men do wear necklets." She cocked her head to the side, her brown eyes sparkling. "What a girl your age needs is beads. You will soon find a man you wish to make a necklet for, won't you?"

Tam's heart leaped at the thought of making Marcalan a necklet. But shook her head.

The woman smiled broadly. "Ah, I think you have a wish. But perhaps it is too soon?"

Tam hesitated. Should she say on about her uncle's wishes for her to wait five years?

Raising a hand with knobbed knuckles, the woman chuckled. "See! Someone yes, but perhaps not too soon?" She patted her own chest with curled fingers. "Itasa knows these things!"

Tam opened her mouth to contradict her, but the woman pushed a small drawstring bag surreptitiously to the front of her table. "You take this and make the necklet. Braid some hair with the string, and choose pretty colors. Then you will have it for when the time is right!"

"I... You are mistaken. I have no one to make a necklet for and besides, I have no coin."

The old woman's brown eyes met hers for a long moment, then her face softened with a smile. She pushed the bag to the edge and whispered, "If you truly had no one, you would not say you have no coin. Take it. No one has to see. You can pay later."

"But why?"

"Ah, old eyes see much, girl."

Tam hesitated. Did this woman have foresight? Was she a Child of the Enaisi? Tam reached out to sense her but felt nothing unusual. No special abilities, but also no guile, just kindness and sadness. She seemed to be honest in her desire to have Tam take the bag.

Itasa patted the drawstring bag and murmured, "I can see a girl in love. Take it. You're a Ranger, I will trust you to pay later."

Tam quickly gathered up the bag and hid it behind her laced fingers, in front of her. "I will pay you. Thank you."

Once back in the gardens, Tam dropped the small bag inside her jerkin. It settled above the beltband and she patted it flat. She slowly trod across Avadhron's Sward toward the Great Hall, remembering what her uncle had told her of necklets, that different colored beads represented love, faithfulness, and other vows important to a marriage. Stars, to actually make her necklet for Marcalan! But she dared not tell him. And Uncle—if he found out, he would be so angry!

She followed the paths of the sward aimlessly, lost in thought until the gathering darkness almost had her lost in truth. Servants came along the walkways lighting the torches. The city certainly ran on a strict schedule.

The horns sounded, signaling evening meal drew near. Tam quickened her pace. Just as she got to the door of the Great Hall, she heard Sarinna call to her and turned. Her aunt walked toward her, holding out her herb book. Tam took it and clasped it to her chest. "Thank you, Sarinna."

"You are welcome, my dear. We have time for a short talk now, if you do not mind."

The two entered the Great Hall and ascended the staircase to Tam's chamber.

"Are you recovered from the wine?" Sarinna closed the door.

"Aye." Tam placed her book on the small table. She thought of the small bag hidden in her jerkin. "Sarinna, how do Rangers get money?"

"We have three coffers here in Zaidhron, but as a Ranger, 'tis best you go to the treasury in chiefs' range. All Rangers' accounts are maintained there."

"Accounts? I have an account?"

"Aye. And you may draw upon it at will. Although not being of Age, if you wish to withdraw a large sum of money, they will likely ask for

Alcandhor to approve. When Rangers are sent on assignment, they take a letter of credit with them so they may pull from the coffers of any Ranger hold they pass near."

"Oh." So Tam could easily pay Itasa. She hesitantly returned Sarinna's smile, hoping her aunt would not ask what she wanted money for.

Sarinna settled on the bed and patted the spot next to her. Tam sat down, twisting slightly to face her aunt. This woman had the sensitivity of the Thane, yet the directness of Tam's father, a strange mix of her brothers' personalities. A disconcerting combination.

"I know you are not used to having a mother, Tam, but you are at an age when you need one. You are growing up and may need the advice of a woman to guide you, do you understand?"

"Aye, Sarinna, but Uncle has already talked to me about all that."

"About what?"

"Growing up."

Sarinna's eyes widened. "My brother talked to you about growing up?"

Tam nodded. "My father told me nothing, and while at Ranger Hold, Uncle decided I needed to know certain things that could not wait, so he talked to me."

"A–about growing up?"

"Aye."

"Such as?"

"The changes happening to my body, and why. And about how men and women are attracted to each other. About marriage and how babies are made."

Sarinna's grey eyes fixed on Tam, and she seemed frozen for a moment. Her mouth opened and closed twice before she asked, "My brother explained all this to you? Alcandhor?"

"Aye. I can sense others easily. That is why Uncle felt he must explain things to me. Some of the Rangers made me uncomfortable but I did not know why."

"They were none forward with you, were they?"

"Forward?"

"Did they say or do anything that they should not have?"

"Like trying to touch me or kiss me? Oh, nay, Sarinna. Well, except Nandhal, but I knocked him topside-down. But I can sense so strongly that I could feel that some Rangers desired me."

"I see..."

Tam gazed at her aunt. Uncle trusted her fully, and she had sensed their love for each other. If only she knew her well as she did her uncle and Haladhon and Marcalan. What was she like as a young lass? She remembered how Sarinna had greeted her father with a kiss and was not afraid to chastise him. "Sarinna? Tell me about my father. What was he like as a boy? You are older, so you remember more than Uncle, do you not?"

"Older than your uncle, and also your father—by a few minutes," she replied with a laugh.

Tam blinked. "By a few minutes?"

"Aye, knew you not we were twins?"

Tam shook her head.

Sarinna smiled. "I used to tease him that if women could be Rangers, I would have been heir to Thane, not him."

Tam's eyes widened. "But Sarinna—"

Her aunt held up a hand. "Nay. I did not truly wish to be Thane. Just to torment him because I was the elder of the two of us. So worry not that I have regrets since you have come as a Ranger." She raised an eyebrow. "I do wonder at his thinking in Training you though. It was not like him. But I suppose we will never know now."

Tam did not know what to say, so she merely shook her head.

Sarinna smiled brightly. "Anyway, you asked about your father. What would you like to know?"

"What was he like as a child?"

Sarinna tipped her head, her grey eyes piercing Tam. "Quiet. A loner. He never cared for other people's company. He never had friends. The closest one to him was perhaps Cordhan. They both enjoyed hard matches and fought often."

Tam nodded, smiling. "Cordhan is a hard fighter. He reminds me of my father when I match him. He says he can tell my father Trained me, as I fight hard, too."

Sarinna gazed at Tam with open curiosity. She softly asked, "Was he very harsh to you?"

Tam shrugged. "He Trained me hard. He said I had to learn all he could teach me of Ranger ways."

"But why?"

"I know not. He would not say."

Sarinna looked thoughtful for moment. "As a teacher then he was hard on you, but as a father, was he harsh?"

Tam frowned. "I know not how to answer your question, Sarinna. He was a Ranger. He Trained me. That was all I knew until Uncle came."

"But he was your father. Surely there were times when you talked of things other than Ranger Training, and you did things together."

"We hunted for food, tended the garden, and did chores. Usually I tended the garden and cooked. We both hunted. He never talked to me except to teach me Ranger ways."

Sarinna's eyes filled with tears. "Not about anything? About your mother? About your family?"

Tam shook her head, her throat tightening, as a tear slipped down Sarinna's cheek.

"Did he ever even tell you he loved you?"

Tam hesitated. Ever since breaking her leg several years ago, she had hoped his worried searching for her when she fell into the ravine, and careful care had meant he loved her. But now, she had felt fathers' love many times. Most especially her Uncle's love toward his children. And Lantalan's for Marcalan, both love and pride, despite his pretense of disapproval. Tam knew now her hope was in vain. "Nay, Sarinna," she whispered, "and I know not whether he did."

Sarinna wrapped her arms around Tam and held her tightly. Her aunt's heartache and anger caused tears to spring to her own eyes, and she just let Sarinna hold her.

A knock at the door interrupted the quiet moment. Sarinna rose and answered the door.

It was Taniss. She glanced at their wet faces, her eyebrows raising. "I had wondered how your first day here was, Tam."

"It was fine. But it is so different here."

"I imagine it is." Taniss smiled. "If my son pushes too hard, you let me know. You need to be allowed to adjust to your new life here."

"Aye, Taniss." Her grandmother could not possibly mean that she could order the Thane around. Even if he was her son.

Sarinna wiped the tears from Tam's face. "We should wash our faces before we go down to table. If you wish to talk about your father, Taniss and I both would be glad to tell you whatever we can. Perhaps later tonight."

"Thank you, Sarinna." Tam did not think she would want to talk about her father anymore. Not if it meant hugs and crying. She found those two things very uncomfortable.

~*~

His children distracted Alcandhor during the meal, and lightened his mood. And he found he did not dread that evening in the Great Hall, knowing he would not have Aleta's moods and tempers to worry about. She had not yet come out of her dorm, and had moaned that she would starve before coming to table in Zaidhron.

After the meal, a few musicians assembled to play tunes at the far end of the hall. Alcandhor relaxed, listening to them as he watched Tam. Haladhon was right. Rangers did tend to gather about her. And not just the younger ones either. Edhron and Cordhan both seemed smitten.

Well, who was not? She was so young and ingenuous, and had a quality about her that made one feel protective of her, even with the knowledge the Ranger-Trained lass could take care of herself.

As Tam sat, surrounded by a swarm of Rangers asking questions and jesting, another group had gathered around Marcalan farther down the table. Alcandhor pondered that, as Marcalan had been at Tam's side almost constantly since leaving Lairdton's Ranger Hold, but not this evening.

Had Marcalan been forward with Tam, making her put him in his place? Just then Marcalan called out and Tam turned, dimpling.

"These Rangers believe me not that you journeyed to the Forbidden Peninsula."

Tam shrugged. "I had to. That was where the Laird was being held captive."

"See?" Marcalan crowed to those around him.

"Marcalan," Alcandhor called down the table. "That need not be bandied about. That peninsula is still prohibited. Tam journeyed there under unusual circumstances, being sent under orders from me. I want not Rangers, nor anyone else, to think the ban on that peninsula is lifted or is to be taken lightly."

"Aye, Thane." Marcalan rose and swept into a dutiful bow.

Alcandhor wanted to box his ears for the mischievous twinkle in his eyes. The Thane gazed at the Rangers nearby who had heard him, to make certain they understood also.

Alcandhor then turned his mind back to Tam. Obviously, from the brief exchange, nothing was wrong between her and Marcalan. Perhaps he had just felt a protectiveness of her while away from Zaidhron, as one would a younger sister. He had said as much at Ranger Hold. Aye, that must be it. Now that they were home, he would not feel the need to hover over her so closely.

Ah well, as long as he behaved himself, it did not concern Alcandhor. He rose to get some ale. Sarinna approached the kegs as Haladhon filled his tankard. His cousin turned to his sister with an engaging grin. "You are looking exceptionally pretty tonight, Sarinna."

She laughed. "Why thank you, flatterer."

Haladhon slipped a hand around her waist. He pulled her close, his voice soft. "It is not empty flattery, Sarinna, as you well know."

"I do know, Haladhon." Sarinna looked up at her tall cousin, still smiling. "But as always, the answer is still 'nay.'"

Haladhon turned a little and sighed at Alcandhor with a woeful expression. "A sad fate for me."

Sarinna touched his cheek then turned toward the kegs with quiet laugh. Haladhon winked at Alcandhor then sauntered away.

It took a moment for Alcandhor's scrambled thoughts to allow him to speak. "Sarinna, did I actually see you allowing Haladhon to flirt with you?"

"Aye. Why?"

"But Sarinna, Haladhon is...is, well, you know."

Sarinna burst out laughing as she filled his tankard with ale. "Alcandhor, my dear, sweet brother, it still amazes me how easily embarrassed you are by such things. Aye, I know what Haladhon is. But remember, I have five years over our cousin, and for him, even in jest, to offer compliments to me, makes me feel young and pretty."

"But you are young, Sarinna. And not just pretty but beautiful."

"Why, thank you, 'Candhor. I would not expect you to notice—or say anything if you did. Think you that I do not desire compliments because I am widowed?" She lifted an eyebrow with a coy expression. "I am not dead, brother. Here." She handed him his ale.

"My thanks. Why have you never married again, then? I have seen you turn away from men who would be suitors."

Sarinna shrugged. "Few have been brave enough to pursue me."

"'Tis a woman's prerogative to pursue. But I would think a Ranger would be considered brave."

"Forget you I was daughter of the Thane and am now sister of the Thane? Most Rangers treat me with deference. Too much deference. And keep distant. Think you I could be happy with a man who has no fire or determination? That is why I loved Teldhrel, he was bold and not afraid to take a chance—even with the daughter of the Thane."

Alcandhor chuckled. "So you know not a man who will take the challenge, is that it?"

Sarinna's lips pressed together, and she took his arm, nodding toward the section of the Great Hall where couples were dancing. "Dance with me, brother."

"I have but one arm."

"'Tis the weaver's step dance, if you would but look. As long as you have two feet, you can manage."

Suppressing a groan, Alcandhor led his sister to the floor. Two feet he had, aye, but the weaver's step took a good memory and much practice as well, remembering which way to turn and around which person to move. Alcandhor had not much practice.

When the music ended, and the calamitous weave wound down, Alcandhor found his sister. She took his arm with a broad smile. "I understand from Tam you had a talk with her. About growing up."

Heat rose in Alcandhor's face. "Aye. I had no choice."

"So she said. My poor brother. How did you manage?"

"We do what we must, Sarinna. I dared not wait. I gave her what basic knowledge I could. I am certain that, between you and Taniss, you can fill in any gaps." He paused. "I mentioned to Taniss at table tonight that she should not hover over Tam. The child is skittish and not used to attention, much less from women who wish to mother her. I would say the same to you."

"I agree. I will try to slowly ease into a friendship with her. But tell me what you told Tam about growing up."

Alcandhor groaned at his sister's teasing smile.

Chapter Nineteen

The evening Training left Tam sore, but she did learn from all the various Rangers she fought. She bathed, appreciative of what still seemed a luxury of a large tub of hot water, then hurried to her chamber to begin her secret task.

Tam mused about Marcalan as she sat on the rug in front of the fireplace and braided her hair with the thin twine of the necklet. He kept distant at the Great Hall, but she understood why. She felt a growing anxiety in him about keeping their secret. His love and loyalty for the Thane made it seem wrong to hide their feelings from him.

She finished braiding and stopped with a frown. The thin strands would make tying off the end a challenge. She bit her lip, concentrating on the task. It took quite a few tries, but she finally succeeded. Now to string the little beads. That took little time, only deciding the order in which to place the colors. Before long, the necklet was done.

With a smile, she held her handiwork up and examined it. Someday, they need not hide. Someday, she could give this to him. She squeezed the necklet in both hands, hugging it to her chest. What a joyous day that would be! A questioning amusement wafted over her. So Marcalan was curious about her mood? She giggled. She had a secret from him, but a good one. Let him wonder!

She hid the necklet under her clean clothes in the wardrobe, then prepared for bed.

The excitement of making the necklet made it difficult, but at length she drifted off to sleep, the warmth of her connection with Marcalan more comforting than her blanket.

~*~

The evening in the Great Hall had relaxed Alcandhor, and he meandered across the sward, enjoying the bracing chill of the night air, and the quiet.

Footsteps pounded along the path, and a voice called, "Thane!"

He stopped, sighing. "Here."

One of the cell guards, Alcandhor did not recall his name, bowed low. "Grave news, Thane. Tanadhon...he has killed himself."

Stunned, Alcandhor ground his teeth then, fighting down bile, replied,

"Is he still in his cell, or has his body been removed?"

"Still in his cell, or was when I was told to find you."

"Then we shall go to the cells."

So much for the restfulness of the evening. Grief now drove out all else. Neither man said word one as they crossed the sward to the gate tower, and descended to the cells. Haladhon, his face grim, waited with the guards by the open cell door.

"We have not moved him, Thane," a guard said.

Alcandhor nodded and entered. Haladhon followed, holding a torch. Tanadhon's body lay sprawled on the floor, his dark hair covering his face. Alcandhor hunkered next to him, and gently laid one hand on his back. *I know not how I failed you, but I feel I did, my friend.*

He rose and turned to the guards. "How did he this?"

The young guard said, "He ripped his shirt apart and braided the strips into a cord, then tied it around his neck—" He stopped and licked his lips. "We found him just as you see."

Alcandhor nodded. "He gave no indication. You could not have known," he murmured.

As he heavily climbed the steps, Haladhon, following, asked, "Are you all right, Thane?"

"As all right as are you, I imagine."

"I would fain tip one or two back."

"Ah, nay. I think 'twould not be the best idea."

They spoke no more words until in the open air. Alcandhor then whirled to his cousin. "How did this happen? How did we fail him?"

"You cannot take it to heart."

"Can I not? I am—was—his Thane!"

"He chose. Just as Monadhal chose. It was not your fault, just as—" Haladhon stopped, his jaw muscles jumped, the rage radiating from him palpable. "Just as it was not my fault."

Alcandhor hesitated, then nodded. "Aye. They chose. Knowing our laws, they chose."

~*~

"Ready?" Monadhal whispered.

Nandhal peered in the dark at the outlines of the other Rogues, hiding in the woods near the home of the family they were going to raid—his third one. With both moons high, he could easily see the farmyard, and his assigned objective.

They would search for recently butchered and smoked meats, harvested vegetables, and any other supplies found that they needed, then be gone. So far no one had awakened, but if it happened, the rule was to down them quickly with a cudgel or fist and flee—murder would bring the Rangers' wrath too quickly.

Monadhal gave the signal, and the men quietly rushed to the outbuildings where the meats and harvest were stored. Nandhal ran from the shed with his partner, carrying two sacks when he heard a loud cry. A bearded man stormed toward them with a shovel in his hand.

"What're you doing on my land! You leave my things be! Get away with you!"

A young man appeared behind the older one, also brandishing an ersatz weapon.

"Bloody Bells!" the Rogue near Nandhal hissed. He swung his cudgel at the younger man, who fell into a motionless heap.

Nandhal ducked the shovel swing, dropped his sack and cudgel, and drew his sword.

"Do not kill them!" Monadhal yelled. "Run!"

The older man fell without a chance to fight. Nandhal withdrew his blade with a quick saccade. Screams came from the doorway of the cottage, and a woman ran into the yard. A lass followed her, yelling "Mam!" From inside, a babe squalled.

Nandhal reached for the woman as she dropped to her knees over the corpse at his feet and jerked her up. She only wore a thin underdress, and his eyes raked up and down her body. He sheathed his sword with a smirk while still holding her arm with one hand. Her eyes widened, and she screamed. He punched her, and she collapsed in a heap as he heard Monadhal call to him. The lass cowered on the ground, shrieking as a Rogue lifted his cudgel. Nandhal stepped forward and grabbed his arm. "Nay!"

"I do not take orders from you!" the Rogue hissed.

"Hang you, Nandhal!" called Monadhal again over the cries. "We must go!"

"You go!" Nandhal yelled over to his leader. "I will not be long."

"Cursed cockerel!" Monadhal shouted. "You would take a chance of getting caught just to feed your lust?"

"Let me worry about getting caught. I will catch up with you before long."

Monadhal wavered then shouted for them to flee. Nandhal grabbed the girl, who yelled, hitting at him with her fists. She looked to be about Tam's age, which pleased him even more. He backhanded her then took out his knife and put it to the girl's throat.

The woman on the ground clawed at his legs. "No! Not my daughter! Not my little girl!"

140

He kicked at her, snarling, "Get up. Or I will kill your daughter right now!"

The woman slowly rose to her feet, cringing and weeping. Nandhal shoved her ahead of him through the door as he dragged the fighting, screaming lass into the cottage.

~*~

A voiceless call pulled Tam out of a dream, urging her to enter the black void. Even while asleep, her heart pounded with dread, but a peaceful reassurance swept over her from Marcalan. She would not face this alone. He would be there.

With a gasp, Tam quit fighting the call. The blackness shot to her, engulfed her, then the glow grew into a bright light. She passed through and then—she again saw that beautiful face, with dark eyes and skin darker than hers, and he smiled at her. At them—Marcalan and her. This was an Elder, an Enaisi. Uncle said she need not fear. She breathed slowly and deeply to keep calm. She must ask this question so important to Uncle, but—could not bring herself to speak.

"Welcome, my children. My name is Mattan. It is good to see you both, Tam and Marcalan."

Tam felt Marcalan's amazement with her own. Mattan laughed softly. "Yes, you are both surprised—I have forgotten you would most likely not be used to my people's ways anymore. My apologies. And I'm afraid you were frightened last time, Tam. It must have been an overwhelming experience for you. I apologize for that, too."

Tam tried not to feel afraid now. She did not know why. Mattan was not fearsome, but warm and open. Marcalan comforted her, trying to give her support. Mattan smiled at them, and Tam managed the courage to actually speak to him. "How can we open the portal?" Relief at having asked that most important question made her feel weak.

"Don't worry about that, Tam. But tell me, how are your people? And do they remember much about mine?"

"We study some books left by the Enaisi, and there is still Enaisi blood in some of us, sir."

"Just call me Mattan. Would your people welcome a visit from me?"

Fear tugged at Tam, but again Marcalan gave her strength. "Uncle would be so pleased. It has been his ambition to meet the Enaisi."

Mattan laughed again. "Tam, you are strong enough to talk with me on your own. If your uncle has questions, he can send you to ask them."

"I know not how to cross the blackness and talk with you. I am asleep and dreaming this, am I not?"

141

"No. It is because you were sleeping that I was able to, shall we say, gain your attention. But you are strong enough that if you concentrate on finding me using empathy, as you would, say Marcalan, or anyone else with my people's empathic ability, you can communicate with me."

"I do not understand. How is that possible?"

He laughed again in his soft, quiet way. "You will see. I'm making plans to visit as soon as I can. I will let you know when. Now rest, both of you. We will meet before long."

Tam fell back through the light, then the blackness, and found herself upright in her bed. Was it a dream? Did she really talk to an Enaisi and did he really say that he would soon come through the portal? She needed to tell her uncle. A horrifying thought struck her. Would Mattan reveal her connection with Marcalan?

Marcalan! Their connection! She concentrated on it, and aye, he was awake. If only they could talk through this connection instead of just *feel*! But what did *he* feel? Confused, agitated, and yet, naturally, amused. A wave of calm passed over her. He wanted to comfort her. Dear Marcalan.

She lay back down and pulled the covers to her neck. Nay, she must tell Uncle! Tam threw off the covers and dressed, then hurried down the stairs and through the Great Hall. She stepped out onto the grounds, her cloak wrapped around her tightly against the chill. The pink in the east fanned out across the sky.

She stood uncertainly. Which family suite was Uncle's, and was he in Family North or East? She sent to him feelings of urgency and her excitement. She felt nothing. He must be asleep. She sent again, strongly, and kept sending until she felt a response and then walked in that direction.

Soon she saw her uncle striding to meet her, his face haggard, with dark circles under his eyes.

"What is it, Tam?"

"I–I am sorry to wake you, Uncle, but you would want to know. I met him, Uncle! His name is Mattan and he—"

Alcandhor's eyes widened, and he straightened. "Who? An Enaisi? Tam, did you dream again?"

"Aye, Uncle! His name is Mattan and—"

"Did you ask about the portal?"

"Aye, Uncle, and he said not to worry about it. He is going to come and visit us!"

Her uncle stood, looking at her, not saying anything. She felt his emotions—so many emotions—like a churning of water over many rocks, but his body remained unmoved as stone.

"Let us go into the Great Hall and have some tea," he finally said, his voice thick. "I want you to tell me all about this."

She matched his long strides as he hurried through the hall and to the kitchen. Servants scurried about, preparing for breakfast. They turned in surprise to the Thane and Tam.

"Is there water hot for tea?" Alcandhor gazed about, as if expecting a kettle would be ready to hand.

"Yes, Thane," answered one of the girls.

"Bring some tea to the early room, please," he requested, then led Tam across the hallway. The small chamber held not much more than a table and chairs. A fire crackled in the fireplace at the far end, and two Rangers sat, drinking tea.

Alcandhor nodded to them, sitting Tam down at the other end. "Now tell me everything he said."

"He asked if we remembered them and asked what we would think if he visited. I told him it would make you very happy. He laughed."

Little of her uncle's excitement showed on his face. He seemed so calm. She realized he was usually this way. His emotions did not readily show in his face, unless he was laughing, or angry, then his eyes would darken and his jaw set like her father's. Why had she not noticed this before? Probably because she sensed his feelings so intently that she had never really watched his face for reactions.

"Did he say when he is coming?"

"Nay, Uncle. He said it would be soon. He said..." She stopped to remember his exact words. "He said, 'I will make plans to visit as soon as I can. I will let you know when.'"

Alcandhor shook his head. "I cannot believe you have spoken to an Enaisi."

"I was afraid, Uncle. I almost pulled back as I did last time. I know not why as Mattan is very nice. He apologized for frightening me."

A girl came in with a tray and set it on the table. Alcandhor thanked her then poured two cups of tea and sipped his, leaning back in his chair with an appreciative sigh. Tam tried hers. It was strong and dark, a morning tea meant to wake up Rangers.

"So he is polite." Alcandhor's eyes crinkled.

Tam smiled. "He is very nice. He was very excited to see—me."

Her uncle chuckled, and Tam hoped he did not realize the catch as she stopped herself from saying 'us.' Lying to her uncle felt more and more wrong. But how dare she tell him about Marcalan?

"I wish I could talk to him. I have so many questions."

"He said I could contact him and ask questions for you."

"He said you could what?" Alcandhor's eyes widened.

"He said I was strong enough to contact him. That I could send to him as I do you, or any other person who can sense."

143

"Through the portal?"

"Aye, Uncle. I did not understand it, and he laughed. He has a nice laugh. It is soft and gentle. It reminds me of Zandhral's laugh."

Alcandhor laughed himself. "You are amazing, girl."

"Why?"

"I sit here, astounded that this Mattan says you can send to him through the portal, and you talk of his laugh."

Her uncle thought it amusing—had she erred? She could not help but smile though. He grinned, the warmth of his love flowing over her.

"So since you seem more interested in Mattan, can you tell me more about him—other than his laugh?"

"He is very kind. He reminds me of you."

"And how does he remind you of me?" he asked, his voice teasing.

"I guess because he is very kind."

Why did her uncle find that so funny? She could see his eyes smiling over the rim of his cup and feel the laughter he held inside.

"So he is kind," he said, setting down his tea, "and you think his laugh is nice. What else?"

"He is very happy that he is coming here. He is excited about it. I think he has wanted to come but did not know about us anymore. If we remembered them. Or would want him to come."

"Aye. It has been about five hundred years. He would not know what changes might have happened in our world. I wonder why they broke contact," he murmured, staring into the air pensively.

"I can ask him if you wish, Uncle."

"I think that is a question best saved for when he actually arrives. I imagine the answer is not a simple one."

"What do you think happened?"

"It is useless to speculate. I am sure Mattan will tell us. It is interesting that he has that name..." his voice trailed off as if he pondered something.

"Why?"

"There was an Enaisi from our beginning named Mattan."

"Oh, aye, I read about him. He was one of the ones who helped us plan and move to this planet. And he married Zaidhron's daughter, Tarnill."

"Aye, he is our direct ancestor many, many generations removed. He helped our leaders come up with our system of governing ourselves. The Rangers, in their current form, were largely his idea from what some of our books say."

"So he lived here—right here with our people?"

"Aye. Right here. In Zaidhron."

"Uncle, the Enaisi have such wonderful knowledge. They know how

144

to make light in a chamber without fire, and so much more. Why did they not give us this knowledge?"

"Our ancestors wished us to live a simple life and not destroy this planet. Granted our own planet Teledhar was unstable, but our history records we were not wise and aided in its destruction."

"I understand not how such knowledge could destroy a world."

"A complete answer would take much time and study for you to understand. But put simply, such knowledge and advanced devices often came with a destructive price."

"What do you mean?"

"To build a fire, you must have fuel. Now granted we have more than just wood for that purpose, but for argument's sake, say we use only wood. This means trees need to be felled. And our laws are strict that for any tree felled, another must be planted, and for any tract cleared, another must be planted with saplings."

Tam nodded. "Aye, to maintain balance."

"Exactly. Now, imagine the cost and imbalance created, if, to make use of a device, it meant cutting down an entire forest. A mountainside stripped bare in, say, one lunation. And another forest gone in another lunation, and so on."

Tam swallowed heavily. "That would destroy the planet before long. We could not replant saplings fast enough, and there would not be time for them to grow to replace the lost trees. Balance would be lost."

"Aye. Now that was a simplistic example, but you grasp the danger. At times it feels we are held back from advances and inventions that could be useful, but we are bound by our laws to not allow anything to be built or used unless we are certain it would not be dangerous. The trouble is, many of resources and references to what might be allowed or not have been lost."

"But Uncle, the Enaisi's books are not made of pulp or parchment as ours are, and do not seem to grow brittle or fade with age. How were they lost?"

"They are missing. Whether they were stolen or destroyed or simply mislaid, I know not. But they have been missing for a very long time. We have copies of some of them, but they have been scribed onto new pages many times and we know not how accurate our copies are now. Some of the books you found in that secret chamber under Ranger Hold are among the ones lost. Rumors have said there had been a vast library underneath Zaidhron and that many of the missing books are there, but we know not if it is true."

"When Mattan comes, perhaps he will know?"

"Perhaps." Alcandhor pushed back his chair and stood. "'Tis almost time for your archery practice. I need a walk to clear my head. Thank you, Tam." He kissed the top of her head and strode out.

Tam sat unmoving, thinking of Mattan and the portal and her uncle's ambition. If this was all such a good thing, why did she still feel so much fear?

"By the Bells, do you ever stop causing trouble?" came Marcalan's voice.

Tam jumped in her seat. Her friend-and-cousin leaned on the doorframe, arms crossed. His eyes twinkled, but his lips pinched into a line instead of the easy smile he usually wore. She had not felt his presence near. Why was he blocking?

"Join me in a walk on the grounds before breakfast, cousin?" He backed up, bowing, but almost bumped into servants carrying stacks of plates. His wide-eyed dance of avoidance in the hallway brought forth rebukes from the women. Tam put a hand over her mouth to stifle her laughter.

"I think we should go outside, Marcalan, before you cause some disaster. I think you would want to avoid Ganill's wrath."

"You are wise for your years."

Tam followed Marcalan outside and breathed deeply. 'Twas not the dewy, scented air of the many types of evergreens and ferns of home, but had a dawn freshness mixed with the toothsome smells wafting from the kitchen. Would she ever stop missing home? She must try. This was home now. And with the gardens of Avadhron's Sward so lovely, why did her enjoyment of them seem constrained?

"Sad state of affairs to be yanked along on a journey yet not have the strength to speak for oneself," Marcalan commented in a low tone.

Tam chided herself for her self-absorption. This was a rare moment of time for them alone, and poor Marcalan had not the chance to discuss the amazing event they had shared. Perhaps that explained his disquieted expression earlier. "Stars, what did you see and hear?"

"I imagine everything you did. I could see Mattan, and hear him, but could not answer. 'Twas a sore trial."

Tam whirled to face her cousin, grasping his sleeve. "He is coming here soon. What if he tells Uncle about our connection?"

The woeful expression on Marcalan's face wrung Tam's heart.

"I cannot keep lying to my Thane, Tam. It slams against my Training and loyalty. And what I feel for you is too deep. It tears at my soul."

"But we cannot tell!"

"Aye, I do understand that, but I feel—" Marcalan broke off, scrubbing his face in his hands. "I must be alone. I am sorry, Tam." He strode off at almost a run.

"Marcalan!"

His shoulders hunched, but he did not turn nor slacken his pace. Tam knew sending was futile, as he still blocked, but she tried anyway. Blinking back tears, Tam headed for the archery range behind the Training halls, following her duty and not her love.

Chapter Twenty

Nandhal hid near the cave entrance and gave the bird cry used as a signal before revealing himself. Two Rogues rose from behind large verga shrubs, bows at ready, faces grim. One jerked his head toward the cave. Nandhal resisted the urge to roll his eyes and obeyed, blinking to adjust to the dark of the interior. He put a hand out to feel the rough rock sides of the passage until it twisted around and he could see the light from the fire in the large cavern ahead.

Monadhal sprang up and grabbed Nandhal by the throat, his face contorted with rage, shoving him backwards until his back slammed against the sharp rocks of the wall. He tried to break the Rogue's grip, but none of the tricks he had learned seemed to work.

"You did not have to kill that man! We are too close to Zaidhron for such risks. They will swarm like pincebugs after us!"

"Who will know who killed that family?" Nandhal gasped, fingers clawing at Monadhal's hands. "I left none alive."

Monadhal's blue eyes blazed even in the dim light. His grip tightened, and he lifted Nandhal higher, jamming his knee into Nandhal's groin, pinning him to the wall. Nandhal tried to scream, but all that came out was a strangled gasp.

"You bloody fool! They will know! I should kill you now!"

"How can they know?" Nandhal managed to squeak, tearing streaming down his face. "You need me. You said so. I can sense and am not branded." Nandhal's face felt ready to burst, and his sight dimmed.

Monadhal dropped him, and he fell to his hands and knees, coughing. The Rogue pulled his head up by his hair and brandished his dagger by Nandhal's throat. "You ever disobey even one order again, and I will kill you. Do you understand me?"

"Aye," Nandhal croaked.

Monadhal twisted his hands through Nandhal's hair and smashed his face into the ground. Nandhal lay, sprawled out and unmoving. He clenched his fists. Curse Monadhal! He would get revenge on him one day!

~*~

Marcalan crossed the sward, knowing not what to do. He must keep his mind off thoughts of that most beautiful girl! And Bells, the amazement at seeing an Enaisi! And he dare say naught of anything.

He wheeled about at hearing Haladhon call his name. His tall cousin swaggered up, smiling. "What are you scheming, enh?"

Years of concealing his newly uncovered secret made dissembling easy. A wide grin spread, and he raised innocent eyebrows in tacit denial. Haladhon rolled his eyes. "Leave off your pranks, for a few days at least. I am off to Thane Valley after morning reports, and as my Second, I need you to keep abreast of matters for the Elites."

"Consider it done." Marcalan swept his arms out with elaborate obeisance.

Haladhon glared. "Are you not going to breakfast in the Great Hall?"

"Nay. I will grab something quick from the Thane Hall kitchen, then report to the Elites' chamber."

His cousin shrugged and continued toward the Great Hall with a mock bow.

Marcalan switched direction and aimed for the chiefs' range. Perhaps receiving the reports and analyzing the details would distract him from worry about Tam, his parents' reactions, Tam, his guilt at lying to his Thane, Tam, that mysterious Enaisi, and Tam.

Tam, Tam, Tam! Bells and stars, nothing could drive her from his thoughts for more than a few moments!

With a quickened pace, Marcalan soon arrived at the chiefs' range. A pile of reports awaited in the basket on table to the right of the entrance to the Elites' chamber.

Marcalan brought the stack to Haladhon's table. No drum messages had come in overnight, which was good. Only the most imperative messages for the Elites came by drum—and using a code only the Elites and chiefs knew. So although the reports were all important, none were dire. Of course, if a message had arrived by drum, the Elites and chiefs would likely all be rushing about like tiny pincebugs whose hill has been disturbed.

The Thane's renewed vigor in wishing to eradicate the Rogues had intensified all the Rangers' efforts, with the Elites at the forefront. Runners arrived every day with updates about the Rogues—where they were, and were not. Some rumors, some fact, and it was the duty of the Elites to ascertain the verity and strength of each report. Hopefully, they would soon be able to narrow the search to a precise area, then successfully bring the Rogues to justice.

The worry that Marcalan shared with all the others was those bloody caves in the mountains that created the border between Lantral Province and Pashelon and Keladar. How many Rangers would it take to scour those endless tunnels and caverns? And how many would they lose, not only to

Rogues who knew those subterranean chambers as their home ('tis said), but to the treacherous dangers of the caves themselves?

One worry at a time. For now, they needed to locate the Rogues. He sat in Haladhon's chair, back to the window, and began to read.

A scuff at the door broke Marcalan's attention on the reports. He blinked and peered up to see Zandhral leaning on the doorframe. His cousin nodded a greeting. "Has Haladhon left for the valley yet?"

"Nay. After morning reports with the Thane." Which were taking place by now just on the far side of the forechamber, with Tam attending. Tam... Stars! He must force his mind off—

"Has Haladhon said anything to you about how he and Alcandhor are?"

"Nay. Why?"

"Why?" Zandhral straightened. "Tell me, Second of the Elites, have you not heard the news that Tanadhon killed himself last night?"

Marcalan stared at Zandhral, mouth open. "Nay, I did not know. I saw Haladhon, but he said nothing."

Zandhral, his expression inscrutable, pushed off from the doorframe. "Would you like some assistance?"

"Aye." Marcalan pushed the one pile of reports toward his cousin. "These appear to be substantiated. Sightings are in a tight scope and need to be added to the map. They are slowly moving north. Still. I cannot comprehend why. One would think they would head to Keladar or lower Lantral."

"They must have a plan. Do you think they—" Zandhral paused, frowning. "Could they be planning another attack like the last year?"

When they killed Bardhor, Haladhon's father. His cousin had raged in his grief, and Alcandhor, livid, had been unapproachable. The lack of any evidence had bespoken the murderers were Rogues. Who else could hide tracks and disappear so easily? And those cursed caves had defeated their efforts. Now that the traitors and the threat to the Laird had been eradicated, all their focus targeted on the Rogues.

Marcalan lifted his shoulders. "Who can say? But this time we shall prevail. Our attention is not splintered by other concerns, and we have engaged all those Rangers who helped with the siege to increase the hunt."

Marcalan need not drop his block and sense to realize Zandhral's misgivings about their chances of success. The man's weak attempt at a smile told all. As Marcalan returned his attention to the reports yet to be read, his cousin took the others to the map table and busied himself with updating the confirmed sightings.

Soon, Marcalan had the rest of the pile sorted, and brought over the ones relevant. Zandhral stared staring at the map.

"Do you see a pattern?" Marcalan asked.

"I search every day when I come here. 'Tis random. They move fast." Zandhral pointed. "See, here, then here. Then"—Zandhral's finger circled a spot—"nothing through this area, and then again they looted here." He stabbed a new flag.

"Aye." Marcalan slapped the last of the reports on the pile with the others. "No sightings from any of these companies of Rangers. Monadhal is keeping his men close to hand. And they must be using the caves to move stealthily from one region to another. I see no other explanation. Zandhral, your hand is neater than mine. Write out a summary for the Thane. I will call out the locations we received today."

Zandhral nodded and sat, pulling a fresh paper to hand.

The far door, where the Elites' files were housed, opened and Gardhal entered. He gazed at Marcalan, then toward the ceiling as if in supplication. "Haladhon has left for the valley, and we must endure you?"

"He leaves after morning reports. We are finishing a summary to send across to the Thane."

Gardhal's dour face hardened as he approached the table. "What news?"

Marcalan updated his moody cousin and at the same time, Zandhral wrote the details. Gardhal pointed to the latest sighting, not but four days' journey from Jessel, muttering, "Too close."

Zandhral set down the quill, then blotted the paper. "Aye, and the information we receive is a day behind at least, if not two or three." He held the report out to Marcalan.

Marcalan stared at the paper, and thought of Tam, just across the forechamber. Bells. "Gardhal, would you deliver this to the Thane?"

With a suspicious frown, Gardhal asked, "Why? Did you do something? Do you need to avoid the Thane?"

Marcalan rarely used his rank as Haladhon's Second, but he was not going to argue. "Deliver it to the Thane."

Gardhal snatched the paper with a glower and marched across the forechamber. Zandhral peered up at Marcalan with an unreadable expression. Scowling, Marcalan picked up the reports from the map table and took them into the back chambers to file them.

Chapter Twenty-One

Tam entered the Thane's Chamber and slid into a chair. Across the table, both her uncle and Haladhon seemed a bit more quiet than usual. Her uncle peered at her. "What is wrong?"

"I just heard about Tanadhon. I am very sorry, Uncle."

"I am, too. But he made that choice, just as he made others. If he had not, we would have hanged him. This he knew. Perhaps he felt it was easier. Or perhaps he felt he wanted to make the choice himself and thus rob the law."

"Have you talked to his uncle, Rondhrel?" Haladhon asked.

"Aye. He had already inured himself to the loss, but I deem he felt more than he let on. 'Tis done." Alcandhor straightened, peering at Tam. "How was archery practice?"

"I was chastised for being late, but Bardhal forgave me when he found I had not known where the archery range was. He says I am very good. He thinks he could make of me a master bowman."

"Good. Very good. But I do apologize. I forgot you know not the city yet. You need only ask."

"Aye. I find I am always asking." Tam clenched her fists in her lap. Everyone must think her simple with all her questions.

Her uncle smiled and waved a hand over the table. "Now, let us on to our task."

He picked up a report, and after a few moments tossed it on the table with a groan. "Those two!"

Tam's eyes widened. "What is it, Uncle?"

He waved an arm toward the offensive document. "Read it."

With a sidelong glance at Haladhon, Tam picked up the report. A farmer in Thane Valley claimed his neighbor had stolen fruit from trees on his land. After reading the first few sentences, she looked up, frowning. "Why is a report of such unimportance being passed up to you?"

"Because they live in Thane Valley." Alcandhor rubbed his hand over his face.

Tam tilted her head, grimacing at her uncle then over at Haladhon in confusion.

"Know you not 'tis not called Thane Valley on a whim?" Her cousin nodded at Alcandhor. "He owns it."

"I thought it belonged to our clan."

"It is beyond any provincial jurisdiction, a territory solely under our clan's dominion, but technically it belongs to the Thane of Ch'shalna clan."

"I..." Tam stopped and wrinkled her nose. Were her uncle and cousin pranking her? Her father said—what did he say exactly? "My father said the valley belongs to our clan. He would not teach me incorrectly. I know he would not. I know he did not."

"Nay, but he often did omit or incompletely teach you." Alcandhor lifted his chin, his blue-grey eyes probing. "Of that you are aware."

"Aye."

"In general terms, aye, the valley belongs to our clan. All those in the valley are tenants, and a portion of their increase is given to support Zaidhron. But in strict terms, that valley belongs to—me, at the moment. To whomever is Thane of our clan. When the Enaisi brought our people here to Elyria, that was a special gift from them to our first and last king on this planet, our first thane on this planet: Zaidhron. Its ownership has passed down all these years, unchanged."

Tam dropped her gaze to the paper she held. "So you must deal with such trivia?"

"Nay. The Rangers who roam and guard the valley must deal with it. But all reports from Thane Valley must be copied and sent here. And since those two farmers are a star-flower thorn in my hide, I feel the need to keep abreast of their feud. Thus this report on my table." Alcandhor leaned back, his breath hissing out through clenched teeth.

"So this is an ongoing problem?"

Haladhon and her uncle both barked laughs almost simultaneously. That was an answer, so Tam asked, "What is their history?"

"The one family has tenanted the land for almost a decade. The parents died and the daughter married and requested that the tenancy be made over to her husband, Lanwin. The other fell vacant, oh, a year or two ago, was it?" Alcandhor peered at Haladhon who lifted a shoulder.

"Closer to two, now I think." Her cousin rubbed his neck. "Aye, because this will be the second season's autumn crops."

Alcandhor nodded. "That family, headed by Sonvil, is new to the valley. The gall between the two started almost immediately with a dispute over who should fix the stone wall separating their lands."

"And then there was the mess about that culvert."

"Aye, and then Sonvil accused Lanwin of fouling the river that runs across both their lands."

Tam straightened. "That is serious."

Haladhon nodded. "And immediately investigated to no result. The water was fine."

"Soon after, Lanwin claimed Sonvil put a dead animal in his well. All very fine to point a finger, but how does one prove the poor creature did not just fall in? The well is left open, not lidded."

"And the reports of sowing weeds in each other's crops."

Tam gasped. "What weeds into what crops?"

"That," Alcandhor spat, "if proved, would have been dire for them. But 'twas shown to be a freak event affecting all the farms in that region along the south-west mountain range. Although the story of how the bindweed—"

"Bindweed! 'Tis a foul affliction to farmers!"

"Aye, truly."

"How did the bindweed get in so many fields if not deliberately sown?"

"That was a mystery that took some investigating by my men."

"But how?"

"Kinchou droppings." Her uncle's mouth twisted.

Haladhon's eyes glinted. "And birds."

Tam glared at the pair of them. "Please explain."

Haladhon chuckled. After a wry look at his cousin, Alcandhor lifted a hand and adjusted his sling. "A herder bought kinchou from out of the valley, and along their journey to their new home, somewhere they ingested bindweed." He grimaced. "Those stupid creatures might have the best hair for weaving fine clothes, but they are not discriminatory about their diet."

"Birds"—Haladhon leaned forward—"then found a nice meal of bindweed seeds from their droppings and spread their treasure through the whole area."

Tam's hand flew to her mouth as her cousin continued, "We had to alert the whole southern half of the valley to scour for bindweed and destroy it. Rangers were dispatched from the city and other nearby bounds to help the tenants and local Rangers in the task."

"Stars!"

"But those two still contend it was the other one responsible for the whole problem."

"It sounds like they should lose their right of tenancy."

"I am pushed to it, but it pains me to cause hardship to two families. If they were but single men, I would toss them out of the valley in a breath and care not."

"This accusation about the fruit, is this not part of the percentage to be sent to Zaidhron?"

Both men shook their heads.

"Nay." Alcandhor smiled wryly. "I need not look up the tenancy to know that, not for these two. I am all too familiar with them. Their land is strictly farming. The fruit trees are incidental, growing wild."

Tam read the report further. "Uncle, this says that the thievery is due to chance. The trees grow near the stone-wall border and the fruit falls to both sides."

"Aye. And the fruit which falls to the other side is picked up by the neighbor."

"But they do not own the land. So the trees belong to you, aye?"

Her uncle closed his eyes and nodded.

"So if they wish to be petty about that fruit, can you not merely claim it all?" Tam hunched a bit at her next thought, as it seemed almost heresy to speak of it. "Or order the trees chopped down?"

Haladhon burst into laughter. "Aye if they wish to fight over their toys, take them away."

"'Tis no laughing matter, Haladhon. I warned them the last time if the feud did not end, I would end it."

"So they continue to feud, knowing you will put them out of the valley? They must have no sense."

"Aye. I cannot believe they are so foolish." Alcandhor patted the table. "Leave that report here, Tam. I will address it tomorrow. Order the rest of these into categories, and Feladhrel can file them."

"But I need to learn, Uncle."

"You will gain much experience in filing reports, believe me. Let the stripling garner his own for the lunation he is here. You just order these for today."

Tam rose and reached over the table, doing as she was told. Reviewing reports, writing them, and sorting them was one part of being a Ranger she did not like. But at least the task had taken her mind off her worry for Marcalan. Well, mostly.

"Think you the boy will decide to become a law-keeper?" Haladhon asked.

Alcandhor shrugged. "Time will tell. He is eager. So far."

A knock came at the door. Alcandhor called come, and Gardhal entered with a bow. "Today's Elite summary of the Rogues, Thane."

"My thanks, Gardhal."

Tam took the paper from the Ranger—the Elite?—and held it out to her uncle. He nodded.

As her uncle read the report, Tam stifled a sigh. So Gardhal was an Elite too? Stars, how many were Elites and how could she know? Chiefs had the Thane's crest embroidered in silver on their leather jerkins over their hearts. But the Elites sported nothing on their jerkins to indicate such status. Surely the Rangers at Zaidhron knew which of their cousins were Elites, but Tam knew nothing. 'Twas not fair!

The Thane grumbled a "hm," low in his throat, and Tam brought her attention back to what she should be worried about. "What is it, Uncle?"

He passed the paper to her. "You may read it. Both of you read it."

Haladhon came behind and read it over her shoulder.

"They are coming closer," Haladhon hissed.

"Aye, they are becoming more bold. I think we need set the Rangers in the city on alert. But I do not rescind your leave. Go to the valley. If you do not hear a drum message ordering you back, stay as long as you wish. You do not have the chance to see them as often as you should."

"But where are you going?" Tam tipped her head back to see her tall cousin.

Haladhon opened his mouth but said nothing. Alcandhor leaned back in his chair with raised eyebrows. Shooting a quick glare at the Thane, Haladhon said, "I have two daughters living in the valley."

Now Tam's mouth gaped. She looked at her cousin's bare neck. "But...did your wife die? Why are your children not here?"

"I am not married, Tam. The mother of my daughters is listed as my legal mistress."

Tam blinked. Too many questions competed to be asked. At last she just blurted, "But why?"

Haladhon rubbed the back of his neck. "I was indiscreet. When Panill came to me that she was carrying my child, I offered to marry her, but she refused."

"Refused?"

"Aye. Her parents were tenants in the valley, and she had a fear of leaving them, and her home. Her mother is gone now, but she will not leave her father."

"I understand not wanting to leave home, but Zaidhron is at the mouth of Thane Valley. Surely 'tis not far to where her father lives."

Alcandhor pulled at his ear. "Thane Valley is huge, but aye, the homestead is less than a half day's journey."

"So then why would she not marry you?" Tam asked Haladhon.

Her cousin's face flushed slightly. "Panill is..." He stopped with a pained grimace. "For all her beauty, she is not...graced with an abundance of intelligence."

"I must not be either, because I still do not understand."

"Her mind is very simple, Tam," Alcandhor said softly.

"I can understand *that*, Uncle, but not why she and Haladhon would not marry. If she would not leave her parents, could Haladhon not have lived there?"

Both men shook their heads.

"All chiefs must reside in Zaidhron," Alcandhor said. "That has ever been the law."

"But my father did not live here."

Haladhon's jaw muscles jumped.

"That was a special circumstance, Tam," her uncle said.

Tam frowned, crossing her arms. "I do not understand."

"Nor I," muttered Haladhon.

The Thane rested his good hand on the table. "I have no understanding of the matter, Haladhon, as I have said. And that conclave session was sealed. The only one still alive with that knowledge is our uncle, and Lamadhel claims he is bound to silence."

"So much is bound to silence or secrecy in the last few years." Haladhon looked away, frowning.

Alcandhor turned his hand palm up and lifted it slightly. "Go see your girls, cousin."

Haladhon inclined his head and left. Tam watched him go.

"He is very angry and sad, Uncle. Is there no way to...to do something?"

"Do what, Tam? How? The woman has no sense. She cannot understand why Haladhon would not wish to live with her and farm the fields and tend the herds. She seems to think the world ends at the edge of their homestead. Perhaps, in her mind, it does."

"Did they ever have *in love*?"

Alcandhor gazed at her, his eyes crinkling slightly for a moment. He grew sober again and shrugged. "He saw a beautiful lass, and she saw a handsome man. I believe that is all it was. He certainly cared not whether she had enough sense to know that if it is dark outside it is nighttime, and she cares about nothing, I think."

Sarinna stepped into the doorway and crossed her arms.

Alcandhor nodded to her then continued, "I will say this for Haladhon. He has provided well for them, and in spite of his ways, has asked her many times to marry him."

"I feel sorry for him."

"I do not," her uncle said.

Sarinna lifted her chin. "Nor I."

Tam looked from her aunt to her uncle.

"He is reaping his own folly," Sarinna said.

A deep simmering resentment burned in her aunt. Tam wanted to ask her aunt why, but the mood reminded her too much of her father, and her voice choked in her throat. With Sarinna's face set thus, and the feelings she presented at the moment, Tam could easily see this was her father's sister and twin. She swallowed, unable to speak, and concentrated on slow, even breaths.

Sarinna's mood lightened a little as she gazed at her brother. "You are to see the healer, Alcandhor."

"I am?"

Her eyebrows raised, her voice firm. "Aye. Now."

With a prolonged sigh, her uncle stood, muttering, "Thane of the Rangers, and I answer to my sister."

Sarinna smiled, and Tam could sense the love they bore for each other, and the humor. This must be a longstanding jest. Her dread eased, and a desire to join in overcame Tam.

"Any other duties before I go to the Training halls, sir?" she asked.

Alcandhor gave her a confused frown. "Sir?"

She gave him an innocent expression, as she had seen Marcalan do. "I am speaking to my Thane."

A slow smile spread on his face. "At least there is one female in my family who gives reverence to my rank."

Sarinna huffed a breath. "That will soon pass. Come, brother."

Tam felt the humor behind the mock sorrow of his expression as he wagged his head. "See how I suffer?"

Sarinna pushed him in the back, forcing him toward the door. Tam watched them walk away, Alcandhor still complaining that he was fine, and Sarinna taking him to task for neglecting himself. The love fueling the bantering made Tam bite her lip to hide a smile.

Now to the Training halls. Tam lifted her face to the sky as she exited Thane Hall. The sun hid behind gathering clouds. To go from this northwest range to the southwest range, she could follow the wide, paved walkway curving along the edge of the ranges or cut straight across Avadhron's Sward in a direct line. Surely that was the best choice.

The paths through the sward wandered this way and that—not a direct line after all, and Tam found herself distracted, stopping to smell flowers and inspect the various gardens. The sun stopped occasionally winking through the leaves of the trees as the clouds grew thicker and darker. All too soon she arrived, and stared up at the massive, glittering white front wall of the Training range that held the barracks and Training halls where Rangers—well, stripling and unmarried Rangers anyway—lived, Trained, and slept.

Where Marcalan slept.

Nay, she must not think of such things. Marcalan was a friend and cousin. But where was her friend-and-cousin? He still blocked. She closed her eyes; she needed to concentrate on duty.

So—where in this huge building fronting the barracks range could she find Edhron's Training chamber? She could wander about searching herself, or be more sensible and ask. Uncle had said to ask.

She picked a random Ranger walking by and did the sensible thing.

He walked past a few steps, then slowed and after a hesitation he turned around. His cold, hard eyes and curling lip would have told Tam what he thought of her even without sensing. He nodded in the general direction of the barracks range, then turned and marched off.

Never had Tam been so tempted to send debilitating emotion to someone! She would remember that Ranger! Fists clenched, she picked an entrance and forged ahead. Another Ranger exited a nearby door and bowed to her. Ah, perhaps she might receive a helpful answer from this one.

"I am trying to find Edhron."

The Ranger pointed to his left. "The more advanced Training and sparring are at that end, nearest the west range."

"I thank you, Ranger...?"

"Deralan."

Tam repeated the name, then smiled. "And how are we related, cousin?"

"We share the ancestor Zandhor, and are ninth cousins two times removed. However," he added, grinning. "I am nephew of Nadinn, your uncle Lamadhel's wife. So, we are first cousins one-time removed by marriage."

"Stars! How can you know all that?"

He chuckled. "I know my relation to your father, so 'tis easy."

Tam shook her head. "I have so many cousins to meet and learn of."

"I am certain the Thane has already undertaken your studies of our kin."

"Aye. History and genealogy are my pursuits after luncheon."

"A sorry aid to indigestion, I would wager."

Tam smiled at his humor, but was unsure how to answer. "I thank you again, Deralan."

They parted and Tam almost felt like skipping as she continued to the Training halls. At least not everyone hated her.

She entered the building, and although a wall blocked her view, the sounds of men sparring—the grunts, calls of encouragement and of mocking, the smacking sounds of blocks and attacks—told Tam she had found the right place. The humidity, the odor of sweat, and of several herbs much used for sore muscles assaulted her. Her mind immediately analyzed the nose-tingling scents: sweet creeper in both summer and winter varieties, zygys, caltus, and other smells she could not identify. She would hazard the recipe would have ch'illeya or umaral. Perhaps she could find someone who could tell her.

But for now, she needed to find Edhron. This inner wall blocked the view from outside, but allowed one to turn either right or left. She rounded

159

the wall on the right-hand side and stopped. The chamber spanned almost the size of the Great Hall. Some areas had been marked off with lines on the floor for sparring, and other areas had thin mats where men grappled. Swords, staves, wasters, and other weapons lined the walls with tables strewn here and there piled high with drying cloths as well as jars and bottles. Most Rangers were stripped to the waist and sweating.

A nearby Ranger scooped something from a jar on a table and smeared it on his shoulder. He grinned at her. "Here to match, cousin?"

"Aye. I was told to report to Edhron."

He wiped his face on a drying cloth. "Edhron Trains at the far end." He nodded to her right.

"I thank you."

He put out a hand before she could walk away. "The Thane usually shows up here after morning reports, but I fear he is not healed enough yet. How fares he?"

"Sarinna is forcing him to the healer just now. Perhaps she could tell you."

The Ranger threw his head back and laughed. "Aye, that she could."

Tam wanted to ask his name, as she did Deralan, but before she could, he bowed and moved off, calling to another Ranger, asking for a rematch.

Ah well, she could not learn every Ranger's name and relation right away, although she still found it difficult to believe every Ranger knew all their kin.

She wove her way around mats and sparring rings looking for Edhron.

From beyond a group of Rangers, Cordhan lifted an arm. "Match, cousin Tam?"

Cordhan was to be one of her match partners. Tam nodded and hurried to him. She enjoyed the match with Cordhan; he fought hard, as her father had.

Two others took their place in the sparring circle as she wiped her face on a drying cloth. Tam turned to see Zandhral smiling gently at her. Though she knew he had trimmed it, she still expected to see his full beard, not the traditional moustache and closely clipped chin-beard.

"Why did you shave?"

Zandhral chuckled. "I prefer my beard, but my wife does not. While out of the city I often let it grow, but then must trim it when I get home. She does not leave off until I do."

Tam studied his face. "I think you looked fine with a beard."

"Do you?" He stroked his chin. "Why? Because it hides more of my not-so-handsome features?"

"Oh, I think you are very handsome, but nay, you just seem a very gentle person," Tam said. "Soft. And the full beard seemed softer than the chin-beard."

"Soft am I?" He grinned.

Tam nodded, not understanding why he found that amusing.

"Shall we match next?"

Tam agreed and when the two sparring finished, they moved into the circle. Someone as kindly as Zandhral did not seem like he should be a good fighter, but he fooled her. He was intense and cunning in his techniques, and very fast.

As they called the match, Tam saw she was being watched. As usual. Would she ever accustomed to being the center of attention? Breathing hard, she wiped her face and neck with a drying cloth. Sweat dripped down her back, and her shirt stuck to her skin and itched. Stars, if only she could strip as the men did.

Leaning against a wall with his arms crossed, Edhron regarded her. "If you are through playing, it is time for some lessons."

"Playing?" Tam's voice rose and broke. He thought she was playing? Stars.

Edhron pushed off from the wall, inclining his head toward his right. Tam followed. They entered a smaller chamber with wall-to-wall mats. He plucked a grey jacket from a peg on the wall and shrugged it on. He tossed a similar one to Tam along with a pair of matching trous. "Wash rooms and privs are that way." He nodded to an archway to her right. "Those are your grappling garments. It should go without saying, but this"—he held up what looked like a blouse, similar to what Tam had worn so long ago when pretending to be a mountain girl—"goes underneath. Go change and we will begin."

Tam did as instructed, wondering about the heavy, quilted cloth of the clothes. She returned to the grappling chamber. The older Ranger looked her over and nodded, then his eyes met Tam's. "Your father, being large and muscular, never saw the purpose of grappling, joint locks, or throws, and although he taught you well, his knowledge was very limited in the techniques in which I shall Train you."

Tam stared, unsure what to say.

"Your uncle has some misgiving about your Training, however. He and I have approved certain Rangers as your sparring partners, mostly older Rangers rather than young ones." Edhron stopped, squinting slightly at her. "I understand you can sense emotions?"

"Aye."

"Your uncle has indicated he wishes you be aware in case your sparring partner should become, eh, shall we say *distracted* by the fact you are female."

Tam tipped her head. "Sir? You have said 'my uncle' twice now, not the Thane."

"Do you ask a question?"

"Do you think his decision is based on our familial relationship instead of as Thane?"

"You are quick. Has anyone suggested you might make a good law-keeper?"

Tam crossed her arms. "Aye. And I have a suggestion of my own."

"What is that?"

"If I sense that my opponents are *distracted*, that will give me an advantage, will it not? And thus offer me the chance to give them a very painful lesson as well?"

Edhron threw his head back, laughing. After bringing his humor under control and wiping his eyes, he replied, "I think your uncle has no need of concern. I cannot say the same for any of your match partners. Now"—he strode to the center of the mats—"let us begin."

Chapter Twenty-Two

The gong for the meal sounded, and everyone sat. Tam leaned over and asked her uncle, "What did the healer say?"

Alcandhor scowled. "I must wear the wretched sling for a time yet."

With a sniff, Sarinna said, "For quite some time yet. The healing goes slowly. And he is pushing."

"How am I pushing when I wear this bloody thing all the time?"

"Watch your language, Alcandhor," Taniss said. "'Tis disrespectful to our Enaisi ancestors."

Tam pressed her lips tightly to keep from smiling as the Thane of Ch'shalna clan murmured an apology to his mother. She craned her neck to see if Marcalan sat down the table, but nay. She ate quietly, missing him so much it felt almost a physical pain.

The meal finished, and they all stood. Tam buried the lonely feelings and asked Sarinna where in the chiefs' range she could find the treasury.

"The first entrance north of Thane Hall itself. You cannot miss it," her aunt said, smiling. "Its entrance is marked by banners."

Tam thanked Sarinna and hurried toward the chiefs' range, wishing to get the money before she was expected at the library for her afternoon studies, and also before it began to rain.

Embrasures and cornices and various traceries embellished the treasury. Not like Thane Hall next to it, or like the Great Hall; both seemed decidedly plain by comparison. Tam would have to remember to ask Uncle why some buildings had such ornamentation, and others did not.

And indeed, banners bearing not only the word treasury, but by an emblem of a chest and coins, marked the entrance.

The layout of the interior was different from Thane Hall as well. No forechamber with doors into various rooms, but a large central chamber with men writing and ciphering at several tables. Behind them a wide archway opened up into another chamber. Shelves filled with books seemed to dominate that room from what little Tam could see.

The writers glanced up and, to a man, peered over at the grey-haired man at the center table. Tam took the hint and approached him. He set down his quill and looked up. His lower eyelids sagged, the pink showing, and his blue eyes watered. *How very old he must be!*

"What may I do for you, young Ranger?"

"I–I need money. Sarinna said to come here."

"Certainly. How much?"

Tam blinked. Stars. She could not ask how much a bag of necklet beads would cost!

The man tilted his head, his old eyes probing.

"I–I know not. I..." What could she say? She must dissemble, but what story could she tell? "I was walking by the market at the main gate, and saw...pretty things."

One of the men at another table snickered then covered it up with a cough. Tam's spine stiffened and she spat out, "I thought to buy something for my grandmother and aunt."

The grey-haired man smiled. "Ah." He rose and shuffled into the back chamber. Tam stood, lips pressed together, purposefully not letting her gaze be drawn to the man who had laughed.

Before long, the older man returned with a small drawstring pouch and a ledger. He reseated himself and opened the book, then squinted up at Tam. "As is custom, all your father's credit passed to you as his only heir. Since he used little of it, the accumulation is right fair. If you wish to withdraw large sums, your legal guardian will have to approve, but for most needs, you may come to me directly."

"Aye, so Sarinna told me."

He smiled, then picked up the quill, dipped it in the ink, and wrote in the ledger. "I have estimated what I think you may need for presents for Taniss and Sarinna with a little extra for yourself because young ladies, Ranger or no, might want something too, enh?" He blew on the page to let the ink dry then turned the ledger around and tapped it. "You sign there."

Tam dipped the quill in the ink and signed. The old man held out the pouch, and Tam took it. "Do I...do I bring back what I do not use?"

Again a snicker from that side table.

"'Tis yours to do with as you see fit."

Tam returned his smile. "I thank you."

Just as she passed outside the doorway, she heard a voice hiss, "How could she ever be Thane when she has no concept of money or the treasury or—"

"Shu!" A different voice urged.

Tam hesitated, her hand still holding the door open. She should just walk away. She was certain 'tis what her uncle would do. Her father, however, would not. She wheeled about and strode back into the chamber, facing the snickering man, whose face paled. "Nay, I know nothing of money nor the treasury, nor many other things that come as breathing to those raised with them. We had no treasury in the mountains where my father and I roamed. You laugh because of things which are strange and new to me, but how would you fare in *my* mountains, climbing paths fit for

164

not much more than a kinchou, tracking a bandit who stole the little bit from a needy woman in a mountain village? How easily would you be lost and at the mercy of ballan or ka'gua? Should I then laugh at you?"

The man's grey eyes widened and he stared at her, open-mouthed.

"I asked you a question."

The man swallowed, his eyes flicking at his fellow treasurers. "I apologize. I spoke out of turn."

"You apologize, *Ranger Chief.* Forget you not I am Confirmed and am Second at Table."

After a blink, the man said, "I do apologize, Ranger Chief Tamissa."

The old man at the center table cleared his throat. Tam turned to see his chin lifted, lips pressed thin, but a twinkle in his eyes. "Young you may be, Ranger Chief, and a female, but I see your father's fire in you." He waved a hand. "Now go buy your presents before you affright my treasurers and melt them in their chairs."

Tam offered a slight bow then left. She inhaled deeply once outside. The chill tang of the autumn air would hopefully cool her emotions before she reached the library. She frowned at the pouch in her hand, and a memory returned of Rangers occasionally having pouches tied through their jerkins' beltbands. She secured her treasury pouch thus, then crossed to Thane Hall, a slight twinge of her left hip from that morning's Training reminding her she would later be feeling the full affects of that morning's grappling lessons. Her shoulders also felt a bit stiff. Stars, how did Edhron still do this day after day for so many years?

She found her assigned book and settled at a table in the library. She could not sense Marcalan; he must still be blocking. And he was not here. Being an Elite, perhaps something important had arisen that he needed to address.

With a sigh, Tam opened her book.

Marcalan soon slid into a chair opposite her, book in hand, his smile haggard. Tam wanted so much to hug him, but dared not. She whispered, "Please, stop blocking!"

"I am sorry, Tam. I must master this, and I cannot if I sense you."

Before Tam could reply, he nodded to her book. "Let us study."

Being bereft of their connection seemed to swell and grow into a knot in her stomach. Tam blinked back tears and concentrated on her book.

Focusing on her studies diminished the sense of loss, but every time she looked up and saw Marcalan staring blankly at the pages in front of him, the sorrow increased again. Concentrating became more difficult and Tam finally closed her book. "Marcalan, we need to discuss this."

Marcalan shook his head but before he could say on, Alcandhor padded to the table with a drawn expression. "I read for hours last night, but this will take much more study. It does seem my understanding is correct. Enaisi traits are encoded across a variety of dominant genes to avoid spontaneous mutation. If your parents do not make a key glow, you should not. But there may be exceptions or reasons why it can happen." Alcandhor rubbed the heels of his hands on his eyes. "I must research much more. I have no answers yet."

Marcalan fidgeted in his chair. "When are you going to talk to my parents about this, Thane?"

"*We* are going to talk to them now. I have asked that they meet us in the Thane's Solar."

Marcalan's face paled. "Stars."

The desire to hug Marcalan almost overpowered Tam. She squeezed her fists tightly and, trying to keep her voice even, asked, "Shall I be there as well?"

"As door warden only, Tam. This meeting shall be completely private."

Marcalan managed a weak smile. "I wager somehow my mother finds me to blame."

Alcandhor clapped a hand on his shoulder but said nothing.

~*~

The rain battered an uneven tattoo against the windows. Alcandhor, although feeling restless and queasy, reclined in one of the luxuriant, upholstered chairs, refusing to give in to nerves. Marcalan pushed back the heavy drapes and peered outside, then turned and paced the solar.

"Sit you down, Marcalan, lest you wear down the rug and shimmerstone beneath."

"This is my life's nightmare, Thane. What shall I say?"

Alcandhor leaned forward. "This is not your fault." He grinned despite himself. "Probably the first and last time anyone shall say thus to you." His cousin's lips quirked but he did not reply. *Aye, Marcalan is truly distressed.*

Alcandhor continued, "You will finally have answers, cousin."

His shoulders hunched as he replied, "And what is the probable answer? Unlikely as it seems, my mother—"

"Make no judgments, Mar," Alcandhor whispered.

A shrill voice pierced the heavy wood of the door where Tam waited as door warden. "Why will you not tell me what is going on, girl? Why in the names of both moons would the Thane need to see *me*? Lantalan, what is this all about?"

"I know not, Kalinna, but now we are here and shall discover the reason, enh?"

The door opened and Marcalan's parents entered. Lantalan, a good Ranger, one of his late father's closest friends, and Alcandhor's second cousin, wore an inscrutable expression. Alcandhor found himself blocking—a years' long habit he must break—and let himself sense. Lantalan held himself in reserve as much as he appeared to. A credit to his Training. Kalinna fluttered, confusion and irritation wafting forth from her.

Alcandhor rose and bowed to them, asking them to seat themselves on the plush settee opposite. The couple stopped upon seeing their son.

"What has he done now?" Kalinna asked.

"Please." Alcandhor gestured with an open palm for them to be seated.

Marcalan said nothing. He stood to one side of the settee, a hand stroking his chin beard, elbow propped on his other arm, his eyes downcast. He blocked his emotions, which Alcandhor could not fault.

Alcandhor turned and met Tam's eyes with a nod. His Second at Table inclined her head, biting her lip, and withdrew, closing the door.

Lantalan stared over at his Thane, waiting. He was taller than his eldest son, with lighter skin. His second son, Loch'alan actually resembled him much more than did his eldest, sharing his height, coloring, and build. Alcandhor did not like the turnings of his mind on these comparisons. He moistened his lips and sat opposite the couple, forcing himself to make eye contact with the husband, then the wife.

"We have discovered something...unusual. Marcalan..." Alcandhor hesitated, but before he could say on, his cousin blurted out, "I can make a key glow."

Marcalan stared at the floor, not his parents. Kalinna sat still as stone, her initial shock twisting into horror. With a strong sense of protectiveness and love, Lantalan reached over and took his wife's hands, forcing them open and holding them between his. He let his breath out slowly. "Well." He said nothing more.

The silence stretched on. Conflicting emotions grew in Lantalan— love, worry, fear, and anger, and in his wife, a sense of shame. This was too intrusive; Alcandhor should not be privy to all these feelings. He put up a block, but it did not ease the anguish he felt for this family.

Lantalan looked up at Marcalan, tears in his eyes. "You are still *my* son. You have always, only been *my* son."

Marcalan swallowed. "I...do not understand. You...knew?"

Lantalan dropped his gaze. Kalinna shuddered; Alcandhor blinked as he realized the woman was silently sobbing.

"We...did not think you needed to know." Lantalan leaned close to his wife, and murmured. She shook her head. "We must!"

Kalinna covered her face with her hands. Lantalan put an arm around her and cleared his throat. "She was attacked. Violated. I found her. We had planned to marry anyway, and to protect her, we married right away so I could bring her to Zaidhron for safety. When we found she was with child soon after our marriage we knew there a chance—" Lantalan looked up, his expression fierce. "I care not for Clan Law. He is *mine!* My son!"

Alcandhor nodded, thinking of his own uncertainty about Amara due to Aleta's indiscretions. "Aye," he said softly. "Love makes family."

Marcalan, face white, stared at his mother. Kalinna kept her hands over her face. Lantalan finally murmured, "I'm sorry, son. I wanted to tell you, but Kalinna felt shame..."

"Shame?" Marcalan's voice cracked. "Why should she feel shame that she was *violated*? Who was the by-blow that—" He gasped to a stop, tears welling in eyes turned black. "Who is he?"

Alcandhor shot to his feet. "Marcalan, ease off!"

"Who?" The young man shook, fists clenched. "By the Bells and both moons, I would know who!"

"So you can do what, son?" Lantalan asked, blue eyes flashing as he held Kalinna. "Think you I did not try to find him and make him pay?"

Lips pressed together, Marcalan stood, chest heaving, glaring from one to another. "Who?"

"Think it through, son," murmured Lantalan. "There are not many with Enaisi blood in our world, and only one who would have done thus."

Alcandhor started as the realization hit him: Uardhel. The leader of the Rogue band that had tried to assassinate him at Lairdton's Ranger Hold. The one Marcalan faced down in the crypt. He lowered himself back into his seat.

"I killed him." Marcalan's stunned expression gave way to a hard sneer. "I killed the by-blow. Bedamn him to the fires of Teledhar!" He let out a humorless laugh. "I killed him, Mother."

Kalinna looked up at her son, her face wet, eyes red. "Does that change what happened to me? Does that stop the pain? He did not just violate my body, he raped my *mind*! I have lived with that for all these years! You want vengeance, but I just want *peace!*"

For the first time, Alcandhor felt he understood the strangeness of the couple's relationship: easygoing Lantalan and the hard, stiff-backed Kalinna, yet he hovered about her protectively. So many offered the opinion he was a fool, and that he allowed her to control him too readily, when in reality, he saw the fragility inside her tough exterior.

So many questions and paths of thought coursed through Alcandhor's brain. And most of them would likely cause more pain for Kalinna. He rubbed his hands together between his knees and wet his lips. "You obviously did not report the crime at the time, and the culprit is now dead.

But I would know details. When it happened, and where."

Kalinna shook her head. Lantalan pulled her more tightly into his arms. "She was in the fields near her family's home, bringing the herdbeasts to their north pasture. Uardhel, we think, must have been hiding in Thane Valley, although why we cannot fathom. It would seem more dangerous when on the run. Easier to become trapped."

Alcandhor nodded but did not interrupt. It was indeed how Uardhel had been caught and branded Rogue.

"I came to visit her and when she was not at home, I went to the pasture looking for her and...and I found her. I will never forget it. She just lay there, unblinking. She..." Lantalan's head bowed, and he took several shuddering breaths. "I carried her to her parents' home. She roused enough to beg me to tell them nothing. I said she was ill, and I was taking her to Zaidhron. Her father harnessed their dray beast to the wagon and brought us to the city. I asked Saldhor for a family suite that same night, and we used the nestling days as a time for her to rest and for me to try to help her recover."

Kalinna hiccupped a sob, shaking her head.

Lantalan stroked her hair, murmuring, "I know. I know." He looked up at Alcandhor, his face one of fury. "What he did to her body paled with what he did to her mind. I cannot imagine the horrors he placed there. She has never recovered. I have loved her as well as any man can love a woman, but he... It is as if he rent her soul."

Alcandhor knew not what to say.

Marcalan's loud, rasping breaths were all that was heard. He clenched and unclenched his fists. Finally he said, "So this is what I am. How you must despise me."

"How can you say that, son?" Lantalan asked.

"Her! I am talking to her. She bore the spawn of that evil by-blow. And I thought her dislike of me was because she had no sense of humor and merely could not understand—"

"How can you say that?" Kalinna cried. "You are my son! I love you."

"Do you really? I cannot see how! Love the son of the man who has tortured your mind all these years? Nay!" He strode to the door.

"Where are you going?" Alcandhor called.

"I know not," Marcalan spat standing in the open frame. "I care not." The door slammed.

Alcandhor rose, but Lantalan held out a hand. "Let him be. He needs time to absorb this."

"'Tis much for him."

"Aye. But he is resilient. He will need time."

Alcandhor hesitated then nodded, not looking directly at Kalinna. He could not bear to see her like this, so different from her normal peremptory self. He took a breath and softly said, "We shall keep this between us. When you feel ready, Kalinna, your husband may take you home. Lantalan, I release you from today's duties." Alcandhor backed up a step. "I am sorry, Kalinna, to have caused such distress. I will leave you now." He bowed and hurried out.

As the door shut behind him, he stopped to let the emotions of that tumultuous scene and the resultant problems it posed wash over him. He closed his eyes with an overwhelming feeling he had just run away, and with no sense of wishing to correct that wrong.

A soft touch on his arm made him open his eyes. Tam, face sober, stood before him. "Uncle, I...I heard."

"I trust you know you are to say nothing." He scrubbed his face with his hand. "I need time alone. To think."

Chapter Twenty-Three

Marcalan needed a place to be alone. Utterly alone. And he knew of one—surely no one would find him in one of the unused guard chambers in the towers along the west range's allure.

His feet dragged as he climbed the tower's steps. Surely this could not be true.

But it must be. Lantalan was not his father. For all the jesting, and the man's taunting that his son was a recalcitrant scoundrel, he held love and pride for Marcalan. Yet he had known.

He reached the tower guards' chamber. Once inside, he sat on the floor against the wall.

That unlamented Rogue, that he himself had killed, was his father. He stared ahead, seeing nothing, remembering...

Holding a torch above his head and his sword in the other, Marcalan pelted down the steps. In the dim, flickering glow he saw his Thane on the floor, Tam kneeling next to him. A tall man, gaunt, with stringy blond hair, stood in front of them, doubled over. A Rogue. Uardhel, if the reports were correct.

"Have at me, Rogue!" Marcalan pitched the torch to the floor of the chamber below, and jumped over the forms of his Thane and cousin, landing before them, brandishing his sword.

The Rogue's teeth bared as he lunged. Marcalan parried and jumped to his right and back, taking the fight farther from his kin. A glance showed Tam trying to help Alcandhor sit up. Stars, man, concentrate! Tam can take care of the Thane. Down this Rogue!

A shot of hatred hit Marcalan, and he stumbled back. 'Twas not as forceful as Tam's sendings, but still! The pain stopped, and the emotion whipped back onto Uardhel. Marcalan felt Tam sending through him and blocking through him as well. Nay, blocking for him! Stars, what that woman could do! He laughed aloud.

Uardhel lunged, hissing, "By-blow!"

"Ha! Nay. Sorry." Marcalan weaved sideways with a diagonal down-stroke. He countered with the flourishes of an advanced technique he had been studying with Maradhor. Uardhel fell back.

"Cannot cheat, can you now? Must merely use your sword skills. Lacking a bit, are they?"

Uardhel's face twisted in hatred as he lunged forward with a downward cut.

Easily sidestepping, Marcalan countered with one strike after another, driving the Rogue back. He hooted at the astonished, increasingly desperate expression on Uardhel's face.

"Stop playing him, Marcalan! Finish him!" ordered Tam.

More footsteps—Rangers clambered down the steps with torches.

Voices yelled, but he only heard Haladhon clearly. "Marcalan, be careful! He—"

"Tam has him blocked. He is mine!"

Uardhel grunted with effort, gasping for breath, his face intent. Their blades flashed, the clanging loud as all noise ceased for an endless moment. Then—Marcalan found his target. Uardhel's mouth opened, but no sound came. Marcalan withdrew his sword with a quick saccade and struck his opponent's from his hand.

The Rogue's face contorted, and he spat at Marcalan. Then he fell, lifeless.

By-blow, Uardhel had said. He had not known the truth of his words. Such a man was his father. His kin was not what he thought. He was not what he thought. Who was he truly?

And Tam. What right had he to love such an innocent lass? Daughter of a chief, niece of their Thane. He deserved nothing so precious and good.

For the first time in his life, he could find no humor in a situation, or in himself.

~*~

Tam said nothing during the afternoon meal. Neither did Uncle. She could neither find nor sense Marcalan. If only Haladhon were in the city. She wandered outside in the drizzling rain after her lesson with Maradhor ended. He had not been happy with her performance today. Focus! Control! He sounded like her father, and it made her miss him more. Which made it harder to do what Maradhor instructed.

Finally, she sat on a bench in Avadhron's Sward, unbalanced and alone, the hood of her cloak over her head. She could not comprehend what Marcalan must be enduring. And since he blocked, she could not comfort him.

She could, however, pay for the necklet beads. Stars, aye! She rose and hurried toward the main gate and Itasa's stall. The old woman saw her approach and smiled.

Tam untied the pouch and opened it. "How much do I pay?"

"Three star coppers is all."

Tam spilled some of the coins into her hand, mostly copper, but a few silver. She found three small ones with stars stamped into them and held them out. They should be star coppers if they were copper with stars on them, aye? She hoped so anyway.

Itasa took them into her gnarled hand. "Thank you. And when you give your young man the necklet, bring him by for me to meet."

Tam smiled shyly and eyed her wares. Various scarves and shawls decorated the sides and back under the awning raised today against the rain. "How much for the shawls?"

Itasa lifted her brows. "Different prices. Depends on the quality of thread and workmanship." She took down a grey one with a bright sheen, then reached up for another with brighter colors of blue and grey and spread them out. "This grey one, see how it almost shimmers? It seems plain but feel how soft. That is kinchou hair, spun into the finest thread! This other one looks fancier with the blue in it, but the thread is not as fine."

The grey of the former shawl seemed almost the grey of Sarinna's eyes. Tam fingered it lovingly. "How much is this one?"

"Four silver stars." Tam looked up at the other shawls. Taniss wore dark colors, but with warm tones in the trim and lace of her bodice-gown. One shawl caught Tam's attention, woven with darker autumn hues. "May I see that one, please?"

Itasa lifted it off it's wooden rod and brought it over. "You have good eyes—and taste."

Tam's fingers lightly brushed over the fine softness. "How much for this one?" she whispered.

"That one is four silver stars and three copper bells."

Tam fumbled her pouch open. Did she have enough silver for these shawls? She again poured coins into her hands, and sighed with relief as silver issued forth as well as copper. She plucked the coins that she needed for both shawls and handed them to Itasa.

The old woman folded the grey shawl then the warm-hued one and wrapped them in a bit of paper, tied with a string. As Tam picked up the package, Itasa handed back the three copper bells. "You need to learn to haggle, my girl."

"But you said—"

"You ask for lessons in haggling. Perhaps that tall cousin of yours. He is winsome, that one, and uses it to good advantage with the vendors. Even me!"

A woman walked up, asking about jewelry, and Itasa waved Tam on.

Confused by the concept of haggling, and cheered by the gifts she had bought, Tam strolled through Avadhron's Sward. Before long, the nagging worry about Marcalan arose, blotting out other thoughts.

An herb garden in need of tending caught her attention. Such work would ease her mind, surely. She hoped her rank would keep her from being chastised but she cared not. She wrapped her package in her cloak and set it under a nearby bench to hopefully keep dry, then knelt in the mud to weed. Soon she forgot the drizzle and her fine Ranger clothes.

Footsteps on the path nearby halted.

"This is how our new heir to Thane spends her time?" a man's voice sneered.

Tam looked up, blinking at the droplets hitting her face, to see a man and woman glaring at her. Their contemptuous expressions stiffened her spine. "And who are you to demand an accounting of how I spend my time?"

"Well said, Tam," drawled Zandhral's voice. Her cousin sauntered over with a hard smile for the two interlopers. "I would fain hear the answer to that myself."

"I would think the new heir would be working hard to learn all she needs to take on her role," the man said, his voice more apologetic than condescending now.

"Ah, I see." Zandhral nodded, then he grinned. "Go tell the Thane that he should be tending to tasks right now instead of poring over books, or go tell Haladhon that he needs to be giving attention to Elite matters instead of smithing at this hour. Should I be improving my bowman skills instead of strolling Avadhron's Sward?"

"I simply meant, that being new to her position—"

"I know what you meant," Zandhral spat. "And so does she. We are both Children of the Enaisi. What you *meant* was sensed without any words. And you should be grateful I am taking you to task and not our new heir. She has much of her father in her."

The couple bowed, mumbling apologies, and hurried down the path.

Zandhral bowed to Tam. "I apologize for interrupting both your gardening, and what would have likely been a good verbal hiding. I have not grown past the protectiveness I feel when I see a lady being treated thus."

"But Zandhral, you know I can fight. And you do not treat me as a female when we match. How can you feel the need to protect me?"

"Ah, my young cousin. Ingrained mores are the problem."

"I do not understand."

Zandhral squatted next to Tam. "As I perceive, there are several different reasons why we have trouble accepting you in your role as both a Ranger and as heir. First, there are those who will not accept you because they feel you are not good enough merely because you are female. Some of those same people have never accepted Alcandhor for the same reason. 'He is not strong as was his brother' and 'he is too soft-hearted.'"

"But he is so very strong! He faced down my father more than once and beat him in a fight on the way to Zaidhron!"

Zandhral's grin broadened. "Did he! I would fain have seen that."

"Aye, he—"

Zandhral lifted a hand. "You can tell me another time. I wish to continue giving our new heir a lecture."

Tam smiled at the humor exuding from her cousin. "Say on then."

"Then there are the rest of us. We trust our Thane, and therefore are trying very hard to accept you. Cordhan and Edhron and others of us who have been assigned as special match partners have discussed this at great length."

"Discussed me?"

"Aye, and how to approach Training you."

"But, why? You know I can fight—"

"This is where our ingrained mores flip us topside-down." Her cousin's blue eyes searched hers. "A woman can do something no man can. Life sparks in her body. We venerate women because of a role so unique— and more important than fighting or anything else a Ranger can be Trained to do. Without women, we are nothing."

Tam bit her lip, unsure of what to say.

"So," Zandhral continued, "we Rangers must master that reverence in order to help Train you for your position. And this goes against everything we are taught. Clan first, kin first, women—mothers or potential mothers— first."

"I suppose that makes sense."

"Edhron was the first to chastise us. We do have some women who choose to learn to fight and wield weapons for protection's sake. But their training is not the rigorous and too-oft dangerous efforts of Ranger Training. He said we needed to learn to match full-on with you, without regard—"

"There are women who learn to fight?"

"Aye. Do not cross Sarinna, for example." Zandhral grinned. "Ah, I expect in this case perhaps she should be told not to cross you, but aye, she fights. She matched with both her brothers at one time. She was wicked with a dagger or sword, and had some sweet grappling moves. The daughter of the Thane should not be an easy target, she used to say."

"You speak in past tense. Does she not match now?"

Zandhral shook his head. "Not in years, to my knowledge."

Tam tipped her head. "Perhaps she would with me?"

"Perhaps. But her duties as city steward take most of her time." Zandhral rose, his knees cracking loudly. He rubbed them with a wry smile. "I need to move on. My wife and children await me."

Tam smiled as he nodded and strolled away. Zandhral's frankness and friendship cheered her, and she returned to her gardening with a lighthearted zeal.

The mealtime horns sounded, and Tam jumped up, wiping the mud off her hands onto her trous. Stars, she would need to wash her garments tonight! She picked up her package and hurried toward the Great Hall. She arrived well before the gong, and wove around servants bustling to finish their tasks before the meal started, standing on tiptoe looking for her aunt and grandmother to no avail.

During the evening meal, any news of import would be discussed by Rangers, so the families did not sit together as during the day meals. Instead the women and children sat at side tables. And many families chose to eat in their own ranges instead of at the Great Hall anyway. Perhaps Sarinna and Taniss sometimes ate elsewhere.

To her relief, the women walked in together from the back halls. Tam rushed to them, holding out the package. "I bought something for you both."

Taniss raised her eyebrows, but Sarinna smiled. "Let us go into the early room." Tam followed them into the small chamber, empty at the moment, and again held out the paper-wrapped gift.

Sarinna placed it on the table and untied the string. Tam lifted the grey shawl, saying, "I thought the shiny grey color was pretty like your eyes." Sarinna's smile widened as she took it.

"And this is for you, grandmother."

"These are very fine," Taniss said, holding her shawl in her hands. "Kinchou, well spun and woven."

Tam nodded.

"These are very fine gifts indeed," Sarinna said. "What is the occasion?"

"Occasion?"

"Was there a reason you wanted to gift these to us?"

Tam shook her head. "I just...wanted to."

"A gift of love, for no other reason. 'Tis the best reason of all." Taniss pressed her cheek to Tam's, whispering, "Thank you."

Sarinna thanked Tam too, but a sense of curiosity lurked behind her smile. Tam kept her feelings light, hoping her aunt could not feel a tinge of guilt that the presents were an after-thought and diversion for her true reason of needing money.

"And what did you pay for these, my girl?" Sarinna asked.

"Sarinna, you know 'tis not appropriate to ask thus," Taniss said.

"Aye, but Tam is new to these things, and I only hope the vendor did not cheat her."

Tam hesitated, but her grandmother nodded.

"Four silver stars each. That one"—Tam nodded at her grandmother's shawl—"was actually four silver stars and three copper bells, but Itasa gave me back the three coppers. She said Haladhon should teach me to haggle."

Both women burst out laughing.

"Aye, indeed, you need to learn to haggle," Sarinna said. "But Itasa is more honest than most."

"And claims she is too old to haggle much anymore." Taniss swept the shawl over her shoulders. "Not that I believe that for a moment." She ran her fingers over the fine work. "But I think she did not overcharge you for these shawls. Indeed, she may have not charged enough."

"But why would she do that?"

"Itasa's story is a long one. Suffice to say, she has been a fixture here since she was a young lass, making jewelry and spinning for her mother and grandmother. Thane Handhor, your great-grandfather, gifted her family that prime location for their stall ages ago after a family tragedy. Handhor was not the most compassionate of men, but he did right by them." Taniss pulled Tam into a hug. "Again, my thanks for such a gift. Now to table before the gong sounds!"

"Hm." Sarinna nodded at Tam's hands. "Gardening, niece? Wash before meal, girl."

Tam looked at the dried mud encrusted in between her fingers and under her nails and smiled. "Aye, that I will."

The meal was subdued, especially so without either Haladhon or Marcalan there, and her aunt and grandmother sitting at a side table. And Uncle did little more than tap his eating knife the whole meal and push the food around his plate. She fiddled with her glass after the meal, only rising when the servants began to clear the tables.

In the far corner, musicians gathered. This must be a nightly occurrence. She wove between the remaining tables and found a place to sit and listen. The music, although soft and soothing, was a bit sad. Tam sighed. If only she knew where Marcalan was. She wanted to comfort him. Swallowing heavily, she thought of the necklet, and how happy the day when she could put it around his neck. *Oh, Marcalan, where are you?*

"You seem quiet."

Tam jumped and looked up. Taniss smiled and sat down next to her.

"Is everything all right?"

So much was wrong, but Tam could say nothing. Not about Marcalan, nor his mother, not about how it hurt to have *in love.*

Her grandmother's gentle, expectant gaze somehow demanded an answer. Tam finally managed, "Life was much simpler back at our cottage."

Taniss huffed a soft laugh. "I imagine it was. You have been barraged with many changes, my girl, and borne them bravely. But everyone has a time when they need to step back and gain their bearings. A time to find a new center."

"How does one do that?"

Her grandmother inhaled slowly, staring into the distance, then just as slowly exhaled. She still looked away, as if seeing something or someone when she replied, "'Tis different for everyone. And does not usually happen quickly." She blinked, then smiled at Tam. "And if anyone, even our Thane, presses too hard, you be not afraid to say it is too soon."

"Aye, you have said thus before. But Uncle needs me to—"

"Your uncle cannot see beyond the end of his own nose about some things. He has personal reasons for wishing to push you, but you are Valdhor's daughter. I know you have the will to push back. Do not let him bully you. Understand me?"

Tam frowned. "U–uncle does not bully."

Her grandmother gave her a wry smile. "Not in the overt way Valdhor would, but he has a strength of character that is harder than shimmerstone underneath his unassuming demeanor."

Tam's fists clenched in her lap. "Uncle is not a bully!"

Taniss twisted to face Tam full, her clear blue eyes intense. She took Tam's hands in hers. "This is why I tell you a second time to not let him push you too hard. You adore him. And rightly so. He is a most worthy man, even if I say thus myself. But when he fixates on a target, 'tis very little that can distract his aim. As much as he loves you, you are a means to an end."

"His desire to not be Thane, is that your meaning?"

"Aye."

"I do understand that, Taniss. And I do not wish to be Thane. Ever. I wish him to be Thane."

"And he knows this?"

"Aye. Even the Rangers wager on who will win in five years."

Her grandmother laughed softly. "Good. Good for you. Push him back as hard as he pushes you."

"So you do not wish me to be Thane either?"

"My dear girl, my concern is that you are healthy, in mind as well as body." She leaned close and whispered, "So *push back!*"

The sparkle in Taniss's eyes made Tam smile. "I will."

Chapter Twenty-Four

Tam scoured the Great Hall one last, futile time for a glimpse of Marcalan before going to the evening Training session. Lonely did not begin to express how she felt. Desolate. Empty. Despite that, she knew she had to concentrate. Fight hard. Fight smart.

Afterwards she dragged back to the western range. She needed to bathe and her clothes reeked. Once done with the washing of both herself and her clothes, she climbed the stairs to her chamber with leaden legs. Her jerkin and boots needed attention too. She rubbed the leather dressing into them and finally finished, set them aside and crawled into bed. She dozed off and after a time, a warmth and presence grew. Although she did not wake, she somehow knew Marcalan must be asleep since he no longer blocked. Marcalan's pain and sorrow along with Tam's worry and love weaved into combined dreams of Tam cradling him as he wept.

~*~

Tam struggled during the morning reports to keep her worry over Marcalan hidden. Her uncle saved the feud for last. She could not blame him. He eyed the report with a curl of his lip that flashed to memories of her father. Another pang to add her to inner distress.

He raised his head with a worried frown. "What is wrong, Tam?"

Stars, he sensed her sorrow! She dare not say on about Marcalan. She bit her lip then said, "Your face. The look on it reminded me of my father."

Her uncle sat back and closed his eyes for a moment. When he opened them, he murmured, "We cannot help those feelings, enh? Or when they strike." He straightened and tapped the report with a finger. "However, we can focus on other things."

"Will you evict them, then, Uncle?"

"I have no choice." He stood and arched his back, one arm above his head. "However, I will wait a few days." He pulled the cord.

"Why?"

"I have only had complaint from one side. The other will soon follow. They always come in pairs. Hang those two for forcing me into such a decision!"

"Most of being Thane seems to be receiving reports and making decisions you do not like. Even more reason why I do not wish to become

Thane one day."

Alcandhor huffed a laugh. "If I wish not to be Thane, and you wish not to be Thane, who then shall lead our clan?"

"We are not given a choice."

"Nay, Tam, and that is the point. I was not. And you are not either. It is a duty fallen upon us."

Tam pressed her lips together. Stars, she would not get into an argument about that conclave decision right now.

Feladhrel entered, and the Thane told him to gather and file the reports. As the stripling straightened the papers, Alcandhor said, "Come, Tam. I wish to show you something. Let us go upstairs to the banquet gallery."

Tam sighed and tried to stuff her miserable mood down as she followed her uncle up two flights of stairs to the hallway behind the upper library level. This led to yet another staircase and wide corridor. Alcandhor opened a door and inclined his head with a smile.

The massive chamber had many long tables and wide windows with more ornamentation than any she had seen yet in Zaidhron. The buttresses and ribs of the vaulted ceiling had elaborate designs overlaid with gold, and the draperies had a complex, ornamental golden brocade throughout the deep purple fabric. Portraits, some larger, some smaller, hung crowded together all along the three walls that had no windows.

"What is this place, Uncle?"

"It used to be used for clan meetings and dinners, but we have rarely had them in recent years. Every Thane and his family are here in at least one portrait. I wanted to show you one in particular."

She followed him along the length of the chamber, gazing up at some of the faces staring down at her. Tam stopped and gasped, pointing to a portrait. "That is Mattan!"

"That is our ancestor Mattan," Alcandhor said.

"That is Mattan! That is the Enaisi I talked to, Uncle! It is him!"

"It cannot be. That portrait is almost a thousand years old. Granted the Enaisi lived longer lives than we do, but a thousand years? Nay. It must be a descendent who looks like him."

Tam stared at the strong, kind face smiling down at her and wished she could actually see him again. She could almost hear his soft laugh in her head.

"That is Mattan," she said again.

"I will not bicker about it, Tam," her uncle said, his voice disapproving.

Tam's back stiffened. She wished she could speak to Mattan, to have him affirm she was right. She froze in realization—she could! He said she could! She closed her eyes to concentrate on sending to him, and felt the familiar pulling. She swallowed her fear as she passed through the blackness and the blinding light. She was aware of her uncle clutching her shoulders, but what she saw was Mattan.

He laughed. "See how easy that is?"

"Aye," she replied. "I am starting to not be so afraid of the blackness."

"That's good. I take it you have come to ask questions?"

"I wanted to know—" she was not sure how to ask the question. "We have a portrait that looks like you."

He smiled. "Yes, it's me."

"But how?"

"It is because we are long-lived. I will be able to explain much that seems to have been lost in your people's history when I arrive. Have you more questions, Tam?"

"When are you coming?" she asked.

"Soon. I have responsibilities here. Work to finish. I am certain your uncle understands that."

"You know who my uncle is?"

"Of course—through you, just as I know his name. Tell your uncle, Thane Alcandhor, that I look forward to meeting him very soon."

He gently laughed at her amazement, then she felt herself falling back. She opened her eyes to see her uncle looking distressed, still gripping her shoulders.

"He is coming soon, Uncle. He has work to finish first. And he is the same Mattan. He says they live a long time. He says he looks forward to meeting you very soon."

He exhaled slowly, staring at her, a shocked look on his pale face. "At the rate you keep turning things topside down, girl, I am going to just give up and go tip a few back. You can just contact him any time?"

"Aye, Uncle. Oh, he knows your name and who you are. Do they read thoughts, Uncle? He knew my name before I told him."

"Aye. It is said they do, anyway."

"And that"—she pointed at the portrait in triumph—"is Mattan."

He chuckled. "Had to prove you were right, did you not, girl?"

Had she been too brash? "You are not angry?"

"Stars, why should I be? 'Tis good to see you assert yourself. But I wish you had warned me what you were going to do. I had no idea at first, and it worried me."

"I am sorry, Uncle. I did not think."

"Aye. The fault of the young. They just do without stopping to think." He smiled but it seemed sad. "Come. Let me show you this one painting."

They walked toward the door at the far end, and Tam looked at the portraits as they passed. Straight ahead she saw one that made her heart almost stop. She quickened her pace to get to it.

It was a family portrait. The man in it had a kind face that reminded Tam of her uncle. It had to be Saldhor. A younger Taniss sat in front of him, smiling warmly. Sarinna, beautiful then as now, stood next to her father, chin raised. The brothers flanked the cushioned chair. Her uncle, handsome, but without moustache or chin beard, sported a reckless smile. Stars, but to see him so young, looking so carefree. A stripling Ranger.

Her father was so very handsome. He wore the haughty look she knew so well, yet no lines of care creased his face. She stared at him for a long time, and he seemed almost to be looking right at her.

"That was done not long before he left," her uncle whispered, putting his hands on her shoulders.

She blinked back tears. "I miss him..."

"I know."

She continued to gaze up at her father. She would never see him stride across the clearing again, or see his face as he matched her, yelling at her to try harder, fight harder. She would never again fix him a meal or sit, listening to him tell her of their laws, then repeating them back to him. Never again see him give terse nods as she answered his questions.

She closed her eyes, turned to her uncle, and hugged him. "It hurts so much sometimes."

"I know, Tam," he whispered, his hand rubbing her back. "I know."

~*~

Not being able to match chafed Alcandhor, but he bore the indignity of it as he needed to see how Tam's Training with Edhron progressed. The senior fight Trainer gave him a glare that clearly said he could watch but not interrupt. Another chafing indignity.

He nearly started forward several times despite the Edhron's tacit order, but held himself in check, trusting the elder Ranger despite his emotional responses. He admitted to himself Edhron knew what he was about, and so did Tam, growing more confident with each match.

The mealtime horns sounded. Tam and her partner stopped and rose to their feet, fists over their hearts. Tam wiped her face on a drying cloth and gave Alcandhor a hopeful look. He nodded. "Go change and wash for luncheon, niece."

Tam skipped to the back washing chamber. She joined him soon after, back in her Ranger garments, face freshly washed and damp hair combed. Her expression begged for approval. Alcandhor smiled at her as they walked to the doors. "That was well done."

Her face lit up, but her eyes wandered to his shoulder and the smile faded. "Will you be able to match soon, Uncle?"

"Very soon, likely."

Her smile returned.

Alcandhor dared not let the dread of the healer's report touch his mood, lest Tam sense it. Hindhal was a master of his craft, but his talk of the injury possibly not healing completely was likely only to slow Alcandhor from trying to do too much too soon. If he truly thought it permanent, why had the healer said naught to Sarinna? He inhaled the brisk tang of the autumn air, blinking as rain spattered his face. At almost the same time, he and Tam flipped the hoods of their cloaks over their heads.

A disturbance to his right caught his attention, and he changed direction, crossing to where some Trainees gathered near a match area at the edge of the sward. Two boys fought, and 'twas not a match.

"Take it back!" yelled the one, and Alcandhor frowned at hearing Teldhor's voice. He fought another Trainee, taller and heavier than him. Alcandhor searched his memory for the boy's name; this was the son of one of Ranger clan's master woodcrafters, Davadhrel, a most excellent joiner, but the lad's name eluded him.

"I will not!" cried the other boy, then grunted when Teldhor's fist made solid contact with his face. He staggered back, then sidestepped Teldhor's next punch and countered with a solid strike to Teldhor's jaw.

Tam took a step forward, and Alcandhor put an arm out to stop her. The boys watching the fight became aware of the Thane and slowly backed away, gaping.

Teldhor threw two punches in succession, successfully landing on the boy's face, then a thrusting kick that knocked the boy back into the grass. Alcandhor noted with guilty pride that the thrust kick was executed well.

The boy wheezed as he got to his feet and came in swinging. Teldhor blocked some of the punches but not all, then he spun and caught the boy with the back of his fist in the face. Alcandhor wanted to grin—that move had become popular since Tam had used it on Loch'alan—but he kept his face impassive.

The boy fell back against Alcandhor's legs. His eyes widened and he scrambled to his feet.

"Your pardon, Thane," he mumbled.

"This looks not like a Trainee match," Alcandhor said in a quiet tone.

"Nay, sir," both boys muttered, looking down.

"So, if you continue this fight will it resolve your differences?"

The boys stared at the ground.

"Well?"

"I know not, sir," Teldhor answered.

"Had you two a reason to fight?"

"Aye, sir," Teldhor said with indignation, his eyes dark as he looked up. "Naladhrel said that cousin Tam is a shame to our clan because a lass should not be a Ranger!"

The other boy would not look up, but his ears turned bright red.

"I see. Think you his opinion will change if you thoroughly thrash him?"

Teldhor squirmed. "Probably not, sir."

"Then what point is served in fighting him?"

"To protect clan honor, and yours for Confirming her as a Ranger. And cousin Tam's, too."

"In what way does one person's opinion affect another person's honor, Teldhor?"

"To say such things is to sully a person's honor."

"What is honor?"

"It is a person's good name. It is his reputation, and the respect others have for him."

Alcandhor grimaced slightly; now was not the time be a pedant—or launch into a lecture on personal honor as opposed to public honor. "Close enough. And how is honor won?"

"It is by a person's merit, by their deeds."

"So it is based on what that person has done, not by another person's opinion?"

Teldhor looked up. "I–I suppose it is."

"Then what purpose does this fight serve?"

Neither boy answered. Alcandhor gazed at them both. "Tam will prove herself to our clan as she has already proven herself to me, to the other chiefs, to all the Rangers who have had duty with her, and to those who have become acquainted with her. There are those who may never accept her, just as there are those in our clan who do not like the fact I am Thane. It sullies not my honor that some few have a bad opinion of me."

Teldhor and Naladhrel both looked up wide-eyed.

"But everyone looks up to you, sir," Teldhor said.

Naladhrel glanced sidelong at the boys nearby. "That is true, sir."

Alcandhor smiled. "You two may have a difference of opinion, but remember, yelling or fighting does not change a person's mind." He looked at Naladhrel. "And remember Trainee, that a Ranger never makes a rash judgment. We look at people's deeds, not outward appearances. Have you not been taught this?"

"Aye, sir," Naladhrel mumbled, looking down with a frown.

"Then you have an assignment. You are to look up all the records of Tam's assignments and missions, and you are to watch her in Training matches. You will write a report, based on what you have read and observed, on whether the Second at Table is worthy of being a Ranger. Back up all statements by facts, not opinions. Feladhrel, a stripling who is attendant to the law-keepers, can help with finding any record or law you may require. The report is due in three days."

Naladhrel's eyes grew wide and he glanced over at Tam, face flushed, then whispered, "Aye, sir."

"And you, Teldhor." The Thane turned to his son. "You are to write a report on fighting. On its merits and disadvantages, and what purposes it serves. When a fight might be worth taking on, and when it should be walked away from. Also, on honor, what it is, and how it may be gained or lost. Both reports due in three days."

"Aye, sir," Teldhor said, staring at his feet.

"Now clean up, both of you. You cannot come to table looking like brawling barn brats." Alcandhor waved them away, not letting himself smile until they were gone.

Alcandhor looked over to see Tam dimpling. "What do you find amusing?"

"What was the purpose in fighting my father? What was the merit in that?"

Alcandhor thought back to that bloody brawl he and Valdhor had on their way to Zaidhron and grinned wryly. "Do you want the official answer or the real answer?"

Tam shrugged. "Tell me both."

"Officially, I was proving I was truly Thane to Valdhor in the only way he would recognize."

Tam nodded, and Alcandhor knew she understood. Her father respected authority backed up with power. His attitude had subtly changed toward Alcandhor after they had fought.

She tipped her head, looking up at him. "And the real reason?"

Alcandhor leaned close and said in a conspiratorial voice, "It felt good to thrash him. And win!"

Tam laughed with him. "And Uncle, what you said to Teldhor was not strictly true."

"What was that?"

"About someone's opinion not affecting honor. Slander spread can affect a person's honor. It says so in the law."

"True, but I was not going to muddy the waters and lose the point I was making."

His niece gazed up at him, adoration in her eyes, but also doubt.

"What is it, Tam?"

"How you dealt with the boys."

"Aye?"

"I would not have known how to handle that and I wonder..." She paused. "Will I ever be as wise as you, Uncle?"

He chuckled. "Much wiser, one day, I hope."

Chapter Twenty-Five

Marcalan stared blankly at the map in the Elites' chamber. He thought not of Rogues, nor of Monadhal, nor of any responsibility he should bear. His mind wound itself in interlinking, ever-tightening circles of confusion and despair. He was the son of a vile Rogue. He did not deserve to be a Ranger. And he could find no good in loving Tam. He could not bear the thought of even seeing her. How dare he sit across from her this afternoon in the library?

Devotion to duty and the Thane warred with the conflict within. Duty won, and he dragged his feet up the stairs to the law library. Tam already sat in a chair reading. She saw him and shot out of her chair to hug him. "Marcalan, I am so worried! You—"

"Do not touch me!" Marcalan shoved her away, his anguish growing to a physical pain that almost bent him over. "We cannot—"

"I care not! You are suffering, and I love you." She stepped close and whispered, "I have made you a necklet!"

A shudder tore through Marcalan, and it took all his effort not to groan aloud. He wheeled about and ran out, leaping up the stairs until he reached the top floor. He took a shuddering breath. What could he do? He rubbed his hands over his face. Again he wended his way to the tower guards' chamber.

She had made him a necklet. By the Elders! Even with the Thane's blessing, how could he accept such a gift? Offering her life to spend with him? Stars, he must not think of that! And the Thane—even without this revelation, he would never approve. Not with Tam's age. But how dare he keep concealing his feelings, and Tam's? Alcandhor would consider it a deception, and aye, truly it was. And he could not deceive his Thane. His oaths, his whole life and Training as a Ranger forbad it. He fell back against the wall and slid to the floor. Digging his fists into his eyes, he fought breaking into open sobs.

~*~

Tam stood by the table, unmoving. She felt as cold as stone, her insides hurting as if punched full force. Her uncle strode around the doorway and stopped. "Tam, are you unwell?"

Tam shook her head. She dared not speak and blinked hard to stop her

187

tears.

Alcandhor took her by the shoulders, the worry in his face making her heart ache all the more. "What is wrong?"

"I..." She tried to breathe, but could not seem to inhale. "I cannot—"

Her uncle put an arm around her shoulders. "Come to my chamber. I will call a healer."

Tam shook her head, even as he drew her out the door. Murmuring that she would be fine, and a healer would be called, he took her down the stairs to his chamber and pushed her into a chair.

He pulled the cord to summon Feladhrel.

"I am not ill. I need not...a healer," Tam managed.

The boy arrived in moments. Alcandhor rubbed his chin, staring at Tam.

"Sir?" the stripling asked.

Alcandhor cleared his throat. "Sarinna. Bring Sarinna."

Feladhrel sped off, then Alcandhor knelt in front of Tam. He took her hands between his. She could not bear to see the worry in his eyes and so shut hers. She dared not say on about Marcalan. She dared not—a sob escaped her despite her best efforts, and then she burst into tears.

Her uncle patted her shoulder and stroked her hair, his hovering reminding her of a protective mother bird. Finally he hugged her. Tam let her head rest on his shoulder, weeping uncontrollably. How could *in love* hurt so much?

"Thane?" Zandhral's soft voice called.

"Aye?" Alcandhor whispered.

"I...I felt Tam's distress across the forechamber. Is she all right?"

"I know not. She says she is not sick. I have called for Sarinna."

Zandhral knelt next to Tam. Soothing feelings washed over her. Her crying abated ever so slightly.

"Stars, aye," Alcandhor muttered. Gentle loving emotions from her uncle flowed through her. Their combined effort helped Tam to calm enough that her weeping slowed to sniffling sobs. She looked up to see her uncle's worried face and almost began crying again. That she should be loved so much—why then did *in love* seem to count for so much more?

From over Zandhral's head, she saw Sarinna enter the chamber. "You needed me? Bells, what is wrong?"

"We know not." Alcandhor grimaced and stood. "I–I knew not who to call."

Sarinna pulled a chair over and sat next to Tam. "You men leave."

Once the door shut, Sarinna said softly, "Has my brother been pushing you too hard?"

Tam shook her head.

"Do not defend him if he has, Tam. He needs—"

"Nay, 'tis not Uncle."

"Tell me. I will try to help."

Tam twisted her hands in her lap and shook her head again.

"I know we are new to each other, but sense me, I only wish to help."

Tam dared not answer. Sarinna urged her twice more to talk, and finally just sat, holding Tam's hand. The silence grew long, but all Tam could think of was that Uncle would be so angry to know about Marcalan. Above all else, she must protect him.

"Is there anyone you do feel you can talk to?" Sarinna finally asked.

Tam yet again, shook her head.

Sarinna inhaled deeply. "I think...I think you need to garden."

Tam looked up, wide-eyed, not expecting such an answer. Gardening had been her escape when her father's foul moods frightened her, or she just wished to just stay out of his way.

Her aunt smiled. "You enjoy gardening. Some time alone, outside, away from everyone, doing what you love will likely revive your spirits. I will tell Alcandhor. Is that all right?"

Tam nodded.

Sarinna rose and opened the door. "Go on, Tam."

She obeyed, quickly, before anyone could say a word.

~*~

Zandhral straightened as Sarinna opened the door, and Tam sped outside like a bird flying free from a cage. Sarinna turned to the Thane. "She would not talk. I know not what is troubling her except it is deep. I suggested some time gardening might help."

Alcandhor nodded, his expression of one lost in Hillsdown. "Whatever she needs. Think you I have been too exacting with her?"

"She says not. Sensing her, I believe her. But I have no idea what is bothering our niece."

Blowing his breath out softly, Zandhral said, "I might know. But I am not certain."

"Tell me."

Alcandhor's dictatorial response made Zandhral raise his eyebrows. He wanted to smile at the paternal protection his cousin had for Tam, but kept his countenance solemn. "Ah, nay, my Thane. I will not pass on what is no more than conjecture. Let me do some judicious sleuthing first."

Alcandhor raked his good hand through his hair, his jaw muscles jumping. Sarinna put a hand on his arm. "Trust our Enaisi cousin, my brother."

After a grimace, the Thane finally lifted a hand. "Aye. Sleuth. Now. Go!"

Zandhral bowed then bounded up the stairs. First, the library. His prey was not there. Where then would that rascal go? Had an Elite duty arisen, causing Marcalan to hie off without saying word one? Nay, for he himself had been in the Elites' chamber. No news had arrived. He pondered what to do next when a stripling rose from a table and came over, bowing. "Elite Ranger Zandhral. You are close to the Thane and also that new girl Ranger, aye?"

"I am. And she not a 'girl Ranger' she is a Ranger, and Second at Table."

The boy gulped. "Aye, sir. I–I saw something—" The boy hesitated and twisted to gesture to the library. "Many of us did. Marcalan came in, and he and she had words. It almost seemed as if they argued. He ran out then she just stood there until the Thane came in."

As Zandhral thought. But he dared not let rumor take wings, so he smiled. "Aye. I believe Marcalan will think twice before pranking our Second at Table, enh?"

The stripling blinked, then grinned. "Ah. Aye, that makes sense."

Hopefully it did, and would forestall gossip. But where then did Marcalan go? Asking the stripling might cause too much curiosity—or perhaps not. "I have need of Marcalan for an Elite matter. Did you see which way he made his escape?"

"Nay. My apologies, sir."

Zandhral waved a hand. "It matters not. Back to your studies, lad."

He turned before the boy finished bowing and strode out, thinking. He reached out to sense, but he had not Tam's abilities, and if Marcalan were blocking, he could not find him if he hid two paces away.

Zandhral rubbed his temples. The city was enormous, and Marcalan amazingly clever. Where might the man be?

~*~

The rain mostly stopped, with just spates of drizzle now and again. The wind whipping droplets off leaves of the trees splattered Tam more than anything. But she cared not. She deadheaded and weeded. Between both the solitude and the familiar surroundings and smells of a garden, her mind found a little ease. But just a little. Worry for Marcalan intruded relentlessly.

A man wearing thick gloves and a cloak walked into the garden and stopped. "What are you doing here?" he exclaimed, his voice cracking.

Tam sat back on her heels, brushing her hair out of her face with the back of her hand. "Is it not plain?"

His face reddened slightly. "Aye, I see that. I meant, Rangers do not usually—have you no other duties?"

Tam shook her head. "I have free time, and I enjoy gardening."

"Ah. I tend the gardens. For the healers." He smiled slightly. "You have made my task easier."

"You do not mind?"

"Forbid! You are my new friend if you like weeding. 'Tis the one part of my duty I dislike the most."

Tam smiled. "Then I will finish this plot if you have others to tend."

"My thanks." He bowed and moved off.

Tam lifted her shoulders to ease a slight ache and reached out to sense for Marcalan. A tiny wisp of sadness taunted her, as if he grew weary and his block faltered, but nothing strong enough to give direction. *Marcalan, I need you!*

With determination, she continued gardening, even through afternooning, even through the time when she should have gone to lessons with Maradhor, only stopping when it became too dark to continue. She slipped back into the Great Hall, bathed and washed her clothes, and then descended for evening meal. Marcalan was not there. She kept sensing and could sometimes get a whisper of emotion. He was near enough, in the city, his blocking still spotty.

She ate quickly and returned to her chamber. She retrieved the necklet from its hiding place and sat cross-legged in front of the fire. Clasping the piece of jewelry to her chest, she wept.

~*~

Alcandhor spent the rest of the day with his children and did not see Tam until the evening meal. Sarinna, Taniss, and Zandhral all warned him to leave her be. She retired to her chamber as soon as the meal was over.

Alcandhor watched her walk up the stairs and beckoned for Zandhral.

The Elite approached, inclining his head. "I told Maradhor and Edhron both that she may not be at lessons this afternoon and evening. I did not want her chastised. I hope I was not out of turn, Thane."

"Nay, nay. Have you learned anything yet about what might be wrong?"

"Nothing definitive. But am I not an Elite? Give me a bit more time."

Alcandhor forced a smile.

"I do have other news for you though."

"Oh?"

"Has anyone given you news of Aleta?"

"She finally did her assigned tasks yesterday, I was told, albeit with a sullen attitude, knowing she would not eat if she did not participate. I cannot imagine her doing menial chores. I think she will not stay long under these conditions."

"You are wise. Aleta is leaving. A dray cart has been ordered for the morning."

"How has she paid for the dray?"

"She bartered jewelry for the hire of the dray cart, beast, and driver."

Alcandhor could not imagine the proud, haughty Aleta sitting on a bumping, rocking cart being pulled by the squat, ugly dray beast, her few possessions piled in the back. Except for substantial loads, folks usually hired a bonded travel-man, or two, for help—and protection, if needed. A dray was slower than walking, and harder on one's bones and body. But Aleta would not have gladly walked anywhere if she could help it.

And although she cared not for her own children, she would know that taking them would crush Alcandhor. "Has there been any talk of the children traveling with her?"

Zandhral shook his head.

"Have a Ranger shadow Jholinn and Amara tomorrow, and one for each of the boys. I would hope she would wish to say good-bye, but I will not allow her to try to steal them from their home."

"She was a cousin to Batrig and maintains ties with her clan, does she not? Might she ask that they give her aid to take the children?"

"She was a distant cousin to that traitor, aye, but neither he nor any of his clan cared for her, as her mother was a commoner. I doubt she has any coin she could draw on from them. And considering she has shown the maternal instincts of a fetil viper, I doubt she would even care to try, except as a way to cause me pain." Alcandhor met Zandhral's gaze. "If she had any feelings, any at all, I would have—" He shrugged, lifting his good arm, palm up. "'Tis done."

His cousin's eyes showed his understanding. Alcandhor nodded thanks and walked outside, pulling his hood up against the rain. Of all his worries as Thane, the two torturing his mind were not matters that would impact their world, but his own heart.

Would his children be heartbroken to find their mother had left the city? Between Taniss, Sarinna, and Jholinn they would try to mend those hurts, although considering the years of neglect, the emotional impact might not be too bad.

And what of Tam? Zandhral was one of Haladhon's Elites. If the man had any indication of what was troubling Tam, he must leave off and just trust his cousin to find proof.

Chapter Twenty-Six

"I know she was moved to my range to be under closer supervision, but Casinn is sullen and difficult to work with." Tilann, mistress of Family Range North, stared with expectation at Sarinna.

"If you feel she is unproductive or uncooperative, then dismiss her. It is not the first complaint against her."

Tilann sighed. "I'll give her warning."

Sarinna nodded but before she could move on, Tilann began a litany of complaints against other servants. Some were legitimate, but Sarinna knew Tilann well; the woman enjoying backbiting others. At this rate, she would be late for breakfast. She held up her hand to stop the woman's harangue. "Tilann, the servants in your range are your concern, and you have the authority to mete out discipline if necessary. Why bring it to my attention when it is your duty to handle it?"

Tilann sighed and pointed down the hall. "There is a perfect example." Tilann raised her voice. "Kallig, you missed that whole section above this tapestry." Tilann gestured to dust strings waving slightly from the ceiling. "I want you to go down this entire hallway again and dust thoroughly this time."

"Yes, mim," Kallig replied, extending the pole he carried as he walked to the end of the hall.

"See? He only works well if he is watched."

"I can see, but again, Tilann, this is your domain. Do as you see fit. Complaining to me does not solve the problem."

Tilann curtsied and stomped off. Sarinna let her breath out slowly, rolling her eyes as she continued on. She heard Zandhral call to her and she turned.

"May I have a word with you?"

Sarinna's smile faded at his grave face. "What is it, cousin?"

"It is Marcalan. I am worried something has happened."

"What has he done?"

"Done? Nothing. Not on purpose anyway. But he has not been to table since the day before yesterday, and I can discover no pranks he has pulled in that time. The few who have seen him report he looks pale, almost sick."

"Hm. Have you any thoughts on what is wrong?"

"Aye, but I would rather not say."

"Oh?" Sarinna's eyebrows arched with curiosity.

Zandhral lifted his hands. "If I can find him, could you speak to him? He may talk to you before he opens up to me."

Sarinna frowned. "*If* you find him?"

"I have not done so yet, but if any duty draws him, he will be in the Elites' chamber after breakfast to gather reports."

"*If* you find him, send him to me, and I will speak to him."

"I thank you." Zandhral bowed.

~*~

Zandhral let out a subtle breath of relief when Marcalan arrived in the Elites' chamber, but his cousin's haggard countenance and unkempt appearance astonished him. This was not like Marcalan, and it further worried Zandhral that his fears were not unfounded.

His cousin muddled through the updates with Zandhral again writing the report. Gardhal took it across the forechamber to the Thane's chamber, and Zandhral seized the opportunity.

"Marcalan, I would like talk to you in private."

"If we are through, I have to leave."

"Cousin, I wish to help—"

"Leave off, Zandhral!"

"If you will not talk to me, you will report to Sarinna."

"Sarinna? She cannot order me."

"Shall I tell her you refuse?"

Marcalan wilted. "Nay," he whispered.

~*~

Sarinna found her mind wandering, wondering about Zandhral's cryptic remarks, and about what could be wrong with Marcalan. With a shake of her head, Sarinna reviewed the accounts before her. She looked up at a noise. Marcalan sagged against the doorframe of the city's steward's chamber, his face drawn. She rose with a gasp. He had not shaved or combed his hair.

"You wished to see me, Sarinna?"

"Where have you been? And what is wrong with you? Have you been ill?" She walked around the table to him and touched a hand to his face to feel for a fever.

He backed up a step. "If I have not neglected my duties, then what does it matter where I have been elsewhile?"

"You have not been at table for two days."

"Aye?"

"What is your explanation?"

"Need I one? Is this all you wished to see me about, Sarinna? I need to go."

She stared hard at him, while trying to sense what he was feeling. He blocked but weakly. She got a sense of grief, but over what?

"Marcalan," she asked in a soft tone, "when was the last time you pulled a prank? Or jested for that matter?"

He shrugged. "May I go, Sarinna?"

"Only if you promise you will be at table this evening."

A burst of gnawing grief and deep agony hit her in the stomach and almost took her breath away.

"I cannot," he managed to say, looking down.

"Marcalan, what is the matter?" she begged, stepping forward to touch his arm.

He backed up again. "I have to go, Sarinna. Please." He grimaced and hurried away. Sarinna could not believe or understand what she had just seen. And felt. What was causing Marcalan such pain? She would ask Zandhral.

~*~

No more! Marcalan could not live with this anguish. If he were away from Zaidhron, perhaps he could find some perspective. But he needed to be honest with his Thane. Tell Alcandhor he loved Tam, that she had made a necklet, that he wished to be far away. Where he knew not. Just far away. Beshalon or Tathelon Province perhaps. Would they be far enough? Andethon to the southwest? Some Rangers roamed to the Great River, although he knew not if they dared cross it. Those few hardy enough or outlaw enough to need to hide lived across the Great River, or so it was said. Would that take him far enough to heal, and to forget Tam?

He knew not. Only that he must take the first step. He must talk to his Thane.

~*~

Alcandhor had trouble concentrating on the book before him. He tossed it aside and chose another—one found recently in that underground chamber Tam discovered. It was easier to understand, although written in one of the Enaisi's languages. The story told of how their people and the Enaisi worked to move the Teldheri to this world. He had never read this from the Enaisi's perspective before, and some points seemed to contradict history as his people knew it.

195

Marcalan walked in, and Alcandhor's mouth dropped open. His cousin was unshaven and disheveled with dark circles under his eyes.

"Thane..." He hesitated, shoulders hunched. He took a step, met Alcandhor's gaze, and took a deep breath. "Thane...I need to talk to you about something very serious."

If his rascal of a cousin did not look almost ill, he would have made light of that statement. Instead he nodded. "Say on."

"I...I love Tam."

Alcandhor stared at his cousin, unable to comprehend what he had just heard. "You what?"

"I love Tam. We had meant to keep it secret, but I cannot. I cannot keep something so important a secret from my Thane. She loves me. She wants to offer me a necklet. Of course, I could not accept—"

"What?" Alcandhor shot to his feet. "Nay! Never. Even if she were not too young, even if she did not have responsibilities to the clan, with your reputation, I will never allow it, Marcalan. You are as bad as Haladhon and know not what love is."

"Thane, my reputation is not what you think it is."

"I do not want to hear this, Marcalan. Do not try to tell me you have changed your ways."

"But Thane, I—"

"Stop. You have broken a trust, Marcalan."

"I have tried to *keep* trust by telling you, instead of keeping it secret, Thane. I love her. Truly. I do not say I would accept the necklet, not being—"

Alcandhor jabbed a finger at him. "Stop. I will not hear it. You do not go near her. You do not talk to her. You stay away from her. Is that understood?"

Marcalan's fists clenched and unclenched. He swallowed then replied, slowly, in a whisper, "Aye, Thane."

"I will assign you a bounds so far away that Zaidhron would be but a memory of your youth that you would never see again if you disobey me."

"But that is what I want, Thane. To be sent far away."

Alcandhor stopped as if punched. "You what?"

"I know I dare not love her. I have no right to—I just had to tell you. But I do want a bounds remote from here. Andethon, maybe. Near to the Great River."

Was the rascal playing him? Daring him to make good on his threat? He shook his head. "You have never wanted a bounds. And you are too valuable as an Elite."

"I need to be away, Thane." Marcalan leaned heavily on the table. "Send me away! Please."

Marcalan blocked so Alcandhor could not sense his cousin, but pain etched his face, and his haunted eyes begged. He considered his words carefully. "You have had a serious blow concerning your mother, and all the rest of this"—he waved a hand, not willing to name Tam or this infatuation outright—"has caused you much conflict. I can see that. Go rest, and eat. Attend your duties, and give yourself time to adjust."

"But Thane, I cannot stay—"

"Go, Ranger. Do as I bid."

Marcalan licked his lips, his shoulders sagging.

Alcandhor bent over the table, resting on his good hand, and stared at the wood. He did not look up and after a few seconds, footsteps padded away.

One thing on top of another. As if he did not have enough on his mind, Marcalan had to pull this? 'Twas not a prank. Marcalan was hurting, he felt it, but Alcandhor knew it was a mere infatuation at most and would soon pass. Marcalan was as bad as Haladhon, flitting from woman to woman like a nectar-bird going flower to flower. Did Marcalan truly think Alcandhor would allow him to play with Tam as he did other women? Alcandhor slammed a fist on the table. Hang the man!

~*~

Alcandhor eyed Tam with worry. She was subdued at luncheon. She barely spoke, and did not even smile. They rose from the meal, and he gestured for her to come over.

"What is wrong, Tam? Is it sight?"

She shook her head. "I have not seen Marcalan yet today, and he was not at table either. And he is blocking me."

Alcandhor considered what he should say. "Perhaps that is good. You have been spending quite a bit of time with him lately. You need to spend more time studying."

"Aye. I suppose you are right," she murmured.

She walked away, and Alcandhor rubbed his face with his hand. Stars! A lass having fifteen years infatuated with a rake having twenty-four? Perhaps he really should send Marcalan roaming until they both recovered their wits.

"We have a problem, brother."

Alcandhor blinked at his sister, trying to refocus his thoughts.

"Another one?"

"Marcalan has not been at table in over a day. I also have not found evidence that he has been sneaking food, which has me wondering what and where he is eating. He looks miserable and I cannot discover the reason. Also, I have had not word one from anyone complaining about Marcalan's pranks. He does not smile, nor jest, and when I tried to talk to him today I felt he was in great pain."

Alcandhor stifled a groan. Should he say on, let it go for now, or try to talk again with Marcalan? He took a deep breath. It would probably be a useless effort, but—

"Aye, I know the problem. Send him to me in my Thane's chamber."

"How, if I cannot find him?"

"Drum."

Sarinna raised a censuring eyebrow, shook her head, and left. Alcandhor resisted the urge to beat his head into the shimmerstone walls.

His children ran to him, eager for their study time with their father, so any skull-bashing must wait. He let himself be drawn into their joy, glad they seemed not much affected by their mother leaving the city.

By the time he reached his chamber, his mood lifted quite a bit.

Despite the drum message, Marcalan did not appear. Alcandhor kept waiting to hear a knock at his door but it did not come. It was not like that rascal to not give immediate answer to a summons. He called Feladhrel and asked him to find Zandhral, then, while the boys worked on ciphering, he read to Amara, from a child's version of the tales of the legendary, and probably mythical, Icandhir. One which gave only his earlier heroics, all with happy endings.

When Zandhral arrived, he merely told him to find Marcalan. Zandhral bowed with a knowing expression and left.

Alcandhor dismissed his children to ready for afternooning then searched for the prankster himself, ignoring the mealtime horns. No one knew where he was and most replied Zandhral had already asked after Marcalan. Alcandhor reiterated that if any Ranger found him, to tell him to report immediately to the Thane. Angry and frustrated—doubly that he missed afternooning, Alcandhor grabbed a bowl of soup from the Thane Hall kitchen then returned to the Thane's chamber to read while waiting for Marcalan to appear, leaving his door ajar.

Footsteps approached and Alcandhor looked up.

"You asked to see me, Thane?" Marcalan asked.

"Where the bloody Bells have you been?"

He shrugged. "Around."

"Around? I asked where you have been. We could not find you."

"I had no duties at the moment. There was no place I was required to be. I was...alone."

"Why were you not at table today?"

Marcalan shrugged again. Anger and worry waged war in Alcandhor over Marcalan's unusual behavior.

"I could not be there."

"What do you mean? Why?"

"Tam was there. I am not to see her or be near her."

"Bloody Bells! Are you sulking over that? Think you it will make me more compassionate about your infatuation?"

Marcalan's shoulders sagged, and he bowed his head. "I am merely trying to obey you, Thane." He took a ragged breath and looked up Alcandhor. "Give me a bounds. Far from here. Please."

Alcandhor sighed. "You know you do not mean it. You have always been happy on assignments. Roaming."

"I am in earnest, Thane. Please. I can leave today."

"Mar, there has to be more than you are telling me."

The cynical, hard expression made Marcalan seem a stranger. He shook his head.

Alcandhor sat back. What could be wrong with his cousin? Marcalan blocked, but poorly, as he was exhausted, so Alcandhor could feel a little. Only snatches of grief. Surely this could not just be about Tam? Nay. It must have to do with his parents—and Uardhel as well. He rose, walked around the table, and put a hand on Marcalan's shoulder.

"Come, cousin. Tell me. Have we not been close friends?"

Marcalan backed up a step, shaking Alcandhor's hand off. "I want a bounds, Thane. Give me it or give me an assignment to take me out of this city. Let me roam far if you will not give me bounds."

Lost, and beyond lost, Alcandhor shook his head. "I will give you nothing until I find out what is wrong."

Marcalan stared at the floor a moment, then turned and left, without ever looking up.

With a groan, Alcandhor rubbed his forehead.

Chapter Twenty-Seven

A sharp tattoo on Alcandhor's family suite door awoke him. He opened his eyes, squeezed them shut with a groan, then blinked, sitting up. It had better be the Ranger on night duty with an important message. "Aye?"

"Thane," a voice called, "a runner has arrived."

"News of the Rogues?"

"Aye. Serious, he says."

Alcandhor threw back his blanket and pulled on his clothes. "Where is he?"

"Early room."

"Thank you."

Good. Hot tea and soup or stew for the runner and for himself too, perhaps, if the news were not so dire that he must hie out of the city at once. Nay, if 'twere that serious, the news would be drummed.

"Papa?" Eladhor shuffled out of his chamber rubbing his eyes as Alcandhor stamped on his boots. Amara peeked out of her door, fingers in her mouth.

"'Tis fine. Just a runner with news. Go back to bed."

"Can I sleep in your bed?" Amara asked.

"Aye, Sweetling."

He swiftly tucked her in and kissed her nose, then rushed out and across the sward to the Great Hall. Tam, Andhrel, and Eladhrel waited already in the early room with the runner. Alcandhor recognized him. Tonalan, both a Ranger and a runner, one of their best. He was bundled in a blanket against the wet and chill, sipping something hot from a bowl. He started to rise, but Alcandhor waved at him to stay seated.

Tam poured tea and pushed it over to Alcandhor. Haladhon should be there, as both a chief of the clan and Chief of the Elites, but was still in the valley. Where was Marcalan? As Haladhon's Second, he should be present to represent him, no matter his personal problems. No time to consider that now. He sat and nodded to the runner.

"Tell me, Tonalan."

"The Rogues are definitely north of Lantral Province, Thane," said Tonalan. "I met scouts sent out to tell of your orders to hurry north as I came in. You were right to send them."

"What is the latest news of what they have done?"

"Supply drays have been raided, and they have stolen weapons too. Swords mostly. Herders in the western hills of Lantral have reported beasts missing. And we found one family slain. From what we could surmise, they woke as the Rogues raided their farm for food. They slaughtered them, Thane. Like animals. Even—" He paused, glancing at Tam. "I am not certain I should say on, Thane. 'Tis horrible."

Before Alcandhor could say anything, Tam spoke, her voice low and emotionless. "I am a Ranger Confirmed, and have seen the aftermath of Laird Hall besieged, and the hangings. I will hear this."

Tonalan still hesitated. Alcandhor nodded, dreading what he might hear. Was certain he would hear.

"The family that was murdered, Thane. It was not just murder." Tonalan looked down at his hands on the table, frowning.

Alcandhor's heavy stomach gave a sickening turn. *Nay. Please, nay.* "Tell me," he whispered.

"The mother and a lass almost grown were forced, Thane. They were raped. Then killed. And a young lad and baby were found murdered in their beds." He shuddered, but Alcandhor doubted it was from a chill.

Alcandhor slammed a fist on the table. He had suspected that was their news, but had hoped he was wrong. Monadhal and his men, being condemned, had been not only branded as outlaw but cut off, and rape had never been a part of their atrocities. Nandhal, however—he thought of Kalinna. Not only raped but mind-raped. Had Nandhal done what Uardhel did, then murdered them after? And a child and baby slaughtered— Alcandhor ground his teeth, swallowing the bile that rose in his throat. He would have that by-blow now!

"Monadhal has murdered before, but never a slaughter as thus," Eladhrel murmured, his face pale.

"Nandhal is almost certainly with them. We must catch these Rogues. I will not let it be put off for any other matter. It is our first duty until every one of these outlaws is captured." He stood and hissed through gritted teeth. "We will meet in the Elites' chamber to make our plans. Now."

The chiefs descended on the Elites' chamber and lit the sconces. They gathered around the large table map. Tonalan joined them to update the information plotted.

"By these dates and rates of movement, they are definitely in the north of Lantral now," Andhrel stated. "If they continue thus, they will be close enough to sniff out."

"But why?" Eladhrel asked.

"It would not be wise for them to stay there very long. But it is advantageous for us. This close to home we have that many more Rangers to draw from at shorter notice, plus the ones we have ordered to head north," the Thane replied. "If we can draw them into our net, we will have them."

"I do not like it," Tam whispered.

"What, Tam?" Alcandhor asked.

"I do not like them coming so close to here. It makes me...uncomfortable."

Alcandhor peered at her, startled to realize how pale she was. "Is that just a feeling, or something more?"

"I know not, Thane. I just know I do not like it. It gives me a very..." She stopped and shook her head. "I know not the word. It is like a fear. This is very wrong."

Alcandhor put a hand over hers. "You are sensing something. A premonition? Are you seeing anything?"

"Nay. I do not think so, anyway. I am sorry I do not know more about how to use these abilities, Uncle."

"Do not apologize, Tam. If you do see, or even think you see, or have another strong feeling about this, let me know at once." He gazed around at the chiefs and Tonalan. "You men be doubly on guard. When a Child of the Enaisi has a premonitory feeling, it had best be heeded."

"Aye, Thane," they murmured, staring at Tam.

"Put orders out for the Rangers to be ready to leave at a drum call. Warn them, too, of Tam's foreboding. Drum out messages in the new code, telling the companies of Rangers on the east of the mountains to continue to head north. We shall leave as soon as we receive confirmation of those drum messages."

"'We?' Now wait, Thane, you should not go," Andhrel said.

Alcandhor lifted his hand. "I will not be at the forefront of the attack, but I will go. Eladhrel, see to it a drum message is sent to the valley for Haladhon to return."

The men all murmured assent and left, although Andhrel glanced back over his shoulder with a disapproving glare. Tam looked up at her uncle wide-eyed. In a choked voice, she said, "Something bad is going to happen. Perhaps you should not go."

Alcandhor put a hand on Tam's shoulder. "I will be protected, Tam, and your sight may have nothing to do with any danger to me. All we can do is try to be careful. You have given us warning. Perhaps that will make some difference. Perhaps later you will see something more. We can only do so much."

"I am sorry I do not know what is going to happen, Uncle."

"You cannot force prescience, Tam. It happens. Let us not dwell on it. Now go, prepare your gear."

Alcandhor lingered alone in the Elites' chamber, rubbing his aching shoulder, staring at the map, willing it to tell him more.

~*~

The expected counter accusation arrived from the valley, distracting Alcandhor from the Rogues. Aggrieved, he ordered a writ drawn up for each family for eviction. Rangers whose bounds protected that shire of the valley would deliver the orders. Hang those two families!

Feladhrel helped to rewrite and order the reports that morning, and he and Tam both appeared subdued, likely by the seriousness of the eviction notices. When the stripling left, his arms filled with papers, Tam rose from her chair to stand in front of his table, twisting her hands together. "Uncle? I need to speak to you. It is about Marcalan. I cannot find him."

Not again! "Tam... leave him be. He is around somewhere."

"He is not. I could not find him for two days but he was here, somewhere. I know because he was blocking me—not well, because at times I could feel him a little but not enough to find him. But now he is gone. He has not been here since yesterday evening. I thought perhaps he had been given assignment to roam, but he is not on the roster of those sent out."

"Why are you so concerned about where that vagabond is?"

Tam straightened her shoulders and set her chin. "Because I love him."

Alcandhor groaned. "Must I go through this with you as well? Tam, he is a rake. He knows not what love is. I know he is a personable man, but he is wanting in what would make him a good husband."

"You are wrong."

"Am I?" He looked at her in amusement. "And how are you so sure?"

"Because I can sense. And I have sensed him. He is not what you say he is. And he does love me."

Alcandhor sighed. "Tam, would you know the difference between love and desire?"

"Aye, Uncle. I do know the difference."

"Oh? Then please, tell me."

"I have felt many men desire me. What they feel is not what I feel from Marcalan."

Alcandhor combed his hands through his long hair, then let it fall down his back. "I am going to get Taniss. Nay, Sarinna is closer. Perhaps she can talk sense to you. You stay here."

~*~

Alcandhor returned with Sarinna to find Tam sitting in a chair, her eyes red, with Haladhon and Zandhral sitting on each side of her.

"What are you doing here, Haladhon?"

"Ah, good to see you too, my Thane! My daughters are well, although Panill is still grieving her mother's death greatly, as is her father, thank you. And I arrive to find the city in an uproar about Rogues and more importantly, all a-chatter of Marcalan hiding and wondering what he has done now."

Through gritted teeth, he said, "I meant, what are you doing in my chamber at this time."

"I came to see you and found Tam here alone. She seemed to need a friend, so I stayed."

"I need to talk to Tam with Sarinna. You two may leave."

Haladhon shook his head. "I have an interest in this. I am staying."

"As am I," Zandhral said.

"What interest would either of you have in this?"

Haladhon glanced over at Sarinna for a moment and it seemed to Alcandhor that a fleeting grimace of pain crossed his face. Haladhon looked down at Tam, and put an arm around her shoulders, a determined look on his face. "Marcalan is one of my closest friends and I wish to take his part since he is not here."

"This is not a trial, Haladhon."

"Is it not?" Haladhon's voice mocked.

"This is a personal matter between my niece and me."

"This is a family matter, and I am staying to take Marcalan's part."

Alcandhor pressed his lips together then turned to the other Ranger. "And you? What part have you in this?"

"I have suspected their romance for some time, and—"

"You knew and did not come to me?"

"I was not certain, Thane. Would you wish me to spread gossip?"

"Stars, how many know of this then?"

"None but us, I would say," Zandhral said. "I doubt Haladhon nor Sarinna knew until now."

Sarinna nodded. "Aye, I suspected nothing."

"I had some early sign." Haladhon shrugged. "But nothing seemed to grow between them that was untoward, so I merely watched."

Alcandhor rounded on Zandhral again. "But you did know. You could have said something. Given me some—"

Haladhon pointed his finger. "I tried to warn you that some Ranger would soon catch her eye. Do not say you were blindsided!"

Alcandhor threw his good hand up in defeat. "So I should just give in to this infatuation?"

"'Tis not an infatuation!" Tam's voice rose shrill, her fists in her lap.

"Watch your tone!" Alcandhor shot back.

Sarinna stepped in front of him, lips thinned.

"Thane," Zandhral said, "she is correct. 'Tis not an infatuation."

"How could you know what it is, Ranger? Are you suddenly so wise about matters of the heart?"

"Nay, but I am wise in matters of those with Enaisi blood. And with an uncle who is feeling fatherhood too seriously, I had to take matters to myself to watch over them." Zandhral grimaced. "Not that I did very well in that task."

"Zandhral—"

Sarinna put her hand on Alcandhor's arm. "Leave off, Alcandhor. Let him talk."

Alcandhor glared at Sarinna for a few moments then threw his hand up. "Say on, then."

"Marcalan truly loves Tam, and she, him."

Alcandhor rolled his eyes. "And you know this?"

"Aye. I have felt it. And forget you that she would be able to sense and know whether he did?"

"She does not know the difference between love and passion. She is but a child."

Tam's back straightened. "I am not—"

Haladhon lifted a hand. "Tam. Allow me to say on. To take Marcalan's part." He crossed his arms. "She is not a child. And I think she does know."

"If he feels anything for her, it is but passion, and I will not have my niece dallied with by a rake."

Tam opened her mouth, her eyes dark. Haladhon raised his arm before her, palm down. "Tam, my words will mean more than yours. Be still."

"But—"

"You need to listen to me, girl." Haladhon nodded at Alcandhor. "As does he. For all three of your sakes."

Tears welled in Tam's eyes again, and her chin trembled. She nodded at her cousin. He inclined his head to her then leaned forward, elbows on his knees, to stare at Alcandhor, his green-grey eyes intent. "He is not a rake, Alcandhor."

"And neither are you, Haladhon?" Alcandhor's voice was heavy with sarcasm.

"He is not. It was a deception. I warned him he might regret it one day."

"What in bloody Bells are you talking about?"

"Watch your temper and your mouth, Alcandhor," Sarinna ordered.

Alcandhor glared at her, but hip-sat on the edge of the table and regarded Haladhon, his good arm folded over his other in the sling. "So. Explain."

"When he was young he wanted to be like me, so he began making up exploits. It got out of control, and before he knew it he had a reputation like mine. I found out about it and warned him he might have trouble making people believe he was able to make a commitment with his reputation, but he did not listen. At the time, he had no interest in marriage."

"You are trying to tell me he is not the libertine everyone thinks he is?"

Haladhon slid forward to the edge of his seat, and despite the seriousness of his reply, his eyes twinkled as he answered. "Alcandhor, I have seen him blush at serving girls who were trying to flirt with him and make excuses why he would not pursue them. I finally got the truth out of him. He said his failing was that he was too much like you to chase skirts."

Sarinna snickered into her hand, and the Thane found himself blushing. Stars.

"So, my dear cousin, if Marcalan says he loves her, and she says he loves her, then I would believe them."

Tam sighed with a grateful glance at Haladhon, then turned her large, pleading eyes to Alcandhor.

How could he have been so fooled all these years? Should he not have felt something amiss from Marcalan if it were a deception? But then, Alcandhor blocked most of the time. Until recently.

True, he had done all he could to turn a blind eye to Marcalan in that area, because if he became aware of anything inappropriate, he would be forced to call Question. He loved Marcalan too much for that. And twice Rangers had attempted to call Question on Marcalan because of reputation, yet nothing became of it. No proof was found. Yet Alcandhor remained oblivious, never checked into it, afraid of what he would find, secretly glad, thinking Marcalan had learned enough discretion from Haladhon to keep that jerkin on his back.

Hang the man! Why did he perpetuate such a thing? How could he not realize the harm it would do? His anger melted into joy that his mischievous cousin was not guilty of breaking laws of both clan and Maker.

What had he felt from the rascal since his meeting Tam? Gaiety—naturally, affection for Tam, but, nothing untoward. Aye, that was why he missed what was happening between them. He waited for Marcalan to behave unseemly and he had not.

He exhaled, and ran his fingers through his hair, then with

deliberation, turned his gaze to Tam, frowning. "You are still too young, you know."

"There are girls my age married in Zaidhron."

"True but not many. And they are not you, Tam. You are too young."

She stood up, her hands in fists at her sides, eyes narrowed. "If I am old enough to go on missions, and old enough to kill, then I am old enough to marry."

"Alcandhor," Sarinna murmured. "They are both Rangers. Who knows what time they might have together? Do not take it away from them."

Alcandhor pushed up from his table, groaning. He walked to the window and looked out. Shafts of sunlight broke through clouds, illuminating the gardens and trees of the grounds. "She is so young. And she needs to study and prepare..."

"What effort are you going to get out of her if she is pining for him? Answer me that, Thane."

Alcandhor turned to look at his cousin, a slight smile at the corners of his mouth. "And what would you know of pining, you vagabond?"

Haladhon put a hand over his heart. "I pine for every woman I see."

Alcandhor smiled then. A real smile, but it faded quickly.

"Thane," Zandhral said. "'Tis not just pining."

With a frown, Alcandhor opened his mouth to ask what he meant, but Tam rushed to him and put a hand on his arm, her golden eyes imploring. "Uncle? Will you let me give him my necklet?"

"You were serious that you already made one?"

"Aye." Tam fumbled reaching into the pouch on her jerkin's beltband and pulled out a necklet. "And I will give it to Marcalan one day. Now, if you let me, or later, if you do not. It does not matter much if you say nay, because he will wear it one day. And besides, we have one thing you cannot take from us and that is our connection."

Alcandhor straightened. "Your connection?"

"That is what we call it. Unless we are blocking, we are connected somehow, sensing each other's emotions all the time, even while asleep."

Shock jolted through Alcandhor. "You what?" he asked in a low voice, grabbing her shoulder. She cringed and he let go, as if his hand burned, feeling her fear. He could never strike her or harm her! Why would she think he would? He held his hand out, palm up, in a gesture of peace. "Tam, I would not hurt you."

Fear, sorrow, loneliness, grief... Alcandhor felt all these from Tam and stepped forward to try to embrace her, but she pulled away, fresh tears spilling down her cheeks.

He backed away, a memory of Aleta pulling away from him going through his mind. What was wrong with him? What was it about him that somehow caused those he loved to pull away? He gave Aleta everything she wanted but she pulled away. He certainly was not doing that with Tam—he was denying her what she wanted, and she was pulling away.

It surely did not take long for him to destroy any chance of a relationship with a woman on any level, whether it be wife or niece. He wondered if Amara would pull away from him some day too. But nay—he had to concentrate on this problem, not himself. He took a deep breath, and tried to find words. "Tam, I need to know about this connection. What you describe is called bonding by the Enaisi."

"*That* is what I was keeping eye on, Thane," Zandhral said. "I could not be certain they had bonded, so I tried to keep close to hand to sense them."

Tam turned to him, mouth open. "So that is why you have been around me so much!"

Alcandhor waved his hand. "But this makes no sense. Bonding can happen only between two empaths when—" He broke off, feeling his face grow warm, then asked, "When did it begin?"

"Remember the day we discovered he could make a key glow? It was that night when we were all playing kingsmen. He and I were sending to each other, as a game, and it just continued on its own."

"But that makes no sense." Alcandhor ran his hands through his hair in frustration. "There must be more than a few sent emotions to begin a marriage bond."

"Try not to make sense of things of the Enaisi, Alcandhor," Sarinna said. "If it has happened, it has happened. If they are bonded, you cannot keep them apart. They will go mad."

Alcandhor's heart froze in fear. He whirled to meet Sarinna's wide-eyed gaze. "Great stars!"

His sister's hands flew to her mouth, and Zandhral rose, face white.

Alcandhor spun back around to face Tam. "You say you can sense he is not in this city?"

"Nay, he is not here."

"Where is he?" Alcandhor took her by the shoulders. "Can you sense where he is?"

"He is far away."

Alcandhor straightened. "Haladhon, have a message drummed out for Marcalan to return to Zaidhron. Sarinna, prepare journey rations. Tam, how fast can you be ready to leave?"

"Now!" she exclaimed, her eyes wide.

"How many are going?" Haladhon asked.

"I know you will want to go, but get that message drummed out—now. And aye, Zandhral as well. Meet me at the gate as soon as you are ready."

"We have the Rogues to worry about, Thane," Haladhon said, "and we know not his direction."

Alcandhor jammed his hand in his hair. "Choose a half dozen Rangers to accompany us. Now. Go."

~*~

Marcalan heard the drum message and stopped. Return? The Thane wanted him to return? How could he? He did not want to see her, be near her. He could not bear it. He dare not go forward when summoned to return, but he could not bring himself to turn around.

He wavered then continued on, his heart torn and broken, not stopping until long after dark to make camp.

Chapter Twenty-Eight

"Be you certain he went in this direction, Tam?" Haladhon huffed as they all ran.

South. Why south, Marcalan? 'Tis where the Rogues are! Tam wanted to cry or rage but dared not take energy away from their pursuit. "Aye," she panted, not slowing. "I can sense where he is. He is blocking but not well. He is in much pain."

They continued at a steady pace in the light of the moons.

Haladhon reached an arm out when Alcandhor stumbled. "I am fine. Keep on," the Thane ordered. "We must find him. I will never forgive myself for allowing this to happen."

"You cannot blame yourself, Uncle."

"Can I not? Haladhon warned me. I refused to listen. I did not want you to—never mind. It is useless to talk of it and talk slows us down. Keep on."

Tam hopped over a fallen branch. "We have Rangers roaming thickly, searching for the Rogues. Certainly they will cross Marcalan's path and stop him, will they not?"

"If he claimed he was on duty, they would not stop him."

"But we have drummed for him to return."

"If the Rangers knew him, they would hold him once we drummed, aye," Haladhon answered. "But this is Marcalan, and he is a Trained Elite. And can sense. If anyone could pass by Rangers unnoticed, I would wager it would be him."

But can he pass by the Rogues unnoticed as well?

~*~

A foot prodded Marcalan awake and rolled him over onto his back. He did not bother to try to draw his sword. In the embers of his fire he saw a familiar face: Monadhal. So these were the Rogues.

The chief of these outlaws had his sword pointed at Marcalan, and the others had their bows drawn.

"Monadhal? What do you want?"

"You did not answer the summons, *Ranger.* Why?" Monadhal emphasized the word with rancor in his voice.

Marcalan groaned and tried to roll back over to his stomach to go back to sleep, but a blade in his ribs stopped him. He looked over and saw Nandhal squatting next to him. He squinted, mumbling, "Nandhal? What are you doing here?"

"You first, dear cousin," Nandhal sneered, his hatred for Marcalan radiating from him. "What are you doing in the wild alone and not answering a summons?"

"What I was doing was trying to sleep."

"And why do you not answer the summons?"

"That is my business."

"What think you?" Monadhal asked Nandhal.

"I know not. He has been Thane's pet for years, and was Saldhor's, too. Getting away with wild behavior and pranks and never punished. Perhaps he went too far."

"What say you, Marcalan?" Monadhal hunkered down. "Did you go too far?"

Marcalan snorted. "You could say that."

The Rogues all looked at each other. Marcalan sighed, his eyes all but closing on their own. "If you are going to kill me, do so. Please. If not, I want to sleep."

"I think we will share your camp, Ranger."

"I care not." Marcalan rolled over, burying his face in his arms.

"He looks unkempt and unfit, Monadhal. I saw him less than a lunation ago at Lairdton's Ranger Hold and all was well then."

"We will get answers in the morning. Keep watch on him."

~*~

Nandhal watched and sensed Marcalan as the Ranger woke. Marcalan's hand strayed to his knife sheath, then he sighed. He slowly sat up, glancing around, the ache in him matching the dull look in his eyes. He hunched over in gut-slashing agony, rocking, his eyes squeezed shut.

Gritting his teeth, Nandhal rose and walked over to Monadhal, never taking his gaze from Marcalan. "Whatever is wrong, he is in great pain. I feel it."

Monadhal glanced over at the Ranger then quickly away. "What kind of pain?"

"He is grieving deeply. Perhaps someone he loved died. I know not. But there is a physical pain as well. I felt the intensity and saw him almost double over from it."

"Perhaps he was wounded and does not wish us to know of it?"

"I know not."

"Stay near, and be alert."

Monadhal walked over and sat down next to Marcalan, but the Ranger did not move or look up to acknowledge it. Nandhal knelt next to them.

"Give me a reason to let you live, Ranger."

"I have done naught against you nor have the desire to. I wish to be left in peace. I know you will not do so, though. So have it done. I care not."

"Why? You did not try to draw your sword or knife on us last night and have sat this morning as if nothing mattered. What makes nothing matter to a Ranger?"

Marcalan grimaced, and Nandhal again fought against the stabbing pain that accosted him from his hated cousin.

"What is causing your pain, Ranger? Is it hunger? You have very little food with you. We checked your pack. Why do you not eat?"

"That is my business."

Monadhal pulled out his knife and, leaning forward, speared some meat from a pan by the side of the fire. He held it out to Marcalan. "Eat, Ranger."

Marcalan turned his head away.

"It is not poisoned. See?" Monadhal bit a piece off the meat and chewed. He held it out again.

"I am not hungry."

Monadhal eyed him, then put the rest of the meat in his mouth and chewed with deliberate slowness. After swallowing, he asked, "Why did you not obey the summons? They have been drumming the message since yesterday afternoon yet you did not turn back."

"That is my business."

"Know you if you disobey the Thane you will be censured or even disowned?"

Marcalan shook his head, both laughing and crying. The pain inside Nandhal sharpened. Monadhal pulled Marcalan's head up by his hair. The Ranger did not even fight him. Tears streamed down his face. Nandhal was tempted to block to stop the anguish he was experiencing, but he might learn something by continuing to sense his cousin.

"You really would not try to stop me if I wanted to kill you right now, would you?" Monadhal brandished his knife at the Ranger's throat.

"Do it."

Monadhal let go of Marcalan's hair and sheathed the blade.

"If we let you go, Ranger, what would you do?"

Marcalan shrugged. "Go to the high mountains to the west, perhaps, and then beyond. Go as far from Zaidhron as I can so they cannot find me."

"With no food? Even if you are a good hunter there is little to snare or shoot in the high western mountains. The northern passes are said to be covered with snow already at this time of year. You will find it is slow going if you get far at all. And if you journey south through Keladar to Andethon, you risk being found."

"I care not. Not how far I go, nor whether I live."

"You tax my patience, Ranger."

"I care not. You are a fool to let a Ranger live. Kill me."

"I would do no favor to a Ranger, so I will not kill you. Yet. But you will come with us until I discover what it is I would do with you. Perhaps use you as sport. What say you to that, Ranger?"

"I care not."

Monadhal rose in a smooth motion and stepped away from Marcalan. He jerked his head, and Nandhal came close.

"Well?" Monadhal hissed.

"He truly does not care. Whatever has happened to him, he cares not if he lives. He wishes to die."

Monadhal curled his lip in a malignant smile. "Perhaps we can make him care. I am certain we can accommodate his wish." His eyes glinted. "Eventually. But for now, get him up so we can go."

Two Rogues hauled Marcalan up by his hair and held him while Nandhal bound his arms behind his back. Nandhal was rough, jerking and snatching on Marcalan's arms, and pulling the rope tight. Curse him, he wanted Marcalan to react to the pain he inflicted, to groan, or cry out, but Marcalan remained silent.

Marcalan plodded with them, head down. At times, he lagged and a man on each side would grab an arm and drag him along. Finally, they stopped by a stream. Nandhal put a hand in his back and shoved Marcalan off balance. He fell like a grain sack and lay still on his face.

"He is slowing us down, Monadhal," Nandhal said. "Kill him now. Or let me."

"You are too quick with that blade. I want answers from him first. Why he disobeyed a summons and ran. Why he cares not if he lives. We may discover something to our advantage."

"Then let us do it now and be rid of him. He did not return when summoned, and they will first assume he is injured, ill, or otherwise unable to return before they assume he has disobeyed. That means they will search."

"You think I know this not?"

"Then why do we continue to drag him along when it slows us down knowing they could be on our trail?"

"He is right," a hoarse voice said.

They turned to Marcalan. He licked his dry, swollen lips. "Kill me now. Scatter and regroup later. It is your only chance."

"I have eluded Rangers for years," snorted Monadhal. "I know more about tracking than any twenty of you self-righteous clan-lovers."

Nandhal crossed his arms. "So what are you going to do?"

Monadhal eyed Marcalan, a sinister gleam in his eye. "He wants to die too badly. We will make him wait. Tonight we will find out what we can from him and make him wish he had died quickly."

"You enjoy inflicting pain too much, Monadhal."

Monadhal's icy blue eyes glinted to match his cold smile. "We all have our little vices. Do we not?"

~*~

Agony bent Tam double, tears streaming down her face. Her uncle and cousins knelt over her.

"He is hurting," she cried.

"He had a good head start on us," Haladhon said later. "Think you we can catch up today?"

"I know not," muttered Alcandhor.

"We must," Tam exclaimed. "He is suffering."

"I know, Tam," her uncle replied.

"You do not understand, Uncle. I feel real pain. He is too weak to block all the time, and I can feel pain in his body."

"What sort of pain? Can you tell, Tam?" asked Haladhon.

"He is hungry and thirsty and his arms and shoulders are burning as if wrenched in a grappling match. I am afraid."

"Think you Rogues—"

Alcandhor chopped his hand. "Shu!"

"I think he is right," Tam gasped. "I think someone is hurting him."

Late that afternoon, a company of Rangers crossed their path. Alcandhor told them no details, merely that they searched for Marcalan, fearing his capture by Rogues. The Rangers joined them, swelling their ranks.

They did not stop when night fell; the light of the moons shining through the bare arms of the trees illuminating their way.

~*~

Marcalan stumbled along, weak from lack of food and water, and at times they had to drag him. His arms and shoulders throbbed with fire, but he did not care. They called a halt to make camp and when the two Rogues let go of Marcalan, he fell to his knees. Again, a hand shoved him and he fell full forward, knocking the wind out of him and jarring him to his bones. He laid still. He wished he could sleep and not dream. Sleep and never wake up...

A sharp pain in his side brought him to consciousness. He was kicked several more times then dragged by his hair. They had started. When they were through he would be dead. He was glad it was almost over.

Tam. Sweet, beautiful Tam. He saw her face in his mind and felt the pain start again. How could love be so strong and hurt so much? He wanted to cry, but the Rogues would think it was from their beating, and he would not give them that satisfaction.

"Why did you disobey, Ranger?" asked Monadhal. "Why were you running from Zaidhron when you should have been returning?"

Marcalan did not answer. He could not have if he wanted to, lack of water parched his mouth, and he could not find his voice. But he would never talk if he could. How could he ever tell of his torment?

"Did you finally do something that Alcandhor could not laugh off? Is that it?" Nandhal knelt, bending close, his face so near that Marcalan could feel his Rogue cousin's warm breath on his skin. "What did you do? What made you run?" He kept staring at Marcalan then with a sneer he whispered, "It was the wench, was it not? Did you make her one of your prizes? Did her dear uncle find out?"

Marcalan squeezed his eyes shut and concentrated on the pain. Nandhal laughed.

"What did Alcandhor do, Marcalan? Or did you leave before he got to you? Is that why they were drumming for you to return? Is that why you refused the summons?"

He drew back, rose, and stood still for a few moments, then kicked Marcalan again. Dropping back to his knees and drawing his dagger, he cried, "Curse you, you in-bred clan-lover!" as he slashed at Marcalan's jerkin over and over.

Fire tore across Marcalan's chest as Nandhal's dagger sliced through his jerkin and skin. Nandhal sat up, his breath in heavy gasps, then pulled Marcalan's head back by the hair. "Feel something, curse you!" Nandhal's knife pressed against his throat. "Does nothing make you feel, you simpering clan-lover? Talk, you randy cockerel! Crow of your exploits now! Brag of your pranks!"

"Leave off, Nandhal," Monadhal said in a bored voice. "I want answers first. Then we will have sport. Untie him."

Marcalan was shoved onto his stomach. The cool blade made contact with Marcalan's skin as Nandhal cut the rope, and blood trickled down his arms. He did not try to move.

"Give me answers, Ranger, and you will die easier," Monadhal promised.

Marcalan stared into the dark. *Kill me. Kill me.*

Hands grabbed him and threw over onto his back.

"Answers, Ranger!" ordered Monadhal, flourishing his dagger.

Death was getting closer. He closed his eyes in relief.

"Curse you! Why do you smile?"

A fist smashed into his face, then again and again. He felt himself being pulled up by his jerkin, then dropped back onto the ground, knocking the wind out of him once more. Pain in his sides, his arms, his back, his head, his legs, his groin as he was kicked repeatedly. He slid into blessed blackness.

Chapter Twenty-Nine

Agony pummeled Tam, and she cried out, dropping to the ground, gasping.

"Tam?" Alcandhor fell to his knees, his arm wrapping around her. "Tam, did you injure yourself?"

"Marcalan!" Tears streamed down her cheeks despite her efforts. "He is in pain all over. I feel his pain!"

"Stars! Can you get up, Tam?" Haladhon asked in a soft, worried tone.

The pain eased, and she managed to rise. "I will try." She ran, keeping up with the men, but then a fire slashed over and over her and a smashing as of hard blows rained over her. She crumpled again, groaning. "I cannot block else I will not know where he is, but I cannot run with this pain!"

Haladhon scooped her into his arms and carried her with seemingly no effort as he ran. A warning cry arose not far in front of them, and Haladhon set Tam on her feet. She struggled to draw her sword as her kin did. She blocked Marcalan and sought to clear her head so she could fight.

Wait—this was not a match, and no rules limited her. She sent an onslaught of pain to her opponent, then struck him down as it incapacitated him. She did the same to the next. And the next. She swung about, but no more enemies stood. The Rangers had fought alongside her, and none of the Rogues survived.

Tam turned to see Marcalan lying on the ground, face down, arms flung over his head. She dropped her sword in horror, afraid to move.

"Stars, 'Candhor," Haladhon groaned as he and Alcandhor approached the body. "Oh, Marcalan." He knelt by his cousin, and with great gentleness rolled him over. His face was swollen and covered with blood. His eyes stared blankly at the sky.

Tam crumpled on the ground by him, touching his face. She could feel no pain from Marcalan, nothing at all. She collapsed on him, sobbing.

"Tam, let us see to him," her uncle murmured.

Hands pulled at her shoulders, and she pushed up from him, trying to control her tears. Her uncle and Haladhon bent over him, Alcandhor putting his ear to Marcalan's chest. He pushed up and exchanged glances with Haladhon, shaking his head.

"What is wrong, Uncle?"

"He is..." Alcandhor's voice broke and turned his head away.

"You are not saying he is dying, are you?"

"'Tis too late. I am sorry, Tam."

Hysteria rose in Tam. "Nay! Help me! Please, he cannot die! Please, help!" Screams ripped from her throat, fists clenched on her thighs, her face hot as if the skin itself would burst, and her throat raw. She fell across Marcalan, her soul riven.

Mattan's presence flooded to her, and she could somehow see his worried face. "Peace, Tam. I will help." He sent to her—nay through her. Marcalan breathed, his torment spiking through Tam, but then, it eased. Somehow Mattan not only felt Marcalan's pain—but was taking it away. Taking away his injuries. She relaxed, feeling the flow through her to Marcalan from Mattan.

She felt her uncle stroking her hair from her face, but she did not move, did not open her eyes. Marcalan's worst wounds, those on the inside, slowly healed and his pain alleviated, and she concentrated on that.

Tam knew not how long she stayed like that, just lying motionless on Marcalan, but finally after a long time, Mattan smiled at her, exhausted.

"I have helped the worst of his injuries, Tam. I need to rest. He should recover now. Tend your husband well."

"Thank you. Thank you," Tam murmured, falling into a dreamless sleep.

~*~

Nandhal stumbled through the dark, away from the sounds of the fighting. He thought he heard the sounds of pursuit and kept running until he could run no more. He stopped, hands on is knees, panting, and sensed for anyone behind him but felt nothing. Stars, but was that close!

Had Monadhal gotten away too? The others did not, he was sure. He would not have escaped if it had not been for his ability to sense; he had felt the Rangers approach. He had warned Monadhal, but they had run off in different directions.

He would circle around, making sure he was not being tracked before heading back to their base camp, which is probably where Monadhal would go as well. If he did not find Monadhal, it mattered not. He could pick up food there before deciding what to do next.

He gulped a few breaths, then continued on.

~*~

Alcandhor sat, twisting his sling in his hands. Tam lay over Marcalan's corpse as motionless as if dead herself. Guilt and grief warred for dominance. He had caused this catastrophe. How could he live with himself, or look his precious niece in the face again?

Rangers moved about beyond the fire. A larger fire had been built for cooking. Some of the men were digging. Two lifted a body. Alcandhor could not make himself stir to even call any orders to them, but one did come over to say they had identified all the bodies and found neither Monadhal nor Nandhal.

Alcandhor did not respond.

The sky grew a light grey, and birds began singing. Alcandhor wanted to rage at them for daring to offer their cheerful morning songs. Silence, or a dirge, would suit. His sight blurred again, but he did not bother to wipe the wetness off his face.

Tam shifted and pushed up onto her hands, her hair covering her face. She took a deep breath and sat up, pushing her hair back. Alcandhor started—her eyes! The whites now were blood red. Her screams must have burst vessels in her eyes.

She stumbled to her feet, gazing about her, looking lost.

"Tam, what are you doing?" Haladhon rose and took her by the shoulders. "Come back to the fire."

"He still has some pain. I need to find herbs."

Haladhon moaned and pulled her into an embrace. "Tam, stop."

"Nay. He needs something for the pain. Know you what panvarin looks like?"

"Tam—"

"Think you we can make something to carry him?" She clutched at Haladhon's sleeves.

Alcandhor could not bear to watch. He dropped his head and stared at the grass between his boots.

"Tam, nay. Stop," Haladhon murmured.

"You do not understand!" Tam's voice rose in pitch. "Oh, how could you? You do not know! He is going to be all right, Haladhon! Mattan helped him. He was very tired and said he had to rest, but he said he healed the worst of Marcalan's injuries. But we still must care for him."

Alcandhor shot to his feet. "Tam, you are overwrought. Come to the fire and rest." He took her by the arm.

"Uncle. Mattan healed him. Sense him! He came to me when I was crying and—"

"Nay, Tam," he murmured, shaking his head.

Tam stomped a foot. "Sense him! Sense Marc—" She straightened, lifting her chin. "Sense my *husband*. That is what Mattan called him. Sense him!"

He searched her reddened eyes, then turned to Marcalan. The man indeed breathed! His cousin was truly alive? He wheeled to Tam and pulled her tight. "How?"

"I know not how, but I could feel Mattan going through me to heal him. He is not well, but he is not dying. We need to care for him and get him home."

"Then gather what you need," Alcandhor ordered. "Recruit any of the Rangers which have knowledge of herb lore to assist you. We will heat water to wash his wounds."

Frenzied activity replaced the funereal atmosphere as Rangers rushed to help. Some searched for pots among the Rogues' leavings, and ran to fill them from the nearby little stream that wound down from the mountains through the forest. Others asked what herbs Tam wanted.

"Ch'illeya and panvarin if you can find it. Or loestis."

Haladhon helped Alcandhor cut away Marcalan's jerkin and shirt, then Haladhon covered Marcalan with his cloak and knelt next to him, a hand on his cousin's shoulder.

Alcandhor fell to his knees and rummaged in his pack. "Zandhral. Our healer packets. Salve, bandages."

"Aye, Thane!" Zandhral called out for the Rangers to bring them any healing supplies they might have then tore into his own pack with zeal.

His men brought over a pile of bandages, several types of salve, and some other oddments.

The foraging Rangers soon brought Tam the herbs she requested.

"Ch'illeya, good! Loestis, this will do for pain, but I would rather have panvarin. Please keep looking!" She dumped loestis leaves in one pan of water and ch'illeya in another and set the pans on the grate over the fire.

Alcandhor and Zandhral each took a pan of water and cleaned Marcalan's wounds.

He glanced up at a young Ranger who approached with several balls of sansil cupped in his hands. Not a man he recognized; the Ranger must be from another province. In a soft voice, the Ranger said, "These should help in cleansing the wounds."

"Set them down here, Ranger," Alcandhor said. "And my thanks."

The man still loomed, shifting foot to foot. "I...how may I help?"

Tam pointed to the pans on the grate. "You can watch these. They only need simmer."

His eyes lit up, and he nodded, squatting near the fire in conscientious duty.

"What is your name, Ranger?" Alcandhor asked.

"Ialdhor, sir," he answered, never taking his eyes off the pans.

"Good man."

Tam walked the short distance between the fire and Marcalan on her knees. She gasped and exclaimed, "Great Bells! What did they do?"

"They slashed his jerkin, Tam," Haladhon said in a low voice, "right through to his skin. Did you not notice?"

Tam shook her head, blinking. Alcandhor handed her a pan of water and some washing rags. She inhaled and held it for a moment, then bent to join them in the task. They worked quickly in the cold, keeping him covered with their cloaks where they were not tending to injuries.

Alcandhor inwardly smiled, but sadly, as he saw how gently Tam cleansed each wound on his upper body and rinsed with the ch'illeya infusion.

"What salves have we?" she asked.

Zandhral held out a jar.

She took it and sniffed. "What is in it?"

"Ch'illeya, crown plant, freyala—"

"With freyala, only use this on the surface wounds, nothing deep. And be certain 'tis cleaned quite well first. Do we have other salves? Uncle, do you have the one I gave you?"

So long ago that seemed. On their first journey out of Zaidhron. His face had been cut and bruised from the fight with her father. She had offered the salve to help him heal.

"Aye. I had quite forgotten about it." He rummaged through the various supplies on the grass next to him until he found it, then leaned over to give her the tin.

She blinked, her mouth dropping open. "You are not wearing your sling!"

"Hang the sling! Help Marcalan."

Tam returned to her task, kneeling over Marcalan's chest, and Alcandhor moved down to his cousin's bloody thigh. "'Tis a bad wound on his leg," he muttered. "They kicked wherever they could get a boot in. We need to get his trous off."

Alcandhor and Zandhral each unlaced a boot while Haladhon used his dagger to carefully cut Marcalan's trous. Haladhon caught Alcandhor's eye and winked, nodding to Tam. Between wisps of hair falling in her face, he could see she was blushing. Alcandhor glared at Haladhon. 'Twas no time for such foolishness! He rose to fetch a large cleaning cloth.

Haladhon folded back the trous and his face paled. "Stars, 'Candhor, they kicked everywhere!"

Wincing in sympathetic pain that only another man could understand, Alcandhor placed the cloth to provide modesty for Tam's sake. He then knelt by the leg wound. Stars, 'twas a deep gash! No boot did this! A dagger perhaps? Tam peered over and gasped. "Uncle, that is too deep and open."

"Aye. It needs more than just stitching." He sighed. The gash would need packing, then wrapping. He called out, "Men, we will need more ch'illeya. Or stach'a."

Tam straightened, nodding. "Oh! Aye. Either can be packed in a wound to stop bleeding and infection. But nay, the weather has been too chill, and stach'a will have died off. Ch'illeya grows until a hard frost kills it."

Alcandhor nodded. "Find ch'illeya, men. And bring more hot water."

Rangers soon hurried back with bunches of the herb and more pans of heated water.

"Know you how to do this, Uncle?" Tam asked. "I have read of it, but that is all."

"Aye. I have some little experience. I will do what I can. Why not see if the loestis has cooled. I set it off the fire when I got the last pan of warm water. And is it safe to give Marcalan both loestis and ch'illeya at the same time?"

"Aye. They serve different purposes and their properties do not contraindicate each other. I will try to give him a mug of both."

Alcandhor bent to his work. Tam bustled by the fire, then came over to kneel again by Marcalan's head. "Haladhon, can you help me?"

"Hold his head up a little, and I will get this down him."

"You have done this before?"

"Aye."

Alcandhor glanced up from the wound. "Tam, how strong is that infusion of loestis?"

"Not nearly as strong as I would like. I wish I had a tincture of it like the healers use. I hope it will keep him asleep. I will need to find more, though. I have not enough for the whole journey back."

"We can help you look later." Alcandhor regarded Zandhral, kneeling opposite him. "You found a wound there, too, Zandhral?"

"On his hip. 'Tis bad. I have cleaned and bandaged it. That one?"

"'Tis deep, but if it does not get infected, it should heal with little to no damage to the muscle." He hoped. From the pattern of wounds, although many kicked, one or more daggers inflicted wounds to cause pain and a slow bleeding. A horrible death—near death, thanks to Tam and Mattan.

Alcandhor set bandages over the packed wound then wrapped more around Marcalan's thigh to hold them in place. He settled back on his heels, exhaling, shoving down the guilt that tore at him. He spread his cloak over his cousin. Several others did the same, tucking the ends in. 'Twas all they could do.

Tam sat next to him. She leaned over and kissed his forehead. "You must get well, my love," she whispered. She reached into her pouch and pulled out the necklet. With an expression that asked permission, yet with a set chin that stated this was merely courtesy to her uncle, she held it up, meeting Alcandhor's gaze.

He could do nothing but nod. Dare he deny any request she made? That either of them would ever make?

She smiled at him, then bent over and fastened the necklet around Marcalan's neck. His eyes fluttered open for a moment. Alcandhor's heart leaped in hope.

"I love you, Marcalan," Tam murmured then touched her lips to his. He was asleep again already. She sat next to him, caressing his hair.

"Tam, come, take a moment to eat," Haladhon said.

Tam shook her head.

"Why not let us sit with him, Tam?" Alcandhor said. "You can eat, then rest."

Tam shook her head again, clenching her jaw, and Haladhon chuckled. "She is in too fine a state to argue with, Alcandhor. Like a ballan standing over its fallen mate."

Alcandhor would not allow her to neglect herself. That would do neither her nor Marcalan any good. He rose and filled a bowl with roasted bata roots, some kind of meat, and pan bread. He brought the bowl and a cup of tea to his niece. "You will eat, Ranger."

Tam obeyed, her eyes not leaving Marcalan's face for more than a few moments.

Zandhral brought over a bowl for himself and one for Alcandhor. Knowing Zandhral would take him to task as he had Tam, he took the food and ate, watching Tam watch Marcalan. Her husband. His hand stopped with a piece of bread halfway to his mouth. Stars, she was married!

Chapter Thirty

Nandhal found Monadhal in the cave that was their current camp, sword drawn. He skidded to a stop, hands raised. Monadhal lowered his weapon. "So they did not get you either, I see."

"Aye. We are the only ones."

Monadhal laughed, and Nandhal seethed. "What do you find so amusing? We are but two now."

"Aye, we are." Monadhal sheathed his sword and sat down. "Tell me, was that indeed a wench charging into our camp and cutting down our men?"

"I told you about her. Tam is her name. Did you not believe me?"

Monadhal waved a hand. "I saw her but not clearly. Of all of them, I recognized Alcandhor and Haladhon. By the stars, I wish I could have dealt with him once and for all. I will see him dead. And that wench—I want her, too."

Nandhal shook his head. "Nay. I will have her, Monadhal." His blood grew hot as he thought of what he wanted to do to her. The older man shot him a disdainful look, and Nandhal sensed Monadhal's scorn.

"You do, do you? We will see. Right now we have to deal with what to do to cover our tracks. They will certainly renew their efforts to ensnare us and we must be away before they can do that."

"So we are leaving here then?"

"Aye. I think we must go higher in the mountains for awhile. There are many places to hide in the mountains of Pashelon."

"Pashelon? But we are in Lantral, on the other side of the mountain range."

"Fool! Do you think I know not all the caves and tunnels that riddle this range? Many of them are not natural, did you know that? Pack what you can and we will leave at first light, after a rest."

~*~

That morning some of the Rangers left to join the hunt for Monadhal and Nandhal. The remaining Rangers worked on building the carry-cot to be used to journey back with Marcalan, cutting saplings for the straight poles and boughs to weave and tie.

However, Tam and Alcandhor did not yet give word they thought he could be carried without endangering him. Several of the wounds worried Tam, and her uncle too, she knew. Tam wavered, both wishing him to be at Zaidhron under the care of a healer and fearing the dangers of moving him, in turns. It would likely be some days before they were back at the city.

Alcandhor worried Tam too. When they had all insisted that their Thane put his sling back on, he reacted by throwing it in the fire. The Rangers then, led by Tam and Haladhon, mutinied and refused to allow Alcandhor to do anything but sit by the fire.

So now, Alcandhor sat, mostly poking the embers and scowling. Tam rested next to Marcalan, only leaving his side when she needed privacy behind some bushes.

Haladhon brought them both tea and sat, sipping his own. "It does not surprise me that Monadhal was not among the dead," Haladhon said. "He is too cunning and quick. But he did not mind leaving all his men to die."

Tam needed not to sense to know how much Haladhon despised Monadhal, she could hear it in his voice.

"You hold too much hate in you, cousin," Alcandhor said.

"Have I not a reason?"

"Reason or not, if you hold on to hate, it only eats you from the inside out."

"I will let go once he is dead."

"Haladhon..." her uncle's voice held chastisement.

"Do not lecture me, 'Candhor!"

Tam rubbed Marcalan's arm, staring into the fire in the thick silence. Finally she asked, "How many Rogues got away, Uncle?"

"Not many. From tracks we saw today, I would say two. Monadhal and one other."

"Then it was Nandhal," Tam whispered.

"You know it was Nandhal?" asked Alcandhor, surprised.

"I felt him here. He is still alive and far away now."

"You can tell?" Haladhon asked.

"He has Enaisi blood, and I can sense him."

"Then we were right. He had joined Monadhal's band."

It was quiet for a few moments then Zandhral, sitting nearby tying boughs together, asked, "How did you best those first men so quickly, Tam? They fell like nuts from a tree during a windstorm."

"I stopped each one by sending Marcalan's pain to him, then I killed him," she stated flatly.

Her uncle's head snapped up, his emotions matching his appalled expression.

"Why do you feel thus, Uncle? You cannot disapprove. There are no rules in a real fight as there are in a match."

"It is you, Tam. It is the first time I have heard you talk of killing and could not feel it bother you."

Tam pressed her lips into a thin line as she brushed Marcalan's hair with her fingers.

"Do not let hatred grab your heart, Tam," he said in gentle admonishment. "Let it go."

"After what they did to Marcalan? I would fain bring them all back to life so I could kill them again, but this time more slowly!"

"Tam!" exclaimed Haladhon.

Tam glared at the distressed look on her cousin's face. "Would you not fain do so to this Monadhal, Haladhon? I have felt your hate for him. If you wish to be the one to kill him, you had best find him first, and Nandhal too, because by both moons and the Bells above, if I find them first, I will fain strike them down!"

~*~

No clouds marred the clear, deep-blue, autumn sky as they descended from the Pashelon Ridge, but the chill breeze offset any warmth the sun might offer. Drums announced their approach as they carried Marcalan down the switchback. On each side of the road, the tall, yellowed grasses rustled in the gentle wind's currents.

Before they even reached the out-wall, Rangers met them, fists over their hearts in greeting. Alcandhor lifted a hand, palm out, offering a small smile.

"What news, Thane?" Gardhal asked. He stopped mid-bow to Tam, his face draining to white under his tan skin. Tam still had some red in the whites of her eyes, likely the reason for his surprise. The sour Ranger peered down at Marcalan's face, still swollen and bruised even after several days. "Stars, Thane, will he be all right?"

"He was sorely wounded, but aye, he should recover."

Gardhal's shoulders relaxed and he nodded. "What about the Rogues?"

"Two still live. Monadhal and Nandhal. We fear they have taken to the tunnels and caves in the Lantral Mountains, and are wending their way to southern Pashelon or Keladar. The search continues with heart-fire."

Gardhal lifted his chin, his lips pressed together. He gestured to the nearest Ranger hefting the carry-cot. "I would fain assist."

A tiny smile tugged at Alcandhor's lips as Gardhal replaced the man. Despite his constant grumbling, the Ranger was not as antipathetic toward Marcalan as he acted.

With a wave toward Zaidhron, Haladhon ordered, "Go to, men. See that a family chamber is made ready so that Tam can care for her new husband properly."

"And that a healer is to hand," Zandhral added.

"Food and drink for all of you as well," Alcandhor said. "You have need of it."

The Rangers obeyed, quickening their strides and outpacing those accompanying Marcalan.

~*~

Tam wrung her hands, her eyes locked on Marcalan as the Rangers settled him in the bed, with the healer, Faldhel, flapping about him to check his wounds. Tam tried to tell the old man about the injuries, but he wished to do his own examination and shooed her off. Sarinna pulled her away and murmured to let the healer be about his tasks. "Let me tell you about your chamber."

"I can see it, Aunt." Tam crossed her arms, peering over Sarinna's shoulder toward the bed.

"Attend, niece." Sarinna's demanding voice cut across Tam's knotted worry. She hooked her arm through Tam's and turned her away from the bed toward the other end of the chamber. "This one is small, a single room, meant for a newly married couple. The fireplace at this far end has a crane and a wall oven, although few do much cooking. Most families eat in meal hall of their ward and store little more than some tea in their chambers. Since you are both Rangers, your duties will likely offer you little chance to cook, although I am told you enjoy the task."

Tam nodded.

"Shall I order pots, utensils, spices, and other staples needed for cooking?"

"Aye, Sarinna, please."

Her aunt inclined her head with a tight smile, then lifted an arm toward a side door to the left of the fireplace. "You have a small wash room there with a basin and a tub. You can wash dishes, hands, or bathe." She pointed at another door, to the right. "That is the priv."

Why did Sarinna wish to bother her with all this when a simple opening of a door would give her the same knowledge? Her aunt drew her to the windows at the one side of the chamber. "This chamber is on the first level above ground, and you have a small balcony. I selected it as your rank should offer you some courtesy. It fronts Avadhron's Sward, so you can enjoy the view as you please. On warm days, the windows on this side and the opposite can be opened to let a breeze through. The curtains are heavy to keep out winter's chill. If you care not for the furnishings, you may request a change from the warder for this section of Family North. Her name is Adrinna, and her work chamber is on the ground floor. Near her chamber are the stores, which should offer any items you need.

"I have sent for a basic garland to be placed on your door to indicate it is occupied. When Marcalan is recovered, you two may plan whatever you wish to decorate your entrance."

Tam's mind, only partially on what her aunt was rattling on about, stopped, and she blinked. "Decorate?"

"Aye. To mark the identity of each family chamber or suite, the doors are decorated as the couple wishes. Some just use a basic garland with their names listed below, but most either create an elaborate garland, a banner, or a small tapestry to hang on the door. Some few, and"—Sarinna smiled—"I think you may be one who would do this, even have small trellises or potted plants outside their doors, or flowering vines adorning the railings near their doors."

Tam managed a small, returning smile at that idea, then turned again to see what the healer was about. The man straightened and turned, peering at Tam with a slight squint. "Your husband is settled. I wish to stay for a time to be certain he rests easily."

Tam's shoulders sagged. "Thank you."

~*~

Tam's sweet face hovered over Marcalan, holding his hand, touching his cheek, his forehead. "I love you!"

He tried to answer but could not.

This was a dream. Not real. Please let it be real! I cannot live like this!

The dream faded, and he stood, hands tied behind his back, a Ranger approaching with a brand in his hand, ready to burn the mark into Marcalan's forehead.

He was disowned.

His hands shot to his head as he rolled onto his side and curled up tightly into a fetal position, crying at the burning pain of the brand in his forehead. He was pulled onto his back and a liquid forced down his throat. He fell back into a deeper sleep.

~*~

Tam sat, watching Marcalan, and noticed a pattern. As the medicine the healer gave him would wear off, Marcalan would start to awaken and before long he clawed at his forehead, groaning. But the pain Tam felt from him was not in his head. She felt intense grief, so intense it was as physical agony. Then when the healer gave him more medicine, he fell back into a deep slumber.

Tam got up and walked over to Faldhel, who scratched his head.

"I am sorry, lass. I cannot understand why he is still in such pain."

"I feel no pain from a head injury when he begins to wake. Only very strong emotions. What is the medicine you have been giving him?"

"It is a mixture of panvarin and loestis. It is very effective for pain."

Tam stared at him, wide-eyed. "Truly, but panvarin and loestis either one can also cause hallucinations if the dose is too strong or the patient has a sensitivity. And you have given him both."

The healer looked at her in surprise. "How know you this?"

"What dosage have you been giving him?"

"I have increased the dosage twice since the pain was not lessening."

"Decrease it."

"Young woman, I do not—"

"I am not a 'young woman,' I am Second at Table, Valdhor's heir to Thane—and you, kinsman, are answerable to me. If you do not obey me, I will order you removed."

"You are not a healer."

"I have studied herbs since I was a small child. I know their effects. And I know whatever he is suffering is not great pain of body but only of spirit."

"But how can you know this?"

"I am a Child of the Enaisi, healer. I can sense. I feel his agony and it is not of his body. This wound is in his mind and heart. Decrease the next dose."

~*~

Marcalan became restless, and Tam rushed over to sit on the bed. He moaned, putting his hands to his forehead while rolling on his side with rending sobs. She wrapped her arms around him, sending her love to him and feelings of peace. His crying subsided, and he soon fell back asleep.

Tam rose, stumbling with weariness, and looked over at Faldhel; she had been through this so many times.

The man shook his head in amazement. "I will chance not giving him the next dose. If he begins to show symptoms of withdrawal, then I will have to give him something. Panvarin, probably, in a very weak dose."

"I agree. But I think within the next day that he will not need any more medicine. Any pain from his wounds should be able to be handled with a mild herb." She fell into the chair next to the bed. "A tincture of umaral, for instance."

Faldhel nodded, and they sat in silence, waiting.

Chapter Thirty-One

Tam jumped awake as someone gave a soft rap on the door. She stood and answered it to find her uncle looking as worn as she felt. His eyes flicked toward his cousin as he entered the family chamber then grimaced, flopping into the chair Tam had just been dozing in.

"How is he?" His voice was hoarse.

"Sleeping more peacefully now," Faldhel whispered. "We have been decreasing the dosage of the herbs, and he is doing better."

Alcandhor's guilt weighed heavily. Tam knelt in front of him, aching for the burden she could sense. "You cannot blame yourself. You did not—"

"If I had listened to him. If I had stopped wallowing in my own problems and truly saw him, I would have seen what was happening."

"You cannot be blamed. You are suffering yourself right now, and you did not know we had bonded. Even we did not understand what was happening. You are the one who is always telling me I cannot blame myself for things beyond my control. If you wish me to believe you, then you had best follow your own advice."

The stubborn look on Alcandhor's face reminded Tam of her father. She felt Marcalan waking a little and rose to go sit next to him on the bed again. It was the same as before. He moaned, grabbing at his forehead. Tam sent him her love and peaceful feelings, and he murmured, "Tam..."

"Aye, my love. I am here," she whispered to him.

His eyes opened, but she could sense he still hallucinated. "Nay! I cannot!" he cried, then he grabbed at his forehead again, doubling up in pain. He pulled his hair as he clenched and unclenched his fists, beginning to weep. "I cannot have you! Ever! I cannot have anything I love! I am lost!"

She held him, sending warm waves of comfort again. She intensified them until she felt him relax. Not being certain how aware he was of his real surroundings, Tam thought it was perhaps a mistake to try to talk to him again, so she just cuddled him in her arms. He soon fell asleep. Tam straightened, and her uncle met her gaze. She need not feel to know of his anguish, 'twas apparent in his expression.

"I caused this, Tam. How do I ever look him in the eye again?"

"He will not blame you, Uncle. I do not."

Marcalan moaned, and Tam turned her attention to him again. After a few moments, he rolled onto his back, his arm flung out against the pillow, and quieted.

"This is the medicine, Uncle," she whispered as she sat up. "It is causing hallucinations. But they are lessening since he has not been given any more. Soon they will stop."

Alcandhor stared at the floor, then finally exhaled and stood. "Let me know."

As he left, Tam blinked back tears. Faldhel stood and walked over toward the bed.

"You seem to have things well in hand, young wo—uh, Ranger. I will leave your husband to your care. Send for me if I am needed."

He bowed himself out the door, shutting it quietly.

Marcalan's lips quivered as if he spoke, but he did not cry out. Tam rubbed her eyes and lifted her shoulders to ease the tension. If only she could rest. Wait—stars, she could! This was her bed, too.

She trembled, biting her lip, then finally undressed. Why should I feel thus, she scolded herself as she slipped under the covers, when this is my husband? His arm still stretched across the far pillow. She touched her shaking hand to his side with hesitance. She had never been close to a person growing up, nor been touched in a loving way. To be close to someone, to love them, to be loved—it seemed strange. And this was her husband with whom she would share total intimacy. She touched the bare skin of his chest and then feeling more bold, moved closer. She gingerly put her head on his shoulder, using him as a pillow, and curled up next to him, her hand still on his chest.

~*~

Marcalan opened his eyes. He was in a large chamber, wide windows lining the one wall with heavy draperies pulled shut across them. Light came only from the fireplace. He remembered the dreams: the branding then, inexplicably, Tam holding him, and he closed his eyes against the horrible sorrow of losing all he loved. No longer a Ranger. And Tam. He would never see Tam again.

He opened his eyes, blinking tears. Why was he in such a chamber? Should he not be in a prisoner's cell? His whole body hurt, but most especially his right side blazed with a stabbing fire, and his left leg throbbed. He tried to remember why. The Rogues. But how did he get here—*here* seemed to be a family suite at Zaidhron—if the Rogues had been beating him?

Despite his weakness and his injuries, he tried to sit up but his right arm was weighed down, and he could not move it. He turned his head and gasped—Tam slept on his shoulder? He tried to jump away. Pain shot through him, and he clenched his jaw to keep from crying out. Tam awoke and sat up with a start, the covers falling away from her. He closed his eyes with a moan and tried to roll over so he could not see her, but froze from an agonizing slash across his torso. He had to settle for turning his head. *Was this another dream?* "What are you doing here?" His hysterical outcry sounded more like a hoarse croak.

"You must be feeling better. This is the first time you woke up without having a hallucination."

"What are you doing here?" he repeated.

"This is our family chamber. We are married now, Marcalan. Do you not remember?"

"Remember what?"

"When we found you. After we cared for your injuries, I put my necklet on you. You opened your eyes when I did it and smiled at me."

"I remember it not. I—" He stopped. "Necklet?" He felt at his throat and indeed, he wore a necklet. He rolled his head toward her in disbelief. She now clutched the blanket in front of her; relief and disappointment battled inside him.

"Aye, necklet." She dimpled.

Marcalan grimaced, his mind whirling. "But, but the Thane!"

"He is so sorry, Marcalan." She touched his face with her hand. "He did not understand. But everything is fine now. We are married." She cuddled back into the spot on his shoulder with a smug smile.

Marcalan stared at her. His wife? It could not be. Another dream? But she felt *real*. "Married?"

She nodded, smiling. Surely this was a dream! He tried to lift his right arm and turn toward her, but again pain speared through his side. Tam put her hand on the exact spot below his ribcage, biting her lip. He felt her worry. "Let me give you some umaral."

He must be sorely wounded if he could not even appreciate, well, not much, watching that beautiful lass rise and don her trous and shirt.

Tam sat stroking his hair after giving him the umaral. The pain soon eased a little, and he drifted into a light doze, vaguely aware of Tam cuddling back onto his shoulder. *Stars, if this be a dream as well, 'tis much better than the others.* And with that thought, sleep overtook him.

~*~

Marcalan woke. The curtains had been pulled back to admit daylight. Where was Tam? Had it been a dream? He felt his throat. Aye, he wore a necklet. But this was not right! He did not deserve her. Not after what he did, and not being what he was. But—he needed to be with her. Why, how, he could not say, but the anguish ripping at his heart eased because she was near, because she was allowed to be near.

He tried to sit up, grimaced, and gave up. Excruciating pain extended from his bloated abdomen up to his side. His ribs hurt—not unexpected from being kicked repeatedly—but this was a separate agony, different and much worse. He sighed and tried to roll over into a more comfortable position.

The door opened, and Tam came in, worry radiating from her. "I am sorry I was not here when you awoke. I was talking with Sarinna and Uncle in the hallway so as not to disturb you. I felt you wake up."

She sat on the bed, and grasped his hand. He took in her face, framed by her straight dark hair, incredulous. This most lovely lass was his wife. By both moons, she was so beautiful! He would endure torment ten times this to be near her! Perhaps that was the price. He could have Tam but must suffer as expiation.

"Oh, stars, Marcalan! Your pain is dreadful! I think you need something stronger than umaral. Faldhel left panvarin here, let me give you a little."

Marcalan was glad of the herb, despite the bitter taste of the tincture. The agonizing stabbing in his side eased, and he fell asleep.

~*~

With Marcalan healing and Tam tending him, Alcandhor had no reason to hover near their chamber, worrying. His duties needed attending, especially days' worth of reports. He would probably not catch up on them all before luncheon, but he hoped to reduce the pile greatly.

He entered Thane Hall and wiped his feet on the mat. Voices murmured from the Thane's chamber. Before opening the door, he recognized the deep, rumbling voice of his old friend and burst in. Haladhon hip-sat on the table, looking pleased. Delgan, still wearing his travel cloak, pushed up slowly from a chair, grinning. "Good to see you, Thane!"

"You finally arrived, I see."

"My wife was ill, and I dared not leave her."

"Is she well?"

"Much better. One of our grandchildren came to stay with her just in case while I am here. And then the Rangers would not let me travel alone for fear of Rogues which might be in my province or Pashelon. So I showed them your letter, and then suddenly they were quite helpful and offered an escort." Delgan's eyes twinkled. "Although we heard you took care of most them just days ago."

"That was mostly due to my niece, the new Second at Table, Tam."

"Ah the lass who found the incredible chamber under Ranger Hold in Lairdton! And also found a way to open the door to the lift and access the Portal Complex from here. I have to see this, and also your very incredible niece that has made it possible."

"That is not the only thing she has made possible, my friend. Sit."

"I am too excited to sit, Thane!"

Alcandhor took his old friend by the shoulders. "Delgan, sit. I will not chance you falling over when I tell you. I did not put all the news in my letter for fear your heart would give out."

The history-keeper grabbed the arms of the chair and lowered himself, his eyes never leaving Alcandhor's. "I am sitting. What is it?"

"An Enaisi has contacted her through the portal."

Delgan's face paled. "You wouldn't play foolsies on an old man, Thane."

"Nay, 'tis true. And he claims to be Mattan."

"Mattan? A descendant of *the* Mattan?"

"Nay, Mattan himself. We know they are long-lived, but can it truly be?"

"He would be well over one thousand years old! Is that possible?"

"We can ask him ourselves. He has told Tam he is going to come here."

Delgan stared at Alcandhor and slowly sank against the back of the chair. "Here? You mean *here* here?"

"Aye. He told her he has duties to complete, but afterwards he is coming through that portal to visit us."

The old man placed both hands over his heart and whispered, "By the Bells and both moons!"

Alcandhor chuckled.

"So where is this remarkable niece?"

With a sober glance at Haladhon, Alcandhor replied, "Her husband was attacked by Rogues, and she is tending to him. I doubt we can pry her away at the moment."

"Oh, yes, I can understand why. And I'm certain you have duties, Thane. Don't let me keep you from them."

"Unfortunately, aye, I have some reports to read. But you know where the law library is. Have Andhrel show you the books and charts we brought back from the Ranger Hold."

"He has not yet been given a chamber, Thane. He came straight here." Haladhon nodded to a pack and carry bag by the door.

Alcandhor laughed. "I see your priorities are still set straight, my friend." He pulled the cord. "I will send word to the Great Hall warder to ready a chamber for you. And unless you have objections, I can have your things delivered there. I think Zaidhron's Chamber would be suitable. It was recently vacated by my niece when she married."

Using the arms of the chair to brace himself, Delgan rose once more, then he bowed. "I am honored."

"Go to, my friend. I will join you when I have finished here."

Haladhon stood from the edge of the table. "Shall I show you to Andhrel?"

"Oh, no thank you, Haladhon. I know where his work chamber is. It will be good to see him again." The elderly man left with a grin and a raised hand.

He was more stooped than Alcandhor remembered. Of course he would look older. He *was* older. But seeing the aging of his friend, that was worrisome. With a deep breath, he turned to Haladhon. "Let us go to ourselves, cousin, and make short work of these reports."

Feladhrel arrived at the door, out of breath. "You needed me, Thane?"

"Send word to Erdissa to prepare Zaidhron's Chamber for the history-keeper, Delgan, and have someone fetch his belongings to his chamber."

The stripling ducked his head and shot off.

Haladhon nodded at the table. "Besides all the other reports that have piled up, you have some from Teldhor and Naladhrel which await you. Some punishment?"

"Aye." He had forgotten about that, with all the worry about Marcalan. Besides, he had been out of the city on the day the boys' assignments were due.

And 'twas not the only thing that he had neglected. He stared hard at Haladhon. "I have been lax, cousin. I know you mentioned Panill not taking her mother's death well, but I have never asked how your girls are."

"You have had much on your mind."

"They are your daughters, and my cousins. How are they?"

Haladhon hesitated. "Well. They worry for their mother. Panill...falters. As I said, she grieves her mother's death greatly, and her father does as well. He seems older. Weaker."

"I am sorry. If they need help with the tenancy, do whatever is needed, with my blessing."

Haladhon inclined his head. "My thanks." He cleared his throat and tapped a paper set by itself on the table. "You will not like this one missive, Thane."

"Oh?" Alcandhor walked around to his chair, eyeing the message and its broken wax seal. "Since you have obviously read it already, say on."

"Gilendhar, the new lord of Keladar, is not best pleased with the influx of Rangers roaming his province."

Alcandhor frowned at Haladhon. "Interesting. We always suspected Paltor of aiding the Rogues, and now his first cousin is aggrieved that Rangers search for Rogues in his province, enh?"

"This speaks to potential leanings as those of Lord Paltor."

"Aye." Alcandhor had met Gilendhar many times, but the man had always been as a silent shadow in the background of his first cousin, Lord Paltor. "But does it speak to hate against us, worry of Rangers hindering aid to the Rogues, or mere concern that our presence impedes opportunity for misappropriated personal gain?"

Haladhon shrugged. "Or all three? 'Tis likely he is as corrupt as his cousin. But we cannot know for certain without more information from within the province."

"Delgan is from Keladar, but I do not wish to bring him into the middle of a political situation, even just by asking questions about his new provincial lord."

His cousin rubbed the back of his neck. "I could send an Elite as spy. Marcalan would be my best choice for his ability to blend in as a commoner and mimic provincial accents, but..."

Alcandhor waved his arm. "Let us see what we learn from the Rangers scouring for Rogues. I am certain they have gleaned much that will be useful."

His Third at Table lifted a hand and turned it palm up in acquiescence. Alcandhor turned his mind to the rest of the reports. If he finished in a timely manner, he might have a chance to speak with Delgan again before lunch.

Chapter Thirty-Two

Marcalan woke, and by the sun's slant through the windows, 'twas late afternoon. He was hot and sweating, his side blazing. And there was an ominous clenching in his stomach. He tried several times before he managed to rise. Dizziness assaulted him as he stumbled across to their chamber's priv. Just as he got there, he began to heave, and it continued violent and unabated, causing fire to spear through his side. Finally, it eased, but he felt too weak to call for Tam's help. Could he make it back to the bed? He lay on the floor, unable to stop the fierce shaking. Through that blessed connection, he felt her awakening and her worry as she rushed to him. They did not need to use words as she knelt next to him, brushing his hair from his face. She managed to help him up and get him back to their bed. He flopped down on it, unable to control his fall.

Tam pulled him over onto the bed and tossed the coverlet somewhat over him. Then she crawled into the bed and laid her head on his chest. He knew she was trying to make him feel better, but he could not tell that she was sending him any sort of emotion. He wished the fiery hot knives in his side would go away. He fell back into an uneasy sleep...

A knock at the door awakened him. Tam did not move. He touched her shoulder.

"Tam?" he managed to croak. She was awake—he could see her eyes open—but she did not respond. The knock came again and he heard Haladhon's voice. "Tam? Marcalan?"

The door opened, and the Thane and Haladhon entered.

"What is wrong?" the Thane asked. "Why did you not answer?"

Marcalan swallowed and licked his lips, trying to moisten his mouth. His throat hurt and he could not get his voice above a hoarse whisper. "I could not, Thane."

Alcandhor sat in the chair next to the bed and put his hand on his cousin's forehead.

"You are burning up with fever. Tam? Wish you for me to call the healer?"

Tam shook her head but did not answer. She closed her eyes.

"Tam?" Alcandhor reached out to touch Tam's arm, his other hand still on Marcalan's head. He snatched his hands away. "Great Bells!"

"What is it, Thane?" Marcalan whispered.

"My child, it is too much for you to do alone!"

"He needs me, Uncle," she murmured. "I must do this."

"Why do you not call Mattan?"

"I have tried. I cannot connect with him."

Alcandhor again touched both Marcalan and his niece. "I can sense what you are doing. I cannot do it myself, but I think I can lend you strength."

What did he mean? Marcalan was too worn out and sick to ask. He closed his eyes.

"Haladhon," he heard the Thane say, "call the healer. And all those who are in the city that have Enaisi blood in them. Have them come here. Now!"

Marcalan tried to stay awake to understand what was happening, but he could not...

The next time he woke, it was dark. The fireplaces at each end of the chamber and a few candles provided a little illumination, enough to see people crowded around the bed. Sarinna curled next to Tam, and Zandhral sat beside the Thane. More gathered at the footboard, but he could not see their faces in the dim light. They were all silent. He had no idea what they were doing. He only knew that Tam was exhausted but determined.

He felt cooler and the pain in his side had lessened. He reached up a hand and touched Tam's hair. She did not seem to have moved at all.

"What is happening?" he asked, but no one answered.

He tried to move and hands pushed him down.

"Be still," the Thane ordered.

He obeyed. With nothing else to do, he caressed Tam's hair and sent her his love. But what was happening? He felt foolish lying there with nothing on—modesty only provided by the thin coverlet—and people sitting all around him and Tam on the bed.

After what seemed like hours, Haladhon stole into the chamber.

"Haladhon?" His voice was worse, his throat parched and sore.

"How are you, Mar?"

"Confused."

Haladhon pulled a chair over next to Alcandhor's and sat, feeling Marcalan's forehead.

"Your fever seems less. How do you feel?"

"The pain in my side is almost gone. Please tell me what is happening."

"You have been very ill."

"I am so thirsty."

"Tam? May I get him a drink of water?" Haladhon asked.

Without moving or opening her eyes, Tam whispered, "Aye."

Haladhon soon had a cup and lifted Marcalan's head so he could sip the water. It trickled down his throat, cool and soothing. After Haladhon lowered his head to the pillow, Marcalan murmured, "My thanks."

Haladhon tousled his hair then bent close to Tam and Alcandhor. "Is there anything I can do for you? Drinks of water? Food?"

"Aye, please, Haladhon. Food and water," Alcandhor replied.

Haladhon left, and Marcalan was left to just stare at the people in the chamber with him. Sarinna smiled tiredly. What in the names of both moons was happening? Zandhral sat, head bowed, his eyes closed. Marcalan sensed him. He was struck by something—not an emotion but a force, a strength. Then he realized everyone one there had Enaisi blood. They all, in some way, concentrated their abilities on Tam. But why?

Did it have something to do with how sick he had been earlier? If only he had some answers.

Haladhon came in before long with a stew kettle. He hung it on the swing arm of the far fireplace. Marcalan's youngest sister Valinn followed him in with a tray. She set the table as Haladhon lit more candles.

"Eat," the Thane said. "Take turns, two at a time."

"You first, Thane," Zandhral said.

"Do as I bid. Eat," Alcandhor ordered.

The Rangers exchanged glances then two of them rose, picked up bowls, and dished themselves something to eat from the kettle. Valinn tiptoed close to Marcalan with a worried smile, then leaned over and kissed his forehead. She backed out of Haladhon's way as the tall Ranger walked over and sat down.

"I feel helpless, Alcandhor. Can I not bring over food? For you or for Tam?"

The Thane shook his head. "I will take a turn presently. Tam cannot leave Marcalan. I do not think she will distract herself by eating."

"A drink then?"

"That would be fine."

Haladhon brought two cups over. He handed one to Alcandhor, then touched Tam's face. "Will you take a drink of water, Tam?"

With effort, Tam raised her head enough to take a sip of the water. Marcalan could feel it relieve her thirst. She was exhausted. And weak. He wished he could do something for her. If he at least knew what was going on.

"Haladhon, will you please tell me what is happening?"

Haladhon gestured to the cup.

"Please," Marcalan said.

Haladhon again lifted his head enough to take a drink. Never had anything felt so good.

"Thank you. Now please talk to me. What are they all doing?"

"They are healing you," his cousin replied quietly.

"Healing me?"

"Actually, we are just lending strength to Tam more than anything else," Aladhon, his father's brother, explained, as he walked to the bed, a bowl in his hand. Wait, had not Aladhon been mustered to hunt for the Rogues? How was he then here?

"How much of the healing we are actually doing, I do not know." Aladhon shrugged and took a spoon of stew.

"I did not know that was a ability those with Enaisi blood had," Marcalan said.

"Only in those strong enough, I would guess. And Tam is strong enough. We can feel what she is doing and lend our strength to her, but even all of us together could not do it without her, I think."

"But why not call the healer?"

"It is something inside you, some internal injury. We did call the healer, and he said from the symptoms you have, that there was damage, probably bleeding inside your gut, and likely infection as well. I know not what. He said he would defer his methods of healing to those of the Enaisi."

Aladhon finished eating, then came back over to the bed and tapped Zandhral. They exchanged places and Zandhral smiled at Marcalan as he got up.

Why were they all helping him? After all he had done, and what he was, he should not have Tam, should not be a Ranger, yet they were all here, healing him. The Thane helping to heal him after Marcalan had betrayed him by disobeying him. He turned his head on the pillow and closed his eyes. He could not bear to look at them.

Chapter Thirty-Three

Marcalan awoke. The chamber was light. Tam slept, curled up next to him, still dressed in her trous and shirt. The pain in his side had all but gone, a mere twinge. He needed to use the priv. He carefully extricated his arm from under her and rolled out of bed, leaning on his hands. He pushed upright, and a stab of pain in his left thigh made his leg buckle. Hands grabbed him.

"Steady," the Thane whispered from behind, "you are weak and have not eaten, and you have a serious leg injury that is not fully healed. Sit and let me help you dress."

"Nay, I–I can do it."

"I will help you."

He sighed, giving in to the tone in his Thane's voice, and sat on the bed as his Thane helped put his trous on him.

"There is food keeping warm at the fireplace. Or do you need to use the priv first?"

"Priv."

Alcandhor supported him under his left arm to the door. Marcalan found bruising and swelling in a certain tender area made taking care of necessities a bit of a chore and incredibly painful. Finally, he limped out. His cousin offered a worried smile. "Let me help you to the table."

Marcalan averted his gaze. How had the Thane not disowned him for his direct disobedience? Why did they not just let the Rogues kill him?

He glanced over at Tam sleeping, curled up like a little girl in that huge bed. She was why. Tam. Tam loved him, and her uncle would not cause Tam to go through suffering that loss. But how was Marcalan supposed to live with that? How was he supposed to face any Ranger, much less his Thane, knowing he should have been disowned? How could his Thane, or any Ranger, trust him anymore?

The Thane put an arm around him and helped him across to the table, then handed him his shirt. "Sit you down and put this on while I bring you food," Alcandhor whispered.

Marcalan did as he was told, easing into the chair. Stars, but his tender bits were...tender.

"There is a broth, if you do not feel ready for the stew. Which do you prefer?"

Marcalan hesitated then muttered, "Stew."

Alcandhor got a bowl from the table, ladled stew into it, and set it in front of him. Marcalan stared at it. His favorite stew, with redfruit sauce and pieces of conju fruit. And on top of it all, the Thane was waiting on him. How could he possibly feel more miserable?

"Eat, Marcalan." Alcandhor sat in the chair next to him.

He picked up the spoon in an attempt to be obedient, but after a few bites, he put down the spoon and sat back.

"Do you feel ill?" the Thane asked.

Marcalan shook his head. "Nay, Thane."

"What is the matter?"

"Nothing."

"Nothing? I can feel, remember? What is wrong?"

"Nothing I can speak of, Thane." He kept his voice low to avoid awakening Tam.

Alcandhor rose and walked over to the window, then just stood, looking out. Marcalan fixed his gaze on the table. He was startled when Alcandhor said in a soft voice, "I am sorry, Marcalan. I know not how you can forgive me, but, please believe me, I am sorry."

"I know not what you mean, Thane. What have you to be sorry for?"

"I did not pay attention to what should have been obvious, especially to me with all my studying. I was too caught up in my own petty problems to see what was happening. And I was overzealous in thinking I needed to play father to Tam. I nearly caused your death. How do I ask you to forgive all that?"

"You were doing what you thought was best for Tam, as Thane and foster-father."

"'Twas selfish. And I was warned. Haladhon took me to task, yet I ignored him."

Marcalan closed his eyes, trying to gather his courage. He must say on. He must. He took a breath. "How can I remain a Ranger, my Thane?"

Alcandhor wheeled about, the astonishment on his face as strong as the emotion that shot from him. "Why would you even ask thus?"

"I disobeyed you. Repeatedly. I was in love with Tam when I knew you would disapprove, yet did not request to leave the city or even try to stay away from her until the very last. I left the city without permission. I refused to return when summoned."

"How are you to be blamed for that? You had no control over your actions."

"I am a Ranger. We are taught control, over our bodies and our minds. I demonstrated neither. I should be disowned, but because you love Tam so much, now you have to show me mercy."

"What in the names of both moons are you talking about?"

"Why else would you spare disowning me and come up with excuses to blame yourself? Because you would not hurt Tam. I have gotten away with everything I have done my whole life. I know not why. But I cannot live with the fact that I disobeyed you. I may have been 'Thane's pet,' but I cannot be any longer."

Alcandhor stepped forward, frowning. "Who did you ever hear call you 'Thane's pet?'"

Marcalan snorted. "Does it matter?"

"I asked you a question."

"Aleta," Marcalan replied, then recalled the Rogues. "And Nandhal."

"Nandhal?" repeated Alcandhor, rubbing his jaw. "How would *he* come to say that to you? It makes no sense..."

Marcalan cared not what did or did not make sense. The Thane was quiet for some time. Finally, he pulled his chair close to Marcalan's and took him by the nape of the neck. "Marcalan, you could not help your actions. You and Tam have bonded. Know you not what that means?"

"Nay, I have not heard of it before, Thane."

"It is what you and Tam have shared since you were at Ranger Hold. Tam called it a 'connection,' but what the Enaisi called it, is bonding. Soul to soul, if you will. You are bound to each other. When I tried to keep you apart, you both nearly went mad. You actually did. You cannot be held responsible for your actions in such a situation. You could have done nothing differently, and you did nothing wrong. Can you understand? It was my fault. I should have seen what was happening. I did not and nearly caused your death."

Marcalan could think of nothing to say. How could anything excuse what he did? Alcandhor shook him by his neck. "Marcalan, you are dearer than brother to me. I allow you more leniency, as I do Haladhon, out of love." He stopped and grinned. "Besides, there has to be someone who can rouse things up once in awhile and keep us from getting too comfortable and hidebound."

Marcalan tried to smile but could not.

"Talk to me, Marcalan," Alcandhor begged.

"I have said it all, Thane."

"You will continue to blame yourself and feel guilt for something you had no control over, then?"

"I was the one who disobeyed. Unless this bonding destroys free will, I am to blame."

"But do you not understand? It does interfere with free will. You have both lost some freedom to choose in situations that affect your bond."

"I believe it not. I have my free will."

"You are both so stubborn."

Tam sat up in the bed and staring at them with eyes dark against her wan skin.

"You cannot see what you are doing to each other, can you?" She scrambled out of the bed. "You love each other so much that you will not let the other accept any responsibility for what happened, so each of you is trying to take all the blame." She looked from one to the other. "You think it is not true? Sense each other. Why can you both not just stop wallowing in your own guilt and accept you both made mistakes, as did I."

"Tam," Alcandhor began, "I was the one—"

"I want not to hear it!" she yelled, her voice shrill, her eyes black.

Marcalan gaped at her.

"Tam, you need not react like a child," Alcandhor said.

"I know not how a child reacts. I have never been around a child. But if I make a guess, I think you are both acting like children. Continue it if you want, if you do not care how you are hurting each other. Or me. I am torn as to whether I should block, or send to each of you what I feel of the other's pain."

Marcalan dropped his head.

"Why are you both not blaming me for all this?" she asked. "I am the cause."

"How should you be blamed, Tam?" Alcandhor asked.

"None of this was your fault," Marcalan said.

"Was it not? I sent to you, Marcalan, and that started the first ties of the bond. I lied about Marcalan to you, Uncle, by not telling you that we loved each other. Why do you both blame yourselves and not me?"

"Tam, you knew not what you were doing when you sent to Marcalan," Alcandhor stated.

"True. And you, Marcalan, did not know about bonding, and how it would affect you. From what Uncle has told me, for you to go to him, when you knew I did not wish it and was afraid of his reaction, showed a great strength of will."

Marcalan frowned at such nonsense.

"And you Uncle, why are you not angry with me for lying to you?"

"Because you knew how angry I would be. It was my fault that I—"

"You simply thought you needed to protect me, and have set your desire on having me become Thane. What is wrong with that?"

"I let my desire overshadow everything, Tam. I wished to see you as a child, not a young woman. I tried to force you to reject all thoughts of a suitor or of marriage because of that conclave vow. I was wrong."

"So, you were wrong. Marcalan was wrong. I was wrong. Should I then react as you both are, and start blaming myself for all that has happened? It has all hinged on me, so I could easily take that blame. You told me once, Uncle, that I should take what lessons I could from what happens and toss the rest on the midden. That I cannot allow myself to be buried by guilt—yet that is what both of you are doing."

"That is true for both you and the Thane, Tam," Marcalan said, "but what I did was different. I disobeyed him. Can you not understand? Can you not see what that has done to me? How it has made me feel about myself? How can I call myself a Ranger when I have disobeyed my Thane?"

It was quiet for a few moments then Alcandhor replied, "Marcalan, I can understand that. Any Ranger could. But you have to understand that your disobedience was tied to your bond with Tam."

Marcalan shook his head.

"If Tam called to you through your bond right now, you could not resist her."

Tam tipped her head. "But, Uncle, how would I call him?"

"Perhaps call is not the word. If you were to send to him. A sense of longing, of needing and wanting him."

"As if I were lonely, or sad, you mean?"

"Perhaps. A strong need of him. Not even that of desire, but what if you were in pain, or great sorrow, and wanted his comfort. Any strong need of him."

"So if I sent that now, he could not resist?"

"Nay, nor could you if he sent to you."

Marcalan pushed his chair back from the table and crossed his arms. "Thane, I know you have studied this matter, but that is laughable. What you claim—"

"'Tis true. A bonded couple is just that."

"You jest."

Alcandhor's brows rose. "You truly think thus?" He raised his chin. "Stand, Ranger Marcalan."

"Thane?"

"You heard me. Stand."

Biting back a groan at the pain assaulting his body, Marcalan pushed to his feet.

"Now, by command of your thane, stand firm in that spot and move not until I order it."

"Aye, Thane."

Marcalan stood as ordered, staring straight ahead, seeing his Thane glare at him out of the corner of his eye. He felt a pull from Tam. She was calling to him in her mind, in her heart—something. He did not move. The sending increased and he clenched his jaw against the desire to go to her. An ache grew deep inside as when the Thane had ordered him to keep away from her; as he had felt when he left the city, thinking he would never see her again. He refused to move, and the pain mounted, his insides twisting around each other, his heart thudding so hard it threatened to cut off his breath. He felt his body shudder involuntarily as he fought her, tears in his eyes. Sweat poured down his face, and trickled down his body but he refused to move. This time, he would obey his Thane!

The pull from Tam intensified, and a moan escaped him despite all his effort. The chamber spun—and then he was holding Tam, his cheek against her dark hair as he held her in his arms. He gasped for air. He did not remember moving, or crossing over to her.

"Stars, Marcalan, you have a strong will!" Tam gazed up at him, her eyes filled with tears.

Alcandhor shook his head. "I cannot believe you held out that long."

Marcalan stared at Tam in disbelief, still gasping to catch his breath. But he did not relinquish his hold of her. Rather, he held her tighter, burying his face in her sweet-smelling, silky hair. If he could but stay in this moment for his whole life, he would be fulfilled. Nay—thoughts of Uardhel and his true parentage crowded in, crumbling that thought.

"You see?" She reached her fingers up to his cheek, a touch of melancholy in her face and within as well. "You had no choice."

Marcalan wanted to ask what suddenly made her so sad, but Alcandhor clapped a hand on his shoulder and turned him around. "I am amazed at you, Mar, and proud of you. I wish you could have seen the look on your face as you fought her in your desire to obey me." He chuckled. "You have come a long way from the child who began Ranger Training only because it meant being able to have Haladhon spend time with you, helping Train you and match you."

Marcalan grinned in spite of himself. "Not the best reason to start Training."

"He lost a wager to me on that, too, you know."

"What do you mean?"

"He wagered me you would not last long."

Marcalan laughed and something inside snapped and released. His guilt faded away, and he was able to look at Alcandhor without dread. He continued to laugh, imagining the two young striplings wagering over him. "What did he lose?"

"A lunation's worth of desserts," Alcandhor said with a chuckle.

Marcalan chortled. "I knew this not. I will have to mention that to him."

Tam hugged Marcalan tighter. "Oh, it is good to see you happy!" She kept an arm around him and helped him to the table. "Now will you eat or do I sit on you to make you?"

"Thane, she is threatening me. Is there no law against that?"

"She is your wife. She is allowed to threaten you."

"Ah, nay, what a miserable life." He dared not fall into the chair with an exaggerated flop as he wished, but instead sat gingerly then leaned back letting his arms dangle. "She ranks me, so as a Ranger she can treat me abominably and give me any rotten duty she pleases, and I cannot even escape such torment at home either. I am resigned to be under the heel of my wife."

Alcandhor chuckled as Tam slapped Marcalan's arm in mock indignation.

"That you are. Get used to it," Alcandhor said.

Tam turned to look at Alcandhor, gesturing to the table. "Join us, Uncle?"

"Aye, Thane, please," Marcalan chimed in, a stray mischievous thought running through his mind. He pushed up carefully from his seat and made a sweeping bow and after a short hesitation, Alcandhor sat.

Marcalan smiled. "I will bring over your bowls."

"You should sit, Marcalan, and let me do that," Tam said.

"Ah, nay. 'Tis only a few steps. My leg can manage that." Marcalan grabbed two bowls from the shelf beside the hearth and filled them from the small pot over the fire. From among the spices, he picked up a small jar of hot spicy sauce made from pimin and made sure his back was to them, covering his actions. He limped to the table and placed their bowls in front of them, then slowly reseated himself.

"Then I will at least pour the tea." Tam filled their cups then sat, her eyes shining. "Our first meal in our chamber."

Ah, to finally be able to openly adore her dimpled smile! And stars, aye, 'twas indeed auspicious, their first meal in their own chamber. Marcalan wavered between the joyous awe of his newly married circumstances and glee as the Thane picked up a spoon. Tam frowned at Marcalan with a waft of confusion. He sucked in his lips and bit them, his eyes on his bowl.

"Stars, Marcalan!" Alcandhor gasped and grabbed for his cup. He downed the tea, almost choking. "You vagabond!"

Marcalan chuckled, then Alcandhor burst out laughing. He pointed at Tam's bowl. "You had best check it, niece."

Tam picked up her spoon and tasted her stew. "It is fine, Uncle."

"What?" exclaimed Marcalan, staring at her.

"It is good, Marcalan. I like this much better than the stew from yesterday. It has lots of pimin in it."

Alcandhor threw back his head cackling as Marcalan stared at Tam, his mouth open.

"She got you, Mar!" he howled. "Oh, how sweet!"

Marcalan joined his cousin in the laughter. Tam stared at them both as if they had gone mad. "What is so funny?"

"How come you to like pimin so much?" Marcalan asked.

"My father liked it. We grew lots of it, and used it in foods many times."

"I am glad you had it not in the stew I ate the day I found you," Alcandhor said.

"We had none to hand, and I had no time to go to the garden to harvest the pimin, as I needed to hunt for meat. That was what I was doing when I felt you coming." She crossed her arms. "But what did Marcalan do that was so funny?"

"He added spicy sauce to our bowls. I do not care for it, nor use it, so it burned me. But you, niece, turned the prank back on him—he did not know you liked it."

Tam sighed, one eyebrow arched at Marcalan. "I suppose I am resigned to having pranks pulled on me every day for the rest of my life."

Marcalan grinned at her. "Not every day. That would be too predictable."

Alcandhor stood, dumped the contents of his bowl into Marcalan's, then returned to the fireplace to get some fresh stew.

Marcalan chuckled at him.

"I would advise you to be careful about your pranks with your wife. Women tend to be moody at times, and can react with the speed and violence of a hungry ka'gua." Alcandhor returned to the table and reseated himself.

"My dear Thane, I have grown up here in Zaidhron, with a mother, three sisters, and our dear Sarinna, not to mention all the other females in our clan. I think I am aware of when to be careful." A thought shot through Marcalan with such insight that he sat up straight. "I just realized something."

"What?" Alcandhor asked, picking up his cup.

"Since you are Tam's foster-father, you are now my father as well."

Alcandhor almost sprayed the tea, which set Marcalan into another fit of laughter. Alcandhor joined him. "Oh, great Bells!"

Tam sat with her hand over her mouth, giggling.

"Stars, should I begin calling you 'Father' now? Or should I say 'Uncle' as Tam does?"

Alcandhor moaned. "This is too much! It was bad enough as second cousins, but this..." He shook his head mournfully. "Life has definitely dealt me a wicked blow."

A twinge of heartache shot through Marcalan. Not second cousins one time removed, but as that Rogue's spawn, he and Alcandhor were fifth cousins two times removed. With effort he brought his mood back up, not wishing to ruin such a humorous moment. "You definitely are put upon, are you not, my dear Thane?"

"My father warned me he foresaw I had hard blows to deal with, but he warned me of nothing so dire."

Marcalan threw back his head, laughing.

Chapter Thirty-Four

Marcalan's laugh cut short, and he sat up straight, his gaze unfocused. Alcandhor leaned forward, hands on the table. Was his cousin suffering some further malady?

"Stars!" Tam closed her eyes.

Alcandhor stared from one to the other. "What is wrong?"

"Can you wait until we get to the portal?" she asked the air, then she said, "We will be there as quickly as possible."

She jerked forward a little, opening her eyes. "Mattan is ready!"

Alcandhor shot out of his chair, and Marcalan heaved to his feet. With a dubious glance at his cousin, Alcandhor asked, "What about your leg, Mar?"

"'Tis sore, but I will not let some minor injury stop me from seeing an Elder in the flesh."

"You still have much pain," Tam said. "And not just your leg."

"I will be there, Tam. Please."

Tam hesitated then ran to the wardrobe. She tossed his jerkin at Marcalan, and he donned it with Tam's assistance. He winced as he sat on the bed, and both Alcandhor and Tam helped pull the boots on and lace them. They grabbed their cloaks and hurried out.

"Let us go to the chiefs' range," Alcandhor said. "'Tis only right we have the chiefs present as well. Stars, and Delgan is here. He deserves to be present for this."

"Who is Delgan, Uncle?"

"A history-keeper who was a mentor and is a very dear friend. He arrived yesterday morning. I hope he is with Andhrel or at least close to hand in the library."

Had the city grown in size? It seemed to take forever to cross the grounds. Marcalan fell behind, and Alcandhor put an arm around him to help him. They burst into the forechamber of Thane Hall. Alcandhor shouted his chief's names, then ducked through the door of the Thane's chamber to pull the cord.

Haladhon came from the Elites' chamber. "What is wrong?"

"Where are Andhrel and Eladhrel? And Delgan?"

"I am not certain where Eladhrel is, but Andhrel is upstairs in the law library, as usual. I believe Delgan is with him."

"Get Andhrel and Delgan. We will wait here. Be quick, man!"

Haladhon bounded up the stairs and almost ran into Feladhrel heading down. He grabbed his arm. "Where is Eladhrel?"

"Teaching provincial law to the—"

"Send him here as quickly as possible." Haladhon continued up the stairs, and Feladhrel pelted toward the back.

Alcandhor paced the forechamber. Marcalan limped over to the bench and sat, face pale. Tam joined him, holding his hand.

"Aye, soon," Tam murmured.

Alcandhor turned to see her staring blankly ahead.

"We were across the city," she said.

She was talking to the Enaisi. Stars! Of all the wonders thrown at him, his first, oldest ambition was about to be fulfilled. If only the chiefs would *get* here!

Soon Andhrel and Haladhon raced down the stairs. Delgan followed more slowly, holding the banister for support.

"You called for us, Thane?" Andhrel asked.

"Aye. We await your brother. I have need of all the chiefs." Alcandhor grinned at his old friend. "And you, sir, arrived at the most opportune time. I have the ultimate gift for you. Although I cannot take credit for it."

Delgan peered at Alcandhor with a puzzled frown.

Eladhrel's voice could be heard from the back of the hall. "But what does he want with me, boy? It had better be important—"

"Eladhrel!" Alcandhor bellowed. "Now!"

Tam giggled.

His cousin arrived, gasping and wide-eyed. "Thane?"

"Follow me, all of you."

Tam took Marcalan in tow this time, and Haladhon teased that she was just the right height to be his walking stick as they proceeded to the Great Hall.

"Shu, Haladhon," Andhrel said, then asked, "What is going on, Thane?"

"We are going to meet Mattan."

"What?" Eladhrel cried.

Andhrel grabbed his arm—fortunately, his right arm. "Do you truly mean it?"

"Aye, now hurry!"

Alcandhor led them to the side entrance to the Great Hall that opened directly to the back corridor. He stopped before the embrasure and before he could say anything, Tam touched the panel, and the door slid open. She ran ahead and touched the panel for the lift. Again the door slide aside. They crowded into the lift, Andhrel touching the walls with reverence, Eladhrel gazing about wide-eyed, and Haladhon looking amused. Of course.

Alcandhor exchanged grins with Delgan. This was the secret ambition for them both. So close they came years ago, but this time, they would not only see Mattan in a hologram, but in the flesh. An impossibility walking out of a dream.

Knowing now the basics of this lift panel, Alcandhor easily found the button for the portal. The lift dropped and Eladhrel gasped. It slowed, moved sideways, then rose. The door opened and Alcandhor barreled out, down the corridor, and through the antechamber.

The frame for the portal blazed bright blue. The center pulsed with a blackness that seemed void yet filled with depth at the same time. Everyone fell silent. Alcandhor's heart pounded so that he felt it would break through his ribcage. This is what he had dreamed of his whole life. This is what he had studied about for years, hoping to learn enough to bring it about, and now, it was going to happen. With a jolt, he also realized this was what he had seen in that vision in the sealed off western entrance of the Portal Complex years ago.

He cleared his throat, hoping his voice would stay steady. "Tam, tell him we are here."

"Aye, Uncle," she whispered, then to the air, "we are ready."

Moments later the blackness shimmered and then a bright, white luminescence took its place as the portal expanded. A man stepped through, and the brightness behind him faded as the portal closed, the center blank, the edge once again a low, pulsing blue. The Enaisi did indeed look as he had in the old portrait. His brown eyes shone in a finely chiseled face which had the warm, deep color as of a darkly stained wood. He had a lean build, but with broad shoulders, his height not much more than Alcandhor's. His straight, black hair, tied loosely between his shoulder blades, hung down his back.

His sand-colored clothing set off his dark skin and hair. The loosely woven, soft material marked him as alien to their culture. Nothing bore colors to mark clan or guild affiliation. His trous fell to his soft-looking shoes instead of being tucked into boots. The tunic, also cut straight, came to his thighs. None of his clothes bore lacings. A small pack slung over his shoulder and across his chest.

Alcandhor bowed, fighting the strong emotions that threatened to overwhelm him. The Thane should not burst into tears as would a babe. This was an Enaisi. *The* Enaisi. And as Tam had once said, he was beautiful.

Mattan smiled. "You flatter me." He spoke their language with the same accent Alcandhor had heard in the hologram. "And you need not bow to me, you know. We are kin." He took a step toward Tam, with a broader smile. "Thank you, Tam."

Her eyes widened, and she backed up. Marcalan put his hands on her shoulders. Mattan held his hands out, palm up, his voice soft. "You needn't be afraid of me, Tam. I am a man, no different than your husband or your uncle."

"I do not mean to be afraid," she whispered.

Still smiling, Mattan turned to Alcandhor, and put a fist over his heart, inclining his head. *Why would an Enaisi do such an obeisance to a Teldheri?*

Mattan laughed. "Because you are Thane. I am still of your clan, and owe you allegiance, isn't this true?"

Alcandhor's mouth fell open. *This man, this Enaisi, has just read my mind!* He struggled to find his voice. "But you are my elder, though it is difficult to comprehend. And you are an Enaisi, not Teldheri."

"Yes. But you have other elders who still bow to you as Thane, don't you? And I was accepted into your clan, which is not pure Teldheri in any case."

Alcandhor nodded. That was true, due to this Enaisi and his sister, and later to Ashani. Mattan clasped a hand to the Thane's shoulder and Alcandhor returned the gesture, trying to control his shaking.

"So now what will you do, Thane Alcandhor, that your ambition has been met?"

Alcandhor huffed a short laugh. "Learn from you, sir, if you will permit it."

"Sir?" Mattan pulled up straight with an expression of mock indignation that reminded Alcandhor of Haladhon. Stars. "Please call me Mattan. And I will gladly teach you if you will allow me to learn from you as well."

"And what could you learn from us?" Marcalan asked with typical impertinence.

Mattan turned to him, grinning. "Much, Marcalan. And I am happy to see you healing well."

"Thank you for healing him," Tam whispered.

Marcalan frowned at his young cousin—his wife, Alcandhor reminded himself.

"He healed me?"

"The first time. In the woods," Tam replied. "We found you and they said—I thought you were dead. I cried, and I guess Mattan heard me."

"It was a mind-scream," Mattan said. "I have not heard the like in many years."

"He somehow used me to reach through..." Tam tilted her head. "I know not how to explain it."

"I used her as a conduit. Your injuries were—" Mattan paused, then continued, "severe. My team forced me to bed for many days to recover my strength. But it's why I decided to come now, despite my their resistance that I had not fully recuperated."

"Then my thanks." Marcalan bowed. "I am very grateful."

"You are welcome. But I sense you are not fully healed. Should you not be in bed?"

"I would not have missed this moment."

Mattan chuckled. "Typical Ranger."

Alcandhor stuck on what the Enaisi had said. "Your team?"

"Yes. I will explain more later." Mattan smiled at the silent chiefs staring at their visitor. "So these are your chiefs, Thane?"

Surely he must know their names, mindreader that he was, but Alcandhor introduced them anyway.

"Aye. These are first cousins, Andhrel, Eladhrel, and Haladhon. One other chief is out of the city at the moment, Lamadhel, father to both Andhrel and Eladhrel." Alcandhor gestured to the history-keeper, who had tears streaming down his face. "And this is a dear friend, Delgan."

Mattan stepped toward them, and they all bowed low.

"Do not treat me as a god," Mattan said. "I am but a man. Granted, my race has abilities yours has not, but we are only men as you are, and all too vulnerable and fallible. Please."

Mattan touched Delgan's shoulder. "Bells and stars, man, I am a scientist too, and can understand this moment for you. To see the portal active, to meet—me."

Delgan's weeping increased. He took Mattan's hand and pressed it to his forehead.

"It is well, history-keeper. I look forward to many discussions with you."

Mattan turned and clasped Andhrel's shoulder in the traditional greeting. Andhrel returned it with some hesitation.

"You must have many questions." Mattan's eyes shone. "About your history? And the law?"

Andhrel nodded.

"I will see if I can answer some of them."

Next, to Eladhrel. "And the quiet one, the rock upon whom others depend." Mattan grasped his shoulder, leaned close, and said a mock whisper, "Whether they realize it or not."

Eladhrel blinked, and his face reddened.

Mattan's smile grew to a grin as he reached up for Haladhon's shoulder. "You are a special one, aren't you? A mischief-maker."

Alcandhor laughed at both the statement and the look on Haladhon's face.

"Nice to see someone is not taken in by your looks, for once," quipped Marcalan.

Mattan turned to Marcalan, chuckling. "I am not taken in by yours either, prankster. Does Tam do well keeping you in line?"

"We shall find out, but so far, for the little time we have known each other, she has not tried."

Mattan looked from one to the other, and his mouth fell open. "You are just married? I thought from your bonding that—how long have you been married then?"

Marcalan shrugged, his expression woeful. "I know not. She slipped it on me while I was injured."

Tam's lips thinned.

"I would advise you to guard your humor on that topic, cousin," Andhrel said. "You may find 'tis one Tam will not find amusing."

"Nay, I do not. We thought you dying. You *were* dying until Mattan"—Tam dimpled at the Enaisi—"healed you. I put the necklet on you that next morning." She tipped her head, her eyes strangely somber. "I can remove it if you—"

"Nay!" Marcalan wrapped his arms around her and buried his face in her hair.

"So you have not had your nestling then?" Mattan looked from one to the other.

"Nay," Marcalan murmured.

"Marcalan only rose from his sickbed this morning," Alcandhor said.

Mattan lifted his chin, his narrowed eyes on Marcalan. After a few moments, he said, "Yes, you still are in much pain. With your injuries not fully healed, you are wise to delay nestling."

Haladhon chuckled, and Alcandhor raised a hand to silence whatever he might say. Likely ribald and inappropriate around Tam, married though she be now. His tall cousin took the tacit command to leave off, but continued chortling softly. Marcalan's face grew red.

Tam looked from one to another, frowning. "What is nestling?"

"A newly married couple is given three days seclusion," Alcandhor said. "It is called nestling. Meals are even brought to the chamber, so they do not have to share their time with anyone. A special garland is hung on the door to mark that the nestling has begun, and they are not to be disturbed."

"And at the end of those days, there is a celebration given in their honor at the evening meal," Eladhrel said.

"So, when does ours start, then?" Tam gazed up at Marcalan, her golden eyes wide.

Chapter Thirty-Five

Alcandhor stifled a smile as Marcalan gazed around, his face growing pink, then lifted his shoulders. "As Mattan said, I am not fully healed. We should have a healer—"

"We just did." Alcandhor nodded at Mattan.

"I think you will not need a healer to know when 'tis time to start nestling," Haladhon said, still grinning broadly.

Rolling his eyes, Alcandhor gestured toward the outer chamber and lift beyond. "Shall we stand here all day or return to Zaidhron?"

"Zaidhron?"

"The city."

"You named it after Zaidhron?" Mattan laughed. "By the Bells, he would spit fire if he knew!" He brought his mirth under control and tipped his head. "It is mid-day here, isn't it?"

"Late morning," corrected Marcalan, inclining his head with a smile.

"Come. Let us go to the city. I am anxious to see it again."

They all trooped after Mattan to the lift. In moments, the doors opened to deposit them in the back hallway of the Great Hall.

"Stars! I wish I could get from one side of Zaidhron to the other this quickly," Marcalan said.

"But then, what of the exercise you need, Ranger?" Mattan's eyes glinted with amusement.

"He gets enough of that running from those on which he has pulled pranks," Haladhon replied.

Mattan laughed. He peered around, his eyes bright. "It is good to be home." He gestured for them to follow him through the back hallway to the side door. "Come, I want to see the grounds."

They all paraded outside and Mattan stopped, looking around, a soft, nostalgic look on his face. "Oh, it has not changed much."

The white shimmerstone of the Great Hall and building next to it seemed a dull sight.

"Stone is not likely to change much, is it?" Marcalan asked, chuckling.

Mattan laughed. "No. Nor hard heads, either."

The Enaisi all but ran down the narrow alley between the buildings to the open center of the city. He stopped, his mouth open. "Oh, my!" He stepped forward slowly, crossing the broad walkway with almost a reverence until he stood on the grass, staring at the trees and gardens, now in full panoply of autumn colors. "Ah, if only Avadhron could have lived to see this. His dream fulfilled!"

"Did he not—" Andhrel began.

With a soft smile, Mattan held up his hand. "Pardon, but I want to hear the sounds."

Alcandhor stopped, paying attention to something he took for granted. Aye, he could hear various birds—dustbirds, mistwings, even the distant call of a curvin. Insects buzzed and chirped. A complex, ever-changing chorus.

Mattan closed his eyes. He inhaled deeply, then turned to Tam and Marcalan. "His leg needs rest. I know you will not wish this, but remain here." He gestured to a nearby bench. "We will return before long."

Marcalan's face set in stubborn lines, but Alcandhor pointed to the bench in a tacit order. Tam led her husband over and pulled him down next to her, murmuring something to him. He sighed loudly, but remained seated, dropping an arm around Tam's shoulders.

The rest of the group followed Mattan in silence as he ambled on the footpaths, gazing about with an expression of longing and joy. They mounted one rise, and Mattan stopped with a swift intake of breath. The flagstone path wound down below them, brown crunchy leaves scattered along its length. A disheveled array of bright yellows, oranges, and deep reds burgeoned from between bare branches and smudges of dark green from the winter-hardy underbrush, giving the spot the illusion of being in the wild. Mattan led the way down the meandering trail, which led to a manmade rill trickling into a small pool. The walk and pool were called Avadhron's Dream, although no one knew why. Mattan paused and huffed a quiet laugh before resuming his walk.

They continued on from garden to wooded area to areas of open sward. Occasionally people passed them and inevitably they halted, shock on their faces, staring at this dark-skinned stranger. Mostly they continued on with backward looks, but one Ranger stopped and in a strangled voice, managed, "Alcandhor?"

"All is well, Bandhral." Alcandhor raised his hands, palm out. "The portal again works. This is our Enaisi ancestor, Mattan."

The alien put a fist over his heart and murmured greetings, but Bandhral looked askance at Alcandhor and at the Enaisi. He shook his head and stamped off.

Mattan's lips twisted. "I see some things do not change."

Before Alcandhor could ask, the mealtime horns sounded. Alcandhor shot Mattan a questioning look. The Enaisi smiled. "Later, Thane. Shall we go to luncheon?"

"Let us return to retrieve Tam and Marcalan."

The couple rose as they approached, and Alcandhor peered hard at Marcalan. "Are you well enough to go to table?"

"Stars, and miss the uproar in the Great Hall when we arrive with an Elder? I will manage."

Haladhon laughed, and Andhrel groaned, rolling his eyes.

Eladhrel snorted. "You will likely try to take the credit for the whole scene."

"Ah, if only I could, but I think I will have to let Tam bear the brunt for this one."

Alcandhor smiled at his rascal of a cousin, then saw Mattan grinning at him.

Andhrel glanced over as they walked. "How is our clan going to handle this, Thane?"

"If they could handle Tam being Second at Table, then they will handle an Enaisi."

Alcandhor eyed the limping Marcalan; he hoped the man did not overtax his strength. Tam held on to her new husband, although how much was to keep him on his feet and how much was her desire to just not let him go, Alcandhor would not wager.

"Delgan," Alcandhor said as they passed through the door of the Great Hall, "as special guest, I wish you at my left hand."

"I am honored, Thane."

Silence fell, the only sounds coming from their boots as Alcandhor and the others strode to the main table. Alcandhor stood by his chair, and Mattan came over to stand next to him with a nod. Of course Mattan would know their customs! By his shining, dark eyes, he was as thrilled to be there as Alcandhor was to have him there.

The hall waited in a hush, every eye on the alien.

Alcandhor felt the need to make a speech, but no words would come. He cleared his throat, which threatened to tighten on him, and fought to control his emotions. He fell back on familiar words, ones he used many times to try to draw understanding from his people.

"As my father saw, as I have seen, our world has been balanced on the edge of a sword, needing to adapt. When Tam arrived, 'twas no longer possible for anyone to ignore that changes were happening, whether they approved of them or not. Now, the portal is open." Alcandhor held out his hand. "I would ask our clan to welcome back—" he stopped, his voice breaking, betraying him. He swallowed and cleared his throat once again. "To welcome back Mattan, our forefather, clansman, and a chief. One of the Enaisi who founded our clan."

He stepped back from Mattan and put his fist over his heart, welcoming him. The silence broke into gasps and susurrations. Every

Ranger and clansman in the hall stood at attention and followed their Thane's example. The women all curtsied low. Mattan smiled as he bowed to the assembly.

Alcandhor gestured to the place at his right and seeing the look on Mattan's face, said, "Tell me of a chief with higher rank."

Mattan laughed and threw up his arms in a gesture that reminded Alcandhor of Haladhon. "You just want me next to you so you can ply me with questions."

"Guilty!"

Tam and Marcalan stood next to Alcandhor, arms around each other. Marcalan lifted his brows. "A conundrum, Thane. Where do we sit?"

Kalinna flounced over and took her son's arm on the side opposite Tam. "Come to table, son. You need to rest."

Tam's eyes grew wide as she gazed up at Alcandhor. "Uncle?"

The Thane rubbed his chin and turned to Mattan. "Stars, are there any precedents from the past?"

"From before your people crossed from Teledhar, and the first generations here, yes. The couple usually chose to sit with the family of higher rank, at least for official functions, to honor rank and status, but it was their choice."

"He should sit with his family." Kalinna's lips pursed, her gaze reproachful. Jealousy radiated from her. Ah, an age-old problem, and one Tam and Marcalan would have to address.

Marcalan wrapped his arms around his wife. "Tam is family now."

Lantalan bent over Kalinna. "They are just married, let them be."

"He is my son, and he nearly died! I want him near me!"

"As smitten as they are, how much attention would you garner?"

The toothsome odors made Alcandhor's stomach rumble. Kalinna would likely create a scene, and he just wanted to eat. Well, and to talk to Mattan. "You two go sit with Marcalan's family for now. Go!"

His normally effervescent cousin pulled his arm from his mother's grip. "Leave off, Kalinna."

Lantalan drew close. "Do not disrespect your mother, son."

"I am not your son!" Marcalan hissed.

"That is enough," Alcandhor spat through his teeth. He glanced around, but fortunately only Mattan and Sarinna stood close enough that they might hear Marcalan. "You go with your family, and show proper respect to your *father*."

"He—"

"Do not say on, Ranger. By all clan legalities, he is."

"How can you say thus? By clan legalities, he is not!"

"I am clan thane, and I make final judgment. I have spoken. Do you hear me?"

Marcalan dropped his head. Tam murmured for them to go to table, and he let her lead him over to where Lantalan and Kalinna sat with Loch'alan and the rest of his siblings.

Alcandhor felt the muscles in his neck tighten at the reminder of that knotty problem. The whole hall awaited, and if Alcandhor did not sit to start the meal, Ganill would likely pelt out of the kitchen like a rabid ballan.

He sat.

The gong rang, and the assemblage followed Alcandhor's lead. The clink of dishes and glasses and chatter filled the chamber.

Mattan shook his head, smiling, as he looked around. "I am glad some things do not change. I have missed this."

Amara crawled into Alcandhor's lap, eyeing the newcomer. She pulled on a lock of her father's hair. "Papa? He looks like cousin Tam."

"Does he, Littlest?"

She nodded and peeked at Mattan from the safety of her father's arms. Alcandhor chuckled as he pulled some food over onto a plate for Amara. She wrinkled her nose. "I do not like greens."

"You will eat at least some of them, girl," Alcandhor said.

Mattan reached for a round hand-loaf of bread, whispering, "So, I assume there is some private situation about Marcalan."

"Aye, I can give you the details later."

Mattan nodded.

Alcandhor took a small loaf and broke it in half. He buttered part of it for Amara, asking Mattan, "Exactly how long has it been since you were here last?"

"I cannot give an exact reference in your planet's terms, but about six hundred of your years. I was just getting ready to visit when the invasion came."

"Invasion?"

Mattan speared a piece of redfruit on his knife. "My people were invaded." He stared at a platter, but Alcandhor did not think he was seeing anything on the table. "We had no prescience of it. The devastation was terrible."

"I–I am sorry." A lame reply, but Alcandhor knew not what else he could say. "But–but certainly you were able to repel the invaders?"

Mattan shook his head as he chewed, then he answered, "Neither telepathy nor empathy was effective against them and we had not their battle technology to fight them either. We did eventually win, if you can call it that. My people are very few now," he murmured, then looked up, grim. "But we had to protect the planets we visited. So we sent some of our people through to close the portals from the other side, then we shut ours down and removed the index key. That way, if the invaders were to gain access to the portal they could not use it, nor could someone from the other side activate it and potentially put their whole world at risk."

Alcandhor stared at him, astonished. "But that would mean your people would be trapped on those worlds."

Mattan nodded.

"Have you found your people again when you contact the worlds through the portal?"

"The portal was destroyed, and has been rebuilt only recently. This is the first planet with which I have tried to make contact."

"So that is what happened. And why Ashani stayed behind when the portal was shut." Alcandhor asked, urging a mouthful of greens at Amara, who pressed her lips together with a scowl.

"Aye. When did she die?"

"Centuries ago." Alcandhor took a breath and asked quietly, "Wish you the story?"

Mattan shook his head. "We have time for many histories later. I wish—Ashani was not the only one." Mattan stared at his plate, his voice soft. "My sister Ismari stayed as well."

The news jolted Alcandhor. "Ismari? I knew that not. Where—" The realization of the truth hit him. He licked his lips. "She is not alive?"

"No. When I activated the portal and sent through it, I couldn't find her." The Enaisi stared at his plate. "My bond with my sister was strong. We were twins. The only ones of our kind," he whispered.

Alcandhor murmured condolences, and Mattan closed his eyes, inclining his head. "Thank you." It was quiet for a few moments, and Alcandhor again urged Amara to eat. Then Mattan leaned toward Alcandhor a little. "Tell me about your niece, Thane."

Alcandhor smiled. "Why do you not call me Alcandhor?"

Mattan returned the smile. "My apologies. Even after all these years and being away from this world for so long, I feel the formality of your rank."

"Even with the rank you hold?"

Mattan snickered. "I was never Thane."

"Your son was," Alcandhor shot back with a wry grin.

Mattan's eyebrows lifted in surprise and Alcandhor laughed. "We may be lacking in some knowledge of our history, but not all."

"I am glad. I was afraid of how much knowledge had been lost. So you know of your line back to the time we came to this planet?"

"Aye. That we do know. You are my direct ancestor. And we know that you and Zaidhron were the ones who crafted our laws and founded our clan."

Mattan held up a hand. "Ah, now that is not correct. I, and others of my people, helped offer choices to Zaidhron, and the elders of your clan, when they came here and began to plan and build new lives here. And your clan existed long before you came to this world."

"Aye, but not as it is now. Our clan ruled, our thane was also king. Now we are but peace-keepers."

"Your role changed, but not your clan. Ch'shalna is as it ever was, even if your first thane on this world gave up kingship." He sighed. "I miss Zaidhron, he was a good friend."

Alcandhor frowned. "Your people live such long lives, how do you manage the pain of outliving friends—and spouses when you marry outside your own race?"

Mattan shook his head. "Not easily, at times. And your race is the only one we have married into, you know."

"Is it? Why is that?"

Mattan paused then said, "First tell me more about Tam."

"I apologize, Mattan. I did not mean to not answer that the first time. What would you like to know?"

"Who were her parents?"

"Her father was my elder brother, Valdhor. I know not who her mother was." Alcandhor stared at Mattan in amazement as a realization dawned. "Stars, Mattan, do you think that her mother was...?"

Chapter Thirty-Six

Mattan's sad, grave eyes met Alcandhor's. "There is no doubt in my mind."

Alcandhor stared in awe down the table at his niece.

"She does not know this, does she?" Mattan asked.

Alcandhor shook his head. "She remembers not her mother." He stared down at his niece, involved in a quiet, earnest conversation with Marcalan. "It explains much."

"What shall her reaction be if I tell her?"

Alcandhor shook his head. "I would tread slowly, Mattan. Valdhor was a hard man and raised her alone in the wild, Training her to be a Ranger. He was not loving toward her. She is still very young, and in some ways she is still unsure of herself."

"So I sensed. I will let her become used to me first." Mattan chewed, a pensive look on his face.

"Excuse me, sir." Sarinna, on the far side of Mattan, lightly touched his arm. "Would you please pass the platter of redfruit?"

"Certainly." Mattan lifted it over to her with a polite smile.

Sarinna murmured, "Thank you."

"I am sorry, Mattan. I have been neglectful. This is my sister, Sarinna."

Mattan inclined his head. "I am honored, my daughter."

"And I, to meet you," Sarinna replied with a slight blush.

Alcandhor's eyebrows raised; his sister did not blush easily.

"Where is Taniss?" Alcandhor asked, sending her his amusement at her discomfiture at the same time. "Has she gone back to the Valley?"

She sent back her chastisement as she replied, "Aye, but only to gather the rest of her belongings to move back to Zaidhron permanently."

"Ah, I thought she would. That is good, although she will not have the chance to mother Tam as she would have wished, since her granddaughter is married now."

"I think she will still find a way. You know her."

They chuckled, then Alcandhor gestured to the other side of the table, relating the names of those within hearing distance to Mattan. Complete introductions could come later. Mattan smiled at them all, inclining his head, then regarded the dazed boys, Alcandhor's sons and those of the chiefs, sitting across from him. "It will be good to again watch future

264

Rangers Train."

"Perhaps you could even offer to teach them, and us, more of our history," Alcandhor suggested, with a side glance at Delgan. His friend picked at his food, his eyes on Mattan. "What say you, Delgan. Shall we sit in with the Trainees and striplings to learn history from an Enaisi?"

His friend straightened a little. "Gladly, Thane!"

"It seems you give me little choice," Mattan said. He winked at the youths. "But it will give me the chance to remember which name is which."

Everyone at the end of the table smiled, then it fell quiet as they all ate. Alcandhor glanced down to see Amara had finished her plate, save the greens. "Amara, you must eat a little of the greens."

"I do not like them!"

Mattan's eyes crinkled as he sipped tea. "Children, enh?"

Alcandhor sighed, rolling his eyes. "How long have you been trying to contact us through the portal?"

"Oh, how I have missed the food of this planet." Mattan reached for another spoon of stewed vegetables. "About seven or eight of your years. I knew someone here was strong enough for me to reach through the portal, but the person fiercely blocked, fighting the contact." He glanced down at Tam then grinned at Alcandhor. "Tam is very strong and stubborn."

Alcandhor chuckled. "That is certain. But you are even stronger, with telepathic as well as empathic abilities. Could you not break through her block?"

"Not without traumatizing her. I had to wait and keep trying."

"But why did you not just come through and visit?"

Mattan shook his head. "It had been so many years. I did not know what the attitude might be toward my people, nor if it was safe. Anything could have happened. I was especially cautious because I knew my sister was dead, and Ashani, and I had no idea why or how their deaths happened."

A diplomatic way of saying he knew not if this planet had grown hostile to his people. Had their been such prejudice by some as to cause such a concern? And if Tam were indeed her daughter, then Ismari only died in the last few years. For Mattan to find her death so recent, for him at least, being so long-lived, must be devastating. How would he feel if he lost Sarinna? Stars. "I am sorry I can give you no answers about that, Mattan."

"Thank you, Thane. I have grieved for her. I miss her deeply. Tam looks so much like her that it cuts me to the heart."

Alcandhor remembered the day of the ambush near Lairdton. "It is the one thing Valdhor said before he died. He said Tam looked like her mother."

Mattan seemed thoughtful for a moment, then looked down at Tam. "She has lost both parents. It has been hard for her."

"I have tried to love her, and be a father to her. I do not know if it is enough. She is still freshly grieving her father's death."

"I can sense her love for you. And for Marcalan. She has many here who love her. I think she will be fine. I just hope she can accept me."

"Does she not accept you? She was so thrilled the second time you contacted her. She woke me in the middle of the night to tell me you were very kind and had a nice laugh."

Mattan smiled. "That is good to know. But I sense a shyness and even a little alarm in her toward me."

"She does get easily overwhelmed, but then she is young. She is also resilient. Give her a little time, and I am certain she will dote on you as she does me."

Mattan cut his eyes to Alcandhor with a smile. "We will have to see. Right now she is doting on Marcalan."

Alcandhor looked down to see the couple holding hands and murmuring together, eyes only for each other. In his mind's eye, he pictured Marcalan bloodied, how he had put his ear to his cousin's chest but discerned no heartbeat. He bent close to the Enaisi and whispered, "Mattan, I checked him. I could not hear his heart. I thought he was dead, and did not try to help him."

Mattan lowered his head, murmuring, "His heart had stopped beating—" He lifted a finger before Alcandhor could utter a sound. "Only just. Not for so long that I was unable to revive and heal him." His dark eyes bored into Alcandhor's. "Leave that piece of information quiet, Thane. You Teldheri tend to either hate us, or want to make us gods. And also, if it becomes known too widely that I can heal to that extent, I will be deluged. And trying to explain how it expends us, and that we can actually weaken and die trying to heal, does not seem to put off those in need of healing. I am still recovering from the exertion of healing Marcalan."

"I understand." Alcandhor straightened and nudged Delgan, saying in a normal voice, "And you should be aware there are some Teldheri who would make gods of your people. We called them the Worshippers. They call your people the Celestials."

Delgan rolled his eyes, nodding. "And other names besides. The Holy Ancients, the—"

"You are not serious." Mattan's horrified gaze flicked between Alcandhor and Delgan.

"Perfectly."

"And you have not—no, I will not ask if you have tried to stop them. People can be tenacious in their beliefs, despite evidence to the contrary."

Alcandhor huffed a laugh and drank tea. That was all too true. "Fortunately, none of this clan are Worshippers, at least, to my knowledge. I think they know the truth too well. And no Worshippers are allowed to live here or in the valley. Visits are rare as well as they know they are not welcome. The last one here was a history-keeper, although I am still trying to ascertain how one can study our history and still be so deluded."

Delgan snorted, his eyes flicking up at Mattan, but his head stayed bowed.

"For my part, I am glad I will not have to deal with them."

Alcandhor raised his eyebrows at Delgan. His friend lifted his gaze as if in supplication to the Maker, and he shook his head. "I wouldn't be too glad," he muttered, turning red.

"And why is that, Delgan?" Mattan asked.

Alcandhor wanted to laugh at his friend's hesitance to speak, but merely pressed his lips together to try to suppress a smile. After a few false starts, the history-keeper said, "Once they know you are here, I am certain they will make a 'holy journey,' whether welcome in this city or not."

Mattan spat, *"Tohni teg'ha."*

Alcandhor choked, almost spraying his tea—that was twice in one day. Delgan covered his mouth, his face flushing deeper. At least no one else here could understand Amhan'ai, one of the Enaisi languages, and not the one most commonly spoken and used. Well, Andhrel might have, but he was too far down the table.

"Is that proper language for table, Enaisi?" Alcandhor asked, trying for a stern countenance.

Mattan shot him a wry look. "My pardon, Thane. I see you, and Delgan"—he nodded at the history-keeper—"are truly well-educated. I thought—"

"You thought we would know Enai, but not Amhan'ai."

Mattan inclined his head in admission.

Sarinna leaned forward, one finger lifted. She twirled it slightly. Stars, Alcandhor had held all his people long at table. Pulling Amara into his arms, he stood, releasing them. His daughter wrapped her arms around his neck.

Sarinna walked around the Enaisi with a stern look. "Could you please, brother, be more aware of the time. If afternooning or evening meal is late, Ganill will wish to serve you on a platter."

Mattan smiled. "Perhaps I can attempt to help the Thane keep track of time, Sarinna."

"If you can, sir, you will earn my thanks." Sarinna curtsied and left, one eyebrow arched at Alcandhor. He shrugged at her, and she rolled her eyes. Grinning, he turned back to Mattan, but the man was watching Tam and Marcalan.

Marcalan sat on the edge of the table, face pale, leaning on Tam, whose arm was around his waist. Blood stained the trous on his left thigh; he needed those bandages changed.

Kalinna, domineering as usual, argued with her new daughter-in-law. Lantalan pulled on his wife's shoulder, murmuring to her, but she remained unmoved.

Alcandhor came around the table. "What is the problem, Kalinna?"

"This girl does not want us to spend any time with our son."

"He is weak, Uncle. He needs to lie down."

"Your daughter-in-law is right."

"Of course you would take her side!"

Loch'alan stepped forward. "Mother, even I can see he needs to rest. Leave off, please."

"How dare you speak—"

"Enough!" Lantalan hissed through his teeth. "If you do not wish to help, then do not hinder. Come. I will accompany you back to your family chamber, son, in case Tam needs a second arm to help."

Kalinna stood, open mouthed, staring at her husband.

Marcalan muttered something, and Lantalan said, "Never say that again! Come, Tam, let us get him home."

Marcalan, with Tam assisting, limped out. Lantalan followed with Loch'alan, and his two youngest—Valinn and Santalan, a stripling Ranger—trailing.

Mattan walked up next to Alcandhor and said softly, "I would like to hear the story behind that scene, Thane, if it is not too personal."

Alcandhor inhaled deeply, held it, and slowly exhaled. "Ah, Mattan, it is a mess. Later, in private. Perhaps your advice could help."

"I am honored you would think I am wise enough to offer advice. But I think we have something more immediate to worry about."

"And what is that?"

"The crowd gathering to gawk."

Alcandhor twisted about and sighed at the assembly. "Mattan, I apologize."

The Enaisi's eyes shone with humor. "No need. I expected it. I fear we do need to let them have a little time, Thane."

"Can we not conjure an emergency so we may flee?"

Mattan chuckled, then turned to face the press of people. "I imagine you are all more than just a little surprised at my return."

A few laughed. The scribe Maradhor lifted his chin. "Not all of us, Elder. For years our Thane has prepared those who would listen. And Tam's dreams of you were a portent that the portal would soon open, of course."

Maker bless Maradhor! A Ranger of utmost loyalty and insight. But then, the man was the scribe for all conclaves and privy to just about anything concerning the chiefs of the clan.

Mattan put a hand over his heart, with a slow bow to the scribe, then smiled at his audience. "I am certain you all have so many questions. I will try to give a brief account to you all. My people were attacked by a vicious enemy, and to safeguard your world from being assailed through the portal, we closed it down. My world was besieged and eventually all but destroyed, and our portal damaged. Once the enemy was defeated, we undertook the effort to rebuild the portal, and as you can see, obviously, we eventually succeeded."

"Will all your people return here then?" someone asked.

"Only eight of my people ever crossed to your world. And the two who remained here to shut down the portal from this side are both dead. Another died in...an unrelated matter. The four remaining members of my team who originally helped to bring your people to this planet may wish to return to visit, but they have duties which would keep them from doing so at this time."

A chorus of voices asked which ones died.

Alcandhor lifted a hand to quiet the crowd. "You should know the one, at least. Ashani." He looked at Mattan. "She died almost four hundred years ago. I can relate the circumstances later."

"My thanks. She was a good friend, and loved your people and your world." Mattan raised his arms. "Many of you are my children. I am so pleased to be back here with you."

A barrage of questions were asked at once. Mattan passed over one asking who the other Enaisi was that died, and chose another. "I don't know how long I will stay. The portal is open, so I can care for my duties and come here often. But for now, I am...recovering my health and have no responsibilities, so I will be spending quite a long time visiting."

Alcandhor jolted slightly at the word visiting; his heart plummeted with the thought. But of course, how childish to think the Enaisi would leave his whole life for this planet. More inquiries pelted Mattan and some were aimed at Alcandhor too. He held up his arms. "There are too many of you talking to sort your words." He picked one query that he had heard clearly. "The Portal Complex is accessible now, but not available to everyone."

"Yes," Mattan chimed in, "the place is too big and there are dangers of getting lost. Besides, I cannot know the whole structure is sound. There may have been ground tremors which affected some of it, even though it appears the section of it housing the portal is solid." He chuckled at the renewed onslaught of questions. "Perhaps tonight"—he glanced at Alcandhor—"we shall have a celebration and I can meet you all and tell more of my story. I do need to speak privately with our Thane at present, though. So with your pardon, I will withdraw."

"How do we know you are really the same man who was our ancestor?" A man called from the back.

Alcandhor frowned, raising on toe to see who the speaker was. Sedhral. No surprise there. Indignation seethed inside, but he hoped he kept his countenance unaffected.

Mattan however, merely smiled. "What evidence would you consider proof?"

Sedhral froze, mouth open. Finally he said, "I know not."

"Then I can give you no answer that would satisfy you."

From behind them, Ganill said, "Perhaps you can give an answer to satisfy me."

Alcandhor and Mattan both turned. The head cook, hands on hips, fixed her icy blue eyes on the Enaisi. "You just stride in here and tell everyone there will be a celebration tonight, do you? And who is going to have to do all the last minute preparation for that, enh?"

Mattan bowed. "My apologies for disrupting your routine, good woman. You are the cook?"

"Head cook, aye."

"May I tell you that I enjoyed that meal immensely. I have missed the food on your planet, and your cooking made me feel I had come home."

Ganill crossed her arms. "Do not try that nectar-flower sweetness with me, Enaisi. Alcandhor and Haladhon have inured me to it."

Amara took her finger out of her mouth. "But he did. He even liked the greens." She made a moue.

Every one but Ganill burst into laughter. Amara buried her face in Alcandhor's neck.

"I will have to pull a city-wide banquet out of nothing. Do not expect too much!" Ganill waved her fingers at the throng in a dismissive gesture. "Leave so my workers can clear the tables and prepare for the *celebration*." She glared until the crowd began to disperse, then spun and marched off.

Mattan watched her leave, his lips quirking up. "She is a force."

"Aye. And she commands here. I am only Thane."

Mattan clapped a hand on Alcandhor's shoulder with a grin.

Teldhor pulled on his sleeve. "Papa?" His eyes cut to Mattan and back. "Are we going to the tutoring class instead of with you today?"

Alcandhor chewed the inside of his cheek. Stars, he would not cut short time with his children, but—

"Perhaps, Thane, may I be shown to a chamber, and then visit stores? I should be given proper attire for my rank, should I not?"

Before Alcandhor could reply, Delgan said, "I would give up Zaidhron's Chamber to the Enaisi, Thane."

"Zaidhron's Chamber?" Mattan looked from one to the other.

With a groan, Alcandhor said, "Stars, if you tell us the chamber we have claimed was the one first used by our famed ancestor is not true, I shall weep!"

Delgan and Mattan both laughed.

"Then show me this famed chamber, and we shall see if I can make you cry. Come, children of the Thane, this may prove instructive." Mattan swept an arm toward the broad staircase.

"This I would see," Andhrel said, "but alas, I instruct a class on law after luncheon."

Eladhrel slapped his brother on the back. "I, however, am free of duty. I shall inform you whether our dear Thane falls into tears." He headed toward the stairs.

Haladhon grinned, joining them as they ascended. "I, as well, would see this."

Andhrel threw up his hands, grimacing with distress. "'Tis not fair!"

Eladhrel turned and mimicked Ganill's finger waving. "Be off, brother. This one time I am not excluded. Feel my pain." He grinned and bounded up the steps. Both of Alcandhor's sons ran after him, giggling.

Alcandhor set Amara down, despite her resistance. "You can walk. Go on, catch up to your brothers."

She took that as a challenge and called to the boys, as she scrambled up the steps after them. Alcandhor stayed next to Delgan, who climbed slowly. "Are you all right, my friend?"

"Oh, yes, Alcandhor. I am just old. I move with less speed and more deliberation than in my youth. You'll see one day."

"No doubt. But if you feel overtaxed, you will tell me, enh?"

"Don't fear that. I wish to be around for a long time, not only to vex my poor, patient wife, but to see all the wonders happening in our world."

"I will hold you to your word. We have fine healers here, if you have need."

"Thank you. My wife insisted I see a healer before beginning my trek here. Slow and measured, those were his recommendations."

Alcandhor nodded. He might ask Mattan to sense for any health problems. He was probably overreacting though. Even those in his clan with no apparent Enaisi blood lived on an average of forty or more years longer than those in other clans—barring accidents or slayings. A man of Ch'shalna clan having Delgan's age would look much younger.

They reached the top of the second staircase, and turned to continue down the hall. Mattan stood at the door of Zaidhron's Chamber. "This was the room first occupied by Zaidhron when this place was initially built. Do I get to see you weep?"

Alcandhor grinned. "Nay, Enaisi."

"Since Delgan has this esteemed chamber, perhaps I can be assigned the one that was first mine, if it is unoccupied?"

"And which is that?"

Mattan pointed to the next door, farther down. "We were neighbors."

Neighbors. He had grown up knowing Zaidhron walked on these floors, dwelled in that chamber for a time, making decisions that would affect not only their clan but all the Teldheri. He knew that Mattan and the other Enaisi lived here too, but this, this swept over him like a deluge. He sagged against the wall, struggling for control.

"Stars, Alcandhor!" Haladhon grabbed his arm—his left arm, but the pain was as nothing.

"I am all right." Alcandhor closed his eyes a moment and took a deep breath. "The reality of one thousand years ago stands before me. Alive. Able to tell me what happened, and tell me of my ancestors. 'Tis much to comprehend."

Eladhor peered out from under Alcandhor's elbow. "Papa, could he not tell us stories? Would that not count as history?"

"Ah, wisdom from the young! Would you boys like that? And you, Amara?"

Eladhor nodded eagerly. After a hesitation, Teldhor assented too. Amara shrugged. Most likely, as long as she retained her seat in her papa's lap, she would be content. He gazed at this amazing man. "Settle in your chamber and visit stores, then join us in Thane Hall. You can tell us all our history."

Mattan bowed. "As you wish, my Thane."

Chapter Thirty-Seven

Tam helped Lantalan ease his son onto the bed.

"Let me help get these bloodied trous off you," Lantalan said.

"I can do it myself."

Tam straightened at Marcalan's harsh reply and saw Marcalan's family crowding in the doorway. They needed not to know about Marcalan's true fatherhood, at least, not yet. Lantalan looked up, pleading, the hurt in his eyes cut deep. Tam walked to the door, shaking her head, meeting Loch'alan's gaze. "The wound is not pretty, and we need privacy to redress it."

Her new brother-in-law nodded. "Aye, Tam." He turned and used his arms to herd his siblings back.

Kalinna, standing behind them, pursed her lips, her eyes glittering. "I should help. He is my son."

Tam hesitated.

"We need not three for this," Lantalan called over his shoulder.

This would cause further tension with the ill-natured woman, but Tam felt he was right. And Marcalan's mother would not cause any ease to her son's heart at this time either. She shut the door, and returned to the bed.

"Leave off, Lantalan, I can care for myself."

"Marcalan, you should not treat your father thus."

"He is not—"

"Why do you say on, Marcalan?" Lantalan grabbed him by the shoulders, leaning over him. "Why take out your anger on me? I have ever been your father. I carried you as a babe, held you many sleepless nights, worried over you—even as a grown Ranger, each of your assignments had me holding my breath, hoping and praying to the Maker your incredible skills would be enough to see you through. You have ever, proudly been my eldest son. Why—"

Marcalan grabbed Lantalan's jerkin and looked up, tears in his eyes. "Because I am not your eldest son! Would that I was, but I am not. And you never told me!"

"In my eyes, you were." Lantalan cradled Marcalan's head. "You can sense. Do you not feel my love?"

Tam knelt on the bed, hands in her lap. The injury on his thigh needed tending, aye, but a deeper wound bled in his soul. Surely the dressing on his leg could wait a little time.

Marcalan hung onto Lantalan as if to be saved from plummeting over a cliff.

"Son. My son," Lantalan murmured. "You are mine. You will always be mine. Do not allow a breach, not now. We have need of each other through this."

The turmoil in Marcalan calmed a little. For all his jesting, her cousin, nay, husband—stars, she was not used to that yet!—had hidden this secret his whole life, no one to share his dread.

"He was so alone," she said softly.

Lantalan met her gaze for a moment, and an expression of understanding grew. "I am sorry, Marcalan. I had no idea you knew you had gifts. If I had, I would have—"

"How could you think I knew not?"

"We are taught that many with the gifts of the Enaisi have them weakly and never know. That is why those with a parent who is a Child of the Enaisi are tested by the Thane's key." He stopped, and in a small voice added, "As I was."

"You truly thought I was ignorant of my abilities?"

"You said nothing. Gave no indication. I would not have let you travel this road alone if I had any thought that you knew!" He pushed Marcalan back and stared at him. "Sense me. Have Tam"—nodded at her—"sense me. 'Tis the truth!"

Marcalan sagged, then hesitantly embraced his father. Lantalan held him fiercely, his eyes squeezed shut. Tam blinked back tears. Her father would never have shown emotion thus. She was happy, truly, that Marcalan had such a father, but a tiny burn of resentment kindled that she never had a father's love.

Uncle loved her. He seemed to try to fit a whole lifetime of love into the short time he had known her. But 'twas not the same. She wiped a tear from her face with the back of her hand, waiting for the two men. They finally both took a breath and relaxed their hold on each other.

To keep her own emotions under control, she switched their attention to what was necessary. "We need to change this dressing."

Lantalan straightened, one hand still on his son's shoulder. "Stars, Tam, you sound like a wife already."

"But we do. He has walked on it too much, and it has bled through his trous."

"Then to the task."

~*~

Of his three children, Eladhor alone did not settle quickly. Teldhor bent to his law studies, and Amara, of course, did not mind reading, as she was in her father's lap. But Eladhor kept bobbing his head up from his book, not to ask questions about the law, but about the Enaisi.

"Bells and stars, son," Alcandhor said. "The answer changes not. He will be here after he has visited stores, and he can answer all your questions."

"He truly is the same Mattan? That was forever ago!"

"Aye, son. Aye. The same Mattan."

Teldhor peered up at him, his head still bowed over his book. "But how can we know?"

"Ask him."

His eldest sighed and returned to his studies. It was a good question. They all took the Enaisi's word for it, but could he be a descendent, someone who just looked quite a bit like their legendary Mattan? Alcandhor knew; he had seen the same man in that hologram years ago. Stars, perhaps that was the answer!

With a tiny quirk of a smile tugging at his lips, Alcandhor set his attention on Amara's reading.

~*~

Alcandhor had almost finished with the day's lessons with his children when—finally!—a soft rap came at the door.

Mattan entered with all the chiefs and Delgan. The Enaisi was now properly attired as a chief. He bowed. "Thane."

"You insist on formalities, Ranger Chief. Were you the same when your son was thane?"

"I was, actually." Mattan pulled a chair away from the wall and sat, facing the boys. "Now again, your names."

The boys gave their names, and Mattan tipped his head, gazing up at Eladhrel, standing at his shoulder. "Stars, Eladhor and Eladhrel. Your parents decided to confuse matters, enh?"

"We are the 'spares,'" Eladhrel replied, with a grin and wink to his young cousin. "Second sons. So we are appended 'el' so everyone knows of it."

"Is that a common practice?"

"In some families," Andhrel said.

Mattan peered at Alcandhor. "Your father did not do that to you, I see."

"Nay." He took a breath, then said, "I think because he knew I was not the 'spare.'"

"Oh?"

Alcandhor ran his hands through his hair. "I knew this not until I was Teldhor's age, but my father had sight that my elder brother would not become thane, but that I would."

"Thus Alcandhor, not Elcandhor, enh?"

"Bells, Father, I knew this not." Teldhor's eyes flitted from the Enaisi to his brother then to his father.

Alcandhor waved a hand to dismiss the topic. "Let us ask our new, *old* chief questions." He carried Amara around to the front of the table and sat in a chair, then gestured for them all to do the same. With scrapes of wood against shimmerstone, the men brought forward more chairs, and they all gathered in a circle.

Amara's interest was more in her father than the Enaisi. She curled up against his right arm. She would probably end up napping.

Mattan's gaze rested on Teldhor. "You begin. First question."

His son straightened, his eyes round. "Me?" He swallowed and looked over at his father. Alcandhor nodded, encouraging his son to ask the question he had on his mind.

"How...how do we know you truly are Mattan?"

"Ah..." Mattan leaned back, crossing his arms. "The question of the day."

"I know not how you may prove it," Teldhor said.

Alcandhor smiled that his son had remembered Mattan's previous reply.

"I could prove it through DNA, since the Portal Complex is now open again. But if no one here understands genetics, that would establish nothing."

"Some of us have limited understanding, but not many, unfortunately," Alcandhor said.

"How could you prove it with—what you said?" Eladhor asked.

"A sample of blood, skin, hair, saliva—any of these can be used in a scientific test which can prove not only who someone is, but to whom they are related. Back on Teledhar, every child was genetically tested to prove parentage, so that every child was claimed by its proper clan. Once your people moved to this world, that was no longer an option, which is when the clan laws became more stringent concerning marriage and infidelity. Among your people, clan has always come first. So a child's heritage must be ascertained."

Alcandhor sat as if frozen, his mind on Marcalan's dilemma. By both moons, they knew the answer must be that Uardhel was his biological father. 'Twas the only explanation. But if they could run a test to prove it— ah, nay, to what end? To increase the nightmare that family must live through? The less said, the better, and his support as thane must be strong and open.

Mattan shot him a quick, questioning look, but then returned his attention to Teldhor. "Back to your question, we do have a quandary. You have the right to know I am who I say I am. After all, you have only my word, and if I am not lying, then I have been alive for over one thousand of your years."

Teldhor nodded.

"Yet, such proof is not easy to attain." Mattan looked around. "Does anyone have a suggestion? I know your people are not always readily convinced."

"The portrait." Eladhrel pointed upwards. "He does look like his painting in the gallery."

Andhrel—ever the law-keeper—disputed this. "He could be a descendant with similar features."

Delgan cleared his throat, his gaze flicking to Alcandhor. "If we had some holographic images from those first years on this planet, that could be considered proof."

Alcandhor glared askance at Delgan. The history-keeper gave an almost-imperceptible shrug.

"That may be the answer." Mattan grinned. "Your people saved their history from Teledhar here, in the computers. I could set up a portable imager. You would be able to see not only me, but Zaidhron, Cosdhral, Avadhron—"

"Great Bells, Mattan," Andhrel exclaimed, "do not tease us thus!"

"I do not. My only question would be, what do I choose?"

Everyone stared at the alien as if he were...an alien. He continued: "Something that included all of us, perhaps discussing moving to this planet." His dark brown eyes settled on Alcandhor. "Thane, perhaps you should help me choose, I think."

Thanes should not blubber hysterically nor should they shriek and run in happy circles. Not that he could with a dozy daughter in his lap. Alcandhor settled for nodding, fists clenched.

Haladhon chuckled. "Our Thane is trying not to faint, I think."

"Imagine seeing Zaidhron himself," Andhrel whispered.

"And Avadhron," his younger son added. "Stars, Haladhon I would think you would desire that. Being Chief of the Elites."

"Ah, Avadhron!" Mattan stared upward. "He distrusted and disliked me from the moment he set eyes on me. It quickly grew into a deep loathing." He smiled. "He was a great friend."

"But you just said he hated you," Teldhor said.

"It did not stop our friendship."

"I do not understand."

Mattan ran his tongue over his lips and shook his head. "Avadhron was...the most singular individual I have ever met. I fear unless one met him, one could not understand him." He paused. "Or perhaps not even then."

Alcandhor thought back to that Airing he and Delgan witnessed in the closed off western section of the Portal Complex. Avadhron must have truly been one formidable individual. And aye, he had accused Mattan with an attitude that he did not like or trust him. Yet this man claimed they were friends. Stars, was Avadhron's suspicious nature contagious? Now *he* was doubting—not who Mattan was, but how truthful, and what twist he might put on the past and his role in it.

Mattan inhaled, leaning back in the chair and gazing about. "Other questions?"

Everyone in the chamber exchanged glances. Eladhor timidly raised a hand. "Can you really read minds?"

"Yes, and that's how I was able to communicate with Tam through the portal. It's also one of the reasons your people do not trust mine. What keeps us from invading your privacy?"

After a silence, Andhrel asked, "What does?"

Mattan shrugged. "Nothing. We have a moral code which is intended to keep us from doing so, but a moral code only is as strong as the morals of the individual. And I do admit, I am not used to shuttering my mind since my people most often talk telepathically." He nodded toward the chiefs. "When I first came through, my mind brushed all of yours, not willfully but just...as a matter of habit. I realized what I was doing, and stopped, but you see the problem? You must take my word for it."

"How do your people keep secrets then?" Teldhor asked.

Mattan rubbed his chin, his elbow resting on his other arm. "For the most part, we don't. We can't. One must block to insure a secret, and then—"

"Everyone would know you are keeping a secret." Haladhon crossed his arms. "I would think that would lead to strife, being able to know what someone is thinking. If you are irritated, or think they are acting the fool."

"Oh, it has caused trouble. But it has compensations. Being able to call to someone from a distance, even through the portal. As with Tam."

"So you could call to your friends through the portal, even now?" Eladhrel asked.

"Yes. I should say 'Aye.'" Mattan grinned. "I must adjust to the shift in your language and syntax. As I did before."

"Before?"

"When I first went through the portal to Teledhar, I could barely communicate. Zaidhron was a student of history and language, and he helped me to assimilate your language. Well, the one most commonly used by most clans. This time it will be easier, since it's more of a drifting of pronunciation, and the change in syntax and in usage of contractions, or of different contractions. Some of these changes had begun before I left, but not to this degree."

"Aye, sometimes you sound like a commoner," Eladhor said.

"And your accent is very different from any I have heard," Andhrel added.

"I imagine it is. You're hearing your language as spoken seven hundred to one thousand years ago. I'm only surprised it hasn't changed more."

Andhrel huffed and dropped his head into his hands. Alcandhor rubbed his lips and glanced over at Delgan. His friend glanced at him, eyebrows raised. Did he, too, feel the secret elation that they had already seen and heard this Enaisi in that hologram, along with guilt that they must keep that a secret?

"What of your own languages?" Andhrel asked. "What we have studied is from centuries ago. Has that changed?"

Mattan opened his mouth to reply but the mealtime horns sounded, interrupting him. His sons vented audible sighs.

"The quick answer is no, not much. Idioms and such have, but the tongues themselves remain unaltered." Clearing his throat, Mattan straightened. "My apologies to you all. I...have a need to speak to the Thane in private before the meal."

Everyone rose, all wearing the same expression of disappointment. Except Amara. She hopped down from her father's lap, her eyes on the Enaisi. She rubbed her small hand on his. "'Tis pretty, your skin. The color is rich."

Before Alcandhor could respond to tell his daughter she was too forward, a wide grin flashed on Mattan's face. "I thank you."

"Come, Amara." Teldhor lifted a hand, wiggling his fingers at his sister. "We shall walk with you to the Great Hall."

"I am a big girl. I need not hold your hand, Teldhor."

"Aye, and I would not wish to since you still fain stick your fingers in your mouth like a babe. You need to wash first."

"I am not a babe!"

"Go, child," Alcandhor said. "Listen to your brother."

"I do not wish to. He is mean to me."

He let his voice deepen and clipped the words. "You will do as you are told."

Amara's nascent tantrum faltered, her pouting lower lip the only sign of her indecision whether to continue or yield. Haladhon lifted her into his arms. "Come, cousin. After you wash, I shall carry you all the way to the Great Hall on my shoulders, then you shall be the tallest of all and see the whole city, enh?"

Protests forgotten by this proffered treat, Amara acquiesced. Alcandhor shot his cousin a grateful smile. Haladhon winked.

As everyone trooped to the door, Mattan rose. "Delgan, please stay as well."

The history-keeper halted with a confused frown.

"Please shut the door," the Enaisi said.

Delgan complied with a wide-mouthed show of teeth at Alcandhor that had nothing to do with a smile. All Alcandhor could do was shrug at his friend.

Fists on his hips, Mattan exhaled slowly. "Now. I could touch your minds and discover whatever this secret is you two have." He raised a hand before Alcandhor could even form a reply. "I need not even sense, it is apparent. I am surprised no one else could tell, but perhaps they are too distracted by my presence. But I would know what this secret is."

The history-keeper pursed his lips, gazing at Alcandhor from under lowered brows. *Leaving the decision with me, are you?* He took a breath and met Mattan's dark brown eyes evenly. "We have seen Avadhron's Airing. And your message as well."

Mattan stared at him a moment then burst into laughter. Delgan's mouth dropped open, bespeaking Alcandhor's own amazement at the man's reaction. The Enaisi fell into a chair, his mirth continuing. After some moments, he wiped his eyes. "I should have known. I should have figured if anyone had found that entrance, it would be you, my most curious son!"

"I cannot take credit for the find. That was Delgan and two other history-keepers."

Mattan snorted, waving a hand between the two. "Teacher and pupil, of the same kind, you are!" He leaned forward, elbows on his knees, hands clasped. "So you have done as I asked, and kept the discovery of the entrance and the Airing both a secret, I take it?"

"Yes, sir. One of the history-keepers was reticent, but we persuaded him."

Huffing a laugh, Alcandhor said, "It took all five of us to persuade him."

"Five?"

"While we explored our find, two chiefs of the Sons of Avadhron arrived to run us off, until they found out I was Thane."

"Ah, they still call themselves that, do they?"

"They are proud of their ancestry. As they should be. Their sept chief,

Ordhral, is also a Child of the Enaisi, and they guard their province, and its secrets, well."

"Do they. I wonder..." Mattan's voice trailed off, then he blinked. "Well, I do thank you for keeping trust in this matter. But I do think you have a point about a holographic imaging being a way to prove who I am. Although"—he nodded at Alcandhor—"one would think Rangers would give their thane more credit, especially with one as you who has such a deep knowledge of your history. I hope dissention does not run deep, my son."

"Deep enough." Alcandhor shrugged off his secret dread over Tam's birth record. No one had brought forth Question yet. Was it a fool's hope that the subject would remain buried?

"I do have one more question I would ask before we go to table. Delgan, may I have one moment alone with the Thane?"

"Most certainly." Delgan bowed himself out.

Mattan eyed Alcandhor. "Now, what in the names of both moons is going on with Marcalan and his family?"

Alcandhor closed his eyes with a groan.

Chapter Thirty-Eight

"Marcalan, shu!" Tam ordered. "You are going to stay in bed. Now take off that jerkin, you cannot rest well in it."

"Stars, Tam." He sat on the edge of the bed, scowling. "I am fit and able to be on my feet."

"I can sense, so do not lie to me. Your leg is throbbing, you have such other pain as well, and you are weak. I do not wish to try to lift you if you fall over."

"I would listen to her, son."

With a sigh, Marcalan unlaced the jerkin.

Lantalan grasped his son's shoulder for a moment, smiling. "I will leave you to the care of your wife. If you need anything at all, Tam, call for me."

She tipped her head. "But do you not have duties you need to attend?"

Lantalan's expression had none of the veiled humor so often present. "None as important as my son and his wife."

With a nod at them both, he left.

Marcalan tossed the jerkin onto the bed. Tam picked it up and hung it over the bedpost, then said, "Boots."

Marcalan grimaced. Sitting next to him, Tam made a point of unlacing her own. After a drawn-out breath, Marcalan followed suit, letting each boot clump to the floor. Tam pushed him back onto the pillows, then hopped over him to kneel on the other side of the bed. He still sulked, and she put both hands on his arm. "You must rest to get well. Please do not be angry with me for insisting."

His expression softened. "I think I could never be angry with you."

Tam smiled. "Then please, rest. Sleep if you can."

"Sleep? With the wonder now in my life? Stars, Tam, I may never sleep again!"

Despite herself, Tam's smile deepened. Was he as smitten with the idea of the Enaisi as was her uncle? "Meeting Mattan?"

Marcalan took her hands in his and kissed her fingers, his eyes shining. "You."

Oh! Tam blinked back tears. She snuggled on his shoulder, pushing her new worry down deep. She had never realized until her uncle forced the demonstration of their bond that she had unfairly trapped Marcalan. If she had not sent to him so often, and played their sending game which started the bond, would he still have *in love* for her? Her abilities were much stronger, so her sending was stronger. 'Twas no surprise that his attachment had been so much more to cause him to be crazed.

His finger traced her face. "What is wrong?"

Stars, he could sense her as well as she could him! She could not say on about her true thoughts, but aye, she now understood some of the guilt that he and her uncle had felt. She met his blue eyes, still puffy with slight touches of purple and green and yellow from the beating, then took in his dark brown brows, the pores on his nose, the shape of his lips, then touched his dark chin beard. How could she love him so much?

She hesitated then said, "I just...I love you, and I want you healed. It worries me."

He pulled her tightly to him, his arms so strong and warm around her, the love from him radiating even more warmly. Ah, it felt so good! But— did he truly love her freely? She could never know. She wrapped her worry tightly and tucked it away as she closed her eyes and just enjoyed the moment.

~*~

Nandhal held his torch aloft, squinting into the dark beyond the illumination of the flame. "Does anything infest these caves?"

"Aye. Better hope we find nothing worse than spinners, tail-stingers, and jastahs." Monadhal paused. "Or ch'irpahs."

Hunching his shoulders, Nandhal spat a crude word. Monadhal laughed. "Afraid of a small rodent?"

"If they merely scurried, I would not care. Those things fly."

"Fear not, stripling, I shall protect you from the frightful creatures."

Nandhal bit back a caustic reply as they continued their march. At the moment, he needed Monadhal to navigate this maze under the mountains.

"Where are we going?"

"To Keladar, as I have said."

"But what then? Paltor is dead. Who will help us?"

"That is my worry. We will keep hidden until the search dies, then make for the Great River."

"Great Bells! No one crosses that river! 'Tis too wide and dangerous. And 'tis all desolation on that far shore. Nothing lives."

Monadhal snorted. "And you know this?"

"Are you saying it is not?" The Rogue did not answer. Nandhal ground his teeth and moved to his next objection. "That journey would take us across three provinces and another mountain range. And you think in all that time, no one will see us—especially you, being branded?"

"That is why we shall wait. And I am accustomed to night journeys when around settlements or towns, although having someone not branded and able to sense would come in so very handy. It is your choice, though. You can go with me or stay. I care not. But for now, keep quiet."

They traveled in silence for quite a long while. Eventually Monadhal's torch failed. He tossed it away and continued without a word. Nandhal could see little in the guttering light left of his own.

"This torch will not last much longer."

Monadhal held up a hand, then beckoned to continue walking. Nandhal bristled at taking orders from him, but kept silent and followed. He put a hand out to touch the smooth oldstone wall, hoping the Rogue knew the way in the dark. They had journeyed for hours in this maze of caves and tunnels, some natural and some, as the one they were in now, obviously not.

The torch sputtered and gave up its flickering light. Nandhal cursed as total darkness closed in on him.

Monadhal's voice hissed, "Come to the middle and keep one hand on the raised center ridge. It will lead us to our destination."

With shuffling steps, Nandhal worked to the center of the wide tunnel, his hands waving before him until he found the strange elevated area, like a spine that followed the length of the immense passageway. What was this place anyway? Why did the Enaisi build such an elaborate labyrinth under these mountains? He did not ask Monadhal; the Rogue would have no answers. Perhaps Alcandhor would. Nandhal's lip curled at the thought of that history-loving by-blow.

For hours, it seemed, they continued on in complete blackness, the only sounds their boot steps and breathing, with the occasional stumble over dirt or stones. The air weighed heavy. Nandhal's heart thudded with the thought of coming across ch'irpahs, or some animal more dangerous. Ka'gua nested in rocks above ground and below too. In desperation, Nandhal let his block down, trying to sense something—anything. Other than Monadhal, nothing was near. Not animal, not man. At least Monadhal's confidence gave Nandhal security. The Rogue did believe he knew his way.

The blackness held tightly around them but after rounding a long, slow curve of the tunnel, the ground inclined, and soon a slight breezed ruffled the hair around his face. He breathed deeply, swallowing his relief. Monadhal would sneer if he gave any indication the dark almost pressed him to panic.

Without warning Monadhal halted, and Nandhal smashed into him. The Rogue nearly toppled forward. "Brainless by-blow!"

"Tell me how to see in this black to know you have stopped walking then?"

Monadhal did not reply to his inquiry, but merely said, "We are at the end of this tunnel."

"What now?"

"Before us is a large circular chamber. Enormous. It has several openings. We need to find the right one."

"And how do we accomplish this in the dark?"

"Scattered along the walls of this chamber are supplies. We can build a fire, eat, and rest before moving on. Help me search."

Nandhal felt along the curved wall, trying to find torches, sheaves of wood—anything to give light and drive away the cursed blackness. Having the chill chased out of the air would be good too.

Afternooning, although usually a light meal, bespoke the industry of the kitchens in preparing for the evening celebration. Simple soups were served with many of the best leftover breads from luncheon. No one dared say word one. Alcandhor certainly would not. And many wise persons decided to take their third meal of the day in their own ranges, judging by the empty tables, although the First Table had a full complement, with all eyes on the Enaisi.

Alcandhor chose a soup of vegetables simmered in a creamy white sauce and ate with slow relish, listening to Mattan ask questions of all those near at table. He rose to indicate the meal was over, so those who wished could leave for their late day activities. For himself, he wished more soup.

As he refilled his bowl from the large chafing urn at the serving table, a sharp voice behind him asked, "When are you going to show us proof, Alcandhor?"

He turned a bit too quickly, sloshing hot soup on his hand, and hissed through clenched teeth. Sedhral postured with arms crossed across his broad chest, reminding Alcandhor of Valdhor.

"Are you speaking cousin to cousin, Sedhral? If not, you will address me as Thane."

"When are you going to show us proof of who this strange man is, *Thane*?"

Alcandhor met the Ranger's eyes steadily. "Ask him yourself for your proof, Ranger Sedhral."

"Why? Afraid that—"

"Ask—him—yourself," Alcandhor spat through gritted teeth.

Sedhral's lips curled back, his chin lifted. He looked at something over Alcandhor's shoulder, spun on his heel, and stormed off.

Mattan stepped up next to him. "That was...interesting." Mattan took a bite of a bread with dried fruit baked into it.

"Life is always interesting in Zaidhron, Ranger Chief Mattan. Know you not this fact?"

The Enaisi shrugged, his eyes glittering with humor.

Alcandhor smiled. "Speaking of interesting..." He nodded behind Mattan to a crowd approaching. He left Mattan to his inquisitors and returned to his chair to finish his soup.

~*~

A knock at the door woke Tam from her unintended nap. She opened her eyes to see Marcalan gazing at her with a tender smile, face inches away. He kissed her forehead.

"You are so beautiful asleep," he murmured.

"You were watching me sleep?"

"Aye. 'Twas the most worthy moment of my life."

"You are teasing me."

"Nay, I am not. You—"

The knock came again, louder. Marcalan sighed, but as Tam tried to sit up, he snugged her back in close. "Must we answer?"

Tam closed her eyes and curled tighter against her husband. Could anything feel better than this?

Another knock, and a woman's voice: "Ranger Chief Tamissa? Marcalan?"

Marcalan groaned. Tam extricated herself from his arms and wallowed to the edge of the soft bed. She padded across to the chamber door and opened it.

A young woman held out a tray. "You missed afternooning." Her face blushed pink. "Mistress Adrinna said to bring food, and to ask if Marcalan needed a healer."

"Nay. He is resting well." Tam took the proffered tray. "I thank you." She backed into the room and used her foot to push the door shut. She turned to find Marcalan standing close. He took the tray from her and limped over to set it on the sideboard by the fireplace.

"We still have redfruit stew from earlier," she said.

Marcalan grinned. "With or without the pimin?"

Rolling her eyes, Tam crossed to the table. "You should sit and let me—"

"Stars, Tam, I am not an invalid!"

"You are! You have great pain all over. And your leg wound will not heal with you walking on it so much. Would that Mattan had not arrived

286

today! You have set back your healing."

Marcalan cleared the dirty bowls from the small table, his lips pressed together.

Tam clenched her fists. "You are being so stubborn!"

"I am a Ranger! We do not give in to trifling pain, and we do our duty, even down to petty chores such as—"

"That is not trifling pain! I can feel it. Do you not realize you nearly died yesterday? You need to rest."

"The pain will ease when I sit to table."

Resisting an urge to stamp her foot, Tam strode to the sideboard and snatched up a phial. She held it out to Marcalan. "It will also ease if you take tincture of umaral. And as soon as we eat, you are going straight back to bed!"

"As are you. Think you I sense not? You are weak from healing me. And I need not sense to see how pale you are."

Despite her best efforts, Tam's eyes filled with tears and her chin trembled at the reflected fierce worry from her husband. "Will you truly rest after we eat?"

Marcalan took the small bottle from her with a tender smile and wrapped his arms around her. She rested her head on his chest, listening to his heartbeat, inhaling the special masculine scent of Marcalan.

"Aye, Love-ling," he murmured. "I will fain rest with you beside me."

Love-ling! Tam melted against him, relishing the sound of the endearment. *Love-ling.*

~*~

Ganill chased the stragglers buzzing about Mattan out of the Great Hall. Alcandhor chuckled at the cook's ire—since it was not directed at him this time—as he followed the swarm exiting the building.

"Where to, Thane?" Mattan asked.

Alcandhor had given this some thought, remembering Sedhral's disbelief. His answer might not satisfy everyone, but it was a start. "To your portrait in the banquet gallery."

Amid a chiming chorus of agreement, they all descended upon Thane Hall, with Alcandhor in the lead. They trooped up the stairs to the third floor above ground.

Mattan strode across the grand chamber, glancing at all the paintings. He found his own and stood beneath it, striking the same pose. Everyone laughed, and various comments and exclamations all showed agreement that this was indeed the same man.

With this determination made by the collective present, Mattan did not mention the holograms. Perhaps Alcandhor could cajole him into showing him some of the recordings at some time though. He was certain Delgan and other history-keepers would assist in the task.

The Enaisi sat on the edge of a table and held up his hands as questions assailed him. He repeated the story he had told previously, of the attack on his planet and why they shut down the portals.

Alcandhor seated himself to the side and watched as his kin grew more and more enthralled with their ancestor. He answered some questions, deflected others by asking engaging questions of various persons, turning the conversation to both events on the planet since he had left and in their lives.

As darkness gathered in the chamber, some of the attendees lit sconces along the walls. Alcandhor allowed himself to relax and let the knowledge seep through his mind that his heart's desire had come to pass. Except for those few who had duties before evening meal, no one left before the mealtime horns sounded.

~*~

Nandhal sat with his back against the oldstone wall, his knees raised, staring about the strange place. Sparks from the fire flew up to disappear in the shadows of the vaulted arches high above them. A circular platform spanned the chamber, and it seemed designed to rotate, aligning the ridge— or spine or whatever one decided to call it—to one tunnel or another. By what means could that platform be moved? And what was the purpose of all these tunnels? His eyes darted to the sleeping Monadhal. He would not ask; the man would not know, and on the rare chance he did, his reply would only be a sneer.

Soon it would be his turn to sleep while Monadhal took watch. Then they would start their journey out of these tunnels into Keladar. This man had eluded Rangers for years. Could he lead them away from danger, to a place where the Rangers could not find them or would not follow?

The Great River. Bells. Did anyone dare to try to cross that mighty water course? Did they live if they attempted it? Nandhal clenched his jaw against his own fears. Curse the Rangers for bringing him to this pass!

~*~

Tam awoke and stared into the dark, disoriented. Where she was came to her as Marcalan nuzzled against her hair and neck, still asleep. She must have heard the mealtime horns. She should rise and light candles, and the fire had burned low. And they would miss evening meal. But she was so tired; 'twas easier to sleep. With no effort her eyes shut, and she returned to her dreams.

~*~

The chill breeze rushing past Nandhal's face refreshed him, even as it guttered their torches. He could not wait to be above ground and away from the dank, dark mountains. Even though night, the black sky would not oppress him as had the caves and tunnels.

Monadhal put an arm out and whispered, "This entrance is in the southern part of Keladar Province. Since you can sense, I will let you ascertain that no one is near before we leave. 'Tis maybe forty or fifty paces to the opening after this bend."

Nandhal kept one hand against the rough rock wall as he padded forward, but stopped before rounding the curve. Several people gathered, not far away. He dropped the torch and stepped slowly ahead, pace by soft pace, until he dared go no farther. 'Twas silent. He closed his eyes and concentrated. At least half a dozen men. Hunters camping nearby? Nay, for he heard no voices, no jesting, no songs. Their mood was one of alert determination. He had felt thus before, the Rangers in wait for prey, as they had on duty at the perimeter during the siege.

Clenching his teeth in frustration and fury, Nandhal backed up, picking up his torch along the way.

Before Monadhal could ask, Nandhal spat, "Rangers!"

"Are you certain?"

"They camp in the dark—silent, waiting."

Monadhal hissed a curse. "To the next exit then. 'Tis a half a day north of here. It means more journeying in the open as we head south, but that one has never failed to be clear. 'Tis quite hidden. Come."

His shoulders slumping, Nandhal followed the Rogue.

Chapter Thirty-Nine

Red, green, and white banners normally saved for the Final Crossing celebration hung across the Great Hall, lending a festive atmosphere. Musicians played happy, lilting tunes and tables of sweetings and tapped kegs lined the wall under the stairs. Mattan grinned at Alcandhor. "All for me? Too bad Avadhron is not here to see it. He would have sharp words!"

Alcandhor took his place by his chair, biting the inside of his cheek, remembering his earlier thought about Mattan's version of history. Dare he broach this with the Enaisi?

His niece and her rascal of a husband were absent from the head table, and after a short wait, Alcandhor finally sat. "'Tis not like either Tam or Marcalan to be late for meal," he said to Mattan.

The Enaisi pulled juicy slices of meat onto his plate, then paused with a slight frown. "They are both asleep."

Alcandhor swallowed his astonishment that the man could sense the two of them all the way across the city. He took a large gulp of ale. "Ah. I am not surprised, actually, considering 'twas only yesterday Tam finished healing Marcalan."

"She what?"

"He seemed to recover, but the day before yesterday he became very ill. The healer said 'twas likely internal bleeding, and that he could do nothing. Tam could not contact you so she tried to do what you did. I summoned every Child of the Enaisi in the city to their chamber. We all sent strength to Tam so she could heal him. If we were exhausted from the effort, she must be more so."

"By both moons! I had no thought I did not properly finish healing his injuries! And if I had known they were both thus weakened, I would have delayed coming."

"'Tis done, and ended well. This evening is for celebrations."

Mattan inclined his head and resumed filling his plate.

The lively, cheerful meal lasted for some time, but finally Alcandhor rose, and the tables on the side nearest the musicians were removed to allow for dancing. Mattan trailed Alcandhor to the kegs. Ganill had ordered the good ale from Keddek in Pashelon brought out. Stars! He nodded toward the kegs with the Hind's End mark, and he and Mattan both filled their tankards.

Mattan's brows raised at the first taste. "Bells, Thane, but this is excellent ale!"

Alcandhor lifted his tankard in agreement and wandered to the edge of the dance floor to watch a ribbon dance, Mattan at his side.

Several women simpered at Alcandhor, which confused him until he saw Mattan receiving the same attention. A young lady approached, blushing yet bold enough to ask Alcandhor to dance, but he kindly declined. She did not look best pleased as she flounced off. The Enaisi also refused, with bows and apologies, stating he knew not their dances yet.

A group of singers performed one of the Crossing songs, and Mattan smiled throughout, although once he muttered to Alcandhor, "Stars, is your history this far off the mark, Thane?"

"The song takes some liberties. Perhaps you can set them straight?"

"Forbid!" Mattan grinned behind his tankard before taking a swig of ale.

Alcandhor raised his own and drained it. Perhaps it was bravado from the ale, but he felt he dared say on. "Mattan, it has occurred to me..." Then he faltered. Perhaps he needed more ale.

Mattan turned to face him full, brows raised. "Aye?"

Alcandhor took a breath. "How do we know the history you give us is true?"

A grin slowly spread on the Enaisi's face. "Wise of you to not blindly trust. But you can sense. Can you feel anything that would give away deception?"

"Nay, but you have stronger abilities, and others besides. And one can create false feelings. Not to mention, some individuals believe their own lies, and thus appear to be truthful."

"Aye, there is that." Mattan took another drink, then pointed at Alcandhor with his tankard. "There are records kept in the computers, and as I said, important meetings and conclaves were recorded as well. From Teledhar as well as on this planet in the early years. Perhaps we should call all the history-keepers together and have a viewing of some of them. You might find the first one of me arriving on Teledhar and being introduced to King Janadhan very amusing."

Alcandhor stared, mouth slack, at the Enaisi. Finally he replied, "I need more drink."

He returned from the kegs to find Mattan—naturally—surrounded by a curious crowd. He stayed back, enjoying the ale. Haladhon wandered over, grinning. "I see Tam and Marcalan are not here. Have they started nestling?"

After another pull of ale, Alcandhor shook his head. "Mattan says they are both asleep. She is weak as well as he, from healing him."

His cousin's smiled faded a moment. "Ah. Well, I am certain they will start soon enough. Great Bells, 'Candhor what amazing events have occurred these past few lunations!"

"My father foresaw this. Not this exactly, but something incredible. He would never say on though, except to ready ourselves."

Haladhon nodded. "And you as well."

"Aye, but 'twas not *sight* sight, just a *knowing*. Perhaps 'tis why I have always had such a desire for history and knowledge of the Enaisi. To help prepare our people."

Lifting a shoulder, Haladhon looked away, but came to vigorous attention with a wide smile as a lass approached. She dipped a curtsey in front of both Rangers. "Thane. Would you join me as partner for a dance?"

Stunned at this second invitation, Alcandhor took a moment to find his voice. "I thank you," he said, bowing, "but nay, not tonight."

Before he could suggest Haladhon as a partner, she curtseyed again, lips pressed together and face pink. Her skirt twirled as she turned away.

"Stars, Thane. What harm is a dance?"

"Harm to her, likely. I do not dance well."

"Practice is the solution to that problem."

Alcandhor snorted and took another sip of ale. Haladhon soon deserted him, and another young lady came over to ask for a partner. He bowed to this one and took her hand, letting the beautiful Amara lead him to the floor. Halfway through the dance, he picked her up and carried her through the motions, spinning her around and sharing laughs.

When the dance ended, he hugged her tight as they walked off the floor.

"Soon time for bed, Littlest."

"Aye, Jholinn said I could dance with you once before she takes me away." His daughter waved at the widow, standing nearby, hands folded. Alcandhor took Amara over to her and set her down.

"Since you are both off for the night then, I will bid you both night's rest." Alcandhor kissed his daughter's hand, and bowed to Jholinn. The woman curtseyed solemnly.

He watched the pair of them cross the hall, then turned to search for Mattan. Still amid the many curious; he would get no more time alone with the Enaisi tonight. One more ale, then he would retire.

~*~

"It cannot be! You are mistaken!"

Through gritted teeth, Nandhal replied, "I told you already, I checked. It is being watched."

"Bloody Bells! No one knew of that entrance. We have used it for years."

"They know of it now, and you assured me that was our surety of escape. What do we do?"

"Quiet. Let me think." Monadhal leaned against the rock wall, rubbing his forehead.

Nandhal walked a circuit of the cave, then sat on the ground. The dim light from the torch created strange shadows on the walls of the cave that, in his current frame of mind, seemed an omen. "Can we not search for another entrance?"

"Aye, but they are all north, and we need to head south."

"We cannot just sit here."

"Will you shut up, you in-bred by-blow! I have outwitted Rangers for years, and am not done yet, but I need to think."

Nandhal jutted his chin forward, fists clenched. "Do not talk to me in such a manner! I rank you, Monadhal!"

The older Rogue laughed, pushing off the wall and snatching Nandhal by his jerkin. He snarled in his face. "You swaggering cockerel! You are no longer a Ranger, and rank means nothing. I am your leader unless you wish to try your fortune outside the caves right now. Now shut up and let—me— think."

He slammed Nandhal against the rock wall once for each time he spat out the last three words, then dropped him and paced.

Nandhal slid to the ground, gasping for air, with a wary eye on Monadhal. "How much food do we have?"

"Food is not a worry for quite a time, as I keep telling you. We have enough stored that would have fed all of us for the winter. But you know they will not cease their vigilance until we are caught. And if enough descend on this mountain range, they may swarm in the entrances to find us."

Nandhal nodded; he knew Monadhal was right. "Curse Marcalan. I am certain his death is the reason we are being hunted so relentlessly. I knew it was folly to get so close to Zaidhron."

"Enough. We have done it before. It was a sad chance that they found us before we were well away."

"Chance nothing. I warned you if we did not kill him and leave quickly they would catch up with us."

"You have all the answers, do you not, you randy, young cockerel? Then find us a means safely away from here. Otherwise, keep your remarks to yourself."

Nandhal scowled.

~*~

Even before opening her eyes, Tam knew the chamber was light. Stars, they had slept all evening and night until morning? She stretched under the heavy covers, and her elbow lightly jabbed something— someone! Marcalan! Her eyes shot open. "Did I hurt you?"

Propped on one elbow, Marcalan shook his head, smiling. "Nay, Love-ling."

Tam smiled, then frowned. "Were you watching me sleep again?"

"Aye."

Before Tam could reply, he bent forward and kissed her. His lips were gentle on hers, but his facial hair prickled against her nose. She winced and drew back, giggling.

"Stars, Tam! 'Twas not the response I expected from our first kiss!"

"Your moustache tickles!"

After gazing at her for a moment, he rubbed his face. "Wish you for me to shave it off?"

"Nay!" Tam sat upright. The thought of a clean-faced Ranger seemed so wrong. Only striplings and young Rangers, like Loch'alan, did not sport moustaches and chin beards. "Let us try again."

Marcalan grinned and pulled her down to him. Despite the tickling, the kiss was very good. Stars, kissing made one want to kiss more. After some time, though, they came up for air. Marcalan held her tight, whispering, "I hope I heal soon, because this is only a promise of so much more."

The kissing definitely made the tickling worth it. Tam pushed away slightly to gaze at him. "Can we practice the promise some more?"

Marcalan laughed and complied.

Some time later, the mealtime horns sounded. Stars, they would miss breakfast! What would Uncle say? Tam pushed up from him, but Marcalan lifted himself almost upright, trying to keep his lips on hers.

"We must rise!" Tam insisted.

Marcalan snorted and fell back onto his pillow, arms splayed. "Would that I could!" He sighed, then groaned and slowly sat up again.

Stars, he fought be to on his feet yesterday, despite the agony of his injuries, so why would he say thus today? "Do you feel you cannot?" Tam tipped her head. "Do you think you should stay abed?"

Marcalan chuckled and rubbed his face. "Nay, Love-ling."

She knelt next to him, biting her lip. For some reason, she felt especially attuned to him. He had less pain than yesterday, but the leg still throbbed. "We should check that dressing."

With a resigned sigh, Marcalan flopped back onto the bed a second time. "Do what you will, my healer."

Tam pulled on her clothes, brought over the bandages and ointments, and again knelt on the bed next to him. The wound did look better and had closed up more.

As she completed the new dressing, she said, "I think you should stay abed, or at least not walk much. Not across the sward to Thane Hall anyway. We can eat here, and I can return after morning reports."

"I cannot neglect my own duties."

Tam crossed her arms. "I rank you."

Marcalan sat up, his face set. "Do not try to bring rank into our marriage."

Tam shrank back, blinking, her mind falling back to her father's treatment of her. Heart racing, she scrambled off the bed, gathering the used bandages and trying not to burst into tears.

Marcalan struggled out of the bed and caught her in his arms. "I would never—" He stopped. "I love you. Never have fear of me. I am sorry, Tam."

Tam could not control her weeping then. He just held her tightly, murmuring softly. Finally he set her back and met her eyes. "I jested to the Thane about it, but please know we must leave rank out as husband and wife. We are a partnership. You should not dominate me, nor I you. I have seen enough of that with my mother. Can you understand?"

Tam nodded. Marcalan snugged her in close, swaying slightly, and she slowly relaxed. But inside, the thought that he truly did not love her freely fought against the love she felt from him. Her conflict stole away the comfort she should feel in his arms.

"Come, Love-ling," he whispered after a time. "Let us see what we have here for breakfast. We should have leftover breads, and we have tea."

Tam wiped her eyes, nodding, then managed a small smile. "But at least pull on trous first."

He laughed and, with her help, complied.

Between the two of them, they soon had their meager breakfast made. Tea and bread, toasted in the embers, was fine with Tam. She did not eat much in the morning. Marcalan stared across at her, worry in his face. "Are you still bothered by my growling before?"

Tam shook her head.

"Then what? I can sense something wrong."

Tam sipped her tea, wondering how to answer, but was saved by a knock at the door. She rose to answer it and found Loch'alan grinning at her.

"Hail, my new sister!"

"Ah, Loch'y," she heard her husband call. "Leave us be!"

Her brother-in-law sauntered in with a grin that was exactly like his eldest sibling. "Ha, nay! I come with orders from our Thane. You are confined here to rest. Breakfast will be brought soon."

"But we had breakfast." Tam gestured to their table.

Loch'alan shrugged with a grin. "Have two then."

"And I need not lie abed." Marcalan rose, and Tam knew the painful cost of standing without at least using the table to push against. But he looked hale to the eye, save being pale and the horrible bruising on his torso.

"I am not fooled, Mar."

Or perhaps he did not look hale to a brother who knew him well.

"This is the Thane's command. And he and Mattan will visit after breakfast." Loch'alan peered at their table with a twist of his lips. "I will leave you two to prepare for a better breakfast than that stingy one." He bowed to Tam and backed out, closing the door.

Marcalan scowled. "I am not an invalid."

Tam decided not to argue the point. She tossed his shirt to her husband. "Then dress and help me clean up and prepare for a proper breakfast."

Chapter Forty

Alcandhor knew not why Mattan insisted on visiting Tam and Marcalan. He merely claimed he wished to see how they both fared. Considering he could sense and tell their health from across the city, the claim seemed tenuous.

As Tam opened the door, Alcandhor was pleased to see the color had returned somewhat to her face. Marcalan, standing at the table, bowed.

"Seat yourself, cousin, and eat."

"Aye, Thane." Marcalan sat but only sipped tea.

"How do you feel?" Alcandhor asked.

"I feel much better. I need not be restricted to our chamber, Thane."

"I will let your wife and Mattan be the judge of that. You cannot fool them."

"He should rest, Uncle."

"I agree," Mattan added.

Marcalan slumped in the chair.

"And you are to stay with him," Alcandhor said to Tam.

"But the morning reports! I have been absent for so long, I know not what is happening."

"I can manage, and will have a summary prepared for you later. Your duty at the moment is to make Marcalan obey his Thane's and his healer's"—he nodded at Mattan—"command to rest."

Tam bit her lips, suppressing a smile.

"Thane, may I at least walk in Avadhron's Sward a bit?"

Mattan set his fists on his hips. "If you find your chambers stuffy, open the windows and set a chair on the balcony. You are not to walk more than the length of your chamber today. If—" He raised his voice over Marcalan's objection. "*If* you obey, you will find by tomorrow that thigh wound has healed greatly. If you fight against rest, that muscle may sustain permanent damage and limit your abilities as a Ranger."

Marcalan's mouth snapped shut.

Alcandhor chuckled. "Never has anything quieted him faster."

With an assuasive smile, Mattan clasped Marcalan's shoulder for a long moment. "Be assured, Ranger, that by resting now, you are doing an important duty—for your future and your clan's."

Marcalan merely nodded. Tam whispered thanks as she saw them to the door.

As they descended the steps to the sward, Mattan asked, "Do you mind if I sit in for the reports, Thane?"

"Why should I mind? You are a chief. But why would you wish to participate in something so tedious?"

"It will help me understand some of the problems of our clan. And our world."

Alcandhor could not fault that.

~*~

Haladhon brought over an extra chair for Mattan. "Tam is not joining us?"

"Nay," Alcandhor replied, separating the reports into piles. "She has another duty. Sitting on Marcalan to force him to rest."

"Would that I could witness that!"

"He was very compliant when we left. Mattan put a fear into him."

"A fear? Of what?"

"If his leg does not heal properly, he will not be able to continue his current duties as a Ranger," Mattan said over his shoulder as he pored over the map on the wall behind the table. "So many more settlements, and new provinces." He ran a finger down the line to the west. "I see you do not list any settlements on the other side of the river."

"Nay, we do not cross the Great River."

Mattan turned, frowning. "Why?"

Alcandhor lifted his shoulders. "We just do not."

"But why?"

Alcandhor stared at Haladhon, who raised his eyebrows, shrugging.

"Because...we do not. 'Tis shunned as is—" Alcandhor remembered the pain on Mattan's face in the hologram at the mention of the Forbidden Peninsula. He took a breath. "We just do not go there."

Mattan grimaced, but before he could say anything, Haladhon said, "Aye. Officially, no one goes there. But some clanless brave that dangerous river and the wild on the far side."

"Aye, Rangers patrol near the ruins of that ancient bridge to dissuade anyone from crossing. And to keep eye for any lawless who might try to cross." Alcandhor straightened a pile of reports, while musing aloud. "Perhaps the shunning of the Great River is a tradition, passed down without reason, or a reason that no longer applies. I shall look into that. But not now." He looked up at the two men and nodded at the chairs. "Shall we see what is happening in our world?"

The three bent over the table, Mattan occasionally asking questions, and Haladhon writing a summary for Tam. Most reports offered no problems that local Rangers could not handle. One missive from Lantral gave good tidings, details on the regrowth of a forest that had caught fire the year before.

"So you still oversee the land throughout all the provinces as caretakers, I see."

"We must safeguard our world, else how can it sustain us?"

Mattan smiled. "Avadhron would be pleased."

Alcandhor wished to ask more about his collateral ancestor but later; he needed to finish this current task. He bent to the next report. Lamadhel sent news that the young Laird was well, and that the training of new guards for Laird Hall proceeded as expected. The more seasoned guards, once recovered from their starvation and ill treatment in the siege, helped train their inexperienced comrades. Lamadhel also commended Capalan, the new steward of Lairdton's Ranger Hold, for his leadership. Considering his uncle had questioned Alcandhor's appointment of Capalan in the first place, 'twas high praise, and doubly intended.

They had almost finished with the reports when a knock came at the door. Zandhral entered, bowing. "I have all the Elites' reports for you, my Thane."

Alcandhor gestured for him to continue.

"No sign of the Rogues has been seen on either side of the mountain range although we know Monadhal and Nandhal entered the caves."

"Are we assuming they are together?"

"We know they were both tracked into the same cave entrance, but the trail was lost soon afterwards." Zandhral shrugged. "But if I were Nandhal, I would stay with Monadhal because he knows those caves intimately."

Alcandhor lifted a hand in agreement. "This is old news. What else?"

"Rangers on the eastern side of the mountains have entered the caves from every entrance they can find, and are working their way through, mapping as they go. One man broke a leg in a rock fall, so they are abandoning their search in the natural caves and merely keeping watch as far in as they dare go, and concentrating on the manmade tunnels found on a lower level."

Straightening, Alcandhor repeated, "Manmade tunnels?" He turned to Mattan. "Your people's?"

The Enaisi nodded. "Ages ago, my people had an underground transportation system that traversed this continent."

"Maglevs?"

Mattan grinned at Alcandhor. "Aye. Maglevs."

"So then, these tunnels are vestiges of that system?"

"Vestiges at least. If they have not collapsed or been destroyed by natural disasters, those rail tunnels would allow these Rogues to travel from

299

one side of the mountain range to the other. If there are enough Rangers to continue to press westward, they could force the Rogues to the other side and out to Rangers awaiting them. But who knows how safe they are. Rangers could still become lost and disoriented underground, get trapped, injured, or worse if the rail tunnels are structurally compromised."

Alcandhor chewed the inside of his cheek for a moment, then gazed up at the Elite. "Zandhral, how many Rangers are involved on the eastern side, checking those entrances and tunnels?"

"Hundreds, Thane."

"Good. Drum word by the new code for them to continue. And send word also for the Rangers on the western side to be alert."

Zandhral bowed and left.

"Think you we will soon capture them?" Haladhon asked.

"I hope so. I want this over." Alcandhor scrubbed his face. "Let us finish these reports."

Soon, Alcandhor pushed back from the table, drained.

Haladhon finished writing and blew on the paper. "Shall I have these delivered to Tam?"

"Aye. I wish to give her no reason to leave Marcalan for now. She is our best method of keeping him at rest until he is healed."

Haladhon pulled the cord for Feladhrel, and ordered the summary sent to Tam, and for the stripling to file the reports.

Mattan stood. "Thane, I wish to discuss something grave."

"And that would be?"

The Enaisi hesitated. "Does Haladhon know of Marcalan's...problem?"

Alcandhor exchanged glances with his Third at Table.

"Aye. As does Tam, Sarinna, Zandhral—"

"Ah. Zandhral is close to hand. Call him, please, Thane."

Alcandhor nodded to Haladhon, who left and soon returned with the Elite.

"You wished to see me, Thane?"

"Nay. Mattan did." Alcandhor raised a hand for the Enaisi to begin.

With a bow, the alien said, "I wish witnesses. Just in case. Thane, we may be gone past luncheon. You may wish to let the Great Hall know not to wait—"

"Where are we going?"

"The Portal Complex. Please."

Confused but compliant, Alcandhor and his two cousins followed Mattan out of Thane Hall and toward the western range. "What are you planning?"

"I am guilty of some stealthy theft, and I need a laboratory in the

Portal Complex for my experiment."

Mattan would not say on, so Alcandhor stopped asking questions as they continued all the way to the back of the Great Hall. The Enaisi stopped a servant. The young man's eyes widened.

"Please pass word that Thane Alcandhor will likely not be present for luncheon."

As the servant hurried away, Mattan shrugged at the three. "I do not wish to anger Ganill."

Alcandhor rubbed his lips while Mattan ushered them into the lift, then set a hand out to steady himself as it dropped. "I would like to know what this mysterious scheme is."

"Your story of Marcalan intrigued me. He cannot be what he is, unless he is the son of this Rogue."

"Aye. Genetics has not been an in-depth study for me, but I know enough to grasp that. We all do. Only a child born of a Children of the Enaisi can make a key glow."

"That is correct. But you told me of the prophecy, that a child would be born of two Teldheri and have Enaisi abilities. Not that I have the faith in foresight that my sister did, but one can never tell."

"His situation does not meet the statement of that prophecy, though. It speaks of a child born of two Teldheri—not ones who are Children of the Enaisi—who has full Enaisi abilities. Even able to read minds."

"Was this prophecy orally handed down or written to preserve it intact? I would know the exact wording."

"All of Zadhras' prophecies were written down, but most have been lost. Much was lost about the time Ashani died. Zadhras—" Alcandhor clamped his lips shut. He dared not say on.

"Zadhras what?" Mattan asked.

"It is said the lost knowledge is somewhere here, in the Portal Complex."

"Ah. Perhaps we can find it then."

Mattan did not pursue Alcandhor's mention of Zadhras, which suited Alcandhor. He changed the subject. "So what is this experiment?"

The lift opened. Mattan walked to a panel at the side of the corridor and the lights came on full. He turned to Alcandhor, his eyes serious and sober, then in turn to Haladhon, then Zandhral. "Marcalan has the look of Lantalan."

"But he has not," Haladhon said. "I mean, not as Loch'alan. Marcalan has his mother's features. His eyes are hers, and—"

"Aye, and his mother's coloring and a slighter build, but certain features are subtly Lantalan's—or appear to be. And believe me, among my people we have been trained to notice such things."

"But your people's genetics were encoded with safeguards against thus happening!" Alcandhor said.

Mattan lifted a hand, his face grim. "Believe me, I know all about my people's genetic manipulation. My twin sister and I were to be the ultimate experiment. We were to be the perfection of all they wanted to accomplish."

His lips drew back in almost a snarl. "But they made the mistake of letting us share a uterine incubator. As we developed, our proximity cause a unique sibling bond." Mattan wheeled around and marched down the hall, saying over his shoulder, "My people do not have families, did you know that? We know who our genetic parents are, and many of us have met them, but there is no sense of family love or loyalty. Not as your people experience."

A door opened as the Enaisi approached. Alcandhor stared about at the lit, fully functional laboratory, feeling light-headed. *Stars*!

Haladhon and Zandhral entered but remained silent and distant, giving serious attention to everything as witnesses.

"My sister used to say the reason we both married into your clan was because we did have familial love. We wanted more." His hands passed over a control panel, activating it.

"But your people bond upon marrying." Alcandhor came over to his side, to see the controls better and to watch Mattan's face. His smooth charm had dissipated as they entered the Portal Complex. He was seeing the real man now.

"Aye, there is that." Mattan stared at the counter in front of him, as if seeing something else. "But it's not based on affection or—" He shook his head and was silent. "We are not allowed to procreate in the traditional way. It is considered filthy. *Filthy*! And that among our own people. To do so with yours—we were both ostracized for marrying and allowing our genes to mingle with yours. Ismari never even tried to go back through the portal."

The Enaisi reached inside his jerkin and pulled out three phials. His eyes glittered. "I said I did some sneaking. I whisked back here in a free moment to grab these, then, last night during the celebration I gathered DNA from both Lantalan and Kalinna. This morning, I managed to pluck a hair from Marcalan, follicle intact."

"That is why you wished to see those two today!"

Mattan smiled—coldly. "And now, we shall see if the impossible has happened."

Alcandhor's eyes narrowed. "Is this for Marcalan or to somehow deliver rebuke to your people?"

"Does it matter?"

Alcandhor huffed a sad laugh. "It does to me."

Mattan dropped his gaze. "I apologize. I do it first for Marcalan. If I am right, we can tell him. If I am wrong, he is as he was. But aye, if I receive a favored result, it will throw over two millennia of my people's pride and arrogance about their perfect science into...into the midden, as your people say." He turned to Haladhon and Zandhral. "Even though I am recording this, be certain you watch, even if you do not understand. Your people demand multiple witnesses, not merely a single witness, and for Marcalan's sake, I would have this done right, not only scientifically but also by your laws."

The two nodded.

Alcandhor watched as Mattan painstakingly worked. Each sample took time and processing before he set a labeled phial in a small machine which, to Alcandhor, resembled a canister. Finally, all three phials were inserted and the lid closed.

"Now we wait."

"How long?"

"Not too long. The computer will do the rest." Mattan leaned against the counter, arms crossed.

With a sidelong glance at the canister-machine, Alcandhor asked, "You have witnesses for this test, but not for the taking of the samples. How do we know whose they are?"

"For this test, I merely wished to ascertain the truth, without causing possible harm to the family. If the results are favorable, I will conduct a second one by more stringent standards later for my people, so they will not be able to contest the findings."

Zandhral stepped forward, glancing about the chamber, speaking for the first time since arriving in the Portal Complex. "So this is what you have wanted, Thane? To see this place open and active?"

"Have you never visited the Portal Complex before?"

"Nay."

"What do you think of it?"

Zandhral inclined his head. "Your pardon, Thane, but I find it cold and lifeless. There is no soul here."

Mattan huffed a laugh. "You sound like Avadhron."

Zandhral lifted his arms. "'Tis all stone and metal."

"But the knowledge contained here, cousin. Think of the knowledge!"

Haladhon chortled, pointing a finger at Alcandhor. "You can think of the knowledge. That is your passion."

Glaring at his cousin, Alcandhor spat, "We all know what your passion is."

303

Haladhon put a hand over his heart and gave a mock bow, winking. Alcandhor pressed his lips together. Hang that man! One day his indiscretions would cause him to lose that jerkin. He switched his attention to Zandhral. "And what of you, cousin? What is your passion?"

"I do not think I have one. Not as you do, Thane." Zandhral paused, his brows drawn together. "My passion is for my family, my home, my clan. To safeguard that which I love."

Alcandhor cleared his throat. "That is a good passion. Perhaps the best."

"And what is your passion, Elder?" Haladhon's eyes twinkled.

"I have had more than one, over time. Now, like your thane, I have achieved it. I am back home."

"What of your planet?" Zandhral asked. "Do you not wish to see it rebuilt now, after the war?"

"My people have left Anatai for another world, which we call Retreat. My team and I are the only ones interested in trying to bring life back to that world, but that is more their dream than mine. I wished to restore the portal and return here."

"And who is your team?"

"You should know some of them, Thane. The survivors anyway. Ashani and Ismari are dead. And Lennai. It is only Treyor, Dassel, Atesni, Telkai, and myself left of the original team. A few younger ones have joined us."

"Stars. I know you said they were still alive, but when you say their names, the reality is more..."

"Real?" Haladhon finished, grinning.

Alcandhor shrugged.

A low, intermittent buzz sounded from the machine, and a holographic display arose over the computer next to it. A crooked smile spread on Mattan's face, and he ran his hands over the computer console. To one side, a sheet of some clear material extruded from another console.

Mattan snatched it up and held it out to Alcandhor with a triumphant expression. The writing was in Teldheri, but few would be able to understand what it said as it was mostly scientific terminology. Alcandhor could understand enough to know that this sheet claimed that Marcalan was the child of Lantalan and Kalinna. His hands shook. "'Tis true?" he managed to whisper.

"You—all three of you—saw me conduct the test. It is valid by your laws, and yes, it is true."

"We must tell Marcalan!" Alcandhor strode out, not waiting for the others, the sheet clutched tightly in his hands.

"Thane, wait!"

He wheeled about. "For what? This is conclusive, aye?"

"Yes."

"Then let us tell him! Stars! We need to tell his parents!"

Mattan shook his head. "Give me a moment to store the samples and shut down the lab."

Alcandhor paced in the hallway, waiting. "We should call all the Children of the Enaisi to hear this. Stars, this must be related to the prophecy. Perhaps our remembrance of the prophecy has been wrong. We must tell all our clan—"

"Great Bells, Thane!" Haladhon said. "One step at a time. Tell his family privately first."

"Aye. Aye," Alcandhor muttered, waving a hand. "You are right."

Mattan joined them, and the lift returned them to the Great Hall. Alcandhor burst forth as the door opened, rushing down the back hall and outside, straight for Family North—or as straight as one could go through the winding paths of the sward.

His cousins and the Enaisi called to him to slow his pace, but he ignored them. Marcalan had lived with this private nightmare his whole life; he deserved peace from it. He skidded to a stop and wheeled about. "Have word sent to both Lantalan and Kalinna to report to me at Tam and Marcalan's chamber." Without waiting for a reply, he took off again.

Chapter Forty-One

Marcalan found he did not mind enforced resting, especially in bed with Tam. And if resting helped his body heal faster, perhaps soon—very soon, if it please the Maker—they could do more than kiss.

Luncheon had been an unwelcome interruption.

Tam set their finished tray outside the door as instructed, then stood, arms crossed, looking about at the covered walkway. She stepped forward to peer over the rail at the courtyard below their door. Marcalan pushed to his feet and hobbled over to join her. Bells, but some things still hurt!

"Stars, this is beautiful. A fountain and small garden, and many trellises. Some people have lovely decorations outside their doors." She turned and wrinkled her nose at the simple woven vine that hung on their door. "I do not like this plain thing. How shall we make our door pretty?"

"I have little knowledge or talent for making things pretty. I will bow to your wishes on the matter."

Tam frowned. "Please sit. You are in such pain and need to rest."

To make his wife happy, Marcalan obeyed, limping over to one of the cushioned chairs set near a window. Tam smiled and stretched out her arms. "Such a large chamber!"

"'Tis small, meant only for a couple. Families have suites, which make this seem tiny by comparison."

"Our chamber is bigger than my whole cottage back home." She lightly ran across to fling open the double doors to their balcony, then stood, hands outstretched. "Ah, fresh air all through! I like this!"

"Be glad 'tis not winter yet."

"But then we will have them closed and both fireplaces lit. And—" Tam wiggled her toes. "Why is the floor not cold? 'Tis shimmerstone. Stone is cold."

"Ask Mattan. When his people built this city, they did some of their magic. The floors are cool in the summer, but when the weather is chill, they become warm."

"Stars."

Tam's happy gaze rested on him, and the slight chill of the late autumn breeze mattered not; he felt warmed through. She spun back around and pointed to the balcony. "What think you? In the spring, I can put pots of flowering vines along here and train them to trail along the railing."

"Whatever you wish, Love-ling."

Tam's smiled widened. Oh, those adorable dimples! He could just watch her forever.

She walked back inside, looking about. "Sarinna said we could choose different furnishings from stores. What colors do you like?"

Marcalan scratched his chin beard. "I have never thought much about colors, except for grey, brown, and green," he said, referring to their Ranger garb.

She rolled her eyes. "Those may be the most wonderful colors to wear, but not for a home!" She turned in a slow circle. "Warm colors, like flowers. And green maybe."

"We could go to stores and see from what selection we have to choose."

"Not today. You are to rest. We could bring chairs to the balcony, as Mattan suggested, and view Avadhron's Sward."

"Or return to bed."

"Think you we can kiss all day?"

"Kissing is very curative. I feel my body healing with every one!"

Tam laughed aloud, a rare thing. "Then I will close our door, and endeavor to heal you."

Marcalan rose as she crossed to the door, but she stopped, tipping her head. "Uncle is coming."

"He is here?"

"Nay, but close. He is excited about something."

With a loud sigh, Marcalan gingerly sat back down. Hang it!

Tam giggled. "I promise to work on healing you after he leaves."

The clomp of running boots soon approached their door, and Alcandhor ran in without ceremony and straight to Marcalan, grinning and holding out a flat, clear...something. "'Tis well! You are Lantalan's son!"

The joy of the day seeped out of Marcalan. "So you have said, Thane, but that is your will and law, not—"

"Nay! Nay! 'Tis but truth. Mattan did a test. A DNA test it is called. He had Haladhon, Zandhral, and me as witnesses while he performed this test in the Portal Complex." He rattled the flat sheet of something that was not paper—unless paper could be made clear like glass—in his hand. "This is the proof, although the language is difficult to understand for all but our most knowledgeable science law-keepers. But it states you are the son of both Kalinna and Lantalan!"

Alcandhor's eyes held an intense joy, and Marcalan felt nothing amiss from him, but this could not be correct. "'Tis a jest."

"About something this grave, Marcalan, believe me, I would never jest."

"But how did he do this? How can he test for parentage?"

"Great Bells, the science is too much to explain, but I will try. Every person has a unique coding in their body, you understand this? It determines such things as eye color, hair color, skin color, the shape and size of our bones."

"I understand we inherit such things from our parents."

"It is inherited through this coding. Bits of coding from each parent are present in the child. Mattan stole a hair from you this morning on our visit, and somehow, I did not ask how, got DNA—that is what the coding is called—from each of your parents last night at the celebration. Today, he took those samples to the Portal Complex and did a test. That test proves you have the DNA, the *coding* of not only Kalinna, but also of Lantalan. He truly is your father!"

Marcalan sat back and gaped at Alcandhor. "But that is impossible!"

"Truly. Mattan said so as well."

"Then how has this happened?"

"Mattan feels either his people's science is flawed, or you are the fulfillment of Zadhras' prophecy. He leans toward the former." Alcandhor's grin broadened. "I lean toward the latter."

"But that prophecy speaks of a child born as if an Enaisi, with *all* their abilities. Mine are weak, as yours." He pointed at his Thane. "And you said you thought that prophecy was not real anyway, Thane. You said so back at Lairdton."

"Aye, but I could be wrong. I am not too proud to admit thus. And all we have of that prophecy is oral tradition. We know not what it actually states, cousin. For now, I shall consider that you just might be the fulfillment of that prophecy."

"Great Bells, you would make of me the center of such a thing? The child whose birth is the cause of great upheavals in our world?"

"Ha, nay, not the cause, but merely the portent of those upheavals. And I would say, with recent events, you seem to fit the description."

"How so?"

"If you had not sewn the laces of Valdhor's trous together and incurred that beating—"

"He what!" Tam exclaimed, wide-eyed.

"When he was a tiny lad, having what, five years, I believe?"

Marcalan nodded. "I had six, because I had just started Ranger Training."

"He sewed the laces of Valdhor's trous together. Your father became enraged and beat him, might have killed him if our father and Lantalan had not pulled him off. Haladhon and I witnessed it. He faced conclave for raising a fist to a child."

"Stars," Tam murmured, staring with horror at Marcalan, her face pale.

"The end of that story is that he was stripped of heirship and sent off, given bounds in Pashelon, despite the law that chiefs must reside in Zaidhron, and I became heir. If that had not happened, he would not have met your mother, you would not be here, and my father's and my foresight of preparing our people for changes in this world would not have come to fruition as they have. Your father set little store by our lectures and admonitions for change."

Tam continued to gaze at Marcalan, as if she studied him. Finally, she asked, "What made you sew his trous' laces together?"

Marcalan shrugged with an innocent blink. "It seemed a good idea at the time."

Tam rolled her eyes.

Alcandhor grinned. "Aye. That is what I have lived with all these years, niece." He pulled over a chair. "Your parents have been summoned here for the news, so you will have to endure me for a little while."

Marcalan stared at his Thane, trying to absorb this revelation. He was not Uardhel's spawn, and he could openly admit being a Child of the Enaisi, and his mother had not broken vows to his father as he had feared for years, and Lantalan was his father in truth. By the Bells and both moons, he felt he could soar, save he could barely walk at the moment.

And that prophecy—it could not be true that he was the child mentioned.

Tam walked around behind Marcalan and rubbed his shoulders, then bent forward, kissing his forehead.

"How is your leg today?" the Thane asked.

"Tam says it has closed up more."

"Your face looks less bruised."

His *facial* bruising was not what Marcalan worried about, but he would not say thus aloud. Instead he quipped, "Ah well, nothing I can do about that right now. I will have to match Tam when I get well, so she can keep me looking like this."

Tam gently shoved his shoulder. "Behave."

He tipped his head back to look up at her. "I always behave!"

"Oh, stars!" Tam murmured, play-boxing his ears.

He took one of her hands and kissed it, then pulled her around and down into his lap. She resisted a little, but he said, "'Tis no hurt to that leg."

She hesitated then settled on his uninjured leg, and rested an arm around his neck, her eyes shining.

He grinned, wrapping his arms around his wife. "Stars, Thane, so this"—he tightened his hold on Tam—"is the result of that prank to Valdhor when I was but a babe?"

Alcandhor crossed his arms, eyeing his cousin. "If I say 'aye,' will that then give you excuse to pull pranks at every turn claiming you are looking for great reward?"

Marcalan laughed. "'Tis a thought, but I could receive no greater reward."

"At the time you thought you had received great reward. Haladhon himself carried you to the healer, then we both helped tutor you in your first Training lessons until you were well enough to attend classes."

"Aye, and Haladhon showed me some fighting moves when I was well enough."

"You worshipped him, though why I could never fathom."

Marcalan shrugged. "I only remember following him relentlessly, hoping he would notice me."

"Causing him great vexation, believe me."

Marcalan threw back his head, laughing.

Tam giggled, then sat up straight. "Mattan is here."

"Bells," Marcalan muttered.

"And Kalinna and Lantalan."

"Thane, with this ability, she should be an Elite. Can you imagine—"

"Why were we summoned here?" Kalinna's voice carried from the walkway outside their door.

Marcalan stifled a sigh.

A second voice—Mattan's—said, "Greetings, Kalinna. And Lantalan."

Mattan breezed through the doorway with a smile, and Marcalan's parents followed. The Elder closed the door, and stood by it, out of the way.

His mother's face paled slightly as she saw the Thane, but her mouth set in a thin line and gazed about the chamber. "I cannot say as these colors are pleasing. And the furniture!"

Marcalan felt Tam stiffen in his lap. He gave her a quick squeeze. "Then, Mother, I suggest you take Adrinna to task for the furnishings."

Alcandhor rose and gestured for Kalinna to take his chair. "We have news, good news."

His mother sat, hands fluttering over her skirt, smoothing it.

"News, Thane? About what?" Lantalan's eyes flicked to his son.

Marcalan needed not sense to know his father's unease. He grinned broadly at him, winking, as Alcandhor said, "About Marcalan's parentage."

Kalinna flushed and glared at Tam. "If we are to discuss this again, why is she here?" His mother jerked her chin up toward his wife, then twisted to glance at Mattan. "And that alien?"

A fierce protectiveness came over Marcalan. "*She* is your daughter now, and you will treat her with respect."

Kalinna spluttered, but Lantalan put a hand on her shoulder. "Let us hear what the Thane has to say."

Alcandhor held out the strange, clear sheet. "Mattan has done a test, and it proves that Marcalan is indeed your son, Lantalan."

Kalinna did not move, nor did his father. Marcalan seemed not to breathe. "How–how can this be? I–I mean, I would fain have this be true, but I see not how."

Alcandhor again explained about this DNA coding. His parents had glazed expressions that must have been what he looked like when his Thane told him. Bells, he still felt confused and stunned.

But the joy on Lantalan's face seemed to dissolve years from him. He bolted to Marcalan, and Tam jumped out of the way just before his father pulled him up by the shoulders and into a hard embrace. "Truly, truly mine! Not just of my heart, but my blood!"

The sharp pain of being hauled up melted at the strength of feeling from his father. Lantalan wept, Marcalan found himself weeping along with him.

"But this changes nothing for me," Kalinna said, hands clenched in her lap.

Lantalan loosened his hold a bit, but Marcalan held on tightly. He was not going to allow his mother to steal this moment.

"A great wrong and grievous hurt was done you, Kalinna," Mattan said, stepping close, "but do you think you were the only victim? Your son and husband have lived with this as well."

Lantalan murmured, "Let me go to her," in Marcalan's ear, and set him back with a sad smile.

Marcalan wiped his face, watching as his father knelt in front of his mother while she answered, "Think you I do not know that? But there, you see? They have a resolution. What do I have?"

Mattan leaned over her slightly. "You have a husband who has doted on you, and many beautiful children, and grandchildren as well, I believe, yes? There are so many who love—"

"You cannot understand what he did to me!"

Mattan put a hand on Lantalan's shoulder. His father rose and stepped away, and the Elder took his place. He talked softly to Kalinna, but Marcalan could not hear what he said.

Next to him, Tam stood with hands clasped under her chin, staring at the pair, her eyes wide. Anger rose in his mother. Mattan said something that seemed to calm her, but then the anger returned, and she hissed something to him. He rose with a sad smile. "It is your choice, Kalinna. Remember that."

Not wishing for his mother to retain the attention she had gained, as she was wont to do, Marcalan lifted his chin. "Father?"

Lantalan turned to him with a questioning expression, and Marcalan grinned. "Stars, I like that."

"What?"

"Saying 'Father.' And having no doubts."

"Rascal."

Marcalan pointed at Lantalan. "Aye, but I am your rascal!"

His father clouted him on the shoulder. Kalinna *tsked*.

Tam tipped her head. "Why do you do that, Kalinna?"

"Do what?" Kalinna's sharp voice cut the air.

"Your son and your husband are so happy, and you are not happy for them. You...you resent that they are happy."

Great Bells, Tam just put her foot into it!

"You know nothing, girl!" Kalinna shot to her feet and stomped out.

Tam bit her lip, her golden eyes wide gazing up at Marcalan. "I just wanted to understand. I thought I should burst seeing you two so happy. 'Twas as if a great darkness had been dispelled by the sun. I could feel your joy, and it made me want to jump or dance. But she was not pleased."

Marcalan snugged Tam close, and looked at his father. "Can you see now? She keeps you tethered to her will. I never understood why, but I could sense it."

"Leave it, my son. You cannot change her."

"I wish to change *you*! Or at least know that you see the truth. She saps the love from you, but what does she give you?"

"That is between me and my wife, Marcalan. I appreciate what you say, but leave it. It is not your concern."

"Not my concern? You are my parents!"

"But our relationship is separate from that. It is private."

"But—"

"Leave it!"

Marcalan dropped his gaze, his lips pressed together.

"This is a happy time," Tam whispered. "Your fears are gone, and you have your father in truth! And he loves you. Do not let a shadow fall between you."

"Wisdom from the young," Alcandhor murmured.

"I had not a father's love, and know the value of it."

Lantalan smiled down at Tam, clasping both her and Marcalan's shoulders.

This was all too serious. Marcalan could not abide it. He looked past his father's shoulder to Alcandhor. "So, Thane, you say I am this prophecy child?"

"I cannot deny that is a possibility."

Marcalan grinned broadly. "I shall have to think how to best put that to use. Skiving duties? Extorting desserts from striplings?" He slapped a hand to his chest in a mocking pose. "A statue next to Zaidhron's and Avadhron's in the sward? I know, perhaps a celebration tonight in my honor!"

Alcandhor snorted. "That you can take up with Ganill."

Lantalan tightened his grip at Marcalan's shoulder and shook him. "Stars, you never stop."

"And you would have me no other way."

His father pulled him close and pounded his back. "Nay, my son, I would not."

"We do have a decision to make," Alcandhor said. "Now that his parentage is established, we need to announce he is a Child of the Enaisi."

"How shall we say we discovered this?" Lantalan asked.

Alcandhor shrugged. "The truth. Tam sensed it. And since Mattan arrived, he confirmed it, and that you are indeed his father." The Thane crossed his arms. "I think I shall see what opinions are offered about the matter, initially, rather than even bring up that prophecy."

"But you truly think Marcalan is the one mentioned, Uncle?"

"Unless we can find the actual prophecy to see what it says word for word, we have only the oral tradition of what it says. And aye, by that, I would say it is possible."

"With the Portal Complex open, perhaps we can find it," Tam said. "Would not Mattan know how?"

Mattan grimaced slightly, almost a wince, and Marcalan felt from him a heartache. But the Elder smiled at Tam. "I will try. But I do have a question. What about Marcalan?"

"What about him?"

"Is he considered a chief now?"

"Nay." Marcalan's response was quick and serious. "I have my own family."

"It does not change your family ties nor rank to be given chief status because of your marriage. It was done for me."

"Perhaps we should discuss this in conclave." The Thane scratched his chin beard. "Aye, we shall have conclave for you tonight. Lantalan, send word for the chiefs to meet here, now. I wish this settled by evening meal so we can explain Marcalan to our kin."

"There is no explaining Marcalan," Lantalan replied wryly.

Marcalan chuckled.

Chapter Forty-Two

Tam eyed Mattan, standing against the wall with a sleeve pushed up, looking at his arm. Nay, at some device on his arm. She wished to ask what it was, but for some reason, felt timid. This alien was pleasant, she felt nothing untoward from him, and he had saved Marcalan's life. She should feel friendship, perhaps even love, for him. He was, after all, her very own ancestor. But something held her back.

She brought her attention to Marcalan, sitting in the chair before her. She stroked his hair. "You should go to bed. I feel how tired you are."

"With the chiefs coming? Nay, Love-ling. I will be fine."

"But your leg!"

Without a word, Alcandhor brought over a small chest from the wall and set it in front of Marcalan, then grabbed a cover from the bed and folded it over the top. He gently lifted Marcalan's leg and propped it on top of the chest, then straightened.

Marcalan started to protest, but Tam stopped him. "Do not argue! Stars, are all men so stubborn or only Rangers?"

"Since most men in our clan are Rangers, I cannot say." Marcalan gave her that infuriating innocent expression.

Tam glared, fists on her hips. "That is not true. I have seen many men of our clan in the city who are not Rangers."

"Statistically, I would say it is at least two-thirds," Alcandhor said. "Perhaps more."

Tam spun to look at her uncle, who grinned. "You are as bad as Marcalan at times!"

Both men burst into laughter, and Alcandhor glanced at Mattan. His laughter faded, and with a slight frown, he asked, "What is that, Mattan?"

The alien looked up a moment, then returned his attention to whatever it was on his arm. "I am checking for Zadhras' prophecies in the Portal Complex's computers. The trouble is, there are many databases."

Alcandhor strode over and stared at the thing on Mattan's arm. Tam lifted on tiptoe to try to see across the chamber what this mysterious device was, but stayed by Marcalan with one hand on his shoulder, afraid he would rise and join them.

"What is it?"

"A way for me to communicate with the computers. I can access almost anything with this," Mattan replied without looking up.

A stunning jolt ran through her uncle, and he stood as if frozen in place. "You have what? Here?"

Mattan looked up from his device, blinking. "What?"

"We do not have such technology here! 'Tis not allowed!"

"You do not have it. I have it."

"But—"

"If Zaidhron allowed it, why should you wish to prohibit it?"

"Because my people could be tempted into wishing thus for themselves."

"Then I shall refrain from using it around them."

Marcalan burst into laughter. "I dare say Andhrel would appreciate this conversation. You would make a good law-keeper, Elder."

"But he is right," Tam said. "We are not using it. Only he is."

"And you would make a good law-keeper too," Alcandhor grumbled.

"So everyone says." Tam crossed her arms. "When will they be here? Marcalan needs to lie down."

"I am not—"

"Shu!" Tam ordered.

Marcalan wilted, and Alcandhor rubbed a hand over his mouth, his eyes twinkling. Tam sighed and paced. It seemed forever until the chiefs arrived, but finally they did. Good. Soon Tam could get Marcalan to bed. For all his seeming lack of discipline, little showed of his increasing pain save a pinching between his eyebrows.

The chiefs all bowed to Alcandhor and Mattan, and asked after Marcalan's recovery. Stars, could they begin? Before she could say on, Marcalan said, "I could have worse confinement, and a worse healer. Although this one can be quite severe at times."

"Intimidating, is she?" Haladhon asked.

"Terrifying! Bells, you have no idea!" Marcalan's miming of shrinking in fear was belied by his grin.

Tam feigned a slap on his arm, smiling at the jocularity she felt from Marcalan. Jesting seemed as much healing for him as sleeping.

"You are an irrepressible scoundrel," declared Mattan. "You must keep things from being too predictable."

"The only thing predictable around Marcalan is that there are going to be pranks," Andhrel retorted.

"You would have me no—"

"—other way. Aye, so you say all the time," Andhrel said, shaking his head. "But believe me, there are plenty who are happier when you are roaming."

Marcalan affected an injured air. "Oh, you say that about me, but Haladhon is almost as bad. I do not hear you carrying on about him."

"He is more jests than pranks, cousin. You are just trouble walking around."

"Besides," Haladhon put in, his eyes twinkling, "how much can Andhrel say about me when I rank him?"

Mattan chuckled.

Marcalan sat up straight. "Rank! Bells, Thane, that is something I would like answered."

"What, you rascal?"

"If Mattan is a chief, and even ranks Tam, how does that affect ascension to Thane?"

"It does not change a thing," Mattan replied. "I was never in line for ascension. I was considered a chief as I married Zaidhron's daughter, and provided an heir, since Zaidhron had no sons and no living brothers."

"Almost as it is with Tam," Andhrel commented, nodding. "Your situation was one we studied when trying to decide what to do about her. We knew not what to do with a female Ranger, much less future Thane, since inheritance is normally through the male line. Which should mean even if she became Thane, her children would not be in line for ascension. But with your example, we had a precedent."

Planting her fists on her hips again, Tam asked, "So then, to the question. Is Marcalan considered a chief?"

Eladhrel and Andhrel exchanged glances, and Andhrel groaned. "Please, no, Thane. Make him not a chief. I could not abide having to listen to him at conclaves."

They all burst out laughing.

"Which begs another question. Mattan, did you then vote at conclaves?" Andhrel asked.

Mattan shook his head. "They wanted me to. I would offer my opinion but not vote. I was not born of your clan, and felt it would be interfering with your people. I had several arguments with Zaidhron over that, and with Cosdhral, Dandhral, and the other chiefs as well. Avadhron, of course, was adamant I should not vote. I think it galled him that we agreed on something." A smile flashed on the alien's face.

His expression serious for once, Marcalan said, "Thane, I would feel out of place voting. And I do have Mattan's situation as a precedent."

"But unlike me, you are a Teldheri and a Ranger—a Trained Ranger who has earned the right to wear this jerkin, not an outsider who was awarded this"—he swept his hands down indicating his Ranger garb—"and the title chief merely as a result of marrying the king's daughter."

"More than just for that, surely," Alcandhor said. "You saved my people from annihilation!"

"I helped, certainly, but no more than any of my team, or countless of your people who worked tirelessly not only in preparing for the Crossing but also in the aftermath of the devastation in that Final Crossing."

"But if you had not opened that portal and visited Teledhar, who of my race would be alive now? If you had not offered this planet to us, and offered to bring my people to safety, where would my people be?"

Mattan lifted a shoulder. "This is all besides the point of this discussion."

"Aye," Marcalan said, "which is that I should not be made a chief."

Andhrel scratched his cheek. "If we follow the only precedent we have"—he inclined his head to Mattan—"you should."

"And you are my Second, Elite Ranger Marcalan," Haladhon added. "Which means you are informed about many things which are the chiefs' business."

Marcalan opened his mouth, but Alcandhor lifted a hand. "You have given your opinion, Ranger. But the decision is the chiefs'. Any other points, for or against?"

Eladhrel shook his head. Tam could feel her husband's resistance. Should she vote against his wishes?

The Thane stared at her. "Tam?"

"Other than his own feelings that he does not wish it, I cannot think of anything that should deny the promotion of him to chief."

"Tam, I should not be made chief!"

"We have a precedent."

"Which is another word for tradition. You have spent years railing against tradition, Thane. This is not law!"

"Does anyone else have an opinion?"

"You have decided!" Marcalan sat up straight. "Great Bells, Thane."

Tam put a hand on Marcalan's shoulder to keep him in the chair.

He shrugged her away. "Why? What reason can you give for wishing this on me?"

"Enough!" Alcandhor's voice, although not a yell, rumbled with authority from deep in his chest. The chamber seemed to echo with the resulting silence. He looked around at everyone. "Any more thoughts on this?" He turned to Mattan, still leaning against the wall, attention on the device on his arm. "Elder?"

Mattan looked up. "I am not voting."

"Your thoughts? You said you gave advice to the chiefs, even if you did not vote."

Without a pause, the alien said, "Marcalan has wit, and I mean not just his propensity for jesting and pranks. He is quick, and sees things clearly, and has a heart dedicated to his clan, and especially to his Thane. I believe as a chief he would be invaluable—" Mattan raised his voice as Marcalan began to protest. "Even if he is a non-voting chief as I am. There, you have my opinion." He returned to his device.

"Anyone else?" Alcandhor waited a moment, but no one spoke. "All right. Then vote. Shall we elect to make Marcalan a chief?"

Haladhon and Eladhrel immediately replied, "Aye."

Andhrel glared at Marcalan, but Tam sensed no animosity. She bit back a smile. With an exaggerated sigh, Andhrel grumbled, "Aye."

"And does he vote?"

"Nay!" Marcalan spat.

"I will take that as an 'aye' that you wish to vote, or you would not have voted just now," Alcandhor countered. "I also vote aye."

Marcalan's mouth fell open.

Haladhon chortled and said, "Aye."

Eladhrel nodded. "Aye."

Andhrel stared at Marcalan for a long, silent moment. "Since it will vex you as you have vexed me all these years: aye."

They all looked at Tam. She bit her lip, trying to come up with something so she could vote the way Marcalan would want. "Why does he vote when Mattan does not?"

"I am an outsider, not born of your clan, " the Elder muttered, grimacing at his arm, his finger touching the device.

"But now you are blood of our clan," Alcandhor said. "We are your descendents. Surely that gives you a heart's desire for what is best for us."

"The only vote I shall ever give is that I do not vote."

Marcalan raised a hand. "Wait. If he decided he should not vote, then why can I not decide I should not vote?"

"Nay, it was a conclave decision."

"But you said they wanted you to. You were the one who—"

"Aye, but in the end, it was their conclave decision, and there were other circumstances that impinged on it." Mattan frowned at his arm.

"Will you give your full attention to this matter, Chief Mattan?" Alcandhor demanded.

The alien lifted his head. "I am. But I am also trying to solve your puzzle about that prophecy. I have found some files that appear to have been uploaded to the computers after the time the portal was shut down, but they are encrypted, which is perplexing. If no one except my people could access the computers, why did they go to such trouble?"

Alcandhor took a step toward the alien. "What sort of encryption algor—hang you, Mattan! Keep on topic!"

"You know of algorithms?"

"Delgan knows as much or more."

"I had no idea any of your people would have knowledge of such things, since you are determined no advanced technology be used."

"We are more likely to be at risk if we know not what we avoid, Elder."

"There is a reasoning to that."

Haladhon snickered. "Never have I seen anything distract you so thoroughly, Thane."

Alcandhor clenched his fists and growled. "Back to the vote. Tam, what say you?"

Tam hesitated, massaging her husband's shoulders. She gazed down at him. "I am sorry, Marcalan, I see no reason why you should not vote. So, aye."

Marcalan slumped in the chair. Tam leaned close and murmured in his ear, "Please, do not be angry!"

"We shall postpone a public announcement that Marcalan is a Child of the Enaisi and that he is a chief until he is well enough to attend an evening meal." Alcandhor spread his arms. "For now, let us leave so our new chief can rest."

"Come to bed now," Tam whispered after the door shut.

"Why did you vote thus?"

"I saw no reason why I should not. Feelings do not enter into conclave decisions, else I would not be heir to Thane!"

Marcalan stared at her, and his irritation ebbed. "So this is how you felt?"

"Aye, my love. That is exactly how I felt."

Chapter Forty-Three

"Would it be easier to work on the encryption in the Portal Complex?" Alcandhor asked. He forbore skipping next to Mattan as a child expecting a treat. Thanes should not caper.

Mattan stopped walking, and turned, with an expression that did resemble that of a parent about to chide— "My son, you are amazingly..."

Alcandhor waited.

"Irrepressible."

"That is what you said about Marcalan."

"You are just as bad, but about knowledge and technology instead of jesting. And aye, it would be easier, but it will soon be afternooning. And Ganill is an excellent cook."

"Do not bother telling her. She will only accuse you of trying to get on her good side."

Mattan laughed.

~*~

Afternooning was soup and heavy, dark bread. As they rose from table, Feladhrel ran to him, bowing. "Thane."

"Aye?"

"Rendhol from Dandrin Shire has arrived, and also a runner arrived with a report for the Elites."

So much for going to the Portal Complex. Stifling a groan, Alcandhor gestured for the chiefs to follow him to Thane Hall. "Let us see what news the runner has brought."

Rendhol stood and bowed as the chiefs all entered the forechamber, his eyes widening at Mattan. The chiefs followed Alcandhor into the Thane's chamber, save Haladhon, who ducked into the Elites' chamber to fetch the runner's report.

Alcandhor sat at his table, and Andhrel and Eladhrel stood one on each side of him. Mattan relaxed in a chair by the wall, again present but not a participant. In a few moments, Haladhon ushered in Rendhol and closed the door.

The Ranger hesitated, his gaze darting to the chiefs, then bowed. "Thane."

"Ranger Rendhol, you wished to see me?"

"Aye. The two families which have been given notice are stating they will not be evicted."

"And you came in person to tell me thus?"

"They have been as star-flower thorns. I have thought my hair would be pulled out in dealing with them, and glad I was of the eviction notices. But I fear now they will become violent. I request Rangers to reinforce the eviction when the day comes they must actually leave."

"And what of Pendhras? He is your shire's steward. Is he not worried?"

"Pendhras...seems unconcerned, and dismissed my misgivings."

"Does he know you have come to Zaidhron?"

"Nay, Thane, but he will find out, and I will likely be roasted for bothering you with such a trivial concern."

Alcandhor considered that tidbit and set it aside, leaning forward. "But why come all this way to make a request? You could have just written."

"I feared you would dismiss it, Thane, thinking we Rangers incapable of handling the affairs in our shire. I have brought copies of reports concerning the two families. I know all valley reports are filed here, but thought a compilation would save time and allow you to review the situation."

"You may not be aware, Rendhol, but I have kept myself apprised of those feuding families. Be assured, I know something of what you have dealt with, and I approve of your firmness—and restraint."

Rendhol's shoulders drew back, and his chin raised slightly.

"You may have assistance, come the day. But I do hope we are both mistaken in the need for it. I would not wish harm to either family or Rangers."

"I thank you, my Thane." Rendhol bowed again. Haladhon, as door warden, let the Ranger out then shut it again.

Alcandhor raised his brows at his Third at Table. "What news?"

"They have narrowed the search. They believe the Rogues are still in the caves, but are being forced north to southern Pashelon Province. I do not think it will be long now. We shall have them." Haladhon's eyes glittered. "You had wanted to be present for their capture, if possible. If we leave now, we may arrive before that happens, and if so, I claim Capture Rights on Monadhal."

Leaning back in his chair, Alcandhor let his breath slowly out. "Aye, so you have always said. I only wish it were justice you sought, not vengeance."

"Will you grant it, Thane?"

"He has fought much in the wild, to the death. I know you have keen skills, but—"

"Do not deny me this, Thane!"

"What I deny is—" Alcandhor stopped and shook his head. "He will be fighting to the death. You will be fighting to capture him. The danger to you is real, man!"

"He tried to kill me. He did kill my father. I claim Right. I claim it!"

Haladhon's one stray lock of hair fell down his forehead, his jaw set, his fists clenched. Alcandhor stared at the table, chewing his cheek. The other chiefs said nothing. Finally he replied, "Aye, you have the right to the claim. You may have it."

His Third at Table exhaled and inclined his head. "Thank you."

"That is if we arrive in time. Did the runner have details on how closely they had them cornered and where?"

"Aye. They think they are here," Haladhon strode to the map and pointed. Andhrel and Eladhrel gathered close.

"They never leave the caves. They come close, then retreat and head north toward the next exit point. We think Nandhal is using his ability to sense, and knows there are Rangers awaiting them. It is what we are doing. Children of the Enaisi are by each opening, sensing full."

"If Nandhal is sensing," Eladhrel said, "he may well be able to tell other Children of the Enaisi are there, which gives him the same advantage as us."

Andhrel stroked his chin beard. "True, but they will eventually run out of places to go."

"I would rather they come out than us going in after them, but I fear 'twill not happen thus," Alcandhor murmured. "Fighting in the dark of caves is more dangerous for my men." He looked at Haladhon. "For you."

His cousin raised his head. "Worry not about that. But when do we leave?"

"Let me think on it. Another runner may arrive, or better yet, a drum message. I will make a decision in the morning."

"But we lose all that time—"

"What time? Leaving at dusk? How much time and distance is lost if we wait till morning and journey fresh the whole day instead of a few hours tonight then make camp?"

Haladhon looked away, his jaw muscles jumping.

"I have promised you your Capture Rights, cousin, if it is possible. And I would not leave without letting Tam and Marcalan know of the situation."

"Aye, since Marcalan has been their victim too, he will want to know."

"Since he is a chief," Alcandhor corrected, "he has the right to know."

Haladhon huffed a laugh. "I had almost forgotten. Bells, things are moving so fast. Perhaps too fast." Haladhon rubbed his neck with a grimace. "I know you always say we must roll with the hard blows, but our clan is still reeling from a female Ranger. And who is also heir to Thane. Now, we add a new chief. And—are we announcing he is also a Child of the Enaisi right away? 'Tis much to take in."

Alcandhor snorted and nodded at Mattan. "You forget this." The alien lounged in his seat with a small smile, legs stretched out before him, both his arms and ankles crossed. "I am looking at an Enaisi, *the* Enaisi, sitting in a chair across from me. And after a lifetime of fretting and studying, without my effort at all, the portal works." His hands splayed on the table. "But for me, surprisingly, the hardest to take in is that my niece is married." *She is so young. Too young.* He took a deep breath. "Nay, let us not announce Marcalan is a Child of the Enaisi just yet. We have not even announced he is a chief."

"Out of all the marvels, we keep this one secret?" Eladhrel asked.

"Not secret. Delayed. I, for one, would like more information as to how such an impossible thing happened. 'Twould be good to have that knowledge to give to our people, if we can. And not just to answer questions about Marcalan, but also..." Alcandhor stopped, grimacing. "Every parent shall want to bring their children to be tested in the vain hope that they also have an impossible Child of the Enaisi."

"Stars, I had not thought of that!" Haladhon said.

Mattan cleared his throat. "I shall put much effort into finding answers. But as to that other thorny problem, I can tell easily, so send any parents to me." He flashed a thin, sharp smile.

Eyeing the Elder, Alcandhor said, "That does sound as if you will be here for a long time."

"I cannot guarantee I can stay all the time, I do have duties. But with the portal working and knowing I have a welcome, I can state that I intend to make this my home and be here as much as possible." Mattan's smile broadened. "Fear not, my son, you shall not be shed of me any time soon!"

Alcandhor swallowed to fight the tightness in his throat. "I call this meeting over."

The chiefs all bowed, and Mattan rose from his chair. Alcandhor added, "I am going to Family North to give our news to our two newest chiefs."

The other chiefs scattered upon leaving Thane Hall, but Mattan stayed by his side. "I shall join you. I can see how Marcalan heals."

"You can tell from here."

"I also want to see them. Not only is he a very likeable rascal, but though she does not know it, I am also her uncle. I keep hoping her reserve will crumble."

"I am certain it will, given time."

"How long did it take with you?"

"Once she knew I was her uncle, it did not take long. She craved love so badly."

"Ah, well, I am a far third in line then, behind you and Marcalan. And behind Haladhon as well, I dare say."

"I would not despair. When will you tell her?"

"I have felt a wall in her mind. She has repressed memories. If they have to do with her mother's death, I could cause her trauma by trying to bring them to the surface. So I wait. For now."

Alcandhor nodded, and they walked silently in the growing dark. Workers lit the torches in the sward, and they nodded in passing.

"Tell me, Thane, how did Ashani die?"

Alcandhor grimaced. "'Twas a dark time for us. And explaining may be knotty. Bear with me. Pandhral, her grandson, was Thane because her son, Zadhras, and who had great foresight—we call him Zadhras the Seer—had disappeared. He was considered strange by all, not wishing Thaneship or the company of others, and it was thought he had gone into the mountains to be alone."

"I follow so far."

"Pandhral's son, Isandhral, murdered both Ashani and his father to become Thane. He also gained a title: Isandhral the Cruel. He was not long Thane. He was executed and his younger brother Sandhras became Thane. He is my direct ancestor."

Mattan said nothing for a few moments. The crunching of leaves under their feet became loud.

"How did he kill her?" Mattan asked softly.

"Poison. She could not tell his thoughts because he blocked, and mostly stayed far away, out of the city. The scheme was complex. He dared not let anyone know his plan, because he knew she could sense intention even if not trying to read thoughts. To make the story brief, a lass who served meals did not know the wine flask had been tampered with."

"It must have been a strong poison. My people can resist illness and some types of toxins and heal themselves."

"Aye, 'tis said she died in moments."

Mattan looked down, frowning. "She loved your people, and her heart was ever kind. How was he brought to justice?"

"It was tricky, as he was very careful of those he allowed near. Sandhras and his followers somehow overcame him—the legend is that Zadhras used his strong mental powers to help overthrow his mother's murderer." A new thought came to Alcandhor. "I wonder now...if your sister was here—I know she did not live in the city. There is no knowledge of her even staying, we only knew of Ashani—but if she was here too, perhaps she and Zadhras both somehow helped."

"That is possible. I suspect she removed herself to Pashelon to be in the mountains Avadhron loved so much. Distance would have been no barrier to her reaching out mentally to one such as Zadhras." Mattan looked at the sky, and murmured, "What became of him?"

Alcandhor hesitated. "Legend says he lived by himself, removed from everyone. Perhaps somewhere high in the mountains, perhaps even in the Portal Complex."

"But he was half Enaisi. He would have lived a very long time. No one knows when he died? Or how?"

"Old age." With a quick mental kick, Alcandhor added, "We assume. He is not alive, or you would have been able to make contact."

"Aye."

Did Mattan give him a more penetrating look? 'Twas hard to tell in the dim, flickering light.

"You know..." Mattan stopped, and after walking several more steps, continued, "you remind me a bit of Zaidhron."

Such a comment struck Alcandhor to the heart. To be compared to such a man, in any way, stars! "How so?" he managed to ask.

"Your love of history and languages, your humility, your wish for peace."

Humility? Weakness was more the target. Before he could gainsay Mattan, the Elder continued, "Zaidhron despised having to make tough decisions. Avadhron knew it, so often stepped in and made them for him, and it was rare Zaidhron would gainsay him."

"And did not the clan scorn him for such weakness?"

"His kindness after the despotic rule of his half-brother Janadhan on Teledhar was a welcome relief. A few tried to take advantage of it, but Avadhron stood as warden most times."

"Until he resigned as head of security and moved to Pashelon Province?"

Mattan grimaced, nodding. "Aye."

Alcandhor was quiet for a few moments, thinking of so many things he would ask. This conversation must be edging on grief for the man. He finally decided on: "How did Avadhron vote in conclave, living so far away?"

"*That* was what brought the conclave decision that all chiefs must reside in the city."

"Until they abrogated that for my brother. Who also moved to Pashelon."

"I would love to know the story behind that. I would wager my sister had something to do with it."

"Stars. I still cannot imagine my brother married to—great Bells, Mattan. She was his aunt!"

The Elder's face twisted in a wry grin. "Almost a thousand years' of generations between them, but aye. Just as you are my son, many generations removed."

"But that is, that should not—'twas not lawful!"

"My sister never allowed law to stop what she felt she should do. She interfered as she pleased."

"Such as placing Avadhron's Airing in a forgotten, even forbidden, place? Was that truly following his wishes?"

"As I said, she followed her heart, which is not a faithful guide of proper actions, regardless of the blandishments expressed by poets and songwriters."

Alcandhor winced; he had not meant to trod into Mattan's grief with both feet.

Two Rangers approached on a side path. They were immersed in their conversation, and obviously did not know their Thane was near. Alcandhor recognized Bandhral's voice:

"First he has the cheek to fall in love with the Thane's niece. Then he runs away from his Thane's command, and instead of being brought to conclave or otherwise disciplined, he is rewarded by being allowed to marry her?"

"Do you have a question for your Thane?" Alcandhor asked.

Both Rangers jumped. The one flushed, but Bandhral asked, "What purpose would be served by asking? Marcalan does what he pleases, even in seducing your niece."

"He did not seduce her," Mattan said.

"And how would you know, Elder?"

"Because I am an Elder. Do you not know I can sense, and even read minds if I have the inclination?"

"So you say," Bandhral shot back.

Alcandhor held an arm out as a tacit warning to the Enaisi, but he paid his Thane as much heed as Haladhon or Marcalan would. With a smile, Mattan stepped close to Bandhral and whispered in his ear. The Ranger stepped back, and without another word, hied away. His fellow Ranger shot a fearful look at Mattan and followed.

"What did you do?"

"Do you not know?"

"How invasive were you?"

"Ah, that would be telling. I will, however, warn you that your fears of having Question called are not unwarranted."

Alcandhor's stomach clenched. "On what grounds?"

"I did not intrude on his mind except to brush his surface thoughts, so I cannot say. Would you like me to—"

"Nay."

Mattan grinned. Was he testing Alcandhor or teasing him? Or both? He scowled at the alien.

"I will say their resentment goes deep. Do you know why?"

"I cannot say there is one reason alone. Many begrudge that my older brother was passed over. He was the strong one, the one who should have been Thane."

"Why was he passed over?"

"He lost control. He beat a young child—Marcalan, truth be told. It is not a short nor an easy tale, but he gave up heirship to Thane and moved to Pashelon Province, despite the fact chiefs have always been required to live in Zaidhron."

"Which also explains their hatred of Marcalan."

And now, Marcalan is married to their future Thane. A female. With no proof of parentage in the family records. Alcandhor paused, then let his breath out in a slow exhale.

"What has you so worried?"

"Not here. Not now. Let us worry about more immediate problems."

"Ah, yes—I mean, aye, the Rogues. My apologies. I know they weigh heavily on you."

"They do." Alcandhor's lips quirked up. "Your accent is much less, but you do still have a mixed syntax and what we could call a bit of commoner vocabulary."

Mattan shrugged. "I am working on it."

Chapter Forty-Four

Alcandhor blinked at the industry in his niece and Marcalan's, nay, his nephew's—stars!—family chamber. Tam scurried about as Adrinna and her workers changed draperies, rugs, tapestries, and the cushioned chairs to ones with brighter colors. Marcalan sat in one of the new chairs, leg propped, with a dazed expression.

"Uncle! All I said to Adrinna was perhaps happier colors, like flowers, and see? Are they not beautiful?"

Alcandhor nodded, and stepped back out of the way.

Mattan hooked a chair and placed it next to Marcalan. "I shall sit here with you out of the way. How are you feeling?"

"The pain is less. I grow weary of resting."

"You shall soon be back on your feet, Ranger," Alcandhor said, then sidestepped, to avoid two men carting out the old draperies.

Tam spun in a circle, her eyes shining. "I never thought I should have a home so fine! Thank you, Adrinna! Thank you, Uncle!"

Adrinna smiled. "'Tis merely your due as a Ranger, but I am pleased that you are happy with your chamber."

And appreciative? Alcandhor wanted to ask, but did not. Aleta had driven Adrinna into fits with her complaints. But that was the past.

The warder curtseyed and followed her last workers out, closing the door.

"So why the evening visit, Thane?" Marcalan asked. "Are folks restless, awaiting my recovery so I may resume my mission to bring laughter to the city?"

"More likely relieved to be spared your pranks for a few days longer."

Marcalan slapped his chest. "You wound me, Thane!"

Alcandhor eyed the rascal, wary of his lilting voice. "You must be feeling better."

Tam whirled around one last time, looking at everything, then rushed over and settled on Marcalan's good leg, arms around his neck. She was so opposite the withdrawn child he met those few lunations ago. He brought his mind to the matter which did bring them this night.

"A runner arrived with news of the Rogues. They are still in the caves, but our men make progress in scouring the caves and guarding the entrances. It is now thought they are in southern Pashelon Province. Or were when this last report was sent."

"If we only had faster means of communication," Marcalan said. "Runners relaying from southern Pashelon are likely dated."

"I await a new runner, or a drum message. I hope by morning we shall have another report. I am considering leaving for Pashelon by then, even if an update does not arrive."

Marcalan straightened in his chair. "I wish to go, Thane!"

"You are not well enough!" Tam said.

"Aye, your leg is not healed," Alcandhor added.

"For this, it is healed enough. I claim Capture Rights on Nandhal!"

Alcandhor groaned. "Not you too! I would not have expected vengeance from you, of all people."

"'Tis not vengeance. I read the reports of what he did to that family. He is a traitor to our clan, and was with the ones who planned the ambush on the chiefs in Lairdton. I was there. I saw Valdhor die, and you wounded. And aye, for what he did to me. But not for vengeance, for justice. For wanting to be the one to stop such a Child of the Enaisi who enjoys inflicting pain and suffering. Enjoys it, Thane! I felt his elation. He needs to be stopped. And I wish it to be by me."

"I have just been through this with Haladhon. You fight to capture, he will fight to the death. And he is a Child of the Enaisi, one who is used to what he can do, and I have no doubt he would try to use emotion to gain an advantage. Even if you were hale, I could not sanction this."

"Tam blocked Uardhel's attempt to use emotion to disable me in that crypt. I now know how to block well, and can do the same for myself with Nandhal."

"But you are not healed!" Tam exclaimed. "Your leg would never allow you to walk for days, much less fight!"

"I will go, Thane. I claim Right."

"You cannot if I do not agree."

The man's set jaw gave Alcandhor warning. He pointed at his cousin. "You felt shamed to be a Ranger for disobeying me only days ago. And now you have set in your mind to disobey me again?"

Marcalan dropped his gaze. "Please, Thane. I beg of you."

Tam leaned into her husband, her face buried in his neck, murmuring to him.

"This is all arbitrary," Mattan said. "We do not know what report may or may not come. We may find out they are already captured, and this will all be moot. Let us wait until morning."

"The Thane has said he will likely leave in the morning, news or not. I would not be left behind."

"I am not likely to change my mind, but I do give my word that we will not leave the city without your knowledge. That is the best you will receive from me, Ranger Chief Marcalan."

The silence grew heavy. Alcandhor finally said, "I will leave and let you rest." He strode to the door and turned, but Mattan stayed seated. He raised his eyebrows at the Enaisi but the man shook his head.

"I wish to help change his dressing, Thane. Not that I do not trust Tam, but I am a trained physician and wish to examine the wound."

"Can you not just sense it?"

"Aye, but that does not mean I do not wish to use my eyes on occasion."

Alcandhor hesitated. "I thought we might go to the Portal Complex and work on those encryption algorithms."

"Ah. Tomorrow, my Thane, if we do not leave for Pashelon. My mind is too wearied tonight."

Alcandhor bowed. "As you wish." He opened the door, and as he passed through, he could hear Tam and Mattan.

"What is a...physician?"

"Another word for healer."

"Oh, good! Then you can tell me..."

He shut the door with a smile. It was not about the wound. It was a way to be with Tam and break down that barrier. Good for him.

~*~

Tam pulled back the new heavy draperies to admit the pale morning light. Stars, but the weaving of the bright flowery hues in them and all the new furnishings and tapestries, gave the chamber a cheerful atmosphere.

Tam turned from the window. Though early, she had light to properly see Marcalan's leg. She knelt on the bed and carefully unrolled the bandages around his thigh. "Bells, it has closed! Mattan said it would, but I thought he was much too hopeful in saying we need not pack the wound at all last night." She concentrated on redressing the wound, which was merely a protective covering now over the tender, newly healed skin.

"Good, then I will be able to journey to Pashelon."

"You will not. Uncle will not allow it. He said thus."

"I will wait until he has come to tell us any news. And let him know the wound is healed."

"It is not fully healed. And you still have pain, all over."

"You do not block to keep from feeling it, do you?"

"Nay. Why should I?"

"Stars, need I say on? Did you not know pain *hurts*? I would not inflict this on you."

"But I am as your healer. I need to know if you need a tincture or assistance, and I know you would not tell me. You are a stubborn Ranger!"

Marcalan's eyes twinkled. "I think we are Trained to be."

Tam sighed and shook her head, rolling her eyes. Her husband snickered.

"You enjoy your jesting too much."

"You would have me no other way." Marcalan sat up and reached for his trous.

Tam slid off the bed and gathered the used bandages. "I would not. I think I did not know how to laugh until I met you."

"Ah, that is an untruth. The Thane told a story from when you first journeyed to Lairdton. He tried to explain how to wear an underbodice, and you laughed at his failing."

Tam turned to her husband, eyes wide. "Stars, he told that story on me?"

"Nay, actually he told the story on himself," Marcalan said, pulling on his trous. "You would not think a man who has been married and sired children would blush about an underbodice."

Tam smiled as she placed the dirty cloths in the bin, remembering her uncle having to explain growing up and *in love* and the embarrassment she felt from him. "He is very private about such things."

"I hope we can be private about such things soon."

"I think we will. You hardly had any problem in the priv this morning."

Marcalan's face grew red. "Great Bells, Tam! Do I have no privacy?"

Now it was her turn to tease. "Nay. I was as your healer. I tended to you, seeing to your wounds, and taking care of your needs. And I used our bond to stay attuned to know if you were in pain or needed care." She need not tell him of her own discomfort in having to learn such things.

"I know, but stars!"

He fumbled at lacing his trous, still blushing. Her uncle, it seemed, was not the only one easily embarrassed. Tam smiled. "Hurry and get you dressed, Ranger. Breakfast will be soon."

"Have mercy, woman!"

"As much as you give your victims, prankster!"

"I am doomed, then."

Tam laughed, then ran to the door to answer a knock. Surely not news from her uncle already.

A young man held out a tray. Tam took it with a murmured, "My thanks."

The meal and washing up afterwards did not take long with both of them working together. Marcalan's pain at each step did not stab today but merely twinged, and most of his other injuries were minor aches now. Surely, they could begin nestling soon. She turned to say something to Marcalan, but a drum message interrupted her. Its echo rolled throughout the city, announcing migrating birds had come to rest.

"The Rogues are cornered!" Tam exclaimed.

With hardly a hitch in his walk, Marcalan strode across the chamber and grabbed his pack from the peg by the door and his heavier cloak. "Let us leave!"

"Uncle has said you will not go."

"Only because I was not healed enough. I am now."

"But you are not! Only yesterday you bled through your trous. Granted the wound healed quickly—"

"Mattan healed me last night."

"He what? How did I then not sense it?"

" I know not. You will have to ask him, but I felt the warmth in my leg as he sat next to me. I know not if he knows that I know, but it is the truth. You saw the proof last night and this morning as well."

Ire rose in Tam. What gave that alien the right to interfere?

"Why are you angry?"

"Now you will insist on going, and fighting Nandhal. What if Nandhal..." Tam blinked hard, fighting tears. "What if you cannot defeat him?"

Marcalan chuckled. He held out his arms, and Tam rushed into them, loving the warmth and strength of him.

He stroked her hair, his lips on her forehead as he murmured, "Trust me, Love-ling. I can defeat Nandhal. We have matched for years."

"But a match is not fighting."

He set her back a little, meeting her eyes, a whimsical grin on his face. "'Tis not?"

She shoved him. How dare he have such a playful attitude over something so dangerous, and potentially deadly! "You know what I mean. A match is controlled. This is not."

His eyes sobered and his smile became melancholy.

Tam's voice lowered to a whisper. "I want not to lose you."

"You will not. I could not say the vows when you put the necklet on me, but I say them now: *I vow by the Maker to love you and care for you. To be faithful to you and devote my life to you. To twine our hearts and lives as your hair was twined into the braid for this necklet.*" He bent close until his nose brushed hers for a moment, then his lips caressed her face in feather-light touches. "And that will be for a long, long time, Love-ling. I promise."

Such love! Did he truly love her thus? Freely love her? It felt so, but—she brought her mind to the immediate worry.

"Is this so important to you? To take such a risk?"

"You can sense me. You know the answer."

Aye, an intense zeal burned in him, his blue eyes so fervent and pleading that her heart softened. She slowly nodded. "I–I will not refuse you. And I will appeal for you to the Thane. But remember, you know how you felt when you thought you could not be with me? What will happen to me if you die?"

"I will not die. I vow by the Maker, I will not die."

Tam clung to him, hoping he was right.

~*~

Tam walked to the gate, Marcalan next to her, a fighting staff doubling as a walking stick. That had been her idea, but he had not objected to it.

Her uncle and Andhrel both stared at them in disbelief. Alcandhor raised a hand. "You two are not going. I sent word to you after breakfast—"

"I am healed, Thane. The wound is closed. Ask Tam. Sense me. There is no reason for me not to go. And being chiefs, we should be there as will all the others."

"It is true, Uncle. His wound has completely closed. He is healed enough to journey."

The Thane glared at Tam. "So you agree to Marcalan claiming Capture Rights?"

She bit her lip, but she had promised Marcalan. She reluctantly nodded. "He must do this, Thane. He must. Please."

"If he claims Right, he battles Nandhal alone. As Haladhon will battle Monadhal alone. You could be a widow before nestling."

Tam nodded again. Her eyes stung, and she blinked hard. Alcandhor's shoulders sagged, his expression one of sorrowful resolution. She needed not even sense to know he would refuse Marcalan's claim. That was his face when he was going to deny something. She clenched her fists. "We are Rangers. First. Before anything else. Do not refuse this based on what you feel, Thane, instead of on what is right."

Alcandhor's face twisted, and Tam held her breath. If he was biting the inside of his cheek, he was considering changing his mind. He lifted his hands. "So be it." He turned away, facing south.

"Thane!" Andhrel exclaimed, looking from Tam and Marcalan to Alcandhor with dismay.

Eladhrel and Haladhon approached, Mattan not far behind.

The two chiefs asked why Marcalan was there. Tam left him to argue with them, striding back to talk to Mattan before he reached the rest of the chiefs.

"Why did you heal him? Would you not know it meant he would want to go and claim Capture Rights?"

"That is why I did it."

Tam dashed a tear of anger away from her cheek with her fist. "Now he is going, and will be in danger!"

Mattan reached a hand toward her, but dropped it. "Tam, I cannot say on, but I do have sight. He needs to go."

"So you can guarantee all will be well?"

Mattan averted his eyes for a moment before meeting her gaze with a smile. "Trust me."

Tam pressed her lips together, shaking with anger and breathing heavily. "I cannot help him as I did against Uardhel. He fights alone. He is not truly healed yet, and you know that. Why—"

Mattan grasped her by the shoulders and whispered, "Trust me. I know you do not know me well yet, but trust me."

Tam spun and stalked back to her husband. The other chiefs all gathered around Alcandhor, discussing his decision to let Marcalan journey with him. He threw up his hands. "I am only Thane, they make the decisions." He hefted his pack and began walking. Mattan hurried to join him, Andhrel and Eladhrel not far behind. Haladhon stopped to talk to one of the gate guards.

Tam ran her thumbs under the straps of her pack, glowering at the back of the alien's head.

"Why are you so angry?" Marcalan asked.

"He should not have meddled. I do not like it."

"Ah, because he healed me? Tam, he is an Enaisi. If he thinks it is for the best, then we need to trust him."

"Why? What makes him more infallible than any of us?"

Haladhon loped up to them, grinning, and tossed Marcalan's hood over his head. Her husband smiled, but did not respond or retaliate. Her tall cousin's brows rose, but he said nothing, merely walked next to them. No one seemed disposed to talk.

They passed through the gate of the out-wall, and the Thane returned a salute to the men on duty there. The trees in the distance had given over to deeper autumn colors. Above them to the right, the tall mountains loomed in majestic beauty. The sun shone in the clear, blue sky, warming them despite the chill breeze. As they journeyed south toward the switchback leading up to the Pashelon Pass, the tall, dead grasses flanking the road seemed to wave at them. Why did the thought nag Tam that they waved good-bye? She bit her lip, pushing down her worry for Marcalan.

Chapter Forty-Five

Night settled over them as they made camp in the woods of Pashelon, not far beyond the pass. From a drum message received that afternoon, only a few hours' journey in the morning would see them to the Ranger camp not far from a small town called Kintol.

The night's bitter cold kept them huddled close to the fire, staring at the flickering warmth, sipping hot tea. Except Mattan. He lay back, staring up at the nebula, the mug resting on his abdomen.

Marcalan wrapped an arm around her and pulled her close. She relaxed against him, enjoying snuggling against his shoulder under his heavy cloak. He had walked too long, and his thigh throbbed, but the skin was unbroken; no bleeding through his trous this time. If only she could heal him a bit, but 'twas a long, slow process, and she would not be fit to journey if she did.

"'Twill be better in the morning after a night's rest," he murmured.

Unconvinced, but not willing to gainsay him when she had agreed to take his part to come on the journey, she looked away.

Mattan looking up at the nebula, a smile playing on the corners of his mouth. What made him so...happy? He glanced over at her. "I have missed it. It is so beautiful."

Had he felt her curiosity? Tam dropped her head. He acted as if she were not still angry with him. Indeed, she felt it difficult to stay cross. How did people like Marcalan's mother hold to such ill feelings all the time? 'Twas wearying.

Her uncle interrupted her thoughts. "We need to think of setting the watch."

Tam arched an eyebrow. "I will take first watch."

Marcalan groaned. "You always want first watch."

"Aye, she does," the Thane said dryly.

From behind her, Marcalan chuckled. "Perhaps we should have her take last watch, then."

Tam pushed away from him, half-turning to see his face, his humor lightening her mood just a little, which irritated her even more. "Oh, nay! I will not take last watch ever again when journeying with you."

Haladhon laughed. "I would not worry, Tam. He does not use the same prank twice. Expect something different this time."

"What prank?" Alcandhor glanced between the two.

337

"When we were bringing the Laird back, he had me take the last watch then did not wake me. He let me sleep all night." Tam set her chin in indignation.

Marcalan snickered. "Only Tam would take insult at being allowed to sleep through watch."

Tam play-slapped his chest. "I never did truly get you back for that either."

"Nay, you walked away from thrashing me. Not good form for a Ranger."

Tam did not know how to answer, so she tossed her head, crossing her arms.

Alcandhor smiled at them. "You two have never matched yet, have you?"

"Aye, we have, Thane," Marcalan said. "But we were both tipped back, so I know not if you would count that."

Haladhon's eyes twinkled. "That is one regret I have of leaving that banquet early. I would have liked to see two sotted Rangers matching on the grounds."

Alcandhor snorted softly. "As if you have not seen it before?"

"Ah," Haladhon said, pointing a finger at his cousin. "But being in the match is not the same as seeing it, Thane."

Alcandhor chuckled. "I concede that."

Marcalan waved his arms. "Oh, now this is not fair. Are you telling me you two matched while tipped back? We must hear the details."

The two Rangers smirked, then Haladhon said, "We had what, perhaps, sixteen or seventeen years at the time? We were both so sotted, I am surprised we found the ground with our faces when we fell."

"We woke up and had little idea of where we both got our bruises from." Her uncle's lips twisted in a wry smile.

"And the Thane had no mercy on us either. We matched hard all that next morning, regardless of the headaches."

"You deserved it," Andhrel remarked. "You saw not what you looked like, trying to match that night. Bellowing at each other and calling names, barely able to stand on your feet. Two young cockerels so full of themselves and drink. Saldhor laughed until his sides ached."

Tam shook her head. Haladhon she could see getting drunk and trying to match, but—"I cannot imagine you doing that, Uncle."

Haladhon winked at Alcandhor. "I can tell you plenty of stories about our dear Thane, Tam."

"Forget not I know just as many stories about you, cousin." Alcandhor's eyes glinted with mischief as they peered over the rim of his mug. Tam found herself smiling.

"Ah, but my dear Thane, I am proud of my accomplishments. You are the one who feels he must maintain his dignity now that he is Thane." He slapped his chest with a pose of mock gravitas.

Marcalan chuckled as Alcandhor's face flushed.

"And do not forget, I can tell stories on all three of you," Andhrel declared.

"Our oh-so-serious law keeper." Marcalan tossed a clod of dirt at him. "You have been known to tip a few back, cousin. I remember the time you, Eladhrel, Alcandhor, Haladhon, and...I forget who else, decided to sneak to the kegs of ale in the cellars."

The three Rangers sat up straight and stared at Marcalan. Andhrel's eyes grew wide. "How did you know about that? We were striplings then and you were but a Trainee."

Marcalan snickered. "I was hiding in there to keep from being thrashed by—hm, someone. I forget who. Probably Ganill. I heard and saw the whole thing. You all got fairly well tipped back."

Mattan burst out laughing. "A fine lot you all are. A good thing you are all friends or you could easily become extortionists."

Haladhon snorted. "The sad fact is that we could not. There are few secrets at Zaidhron. Gossip grows wings in that place."

"It always did," Mattan replied. "If those walls could speak, the stories they could tell."

"Why not tell us some of them?" Marcalan asked. "Or stories of your people. There is so much we would love to hear about."

Mattan paused, his eyebrows raised. "Aye, and so much I want to know about all of you and what has been happening here for the past six hundred years or so."

"Stars!" Marcalan exclaimed. "I cannot get used to that. It seems so strange to think your people live so long."

Mattan stared into the fire, shrugging. As he spoke, it seemed he spoke more to himself than to them, remembering. "It surprised us when we first began exploring through the portal and ran across races on other planets that were so short-lived. It seemed sad to us that their lives ended as they only seemed to begin. And it was an adjustment to watch how they rushed at things, but then we realized, their life pace was tied to their life span. We approach things at a more casual pace, knowing we have much time. It also caused us sorrow. When I befriended your ancestors, and stayed here to live, it became so difficult to watch friends and those beloved to me grow old and die. I could not stand it anymore and left."

"How long were you here?" Marcalan asked.

"The first time? For over three centuries. But I could not stay away and came back periodically. As I said, I was readying for another visit when the invasion came." Pain crossed his face, and Tam could feel, as well, how much the memories still hurt. "I wondered all these years how your people fared. It is good to know you have done well." He picked up a stick from the edge of the fire and poked the ground with it, a pensive expression on his face.

"What family have you?"

By both moons, Marcalan was forward in asking so many questions! She glared at him, nudging with her elbow. Her husband grinned at her, and Mattan looked up as well, and smiled. "I do not mind, Tam. Do not try to yoke him, as you would a dray beast. It will not work anyway. Marcalan is meant to be Marcalan, and I sense that it is good for your world that this is so."

Alcandhor's head snapped up. "Sight, Mattan?"

Mattan continued to both smile and poke at the ground with the stick.

Marcalan chortled. "It seems Mattan can be as close-mouthed as our dear Thane. So if you will not answer our Thane's question, how about answering mine. What family have you?"

Mattan chuckled, and Tam sensed his like of Marcalan. She found it more and more difficult to remain cross with the alien.

"Unlike you, family means little to my people. I know who my parents are, but it ends there. My mother died in the invasion and my sister—my sister..." Mattan paused. "My sister and I shared a strong bond, unlike most of our people. She was lost to us because of the war, and is now dead. Only my father is left and we never speak. I have some small attachment to my uncle, despite disagreements of how I live my life."

Marcalan's arms wrapped tighter around Tam. "You have no wife or children?"

"I only married once. To Tarnill. The only children I can claim would be all of you. Since your Thane's line is unbroken, you are my direct descendents."

Alcandhor and Mattan shared a smile, and Tam felt a kinship between the two. They had already built a strong bond.

The fire crackled in the silence. A pop sent an ember flying into the dirt. Mattan tamped it with the heel of his boot. "Now, it is my turn for questions. Let me start with you Tam, if you do not mind, since you are the one with whom I first made contact. Can you tell me of your family?"

Surprised, Tam glanced at her uncle as she hesitated.

Mattan gave her a curious look. "Does it bother you? If so, I will not pry."

"It bothers me not. I know not what to tell. I remember not my mother, and my father was a Ranger. He was the best Ranger there was."

Mattan smiled indulgently, but it faded, and he looked around at the

Rangers, surprised. "He actually was. I sense it strongly from every one of you, that he was considered a great Ranger."

Marcalan snickered, giving Tam a playful push. "We have not yet got used to you being able to sense us, and now we have to learn to deal with Mattan as well." He grinned, tugging her hair, and tightened his embrace. She relaxed into his arms again as he answered the Enaisi. "He truly was a great Ranger, Mattan. He was a hard, skilled fighter and the missions and assignments he went on have become almost legend."

"What missions?" Tam tipped her head back to look at her husband. He kissed the tip of her nose.

"He would come to Zaidhron from his bounds occasionally and was sometimes sent out on missions," Alcandhor explained. "He would not accept long ones as he did not want to leave his bounds for too long."

"I never knew that," Tam murmured.

"He discontinued coming to Zaidhron, and Rangers were sent to try to find him. He found them instead, and told them he would meet with them at certain times and at a certain place, but that he could not leave his bounds any longer. He would not explain." Alcandhor stopped, his gaze on Tam. "But I think it was because your mother died, and he had to care for you. You were too young then to journey so far."

Tam shook her head, staring at the fire as she tried to recall anything from so far back. "I remember it not. None of it."

"Who would have thought his reticence to return was a daughter rather than just being a recluse?" Marcalan said. "A Ranger-Trained daughter who is now heir to Thane."

Tam straightened. "Heir for now."

Alcandhor pointed at her. "It was a conclave decision."

"But that does not make it law."

Haladhon chortled. "Wish you to join the wagering, Mattan, on which of these two wins?"

Mattan shook his head, smiling. "I will stay out of it altogether. I see that it would be safer for me that way."

Haladhon and Marcalan both leaned forward with eager expressions, and Tam knew they both caught the wording Mattan used, as she did. Did he truly mean he had sight, or did he jest with them?

"Ah, cousins, we have a rare opportunity!" Marcalan exclaimed. "Now tell me, Mattan, what bribe would it take to get some early information from you?"

"Now, wait, there is more than one ready to bribe," Haladhon countered.

Mattan laughed, and Alcandhor exhaled with an exaggerated moan. "Be apprised, Mattan, that these two will take any opportunity offered, and make a few new ones on the way, if possible."

"So I have seen," Mattan replied. "But for now, I was the one asking questions."

"No fair," Marcalan retorted. "Tam answered about her father, now it is your turn again. Tell us something about your people, or about our past."

Alcandhor held up his hands, shaking his head. "We shall be up all night and Mattan shall still be answering our questions. Let us set watch, and get some sleep tonight. Tomorrow we can ply our new *old* chief with many questions as we journey."

The watch was settled, and much to Tam's dismay, the Thane ordered that she and Marcalan not watch.

"But why?" Tam asked.

"Oh, great Bells, Thane," Marcalan moaned. "She will argue until dawn with you over her right to have watch! Believe me, I know!"

"Because we wish to sleep," Haladhon said. "If either of you are on watch, the other will be awake as well. And I have journeyed with you enough to know if you are awake, you will be talking and jesting."

"Aye," Eladhrel murmured. He was already wrapped in his cloak, head resting on his pack. "Marcalan never shuts up."

"That was not the reason, but it will suit," Alcandhor said. "Now try to get you some sleep." The stern look on his face forbade any discussion.

They all but Andhrel settled into their cloaks. Marcalan held up both of theirs, and with a shy glance at the men around the fire, Tam hesitantly moved close. He wrapped their cloaks over them, then settled onto his back and gently pulled her over onto his shoulder. "We may not be able to start our nestling, but we can at least be together," he whispered with a lilt, his blue eyes shining.

"Do you think soon you will be healed enough for us to nestle?" she whispered back.

"I fervently hope so! To know I can now hold you, kiss you, and yet my body is too weak to respond—"

"Yet you expend your energy on this journey instead of staying in Zaidhron and healing!"

"I have to do this. I thought you understood."

"I sense how deeply you are driven in this, but not why. And I will worry for you until Nandhal is safely captured."

"I cannot explain why. I can name reasons, but not why I have the burning need."

Tam bit her lip. "Perhaps...it is somehow, some kind of sight?"

"I know not. I have not much knowledge of foresight. But I know I must do this. And 'tis not vengeance. It is..." Marcalan gazed beyond Tam, as if seeing something in his mind. "It is as if, by capturing him myself, I bring balance to...something. One Child of the Enaisi capturing another." He closed his eyes with a headshake, then smiled at Tam. "I know not how to make you understand, when I understand it not myself."

Tam reached up, her fingers tracing Marcalan's face. "You jest, and you laugh, and you make a show of being frivolous and lighthearted, but there is a depth to you that few, I deem, have ever realized."

He snugged her in tighter. "Ah, do not reveal my secret, Love-ling!"

She smiled and let herself cuddle against his side, loving the warmth of their connection as well as the warmth of being next to him.

"Are you still angry at Mattan?"

She tipped her head back to see her husband. Of course; he could sense her emotions. She hesitated. "Nay. But if you are hurt, I will be more than angry."

"An irate, Ranger-Trained female who is a Child of the Enaisi? I can imagine nothing more frightening. I would not wish to unleash such fury on anyone. So I guess I should best be very careful, enh?" He kissed her nose.

Tam's lips quirked despite her best effort to not smile, and she snuggled against his shoulder again. His words were not a guarantee, but they did make her less worried.

Chapter Forty-Six

Tam blinked and rubbed the sand from her eyes. Morning noises now replaced the sounds of night, and the woods around them showed vague shapes of trees in the dim grey. The happy birds known as dawn-singers lustily chirruped at the breaking of the new day. She blinked again, and yawned.

Mattan sat in silence as morning arrived, his eyes bright. But aye, Haladhon huddled by the embers on watch. Why then was Mattan already awake?

The alien nodded to her. "My planet no longer has such things. Dawn is not beautiful. There are no birds, no trees..." His voice trailed off, then he smiled and took a deep breath. "Can you smell it? There is a smell at dawn, a sweet freshness."

Tam sat up, her breath misting, the cold waking her completely. Marcalan moaned.

"Aye, there is. I have always enjoying being up to smell the dawn."

"Smell or not, do not rip the cloaks off me. 'Tis like ice," Marcalan muttered. "Stars, the way you can just be wide awake at an instant makes me tired."

Tam reached around and pulled both cloaks off Marcalan. "That should help you wake up."

"Oh, you are cruel!"

Andhrel groaned and rolled over. "Bells, Marcalan, you never shut up, do you?"

"If I did, you would think I was ill, would you not? I would not want to be a cause of worry to you, my dear cousin."

Andhrel grimaced and rolled his eyes as he sat up. "My thanks for your concern."

Marcalan chuckled.

Before long, they broke camp. Mists covered low-lying areas and in spots it wrapped around them, dampness seeping into them as they walked. Leaves crunched under their feet. The freshness and sharp chill invigorated Tam, as did walking in a real woods in Pashelon, although they were on the other side of the province from where she grew up, and not high in the mountains. Still, it felt almost like home.

"Tell us about your world and people," Marcalan said. "You said that your world was destroyed, and your people now live on another world?"

Mattan smiled. "You are insatiably curious. Aye, we live on Retreat. It is beautiful and lush but it holds no special place in my heart as this world does. I think because it was just that, a retreat. It has no special history and no challenges. It was almost like a prison. We lived there for so long. Our leaders were afraid to allow us to use the portal in case our enemy was still alive and on our planet. Finally I convinced them to let me go through."

"And your enemy was gone?" Marcalan asked.

"Yes. We had succeeded in defeating them but not soon enough. They had started their campaign to make our world uninhabitable, and when I returned, it was. There were no trees or plant life, no animals, no people. All surface dwellings had been demolished. We have been trying to find a way to bring our planet back to life, but so far we have had limited success."

"It must be horrible to see your home world destroyed," Tam whispered.

Mattan shook his head. "It is not our home world, not if you mean the world we originated on. We were forced to abandon that many ages ago. But this world we have called our own, where we built our lives and invested of ourselves. Our Central Portal Complex was there. It would be unfeasible to move that. I cannot see giving up that planet as lost, but not many have the ambition to continue the Planet Reclamation Project. That is why I must keep on with my work."

"But surely your people can see whether it would be successful. Do they not have sight?" asked Andhrel.

"Prescience is a strange thing." Mattan's brow furrowed, his head tipping to one side. A memory of a woman doing the same thing flitted through Tam's mind, and an ache, almost a sorrow, grew within her. She concentrated on stepping over roots and crunching through the leaves, and both the strange ache and the memory faded.

"It is not certain," Mattan continued, "and there are often many variables that can hinder or help a vision in coming to pass. Prescience is tied as much to the seer as to the events."

"I understand not what you mean," Andhrel said.

Mattan grimaced. "Prescience is not exact. It is not like looking up at the sky and knowing the sun will shine when the clouds have passed by. I can see a future where my planet is green and livable, yet another man whom I greatly admire cannot see that. My future is one I will attempt to bring about. He has no hope and so he sees it not. Whether his sight or mine is the one that will come to pass is yet to be seen."

"But I have seen, or felt, things that have come to pass," Alcandhor said, "and I see not how I could have affected them."

Mattan nodded. "There are some things which very likely will come to pass. Like seeing an object bobbing in the tide and knowing it is likely it will come to shore. But yet it is not certain—it could get swept out to sea unexpectedly.

"But then there are others which are much more subject to personal decisions and these are the ones which are harder to see. And it is ironic that they are usually the ones we would really like to see more clearly, too." Mattan's voice dropped low and he paused, a sadness coming over him. "And then it seems that rarely does one have prescience in personal matters, either. It is usually larger events seen, not personal ones." Mattan paused. "There are exceptions, though."

"How often do your people experience sight?" asked Marcalan.

Mattan shrugged, shaking his head. "It varies. Some have it stronger, and others hardly at all. And this is the strange part: it is the least of the abilities we have that the Teldheri do not. Yet among you who are our descendents it is often the strongest ability, more so than empathy in some of you."

Haladhon gazed at Alcandhor. "Our Thane seems to have it very strongly."

Marcalan lifted his brows. "Perhaps it is why he has been so adamant that we would one day contact the Enaisi again? Perhaps it was sight, Thane?"

Alcandhor shrugged. "I know not. I have found that I often overlook sight when it happens. I only know I felt that trying to find a way to contact our old mentors was something I had to do."

"There is much you have in common with Mattan, Thane. You both are compelled to try to do things that others see no point in." Marcalan grinned over at the Enaisi. "And if the Thane's ambition has come to pass, perhaps it is a sign that yours will too, Mattan."

Mattan smiled. "You encourage me. I thank you."

"Aye," Andhrel said. "And from where has such depth of character suddenly emerged?"

"I know not. Perhaps Tam's influence. I shall endeavor to correct this new failing."

Andhrel and Eladhrel groaned.

~*~

The sun had long ago dispelled the morning mists, and the biting chill eased, making the journey one of ease—if one did not think of the Rogues.

Tam eyed Mattan and, after a moment's hesitation, moved closer to walk next to him. "I need to ask you a question."

"Yes?"

"How did you heal Marcalan, and I felt nothing?"

"It's much harder to sense healing. It's very subtle. If all had been quiet, and you had not been distracted by all the commotion and the discussion, you probably would have felt something. Are you still angry with me?"

Tam sighed. "I guess not. But it was sneaky."

"Yes, it was. I can only say I had sight, and knew Marcalan needed to be with us. Am I forgiven?"

"I suppose so."

Mattan smiled, and Tam reluctantly returned it. If his trick had not resulted in Marcalan facing danger, she would not have cared so much.

Her hood flipped up over her head, and she turned to see Marcalan, grinning. She glared at him as she tossed the hood back, but stars, how could anyone stay irritated when he smiled so winningly?

Her own smile faded as she sensed someone not far away. After a few moments, the Thane and Marcalan both slowed, peering ahead, obviously also sensing an approach. Mattan did not react. But then, he would be able to tell if it were friend or not.

"Is it a Ranger?" Tam asked.

"Aye," the alien said. "If we keep on, we shall meet him soon."

True enough, not long afterwards the Ranger Tonalan strode forward, hand out, calling, "Well met! You made good time." He bowed to the Thane, then stopped, mouth gaping, as he saw Mattan. His shock melted into a grin. "*Changes coming*, Thane, so you and your father always said. And I thought our new, female Ranger chief a surprise."

Amid grins and chuckles, Alcandhor made the introduction, then they followed Tonalan toward the camp.

"Any updates?" her uncle asked. "You are farther north than I had anticipated. The drum message yesterday afternoon was unexpected. I had thought we would journey a full day south in Pashelon today."

"Aye. We are not certain, but we think this is the northernmost exit, and they have nowhere else to go. Our men proceed north and west in the caves, so they cannot turn back without a fight. We feel we may truly have them cornered, Thane."

"Have they communicated with you?"

"Nay. How close they are to the cave opening, I cannot say. So far they have kept to the lower, manmade level. We have drummed a message to surrender peacefully, as well as called out to them, but no reply."

The smell of wood smoke and spiced meat bespoke a camp nearby. 'Twas not quite luncheon but Tam's stomach gave her notice food would be most welcome.

"I see you are using hunger as an incentive."

"Aye. The body's needs can overcome the strongest resistance. If they are close enough to an entrance to smell the food. We doubt it, but thought it worth the effort."

"Assuming also they do not have supplies."

"They may have some, aye. We came across many caches, in the manmade level. How much they carried with them, and what they might have stored wherever they are, we cannot know, however."

As they entered the clearing, the Thane hailed the camp, if that is what one would call such an assemblage. Tam had not seen this many Rangers gathered in the wild since they journeyed back to the city from Lairdton.

The Rangers all rose, fists over their hearts. Then they saw Mattan and just stared. Tam felt her uncle's joy and pride as he announced, "This is Ranger Chief Mattan, men. He is an Enaisi who has come back to us."

A hush fell over the entire camp, then the Rangers all put their fists over their hearts a second time, saluting the Enaisi.

A tall, older Ranger with blond hair strode forward. "We did not know when you would arrive, Thane, but we prepared extra food, just in case. Stew is in that pot, tubers are set in the fire, and we have sausage, pan bread, and tea as well."

"Ordhral!" Alcandhor lifted a hand in greeting. "You are in charge?"

"Aye, Thane." The Ranger bowed, while at the same time, Marcalan exclaimed, "A feast!"

"Well met. We shall confer after the meal."

The blond Ranger bowed. Tam had seen him before. He was one of the Rangers her father used to meet to exchange news. And she knew now by how easily she could sense him that he was also a Child of the Enaisi. He turned to her and bowed. "Well met, Tamissa. It is good to see you."

He knew her name? She had never even been allowed to speak with him. Jonadhan stepped forward, before Tam could even respond.

"Marcalan, what are you doing here, you rascal?"

"Eating soon, I hope," Marcalan quipped with a laugh. "Well met."

Jonadhan smiled at Marcalan, then at Tam. "Greetings, cousin Tam. Have you found a way to tame our dear Marcalan yet?"

Tam smiled, her eyes straying to her husband, and she shyly replied, "I think so."

Jonadhan's eyes followed hers, and he saw the necklet. He hooted at Marcalan, then shouted out, "By both moons and the Bells! The story is true! It is a miracle surpassing an Elder in our midst!"

Haladhon almost fell over laughing and nearly dropped the ladle he used to serve stew to his Thane. Rangers gathered around Marcalan, shoving him and laughing at him, while he laughed with them.

Tam felt herself blush but could not back away as Marcalan put his arm around her and drew her close.

Alcandhor smiled. "Let them come and eat. But you will have to wait to torment Marcalan until the chiefs and I confer with the camp leaders."

As Tam and Marcalan sat, several Rangers, one getting stew, another tea, yet another offering pan bread, served them. Each one bowed formally to Tam in a game of worshipping her as the one who tamed Marcalan. She found herself both blushing and giggling, while Marcalan just smirked, obviously enjoying the scene.

"I must say, my dear Thane," Haladhon remarked, "that any hope you had of gaining attention to the fact that we have an Enaisi in our midst is overshadowed by Marcalan's marriage."

Alcandhor grimaced. "Or even discussing the Rogues, it seems."

Chapter Forty-Seven

After the luncheon, Alcandhor gathered the camp leaders and the chiefs. The Thane sat on a log, with Tam seated on one side and Mattan on the other. The rest stood or sat around him. He nodded at Ordhral, whose eyes kept flicking to Mattan. "Tonalan briefed me earlier, but I would have any updates now, if you have them."

"Nothing new, my Thane. They are trapped between us and the Rangers swarming tunnels behind them, but have stayed in that lower manmade tunnel. They do not respond to verbal calls or drums messages, perhaps they are trying to avoid giving us any assistance in finding their exact location, although 'tis not difficult to ascertain where they are. They have not moved, and we think the tunnel is blocked, but we cannot be certain."

"They are not far. I can sense Nandhal," Tam murmured. "He is not happy."

Haladhon snorted. Alcandhor lifted a hand to silence him.

"They are neither happy." Mattan smiled grimly. "They are both fearful, angry, and bickering with each other."

"Stars, aye, you can sense them both, or even read their minds." Ordhral smiled grimly.

The Elder tipped his head in a way that reminded Alcandhor of Tam. "You are not overly surprised to see me."

Alcandhor cleared his throat. "Shall we keep to the Rogues?"

Ordhral's blue eyes snapped with amusement, but he bowed his head. Mattan rested his chin on his fist, lips pursed in an obvious attempt to hide a smile.

Alcandhor shot him a glare before continuing. "If we have our men engage them in the darkness of those tunnels, it is more dangerous."

"They have torches, Thane. And so do we."

"But still, 'tis an uncertain, dim light."

"Aye," Ordhral said, "and you have sent word you wish them taken alive. That is made more difficult in those circumstances. They would fight desperately, and our men would be forced to cut them down."

Alcandhor nodded. "If they refuse to come to the surface, we will have no choice but to do just that."

Haladhon and Marcalan both protested, and Alcandhor raised his hands to silence them. "If you have suggestions as to how force them out—"

"Let us go in," Haladhon said.

"No!" Tam slammed her fists on her knees. "I will not allow it!"

Alcandhor turned to her, surprised.

"But Tam, it only makes sense," Marcalan said.

"I will send pain to them both to make it impossible for them to fight before I let you go into those dark tunnels to fight alone."

"Great Bells, Thane, that is the answer!" Eladhrel said. "She could do that. Incapacitate them. She has done it before."

Alcandhor chewed his cheek. "Aye, perhaps..." He met Ordhral's gaze. "You said your men know approximately where they are?"

"We know they are in a tunnel, however we know not how far the tunnel goes, if it has any offshoots or is a dead end. And we know not exactly where they are in it."

"How long would it take to get to that tunnel?"

"Perhaps an hour. 'Tis deep within the mountain, and one must climb down a shaft with crumbling remains of what was a staircase."

Alcandhor straightened and nodded at Mattan. "Truly part of your maglev rail system, then."

"Aye, but I already told you that."

Alcandhor stood. "Then let us go into these caves and down to this rail tunnel."

"Us?" Haladhon asked. "You do not mean to go down, do you?"

"I will be there when these Rogues are captured. I am Thane."

"How can you think of taking such a chance?"

Mattan raised both hands. "Haladhon, you are allowing your personal concern for your cousin to cloud your mind. This man is Thane, he must be there. Besides, you have Tam with you, and am I right in assuming she would not allow harm to come to her uncle?"

"I have already protected him from an ambush once." Tam lifted her chin. "I will not allow harm to come to him."

Mattan grinned. "And also, you have me with you. It is my duty to protect my Thane, and you should know I can do it."

Haladhon hesitated. "That is fact."

"So now, is your mind at ease?" Alcandhor asked, his tone sharp.

Haladhon smiled, shrugging. "I will not win a fight against both my Thane and an Enaisi."

Alcandhor relaxed as he turned to Mattan. "Thank you."

Mattan grinned. "Just doing my duty as a chief."

"Then if we are through talking, let us delve into the mountain, and into the past, and capture these Rogues."

~*~

They clambered and almost fell on the tumbled stones. This obviously was not one of the openings the Rogues had used often. Alcandhor gazed upward. Either that or a recent rockslide obliterated whatever path existed. Fallen rock and trees shielded the entrance; finding it by chance would be difficult.

A young Ranger awaited them, bowing. He seemed familiar. Ah—Ialdhor. He had worked tirelessly to aid them in bandaging the wounded Marcalan in Lantral.

"You are our door warden, Ialdhor?" Alcandhor asked. "And our guide?"

The lad's eyes widened. "Aye, Thane. This way. Torches will mark the way so we do not get lost. And there are some for each of you as well. We must guard our steps as the ground is uneven and strewn with stone." He handed each a torch and then they all lit theirs from his.

Wordlessly, they trooped through the dark, the flames causing strange shadows to jump and dance on the jagged rock walls. Every so often a Ranger stood guard to show them which way to turn.

They came to a halt, and Ialdhor said, "The steps in the shaft are treacherous. We have a knotted rope hanging down. 'Tis best if you hold on to it at all times while descending."

The climb down was, indeed, a tricky affair; feeling for each step, one hand on the rope, the other still holding the torch. Some steps were missing, others only partially there. Alcandhor's shoulder throbbed by the time they reached the bottom. Suppressing a grimace, he asked Mattan, "Is this how your people got to the maglevs? By these stairs?"

"Nay. These would be for an emergency, or maintenance, to be used if the power were out."

Alcandhor turned and almost gasped. Not at the many Rangers, most with torches, but because of the size of this tunnel. The curved walls rose higher than the light of the torches reached and the ceiling remained shrouded in darkness. The guideway in the center of the floor stretched into the distance in both directions. Alcandhor stepped closer and touched it with a feeling close to reverence. He inhaled and gazed about at his Rangers. "You men have done a commendable task. Well done. Any news on the two Rogues?"

The Rangers muttered nay amid much headshaking.

"They are trapped. We believe this tunnel ends in a cave-in, Thane,"

Ialdhor said.

"Then it is finished save the actual capture." Alcandhor gazed about at the faces before him. This was his one chance to deny each of his cousins their plea. "I have claims for Capture Rights, one for Nandhal and one for Monadhal. If no other Ranger makes claim, I will send the two Rangers ahead of us."

"Stars," a Ranger said, "who would make claim for Monadhal?"

Haladhon stepped forward, chin lifted. "I would."

The Ranger swallowed, then bowed. "May your sword be righteous."

Haladhon inclined his head. "Which way?"

The Rangers pointed to their right, Alcandhor's left.

Haladhon and Marcalan, with Tam close behind, led the way through the curving tunnel, torches held high. Rubble and mounds of dirt on the ground grew more frequent.

"Just ahead," Ialdhor said, after they had walked for some time. "They have a torch or torches, or did. We called for them to come out, but only once did we get an answer. It was..." The Ranger hesitated, his eyes flicking to Tam. "...rather vile."

"Monadhal, I would guess," Haladhon said. "Threatening to kill as many of us as he could, enh?"

"Aye, close to the mark, Ranger Chief. After that, we have received no replies. Some thought perhaps they had killed themselves, or each other, but we have some Children of the Enaisi with us, and they tell us they can still sense them."

"Aye, they are there," Mattan murmured. "Not far ahead now. Feeling cornered. The older one will fight hard, I feel it in him."

"As will I," Haladhon spat. He strode forward, torch high until a darkness separated his light from the many Rangers behind. "Monadhal! Time to end this! I claim Capture Rights. 'Tis you and I."

Alcandhor strove to remain calm as they continued ahead; the Thane observing his Rangers capturing their former kin. The light of many torches filled the tunnel and finally, they grew close enough to Haladhon to see the blocked end of the tunnel and the two Rogues. Nandhal crouched, hand in front of his face, blinking at the brightness, but Monadhal stood, feet apart, lips peeled back in a malicious grin. "Haladhon!"

Monadhal had weathered much, having to live in the Wild, but his eyes remained the same icy blue, and that sneering smile had not changed.

Both men drew their swords.

With a slight effort, Marcalan swung up to the top of the guideway and called to Nandhal. The young Rogue straightened, his eyes wide and called out that Marcalan should be dead. He cursed his cousin, drawing his sword, and clambered onto the guideway.

Alcandhor glanced from one pair to the other. As much as he cared for Marcalan, his main worry was for Haladhon. Monadhal was a wicked fighter, and Haladhon's blind hatred could lead to a fatal mistake.

Monadhal swung his sword in a ceremonious circle. "So this is how it ends, is it, Haladhon? Think you that you can best me?"

"We shall see."

Monadhal's laugh cut with viciousness as the men closed on each other. Haladhon fought with a dour determination. Alcandhor clenched his fists as he felt Haladhon trying to control the burning hatred that filled him.

Monadhal drove Haladhon back. His cousin stumbled over a rock as he back-stepped, lost his balance on the uneven ground, and fell. He rolled as Monadhal struck with his sword, and as the blade hit the ground, he kicked, striking the Rogue in the back of the thigh. Monadhal's leg buckled and he fell to his knees. As he landed, Haladhon kicked again, knocking the sword from his hands, then hooked his leg immediately into a second kick to Monadhal's face.

The Rogue landed flat on his back. Haladhon picked up Monadhal's sword and tossed it to a Ranger, then he stood and waited for his former friend to get to his feet.

Monadhal rolled up, blood trickling from his nose and mouth, and they faced each other.

"Think you I can be bested easier hand-to-hand? I need not a sword to kill you."

"End this. You know if you continue to fight you will not live out this day."

"You do not wish to kill me then, cousin?" Monadhal spat out the familial name with animosity.

Haladhon answered him not. Good. For him to say thus would bring him to conclave to answer for inappropriate motives: a chief was required to be a symbol of the law to his clan. Rangers did not act out of malice or for personal vendetta.

Monadhal's knowing laugh rang out. "Would you wish to kill me if I told you it was my band that killed Bardhor last year? Shall I tell you how we did it? He did not die an easy death, Haladhon. He lived for two days—"

Haladhon rushed Monadhal with a strangled cry and grabbed him by the throat, squeezing as hard as he could, lifting the Rogue off the ground. Alcandhor ground his teeth. He remembered all too well finding his uncle's body, as well as the other two Rangers who had been with him. He saw the sword and knife wounds and the almost ritualistic slicing that had been done to the body. He knew Haladhon remembered it all too.

Monadhal struggled for a moment, his face turning brilliant colors, then he snapped a sharp blow to Haladhon's throat. Haladhon dropped him, falling back, coughing and gasping for air.

The Rogue landed hard, also gasping, but surged up and aimed a kick at Haladhon's face. Haladhon ducked and Monadhal's kick missed, throwing the Rogue off balance. He twisted away trying to catch himself to keep from falling. Haladhon rose, punching to Monadhal's kidney. He followed it with a kick to the back of Monadhal's knee, dropping the Rogue to the ground again.

Haladhon grabbed him by his collar and hauled him to his feet then punched him in the face. Monadhal fell again, but this time, quickly recovered, sweeping Haladhon's leg.

The tall Ranger rolled as he hit the ground. Monadhal already gained his feet as Haladhon struggled to rise. The Rogue's mocking laugh rang out. "Can you do no better than that, Ranger? Your father fought better than this, even with many knife wounds in him."

Haladhon lunged in fury at Monadhal, anger besting him. Monadhal sidestepped his attack, countering with sharp blows to the ribs and kidney. Haladhon fell, landing on sharp-edged rubble with an audible grunt. The Rogue kicked him in the ribs, then a blade flashed in his hand, pulled from his boot.

Alcandhor nearly dove at Monadhal, but a hand on his shoulder checked him. Haladhon twisted and his hand fastened over the Rogue's. They wrestled for a moment, Monadhal squeezing a pressure point on Haladhon's wrist, but Haladhon twisted and got his weight on the Rogue, his forearm across Monadhal's throat.

Monadhal sneered in his face, and hatred and a burning vengeance filled Haladhon. Again, Alcandhor nearly stepped forward. He held his breath, hoping Haladhon did not succumb to the temptation to kill. His cousin smashed his forehead into the bridge of the outlaw's nose, then wrested the blade away from him and tossed it away. Again, Rangers retrieved it.

They both began to rise, then Monadhal dove into Haladhon's midsection, knocking them both back. With a growl, Haladhon grabbed the Rogue by the throat, hauled him up, and threw him through the air as though a child's doll. Monadhal hit a wall of rocks, fell to the ground, and was still. Haladhon strode toward him, his fury still mounting. He reached the still form on the ground and seized him by the front of his tunic, hauling him up. Monadhal opened his eyes for a moment, sneered at his opponent, then his eyes closed and he fell limp.

Haladhon's lip curled in disdain. His rage as potent as ever. Alcandhor licked his lips and called out his cousin's name. "You have done it. It is over."

His Third at Table lifted a fist to smash into the face of the unconscious man.

"Haladhon!"

His cousin froze a moment, then dropped Monadhal and turned away.

Chapter Forty-Eight

Nandhal glanced over to see Monadhal draw his sword. Should he draw his sword as well, and die now, or be taken back and hanged? His mouth dropped open as he realized one of the Rangers at the front was Marcalan, and he was walking next to a grim-faced Tam. With a slight grunt, Marcalan leaped up to the top of the wide, center ridge and called his name.

"You are dead! You should be dead! Cursed prankster!" He drew his sword and brandished it, while blasting emotion at his hated cousin.

Marcalan drew his own sword with calm. "If you are trying to send to me, know it is futile."

Truly. Marcalan was not affected. He should be. It must be that wench. She was blocking him! "You bloody bawd!"

Tam did not respond, not even a flinch. She merely stepped back. No other Rangers moved forward.

Nandhal sneered; for Marcalan to approach him alone meant he claimed Capture Rights. "If you claim Right, she cannot help you by blocking."

"But she does not block." The maddening, innocent smile spread on Marcalan's face, and he spread his arms with a slight bow.

Nandhal bounded onto the ridge, and metal rang against metal as Marcalan parried Nandhal's thrust. Nandhal had matched Marcalan many times, and they knew each other's weaknesses all too well. However, the light-hearted prankster would not readily use the dirty tricks Nandhal would, even in real combat. Smiling with this knowledge, he swung his blade in again, using moves he had practiced in private and new ones he learned from Monadhal.

He had Marcalan on the defensive, his cousin backing up with every thrust and counter. Nandhal almost grinned as he sidestepped Marcalan's thrust, his blade low and arcing up in a vile move that should disembowel his cousin.

Marcalan's unexpected backwards hop saved him then before Nandhal could recover, he swung his sword in faster than Nandhal had ever seen him move, slicing Nandhal's arm deeply.

Wide-eyed in shock, Nandhal stared at his bloody right forearm while attempting to hold his sword steady. He tried to bring the blade up but Marcalan's sword slammed down on his and he dropped it, his arm throbbing from the jarring blow.

Marcalan pointed his sword at Nandhal. He sneered at his Ranger cousin. "Would you run me through if I do not yield?"

"I would, but I have no need," Marcalan replied.

"Why say you that?"

Marcalan just smiled, his eyebrows raised. Tam stepped closer. "You will yield. You have no choice."

Nandhal laughed with derision. "You think so, do you, wench? Shall I tell you what I think about at night. About you. About what I would like to do to you—"

Marcalan's sword came up to Nandhal's throat as he took a step closer. "Dare you say on about my wife?"

The necklet at Marcalan's throat almost caused Nandhal to laugh, but then he met his despised cousin's eyes. They did not snap with humor but instead were grave and—black. A Child of the Enaisi? What? *How can this be?*

From the shadows, a strange man emerged to stand behind Tam. Nandhal had never seen thus a one before, with such deep brown skin and black hair and eyes. And dressed as a Ranger chief.

You should wonder who I am, Nandhal. Can you not guess? Did you not have to learn of my people when it was discovered you had our blood in you?

Nandhal's heart thudded in terror as the voice continued to speak in his mind. This could not be! He could not be real!

It sickens me to think that one of my children could be so callous and cruel. Aye, I am real, Nandhal. Why do you fear me when I am your ancestor?

Nandhal stepped back in fear. He felt a burst of agony inside him, of sent emotions, and he moaned, falling to his knees. It increased, and he felt tears spring to his eyes as the horrible anguish and grief caused his body to shudder. The pain was familiar—he had felt this from Marcalan when they had captured him.

Tam stepped forward, her eyes black, as they stared into Nandhal's eyes.

"Tam," the Enaisi said, his voice soft, "you do not need to do this."

"Let him go, Tam," urged Marcalan. "Rangers do not seek vengeance."

Nandhal felt the pain ebb away, and he slowly straightened. He looked up at the Enaisi—for surely he was—dread and wonder battling in him.

Haladhon's fight with Monadhal ended, and the tall Ranger dropped the Rogue's limp body into a heap. Fear grew afresh in the pit of Nandhal's stomach. It was over. His life was over. He had plotted the ambush on the

Thane and the chiefs, and had tried to kill Marcalan. He would not receive a punishment. For his crimes, the penalty was death.

Rangers pulled Nandhal off the ridge and bound his arms. Beyond them Alcandhor watched, his face expressionless. Nandhal sneered at him then at Marcalan, who now stood with an arm around Tam. Curse him! And her! He sent an onslaught of hate to prankster cousin, then to her, but it slammed back so intensified that he groaned, his knees buckling. Rangers held him up by his arms.

"Get them back to camp," Alcandhor ordered, "then make ready to start back to Zaidhron."

~*~

The Rangers milled, readying to journey. Some would travel with them through the pass, but those whose home provinces were west of the mountains in Keladar and Pashelon would leave them now. Alcandhor did not wish them to depart without a word from their Thane. He leaped up to a small boulder and lifted an arm, calling out for their attention. "Men, you have done excellently and are a pride to our clan, and to me. This year you have dealt not only with traitors and a siege, but have ended the threat of the Rogues. You are all to be commended, and I bow to you." He dropped to one knee, inclining his head.

Some few Rangers exclaimed that their Thane should not do obeisance to them, but most returned the gesture or saluted. One stepped forward, chin raised. "We could have achieved nothing without the wisdom and foresight of our Thane."

Rangers shouted agreement and a cheer rose, echoing through the woods. Alcandhor bowed to them again, then waved his hands, granting permission for the western province Rangers to depart.

He lightly leaped down and grabbed his pack. He slung it over his right shoulder, not wishing to put a burden on the left, not after the climbing earlier.

"Well done, Thane," Mattan murmured as they all moved out.

"I would not take their toil and loyalty for granted."

"And they do appreciate it."

"And I assume you could sense that?"

Mattan's chuckle was his only reply.

Ordhral strode over to Alcandhor, with a nod to Mattan on his other side. "Thane, may I join you in your journey back to Zaidhron?"

"Your province does not need your immediate return?"

"Nay." A smile quirked on Ordhral's lips. "Did I not tell you to hold fast, Thane?"

359

"That you did. How strong is your foresight? Did you see all of this?"

"Nay. But I knew. Have you informed your history-keeper friend?"

"Aye, he is at Zaidhron. He was there when the portal became active, and Mattan walked through."

"I am happy for him. And Thane, now you may ask an Enaisi how a Teldheri like Avadhron can have foresight, and I need not break my vow to my first parent."

Mattan snorted. "Oh, Ordhral, you like to dive straight to the heart. A gift inherited from your famed ancestor, no doubt."

"I will take that as a great compliment."

"And I will turn your question back on you. What have you been told is the reason a Teldheri might have foresight such as the Enaisi have?"

Ordhral hesitated, glancing around, then softly replied, "That we were once one people."

Mattan's brows lifted. "Your sept's history is very extensive."

Stunned, not only at Ordhral's statement, but Mattan's reply, Alcandhor knew a serious discussion would be forthcoming with this Elder.

"Say rather, my history is extensive. I spoke with Tamissa's mother for many years."

"You knew who she was?" Alcandhor asked.

"Aye. And I am sorry for the loss of your sister, Mattan. She grew to know she would not live to see the portal open and be reunited with you."

Mattan stared at the ground in silence as they walked. He cleared his throat. "How did she die?"

"I cannot give you details. Valdhor was tight-lipped. All I know is it was a fever. They were gravely ill. Ismari healed Tamissa and Valdhor, but had not the strength to also heal the babe or herself."

"Babe?" Alcandhor choked out.

"Aye. A son. They named him Sandhor, and he would have had, I think, twelve years if he had lived."

"Tam knows this not. Not who her mother is, nor that she had a baby brother."

"She was a little girl, not much more than a babe herself. She protected herself from the grief and trauma of her mother's death by blocking out the memories," Mattan muttered. He drew his sleeve across his face. "If you will, Thane, I would like time to myself."

Alcandhor inclined his head and watched the Elder, shoulders sagging, walk on alone.

"Think you I said too much?" Ordhral asked.

"Nay. He has wanted answers. Now he has to deal with having received them."

~*~

Despite their somber task of escorting the two Rogues to Zaidhron, the mood of the Rangers was light-hearted in camp that night. Alcandhor leaned against a tree watching the men, but he was distracted from enjoying their cheer by what Ordhral said earlier. He rubbed his knuckles against his lips, lost in thought.

The Elder wandered over with a questioning smile.

Alcandhor nodded in greeting, then asked, "If what Ordhral said is true, then is Marcalan truly an impossibility or aberration?"

"Ah, I wondered if you would ask about that. No. What Avadhron had was extraordinary, the original genes from which my people began their modifications and enhancements. Those genes were rare in the first place, not being present in but a small portion of the population, and according to the geneticists, their culling was complete. Nothing of those traits should still have existed in the Teldheri, which meant—"

"Avadhron should have been as impossible as Marcalan."

"Exactly. But Marcalan's abilities are not the natural ones Avadhron had, but enhanced."

"Are you certain?"

"Yes. His abilities are too strong, and besides, his eyes turn black when angry."

"So that was engineered?"

"Oh, yes."

Alcandhor sighed. "So much knowledge is lost. Or was it meant to be lost?"

"Concerning my people's past, most was meant to be lost. But as to the knowledge lost since the portal closed, I cannot say."

Laughter rose from Rangers. Several rocked back and forth with mirth as Haladhon half-rose from his seat on a log and gestured in his storytelling.

Alcandhor grinned. "Can you feel it, Mattan? I believe it is because we have captured the last of the Rogues. They have been a star-flower thorn in our flesh for so long."

"There are no other Rogues at all?" Mattan asked.

Alcandhor shook his head. "There are a few Rangers who have been tried, stripped of Confirmation, and are tied to limited duties, as well as several who gave up Ranger status voluntarily. One such man lives in Thane Valley and has earned the respect in the village he lives in. He has made a good life for himself." Alcandhor sighed from deep in his soul. "It is a hard cost to start Training. Once a stripling, Training has gone too far to give up without a price to pay. Monadhal rejected any attempt to be kept

361

in the clan and try to redeem himself. The same for the others. They chose to be clanless and lawless. But the Rogues had rarely ever been a star-flower thorn in our trous until Monadhal. He had an uncanny ability to draw other Rogues to himself. I believe we need to rethink how we handle those that choose to be lawless, but we are restricted in what we can do as far as revising laws."

Mattan set his fists on his hips with a pensive expression. "No matter how fair we feel the laws are that we craft, there will times when we wonder if they are correct, and will feel the need to review and perhaps revise them."

"Aye."

"Your ancestors went through much soul-searching in crafting your laws. They knew they were not perfect, but they felt they were good."

"Aye. And I do too, most of the time. But when dealing with this, I feel we have not done enough and that because of it, innocent people have suffered and died."

"You cannot carry the burden and blame of every injustice upon yourself, Thane."

"A family lies dead, Mattan." Alcandhor flung his arms out. "Who should I blame? I am Thane, it is my responsibility to safeguard—"

"It is not your responsibility to personally protect every individual of your world! That is the duty of your entire clan. You do your best, as do your Rangers, but sometimes no matter your efforts, you fall short. You cannot destroy yourself with guilt over that which is out of your control."

The two men stopped, realizing their voices had become loud and the Rangers could hear their conversation. Alcandhor walked off to the side, and Mattan followed him. He put a hand on his shoulder. "Listen to me, Thane, please."

"You have already said enough."

"Nay. I want you to hear me."

Alcandhor turned to look at him, crossing his arms. "So. Say on then."

"I have lived with guilt for centuries. For much longer than that, but I will not dwell on that cursed time and place or those memories. The more recent guilt is this: most of my race is dead. I could not save them. We evacuated all we could to Retreat while working on a way to defeat the invaders. Eventually the lands around the Complex were razed, and it became impossible for any more people to reach us. Any who tried were targeted. I could not save them. I heard their mind-screams as they begged for help and were killed. I released our counterattack, but could not stay to see if it worked, because the invaders began a method of destruction that affected the Complex itself, though it was built deep underground. And so I had no choice but to go through, then shut it down." Mattan grimaced in pain. "Tell me how I live with that?"

The Thane stared in horror at Mattan.

"It was not your choice to leave those people," Alcandhor replied, his voice hushed. "You did what you must."

"Do you think that makes my guilt less?"

Alcandhor grasped Mattan's shoulder, his eyes averted.

"So tell me not about guilt, Thane. My mind tells me one thing but my heart another. I battle it all the time. But you do not. You let your guilt consume you."

Alcandhor was silent then finally replied, "My thanks for sharing that." He turned and walked away.

~*~

Tam sat in front of Marcalan, his arms around her. With the Rogues captured, and her fear for Marcalan's safety no longer a concern, her secret worry would not be pushed away. She leaned back against him, closing her eyes. *He loves me. He truly does.* But the nagging doubt would not leave.

"Tam," Marcalan whispered in her ear. "What is bothering you?"

"Nothing."

"Stars, I can sense. You are troubled. Is it my injuries? I am all but healed now."

"It is not that. I–I mean, it is nothing."

"Please, tell me. We are husband and wife now. If something bothers you, I wish to help. I love you!"

Tam bit her lip, a tear falling down her cheek. She twisted to face him. "Do you?"

"By the Bells and both moons, Tam, why would you think I do not?"

"I know you do. But...I started the sending, and I am much stronger than you. If I had not, if we had not played our sending game, then would we have bonded? Would you have *in love* for me without it?"

Marcalan's stunned expression melted into a gentle smile. "Stars, Tam, did you know I pleaded and cajoled to be sent on the mission to meet you and the Laird? I had known since I was young who I was going to marry. I suppose it was foresight."

Tam straightened, her eyes widening. "You knew you would marry me?"

"Ah, nay. Not exactly *who*, but that I would know who she was when I met her. And when I heard of you, I knew. I *knew*!" With an adoring expression, he brushed back her hair with his fingers. "I loved you before I set eyes on you. And when I did—do you know the thought that went through my mind when I first saw you, stepping out from those brambles, sword drawn? *She is so beautiful! She is going to be my wife!* Of course, 'twas not just my mind affected by you." Marcalan's eyebrows twitched up, and Tam's face warmed by the implication. She remembered the unsettling sensation that ran through her when they met. She knew now what it was.

"So I did not make you have *in love* by sending to you?"

"By the Maker, Love-ling, nay." He snugged her close in his arms, and she closed her eyes, her dread fading into a peaceful nothing.

That unsettling feeling—she felt it now, strongly, as she did when they kissed—practicing the promise, a fire tingling through her but this time echoing from his body to hers, growing in intensity. Her eyes flew open. Stars!

He chuckled softly in her ear.

"Marcalan...is that...?"

His breath was warm on her cheek as he murmured, "Here we are in a large camp of Rangers, with no chance of privacy. The Maker must have a sense of humor."

"So we...we can nestle when we arrive in Zaidhron?"

"Oh, Bells, Tam. Believe me, we will nestle!"

Chapter Forty-Nine

Wrapped tightly in his cloak against the cold, Alcandhor walked alone in the woods, pondering many things, his breath misting. Eventually he came back and got a mug of tea to try to keep the frosty chill away, then wandered through the camp. He came to where the Rogues were kept. Monadhal sneered at him, his icy eyes narrowed. Nandhal's blue eyes darkened with anger, his handsome features contorted by his hatred. He grieved for them but he knew talking to them would be futile. He walked on.

He finished his tea and toss the dregs in an arc on the grass, then sat, leaning against a tree.

Mattan walked over. "May I join you?"

Alcandhor smiled. "It depends on whether you wish to lecture me again."

Lifting his hands, Mattan said, "One lecture a day is my limit."

Alcandhor gestured to the ground next to him. Mattan sat, his hands clasped between his raised knees, and they rested in companionable silence for some time. Of all the questions Alcandhor wished to ask, how to choose? And would the Elder answer? He decided and took a breath. "Mattan, what did Ordhral mean that we were once one people?"

"Stars, Thane, you always ask the hardest questions."

"Meaning you refuse to answer?"

"Meaning a full explanation would take more than one evening."

"This is the planet of your people's origin. Is that not correct? And you abandoned it for some reason—a shameful one, if my guesses be correct. Then you rescued us from our planet, and brought us here, gifting this world to us."

"It is mostly correct. We did originate here and did abandon it, and we did rescue your people from Teledhar as it was destroying itself and settle them here."

"But then how could your people and my people have once been one?"

Mattan looked ahead. "To answer you is to admit our shame."

"I would not cause you pain."

"But you would have answers?"

Alcandhor lifted his shoulders.

"I will tell you," Mattan whispered, "that Teledhar was not the planet

365

of your people's origin."

"This was?"

"Aye."

"Great Bells, you have opened my mind to more questions than stars in the sky!"

"Let those questions rest, for now, Thane. They will not fly away. We have more immediate problems."

"Such as?"

"Tam. I sense the wall she built is weakening. The memories must soon break forth."

"Bells." Alcandhor raised his head to see his niece. She rested against Marcalan, who had his back against a boulder, and they chatted with Jonadhan and several others seated near them by the fire. One of the Rangers said something, and Marcalan replied, making them all laugh. Tam included. Marcalan wrapped his arms around her and must have tickled her, because she gave a small shriek.

"When I first met her," Alcandhor murmured, "she never even smiled and was fearful around groups of people. Now look at her. 'Tis a joy to see her."

"I can sense the underlying hurt, but she has some good measure of healing already. Knowing many people love her will give her support when that mental wall breaks."

A loud burst of laughter and hoots interrupted their conversation. Naturally, the commotion was centered around Marcalan. He rose to see what the scamp had done now, the Elder following.

Tam, red-faced, swatted at her husband. Poor lass! She had best become inured to his jesting. He was snickering, his arms thrown over his head and one leg raised in protection as well.

Mattan grinned. "It seems she needs our support now."

With a chortle, Alcandhor replied, "I think perhaps he is the one in need of support."

"Give him his due, Tam!" called out a Ranger.

"Thrash him!" called another.

"Have pity," Marcalan moaned in mock sorrow, a grin still on his face.

"Not until you promise to behave!" Her giggles belied her fierce words.

"But I always behave," he protested, which inspired groans from every Ranger there. "I will not say how I behave, but I always behave."

Jonadhan laughed. "You are incorrigible, Marcalan."

"Aye, and proud of it." Marcalan grabbed Tam around the waist from behind and pulled her close, one leg on each side of her. She twisted around onto her knees to swat him again, but he kissed her with abrupt passion and slowly her arms wrapped around his neck. She finally pulled away, gasping, her face red. "That was not fair."

He grinned. "Is anything in life fair?"

"Be careful, Marcalan." Mattan's brown eyes sparkled. "She has abilities that could make you pay."

Tam twisted around to see Mattan then smiled, dropping down to sit in front of Marcalan. "Aye, I do." She settled back into her husband, tipping her head to give him a smug look.

"Stars, Tam, you would not!" Marcalan exclaimed, then he groaned. "You are cruel."

Haladhon gave a low whistle, then grinned. "Be nice, Tam. We shall not arrive at Zaidhron until late tomorrow."

"Aye, be kind to your poor lowly husband," Marcalan moaned, tightening his embrace.

Jonadhan tilted his body forward. "What is she doing to you?"

"You want not to know." Haladhon crossed his arms with a broad smile. "Remember, she can send emotions strongly."

"Stars!" Jonadhan stared at Tam, then grinned at Marcalan, who sat now in silence, his arms around Tam's waist, his face buried in her hair. "So I see you truly have tamed him then, cousin."

"'Tis a pitiable life I shall lead from now on." Marcalan gave a mournful shake of his head.

Haladhon chuckled. "Oh, aye, we all grieve for you. I would not mind such a pitiable life."

"You?" Marcalan looked up in astonishment, all pretense of sorrow gone. "You would say that when you have vowed to never marry?"

Haladhon shrugged. "I think a Child of the Enaisi might tempt me."

His cousin's careless attitude—about marriage and about the intimacy of an empathic bond—irritated Alcandhor. "I know you merely jest, but you know not what that means, cousin." Alcandhor stepped closer to the fire. "And I would suggest we all say night's rest. We shall break camp early."

Rangers scattered to various places and spread their blankets to sleep.

"I take it I have been reprimanded, Thane?" Haladhon asked, rising.

"Take it however you wish."

His tall cousin's lips thinned, and he turned away, but then Mattan called to him. Haladhon hesitated, jaw set, as the alien crossed over and placed a hand on his arm. "Monadhal lied to you. Your father did not suffer for two days. His death was not drawn out—it was fairly quick."

Haladhon stared at Mattan, swallowing heavily. "I thank you, Mattan. I...truly thank you." The tall Ranger strode off into the darkness.

"That was well done," Alcandhor murmured.

"I just told him the truth."

Alcandhor nodded, his eyes straying to his niece and Marcalan. "Mattan, I do have a question."

"Just one, Thane?"

"For tonight."

The alien smiled. "And what is it?"

"Tam claims their bond started soon after we taught Marcalan how to send emotions. They made a game of sending, and the beginnings of their bond began. They had not..." Alcandhor cleared his throat. "I always understood a marriage bond involved...intimacy. Yet Tam says you called Marcalan her husband when you healed him."

"Aye, I could sense their bond, just as I did when I spoke to them before. He was present but has not the strength to mind-speak as she does."

Alcandhor blinked. "Before?"

"The night I talked to her. The first time I made contact, she broke it almost immediately out of fear, but the next time she did not. Marcalan gave her the courage to keep talking to me."

"But how then did the bond occur if they had never been...close?"

His head tipped, Mattan slowly replied, "I can only surmise, but I would not wish to speculate without first talking to both of them and finding out details of how the bond started. I imagine that will have to wait until after their nestling."

Alcandhor huffed a soft laugh. "Aye, you have likely hit the mark. I wish you night's rest."

Mattan bowed. "Night's rest, Thane."

~*~

Tam and Marcalan hurried the next day, and the Rangers, with great understanding and even greater humor, kept pace.

When they finally approached Zaidhron, Marcalan and Tam increased their stride. Before they even got to the gatehouse, Marcalan whooped. He picked Tam up, slung her over his shoulder, and took off through the gate, and across the sward for Family North as she shrieked and laughed.

The Rangers all cheered.

Haladhon slapped Alcandhor in the ribs, chuckling. "I got them, Thane."

"What? How?"

"When I saw that Tam and Marcalan were going with us, I took one of the gate guards aside. He has wanted to get even with Marcalan, so I gave him the chance. I ordered him to saw almost all the way through the legs of their bedstead."

"Oh, stars!"

~*~*~

Thank you for reading *Children of the Enaisi*. If you enjoyed it, I'd love for you to leave a review at your favorite retailer.

~L.S. King

ABOUT THE AUTHOR

L.S. King has novels published in two series: Deuces Wild and the Sword's Edge Chronicles.

Besides having short stories published in *Deep Magic*, *The Sword Review*, *Dragons, Knights & Angels*, *Digital Dragon Magazine*, and *Residential Aliens* (the fact that several of the publications which have released her stories are now defunct has nothing to do with her, honest), she also authored a column for writers, has worked as a submissions editor and a copy editor on several magazines, and was a founding editor of the semi-pro online magazine *Ray Gun Revival*, currently on hiatus.

~:~

Check out my website: http://loriendil.com
Follow me on Twitter: @Loriendil
Facebook author page: @AuthorLSKing
Facebook fan group: Loriendil's Lair
Subscribe to my blog: http://loriendil.wordpress.com/

www.ingramcontent.com/pod-product-compliance
Lightning Source LLC
Chambersburg PA
CBHW060151260626
47160CB00001B/223